PAYBACK

GREETINGS FROM THE USA!

A JOHNNY SPICER CAPER

H. P. OLIVER

HPO Productions
8698 Elk Grove Boulevard, Suite 1-271
Elk Grove, California 95624

Cover art and book design by Steve Eitzen

Printed in the United States of America

ISBN-13: 978-0-9994150-1-6

MYSTERIES IN HISTORY

DEDICATION

Respectfully dedicated to the often anonymous men and women who worked in the intelligence services of the United States and our allies during WWII. Whether serving at home or abroad, they were the heroes behind the heroes.

AUTHOR WEBSITE

You are cordially invited to visit the author's website at http://www.hpoliver.com for many free features related to this and other H. P. Oliver books. These include a unique VISUALIZATION section with illustrated quotes from PAYBACK that will increase your reading enjoyment by allowing you to "see" parts of the story. (use link below.)

http://www.HPOliver.com/BOOKS/PAYBACK/VISUALIZATIONS/index.html

ACKNOWLEDGMENTS

The author gratefully acknowledges the following primary research sources used in the writing of this book: The Doolittle Raiders organization, American Gas and Oil Historical Society, the men and women of North American Aviation (now Boeing), Sacramento Public Library, Los Angeles Public Library, Sacramento Air Depot Archives, *Los Angeles Times* Archive, Flight Path Learning Center (LAX), California State Military Museum, Cedars-Sinai academic healthcare organization, Golden Gate National Parks Conservancy, San Francisco Presidio Trust, McClellan Park, and Catalina Island Museum. Also appreciation to Gary Weisenberger for keeping the author honest.

PLEASE NOTE

This novel occasionally refers to individuals and groups with terms that are considered disrespectful and inappropriate today. These terms, however, were in common usage during the historical period in which this story is set and are included here solely for the purpose of accurately depicting the attitudes and customs of the day.

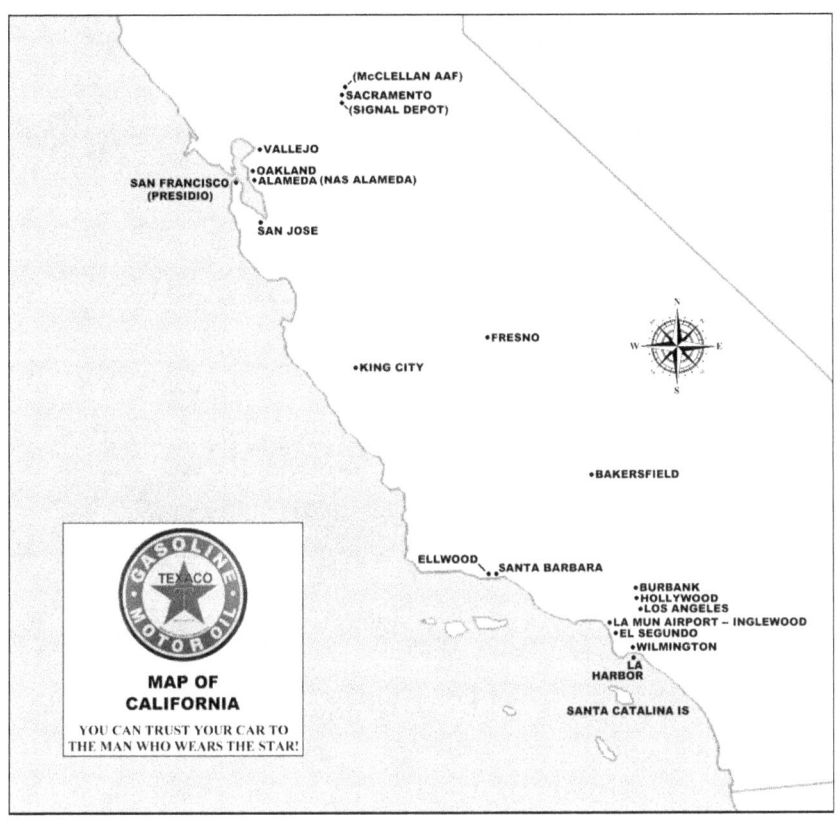

MAP OF
CALIFORNIA

YOU CAN TRUST YOUR CAR TO
THE MAN WHO WEARS THE STAR!

OFFICER RANKS

ARMY/MARINES	NAVY/COAST GUARD
SECOND LIEUTENANT	ENSIGN
FIRST LIEUTENANT	LIEUTENANT JUNIOR GRADE
CAPTAIN	LIEUTENANT
MAJOR	LIEUTENANT COMMANDER
LIEUTENANT COLONEL	COMMANDER
COLONEL	CAPTAIN
BRIGADIER GENERAL	REAR ADMIRAL (1 STAR)
MAJOR GENERAL	REAR ADMIRAL (2 STAR)
LIEUTENANT GENERAL	VICE ADMIRAL
GENERAL	ADMIRAL

One

US Route 101, Goleta

All right, I'll admit it. I was driving a US government vehicle and burning up US government gasoline for private business. No, that's not quite accurate. This wasn't even private business.

Uncle Sam and my boss, Major General Chester Davis, needed me in Los Angeles on Tuesday, so I left the Military Intelligence Division's west coast headquarters at the Presidio in San Francisco a day or two before I really needed to in order to make a stop in Santa Barbara.

Why Santa Barbara? Because that's where Susan Jackson lives, and Susan is the future Missus Johnny Spicer. Angel—my pet name for Susan—and I met a little over two years ago while I was recovering from a gunshot wound in the private hospital where Susan is the head nurse, but that's another story.

Suffice to say my recall to active duty as a Major in the Army's Military Intelligence Division a few months back put a heck of a crimp in our love life, so now we had to grab a little time together whenever my assignments permitted. Since my assignments for MID were in the realm of counter-espionage on the homefront and mostly involved installations and facilities on the west coast, we actually managed to see each other a lot more often than guys who were fighting the shooting war in far off corners of the world got to see their wives and girlfriends.

That bothered me sometimes, but only when I wasn't being a target for some Jap or Nazi spy I'd caught with his hand in Uncle Sam's cookie jar. Yes, I'm in a shooting war, too, just one a lot closer to home. Unfortunately, bullets in the good old U S of A are just as deadly as the ones being fired at Americans in those far off

1

corners of the world.

Anyway, Susan and I decided to take advantage of a pleasant evening by driving along the coast a ways northwest of Santa Barbara to see the sights. By the time we'd wandered up to Las Varas Canyon beyond Goleta, the sun was setting and there wasn't much light left by which to see sights, so I reluctantly turned the Army's Dodge business coupe around and we headed back down US 101, which in these parts is also California Route One.

Susan was cuddled up next to me and I heard her sigh. "I love just riding along like this. I wish we could keep going and going."

"Sounds good to me. Maybe we'll be able to do that . . . ."

WHUMP!

I felt the explosion shake the road under our tires and a brilliant orange flash lit up the sky a half mile or so ahead of us.

Susan jumped. "Johnny! What was that?"

"I don't know, but I'm pretty sure it wasn't anything good."

Taking my foot off the gas, I let the Dodge coast as we drew closer to whatever was going on up ahead. Charging into the fray, whatever the fray was, didn't seem wise until I had a little more information.

WHUMP! . . . FLASH!

"There it goes again, Johnny. Please tell me when I should get scared."

"Hold off on that a little while longer, Angel. Let's see what . . . ."

"What, Johnny?"

"We passed an oil pumping facility on the way up here. Those flashes are right about where it was."

"That's right, the Bankline Oilfield and Refinery at Ellwood. What are you thinking?"

WHUMP! . . . FLASH!

"Johnny!"

"Relax, Angel. If my guess is right, we are witnessing something that hasn't happened in this country for a 130 years."

"Oh, wonderful! You pick such swell times for history lessons. What are you talking about?"

"Unless I'm mistaken, the continental United States is at this moment under attack by a foreign enemy, which hasn't happened since the War of 1812. A ship, probably Japanese, is shelling your oilfield."

WHUMP! . . . FLASH!

"It's not MY oilfield!"

This time I was looking out to sea, watching for the muzzle

flash. The flash I saw looked like it came from a five-inch gun, and it illuminated a low profile, probably a submarine, a thousand or so yards out.

Figuring there was nothing official I could do about a Jap sub at this point, I saw no need to get any closer until things calmed down. I braked to a stop on the shoulder of the road and pointed to where I'd seen the muzzle flash, "There's a submarine out there, Angel. She looks to be a little less than a mile from the beach and her skipper is trying to blow up the oilfield."

WHUMP! . . . FLASH!

Being the trooper that she is, Susan no longer jumped with each round fired, nor had she lost her sense of humor. At least I assumed she was joking when she said, "Johnny, you are an officer in the United States Army. Make them stop that!"

"I can't do that. Enemy submarines fall under the jurisdiction of the Navy and Coast Guard, speaking of which, I bet Jack's telephone is ringing off the hook right now."

"Oh, God! I didn't think about that!"

Jack was Orville "Jack" Jackson, Lieutenant, United States Coast Guard, assigned to the Santa Barbara station. Jack was also Susan's big brother.

"Don't worry, Angel, Jack knows his business. Besides, that sub isn't going to hang around in shallow water much longer risking an encounter with an American destroyer."

WHUMP! . . . FLASH!

"I hope not, but I'll bet Jack is itching to get a shot at it. I wonder how much damage they're doing to the refinery."

"Probably not much. If they hit anything important it will be more by accident than a result of marksmanship. That sub is bobbing around like a cork out there in the offshore swells, which somewhat hinders accurate aiming at targets smaller than a battleship. Besides that, to really cause substantial damage they need to be firing incendiary rounds. I'm pretty sure what they're shooting are armor piercing anti-ship shells."

I could see Susan grinning in the dim light from the Dodge's instrument panel. "Gosh, you're smart, but do you know anything about raising kids and mowing lawns?"

"Sure. I used to be a kid, and I mowed a lot of grass back then."

I had no sooner said that when it occurred to me this was a strange time to ask such a question. I wondered if she was trying to tell me something."

"Ah . . . any particular reason for asking that question right now?"

Susan laughed. "No, Johnny. I'm regular as clockwork, but I sure got your attention, didn't I?"

"Yes, Angel, you surely did."

"Good. I need to keep you on your toes."

In addition to keeping on my toes, I kept an eye on my wristwatch. When fifteen minutes passed without a round being fired, I put the Dodge in gear and pointed it down the road toward the Ellwood Oilfield.

"Do you think it's over, Johnny?"

"I think so. They haven't fired a round in fifteen minutes."

"Is it safe to go down there?"

"I hope so. This is the only route home. Besides, if I inventory the damage and call in a report on the shelling into HQ, I won't feel so guilty about joyriding on the Army's gasoline."

"You're feeling guilty about that, are you?"

I grinned. "Not terribly."

The highway alongside the facility was lined with automobiles that must have arrived during the shelling, proving without a doubt that all the fools aren't dead yet. I pulled up to the entrance gate, which was well protected by a fellow in a security guard uniform and a Santa Barbara County sheriff's deputy.

The deputy came up to my open window. Since I was not in uniform he had no way of knowing I was an important military guy. "Sorry, sir. We have orders to keep the public out until further notice."

Like a good boy scout, I was prepared for that. I held up my MID ID card and said, "Army Intelligence, Deputy."

MID ID cards are impressive. They have our pictures on them, along with the Great Seal of the United States of America and some important looking signatures and numbers. They are also laminated in clear plastic. Anything laminated in clear plastic must be official.

The deputy looked my ID over thoroughly, and then he handed it back to me as he leaned over to look further into the Dodge. Of course, he saw Susan.

"Who's she?"

"Deputy, as long as she's with me, her identity is none of your concern."

He looked ready to argue that point, but Susan smiled at him and that was the end of that. I asked, "Who's in charge here?"

"Walt Potter. He's the plant manager. Follow this road around to the beach and look for a big guy in a red plaid shirt and one of those tin hats construction workers wear."

I did as instructed and because the entire facility was lit up like Bullock's Wilshire at Christmas, we got a good look at the place along the way. The most impressive building was the refinery itself, a large white structure bristling with smokestacks and pipes going in all directions. The refinery was at the north end of the property. South of it six wooden docks poked out into the water. These I gathered were used for loading ships that transported the refined gasoline to wherever it was needed.

Across the beach from the loading docks were several large round storage tanks. They were white, and the large signs they bore said things like, "Richfield Hi-Octane Gasoline." No attempt had been made to camouflage the tanks and their critical-to-the-war-effort contents.

South of the storage tanks were more piers. These were longer and because they sprouted wooden derricks over the water, I guessed they provided access to the oil wells. The rest of the plant consisted of a few small wooden tool shacks and oily dirt roads with leaking pipes running along next to them.

The most visible damage from the shelling were some splintered holes in the piers with the derricks. Also, one of the derricks was down and busted up from what looked like a lucky direct hit. There were also shell craters in the ground, but they were hard to see unless there was a light nearby. The place would look a lot worse in the cold light of day.

I finally spotted Walt Potter, the plant manager, at the foot of the pier with the damaged derrick. He looked like he had enough problems without adding me to the list, so I decided to quickly introduce myself, ask a couple of questions that were on my mind, and get out of his hair.

"Angel, do you mind waiting in the car for a few minutes? I just have a couple of questions for that guy over there, and then we can get out of here."

Shaking her head, Susan said, "I don't mind. Just be careful where you walk. There are puddles of black oily goo everywhere out here."

"Thanks, I'll watch my step."

I threaded my way past the oil puddles to Potter and he eyed me suspiciously, as if I was bringing more grief. I said, "Welcome to the war, Mister Potter. I'm Spicer with Army Intelligence. I have a couple of questions for you and I promise not to take more than two minutes of your time."

"That's okay, Spicer. Take all the time you need. I could use a break. Let's go over there and have a smoke while we talk."

I'd found a willing witness. I was nearly in shock.

Potter and I walked to a small wooden shack across the road from the piers and I offered him a Lucky Strike from my pack. He took it and we shared my Zippo to light up. Then I got down to business.

"First, was anyone hurt during the shelling?"

"Nah. We only have a skeleton crew on at night unless we're loading a ship. The guys all hightailed it to the concrete wall behind the refinery and rode it out there."

"Good thinking."

"Yeah. They ain't no dummies."

"Were all these lights on during the shelling?"

Potter looked at me and made a face. "Yeah, I know. There ain't much else we can do, though. The crew needs light to keep an eye on things. There's a lot going in a combination facility like this. A bunch of things can go wrong in a hurry unless we stay on top of things."

"Along the same lines, has anyone given thought to painting those storage tanks and the refinery buildings with colors that blend into the scenery around here? Like camouflage?"

Potter cocked his head to one side. "You think that would have made any difference?"

"Tell me, Mister Potter, do you have a small surf boat around?"

"Sure. We have a couple of 'em."

"Good. Go out a few hundred yards tomorrow and take a look back at this place. I'm pretty sure it stands out like a sore thumb. A little camouflage paint won't hide it entirely, but it will make the place a little harder to spot from a distance."

"All right, Spicer, I'll do that. Do you think this is likely to happen again?"

"I don't want to say for sure it won't, but this attack seems like it was intended as a scare tactic to panic civilians. There are plenty of targets up and down the west coast the Japs could pick for that purpose, so it isn't likely they'll come back here. Still, it always seems to me the best approach is to take whatever steps you can to make it tougher for the enemy."

"Yeah, that makes sense. Say, I've got a question for you. A while back we heard the Navy was going to start patrolling the coast with blimps, but so far, we haven't seen any. Whatever happened to that idea?"

"They're still working on it. The Navy had to build a new

facility to house the blimp down near LA, and they're busy training guys to use super-secret gizmos for spotting enemy ships. You should be seeing blimps floating by before much longer."

Potter nodded, and I said, "Okay, last question. How would you rate the damage done tonight?"

Potter almost laughed. "Minor. Less than minor. Hell, if they let us get back to work, we can have what little damage was done repaired by tomorrow or the next day. Those Japs can't hit the broad side of a barn!"

I nodded, but said, "You know, Mister Potter, it's never a good idea to underestimate an enemy. If the Japs really wanted this facility destroyed, they could easily do it. Remember December Seventh. This little oilfield apparently isn't that important as a target, but rest assured, if it were, the Japs have the resources to blow it to smithereens.

"Now I'll get out of your hair. Thanks for your time, Potter."

Half an hour later I followed Susan through the front door of her apartment at the north end of State Street. Mister Whiskers, Susan's hefty orange tabby greeted us at the door with loud complaints that we were gone much too long. I told him it was business. He wasn't impressed.

I knew Susan wanted to check on Jack, so I suggested she do that because I needed to tie up her telephone for a while calling in my report to HQ. She made the call and talked with her brother for several minutes. When she hung up and I gently nudged Mister Whiskers off my lap, where he had just gotten comfortable. I was sorely trying his patience tonight.

Susan said, "Jack says 'hi.' When I told him we had a front row seat for the excitement at Ellwood, he said he should have known you were somehow involved in all the commotion."

"You should have told him if he was doing his job and keeping the Japs away, there wouldn't have been any commotion in the first place."

Smiling, Susan said, "Hey, I'm not getting between you two and your inter-service bickering."

"Oh, it's all in good fun."

"I know, Johnny, but like FDR, I'm trying to stay neutral."

"Yeah? You can see how well that's worked out for him."

"Oh, go make your phone calls so we can go back to enjoying your last night here before you have to leave again."

"Good suggestion."

"I thought you'd think so."

I'd been assigned a new immediate supervisor back in

December after I caught my previous boss trying to hand over a secret gadget to the Nazis. Then I made a nervous wreck out of his successor and got him transferred to DC where he couldn't get into too much trouble. Apparently, I'm hard on bosses.

I was connected to the new guy—a tough veteran Colonel named Dwight Beecher—almost immediately because he was still in his office at seventeen-hundred hours. In a gruff voice that probably made junior officers snap to attention even when talking to him on the telephone, Beecher said, "Whatcha got, Spicer?"

"Just a brief after-action report on the oilfield attack down here. I was . . . ."

"What oilfield attack down where?"

That surprised me. I figured he would know all about it by now. "The one that happened two hours ago at the Ellwood Oilfield and Refinery just north of Santa Barbara. A Jap sub parked off shore and shelled the place for about twenty minutes."

"Holy shit! How come we're just hearing about it now?"

"I can't answer that one, Colonel, but I can give you a fairly thorough summary of the event because I had a front row seat for the show."

"All right, Spicer, tell me what you've got."

I gave Beecher my report, along with the answers to the questions I asked the plant manager. When I finished, the Colonel complimented me.

"Good report, Major. Obviously, we need to step up our camouflage security program to make facilities like that harder to see. Also, I need to give our news gathering network a good swift kick in the tail. We get information faster from clear across the country than we do from right here in our own backyard. That changes starting tonight.

"Now tell me what the hell you're doing in Santa Barbara. You and your sidekick are supposed to be at that plant in LA."

"Our orders say tomorrow, Colonel. I left a little early to take care of some personal business here. It's all in the sign-out roster."

"Oh. Okay. Spicer, do me a favor, will ya?"

"Sure, Colonel. Name it."

"From now on check in with me before you leave for parts unknown."

Feeling like the leash was tightening around my neck, I said coldly, "Yes, sir."

"Now don't go getting all uppity with your Colonel, Major. I know you aren't career Army, and I know General Davis thinks you're the greatest thing since cannons on wheels. In fact, I'm coming around to the same opinion, but I'm an old war horse. I need a little discipline from my troops to keep them thinking I run this show. All right?"

I couldn't help grinning. In a much friendlier tone, I said, "Yes, sir. I'll do a better job of keeping you informed of my wanderings."

"Thank you, Major Spicer. Talk with you soon."

Of course. Susan had been listening to my end of the top secret conversation. "Oh, oh. Are you in trouble, Johnny?"

"No, I just got a compliment. I think."

"Oh good. You get grumpy when you're in trouble, and if there's anything I don't want you to be right now, it's grumpy."

I smiled my most ungrumpiest smile.

Two

North American Aviation Plant, Inglewood

The first item on Tuesday's itinerary was an 0900 meet-up with Staff Sergeant Russell Pierce, my aide-de-camp as the Army calls him, at the North American Aviation plant on Mines Field, LA's municipal airport in Inglewood. That made Susan's habit of rising early particularly convenient, because the distance between Santa Barbara and Inglewood is just under a hundred miles and takes a good three hours to drive during the morning hours when everyone in LA leaves their home and drives somewhere else. Mister Whiskers even left the comfort of Susan's bed long enough to see me off and deposit a few hairs on my uniform trousers to remember him by.

Mines Field is roughly twenty miles southwest of downtown LA and only a few miles from where Sergeant Pierce and I first met when he was a member of the MID team assigned to provide security for a small manufacturing plant in El Segundo where a top secret gizmo for spotting submarines from blimps somehow wandered out the door. Russ and I ended up working closely on the assignment and when we completed it, Chester Davis assigned Pierce as my ADC because we worked well together. That was just dandy with me. Pierce is tough and savvy, just the sort of fellow you want watching your back in a tight spot.

As to our specific job on this assignment, I was completely in the dark. Sometimes government spook outfits are like that. Everything is so secret, not even the guys carrying out the assignment know what they're doing. All I knew was Russ and I were to appear at the North American plant on the assigned date at the assigned time. Presumably, if we stood around the place long enough, a clue as to what the hell we were doing there would show up. If not, there was always the beach a few blocks to the west.

North American Aviation makes airplanes, specifically military airplanes. They are best known in aviation circles as the manufacturer of the T-6 Texan advanced pilot trainer and the B-25, a twin-engine medium bomber named the "Mitchell" for General Billy Mitchell who demonstrated the importance of air power to the US Army and was court martialed for his trouble. All was forgiven when he was proven right.

Another plane they have in the works is a single-engine pursuit ship called the "Mustang." North American designed it for the Brits, so they got to name the ship. The Army calls the Mustang a P-51. What little I know about the Mitchell and the Mustang beyond that is classified, so don't bother asking.

The North American Aviation plant is located at the intersection of two major roads—Aviation Boulevard and Imperial Highway—which puts it precisely in the southeast corner of the LA Municipal Airport's property. My route there was easy, even if traffic wasn't. I came down 101 to Sepulveda Boulevard in the San Fernando Valley, then followed Sepulveda south through the aptly named Sepulveda Pass in the Santa Monica Mountains and on to Imperial Highway down in Inglewood.

When I rolled into North American's parking lot and found an empty spot marked "Visitor Parking," Russ Pierce was standing near the entrance waiting for me. I'd have been surprised if he wasn't.

As I climbed out of the Dodge, Russ picked up his duffel and greeted me. "Good morning, sir. Welcome to Los Angeles. Okay if I toss my gear in the trunk?"

I unlocked the trunk, and as he tossed his duffel in alongside my B-4 bag on top of the built-in security compartment on the floor of the trunk, he said, "Did you have a good trip down, sir?"

"It was as good as nine hours in an automobile can be. The stopover in Santa Barbara, however, was much more pleasant. How did you end up getting down here?"

"I hitched a ride with Captain Irvin in his AT-7 this morning, and then I walked over here from the terminal. It's not far. Say, did you get in on the excitement at that oil field that was shelled up near Santa Barbara last night? That's all anyone could talk about at HQ this morning."

"I sure did. Susan and I had front row seats. In fact, I called in the first report Colonel Beecher got on it."

Russ shook his head in something like amazement. "Makes me wonder where those Japs are going to show up next."

"That's the kind of question we get paid to answer. Speaking of which, do you have any idea what the hell we're supposed to do here?"

Frowning, Russ said, "Well, sort of. Miss Ashley at HQ gave me a piece of paper with instructions, sort of."

"Sort of?"

"Yes, sir. All the note says is to contact S. MacLure here at the plant."

"Well that's a start. Let's give it a try."

We walked through a double glass doorway and into a large lobby decorated with aircraft photographs and a large replica of the North American Aviation logotype on the wall. A woman stood up behind a snazzy glass brick counter and said, "Good morning, Major. How can we help the Army this morning?"

"We have instructions to contact an employee of yours named MacLure, first initial S. Would you please let him know Major Spicer and Sergeant Pierce are here?"

She looked at me with the beginnings of a smile playing at the corners of her mouth. "Certainly. I assume you have not met S. MacLure before."

"No, we haven't, and by your expression I suspect we might be tuned to the wrong wave length here. What don't I know about S. MacLure that I should know?"

"Only that it's MISS S. MacLure. Sally MacLure to be more exact. Sally is one of our production design engineers. Please have a seat and I'll call her."

We plunked ourselves down on the couch indicated by the receptionist and I said, "I bet Pauline Ashley did this deliberately. She gets a lot of grief from the Army guys at HQ. This is probably one of her little ways of getting even."

Russ nodded and, at almost the same time, a door in the wall near the reception counter opened. We both looked expectantly in that direction. What we saw there was a far cry from the engineer sort of person I was expecting.

Sally MacLure was an honest to goodness California blonde with a beach tan and a quick smile. Like many women working in assembly plants these days, she wore slacks. They were tailored and fit perfectly. It was the first time I'd seen a woman in trousers that did her justice, or vice versa.

All in all, Sally MacLure had the sort of wholesome girl-next-door air about her that makes young fellows want to take a gal home to meet mom and dad. Glancing at Russ, I got the definite impression this quality had not escaped his notice.

"Good morning, Major Spicer, I'm Sally MacLure." The tone of her voice matched the big smile on her face.

Standing, I said, "Good morning to you, Miss MacLure." We shook hands and, gesturing toward Russ, I added, "Meet Staff Sergeant Russell Pierce."

She offered Russ her hand. "Good morning, Russell. I'm pleased to meet you."

As they shook hands I chuckled to myself over the differences in the ways Sally greeted us. I was "Major Spicer," but Russ got first name treatment. I didn't think for a minute that distinction had anything at all to do with the difference in our military ranks.

It was also clear that in less than a dozen words Sally had completely enchanted Russ. Still holding her hand, he said, "Good morning, Sally. It's good to meet you, too."

I interrupted, fearing I would disappear from the room entirely if I didn't. "Miss MacLure, I'm afraid we are at somewhat of a loss here. The folks at Military Intelligence Division failed to tell us what it was we were supposed to do when we got here. I'm hoping you have an idea about that."

Looking at me intently through the biggest, bluest eyes west of the Continental Divide, she said, "Well, sort of."

Russ and I looked at each other and laughed. I said, "That sounds familiar."

Sally looked a little confused about what we found so humorous, but she was not one to let a little confusion deter her from the task at hand. "My instructions were simply to familiarize you with the B-25 as thoroughly as possible in the time available. I was not told exactly what about the B-25 you needed to know or how much time we had."

I glanced over my shoulder at two fellows in suits who were entering the lobby through the same doors Russ and I used. "I'm afraid I don't know those things either, but maybe we can piece an answer together. First, though, I suggest we take this discussion somewhere less public."

Sally MacLure nodded and turned toward the door through which she had come a few minutes earlier, saying, "This way, Major."

Once in the hallway on the other side of the door, I stopped. Sally turned with a question on her face."

"Miss MacLure, this is a secure facility, is it not?"

"Yes, it is."

"Then it might be a good idea for you to inform your security people that we're here and let them take a look at our credentials, especially after the excitement up in Santa Barbara last night."

Sally smiled again. "That is exactly where we are going. Security is the next door on the right."

"My apologies, Miss MacLure. You obviously know the drill."

"No apology is necessary, Major Spicer. It's always best to be sure."

We presented our MID IDs to a uniformed security officer and he looked them over. Then he had us fill out and sign plant visitor forms. Finally, he handed us VISITOR badges with clips like miniature clothespins so they could be attached to the lapels or pocket flaps of our uniform blouses.

The officer said, "Please wear these badges at all times while you're here and turn them in when you leave."

Attaching the badge to my lapel, I said, "Thanks."

"You're welcome, Major. You fellows being here is quite an experience for me. You and Sergeant Pierce are the first Army MID personnel I've met. Those shoulder patches you fellows wear carry a lot of weight, especially nowadays."

Back out in the hallway, Sally stopped Russ with a hand on his arm and looked closely at the yellow, blue, and gray shield on his right shoulder. "Russ, exactly what is this emblem you wear?"

"It's the Army Military Intelligence Division shield."

"Well, it certainly got our security guard's attention."

Russ grinned. "It should. MID is an elite outfit. I'm very proud of that patch."

I chimed in, "Russ has good reason to be proud of that patch. With the exception of a few guys they overlooked, like me, the Army is very careful about who wears the MID shield. Believe me, Sally, earning the right to sew that particular piece of cloth on his uniform took some doing."

"Wow."

"Maybe Russ can tell you a little more about MID later, but right now, we need to figure out what we're supposed to be doing here."

"All right, let's go out back. The run-up line would be a good place to talk."

As we walked along endless hallways with countless doors, Sally gave us the lay of the land. The building we were in was divided into two sections. Administration and engineering offices occupied the two-story front third of the structure. The rest of the building, open from floor to roof, housed sections of the B-25 assembly line.

The "run-up" area turned out to be a strip of concrete at the north or runway end of the building. Four silver twin-engine ships with double rudders on their tails were parked in the run-up line. It was the place where final engine tests were performed on ships before they were delivered. I noted that B-25s must be in high demand. North American hadn't even taken the time to slap a coat of olive drab on these ships.

Sally gestured toward the gleaming bombers and said, "Camouflage netting is on order for open areas like this, but we haven't received it yet. Every time I walk out here I expect Japanese bombs to come raining down, particularly after that business in Santa Barbara last night."

I looked around at the exposed area. "I don't blame you. Tell you what, if that netting doesn't show up by the end of the week, I want you to give us a telephone call with the name of the supplier. I imagine we can get you some priority. Russ, give Sally one of your MID business cards so she'll know how to get in touch with us."

Sally accepted a card from Russ and took a few seconds to read it. Dealing with slow providers of camouflage netting was more the job of local civil defense authorities, but I was pretty sure Russ would not object to letting Sally know how to get in touch with him.

Slipping the card into the pocket of her slacks, Sally looked up at the nearest B-25, and then turned to me. "I guess I should begin this orientation by finding out how much you already know about Army bombers in general and the Mitchell in particular."

"Well, besides crossing the Pacific Ocean to Hawaii in a B-17 last December Seventh, I have to admit complete ignorance on those subjects. First, though, I'd like to try to solve the mystery of why Russ and I suddenly need to know all about this particular aircraft."

Our guide nodded. "All right, how do we do that?"

"It might help if you could answer a few questions for me."

"Okay, I'll try."

"If you don't know the answers or don't feel comfortable with my need to know classified details, just say so."

Sally smiled. She did that a lot. "All right, what are your questions?"

"This one is a little vague, but do you know of any unique missions coming up in which B-25s will play a key role? I mean out of the ordinary missions?"

After considering my question for a few moments, Sally said, "I really can't think of anything. Of course, I'm not privy to that sort of information as a general rule."

Nodding, I asked, "Exactly what is a . . . forgive me, but what is your title again? Production design engineer?"

"Yes, that's me. At an aircraft assembly plant, production design engineers figure out systems for the most efficient assembly of the product, like the sequence of assembly line stations, part movement within the plant, and details like that."

Assembling the puzzle pieces Miss MacLure was giving me, I was beginning to see a picture of why we were at North American Aviation. Darling as she was, Sally didn't know squat about what happened to the B-25s assembled on her assembly lines once they left the plant. That meant our orientation on the B-25 was intended to be general information that might be somehow helpful later in our assignment, whatever it might be. One other possibility occurred to me, so I asked another question.

"Sally, are you working on any ships that are equipped differently than usual? I mean aside from the usual production improvements that come with new variants?"

Again, she thought about my question for several seconds before answering. "Not that I know of. Sometimes modifications are made in the field, though."

What Sally MacLure was telling us, or not telling us confirmed my suspicion that Russ and I were at the North American plant for general schooling on the B-25. That was fine with me. In my experience too much useful information is seldom a problem in the intelligence business.

Frowning, Sally asked, "Are my answers helping at all?"

"Yes, Miss MacLure, they are. I think what Russ and I are here for is simply a general orientation on the Mitchell—enough information so we know what to look for and where to look for it in the event someone attempts to sabotage one of them or something along those lines. We don't really need to be experts on the aircraft because it's unlikely a Jap or Nazi saboteur will be an expert either."

Sally nodded slowly. "I think I see what you're getting at, Major. How would it be if I started with the basic specifications, and then we can climb aboard and take a look around?"

I smiled. "That would be just peachy keen, Miss MacLure."

Pointing to the aircraft on the run-up line, Sally began her orientation. "These are all C models. There is also a D model. It is identical to the C, except Ds are built at the new Kansas City,

Kansas plant North American just opened. There were three models before the C and D, the B-25, the 25A and the 25B."

"The B-25 is a designated by the Army as a medium bomber. The first production model took off in August,1940. The current models—the C and D—are powered by a pair of Wright R-2600-13 Cyclone 14-cylinder radial engines rated at 1700 horsepower each."

Since it sounded as if Sally was going to throw a lot of numbers at us, I got out my notebook and began taking notes. "You said the engine designation is R-2600-13?"

"That's correct . . . Wright Cyclones. They power the ship to a maximum speed of 286 miles per hour and give it a service ceiling of slightly more than twenty-thousand feet. The B-25C's cruise range is about 1,500 miles with standard fuel tanks. There are two tanks in each wing between the fuselage and the engine nacelle. All four tanks add up to 1,340 gallons.

"Fully loaded, the C model weighs in at around thirty-four-thousand pounds. The wingspan is sixty-four-and-a-half feet, overall length is nearly 53 feet, and the overall height is just under 16 feet.

"The ship is equipped with six 50-caliber machine guns and it can carry a bomb load of three thousand pounds. The typical crew compliment is five: pilot, copilot, bombardier-nose gunner, radio operator-lower turret gunner, and dorsal turret gunner. Depending on the mission, the C and D models may also carry a flight engineer or navigator.

"I have heard, though, that many of the lower turrets are being removed in the field because they are impractical and ineffective. There is also some talk about adding a rear gun turret in the tail of the next variant."

Russ was obviously impressed with Sally's B-25 knowledge, and said as much. "You sure know all about B-25s. That's a lot of technical information to keep in your head."

Sally smiled at Russ. "Thank you, Russ. Knowing all that stuff is part of my job. Mister Kindelberger—he runs North American—insists on his engineers staying current on all the variants of the aircraft we build. In my case that's important because a significant change in a ship's size or weight could require major changes in the assembly process. For example, the C and D models are ten inches shorter than the B models. Multiply that by ten ships on an assembly line, and it shortens the length of the line by eight feet."

Russ nodded. "That makes sense. There's a lot to this

airplane building business that doesn't meet the eye."

"That's true, and I never want it said that a North American aircraft let a flight crew down. Combat fliers have it tough enough without worrying about whether or not their ships are up to the job they have to do."

The expression on Sally's face said she meant what she was saying, and her words brought to mind a B-17 that literally broke in two after it landed at Hickam Field, Hawaii, yet despite all the battle damage it sustained, that Boeing ship got its crew, and me, down safely. You couldn't ask more than that.

Sally was looking at me curiously. "Something on your mind, Major?"

"No. I was just remembering a ship that was assembled by folks who have the same idea as you about the quality of their aircraft. If they did not, I wouldn't be standing here taking up your time."

From the corner of my eye I saw Russ nod. He wasn't at Hickam that day, but he remembered the story.

Sally also nodded, and I could tell she was curious, but I could see no reason to delay the proceedings with ancient history. She can buy a copy of my memoirs when they're published.

To change the subject and move on with the job at hand, I said, "May we go aboard one of these ships now?"

"Certainly." Leading us toward the nearest ship, she explained, "Normal crew access is by way of a hatch and ladder on the bottom of the fuselage between the cockpit and the bomb bay. There are also three emergency hatches located throughout the plane."

The crew hatch was open and stepping up onto the first rung of the ladder attached to it, Sally said, "This is a little tricky to do without hitting your head or bumping into something, so do what I do as you follow me up."

I ushered Russ ahead of me and I hoped he was paying attention to where Sally was placing her hands and feet. From below, it would be easy to become distracted by the trim little bottom in slacks ascending the ladder ahead of him. If you'll pardon the expression, I brought up the rear.

Inside, we discovered that, while the ship seemed large from the ground, the crew areas were cramped. At the top of the hatch ladder the view forward and up looked into the flight deck where the pilot and copilot bumped elbows as they did their jobs. Below the flight deck there was an opening leading to the bombardier's position in the nose of the plane.

Aft of the crew hatch was a narrow passage way—more like a crawl space—leading over the bomb bay, lower gun turret, and back to the dorsal gunner's position, which consisted of a bicycle seat atop a post. Sitting on the seat put the tail gunner's head inside the top turret, from where he could aim and fire a pair of 50-caliber machine guns.

Compared to the B-17 I'd flown in, the B-25C was closet-sized. A claustrophobic crew member would not be happy in this flying aspirin tin.

For the next hour or so Sally showed us equipment within the ship which she considered susceptible to sabotage. These included components of the 24-volt electrical system, the bomb bay racks, the oxygen system, and the hydraulic systems for the landing gear.

When we finally climbed back down the crew hatch ladder, Sally said, "I think the next thing we should do is go over the outside of the ship and look at some of the more likely places for sabotage to occur, but before we do that, North American Aviation would like to buy you gentlemen lunch in our commissary. The food is the best you'll find around Mines Field."

"Thank you, Sally, but I need to take care of some business, so I hope you won't mind if I pass on lunch and leave you to finish the orientation with Sergeant Pierce this afternoon."

Sally gave Russ a sweet smile and said, "I don't mind at all."

Mind, hell, I could not have said anything that would have pleased Sally or Russ more. See what a swell guy I am?

"Before I leave, Sally, I want to thank you for your time. I feel like I could darn near fly one of these things after your briefing."

Turning to Russ, I said, "I'm going to get us a couple of rooms at the same place we stayed when we were here back in December . . . that Patmar joint on Sepulveda. I'll come back here and pick you up around four. Will that be okay, Sally?"

Still grinning like a Chessie Cat, Sally said, "That would be fine, but I get off at four-thirty and Patmar's Motel is just a stone's throw from here. I would be happy to drop Sergeant Pierce off on my way home."

"That okay with you, Russ?"

"Sure, it's swell. I mean. . . . ."

I said, "I know what you mean, Russ. I'll see you around 1700 hours. In fact, if Sally can find us a decent watering hole nearby, the drinks are on me."

Sally's cheeks had to be getting sore from smiling so much. "I think I can come up with a cocktail lounge that will serve the purpose. Thank you, Major Spicer."

"You're welcome, Sally, and thank you for a great orientation. See you two later."

Three

Inglewood, Westchester, & El Segundo

I didn't really fib to Sally and Russ. I did need to make a telephone call, but I also had about all the B-25 I could take for one day and I figured, one way or another, Russ and Sally would make better use of the time without me putting a damper on their fun.

Leaving North American Aviation, I wandered through the small communities surrounding Mines Field—Inglewood to the east, Westchester north of the field, and El Segundo to the south. I wasn't just killing time, though. I noticed something amiss when I first arrived at Mines Field and it seemed important to find out what it was.

The anomaly was nothing specific or tangible, just an uneasiness in the air. I saw nothing through the Dodge's windows to account for the feeling, but I did notice a larger military presence in the area than I remembered from last December. That was to be expected since we were now engaged in a war and Mines Field was considered a primary target.

I also noticed more small gatherings of folks standing around on street corners. They weren't doing anything in particular, just standing there and talking. That sort of thing isn't uncommon in small rural towns where everybody knows everybody else, but few parts of Los Angeles County could still be considered rural and the alfalfa fields that once filled most of Inglewood were long gone.

After an hour of driving around, though, I began to wonder if my uneasy feeling wasn't a figment of my imagination. I couldn't quite convince myself of that, but my stomach convinced me it was lunch time. I skipped breakfast at Susan's, so the needle on my fuel gauge was hovering over E. I found Sepulveda Boulevard and pointed the Dodge toward Patmar's.

Patmar's is a modern motel and coffee shop in the first block of Sepulveda south of Imperial Highway, which makes it quite convenient to Mines Field and the North American Aviation plant. I stayed there while working on the Optitronics caper back in December and found the place quite comfortable. The food at the coffee shop was decent and it all came at a reasonable price, so Patmar's suited our needs quite nicely.

[Author's Note: The "Optitronics caper" referred to in the previous paragraph is described in the novel S.N.A.F.U. by H. P. Oliver.]

I registered for two rooms, stowed my B-4 bag in the room I planned to use and tossed Russ's duffel on the bed in the other room. That done, I made tracks for the coffee shop. I ordered a cup of the chef's special French onion soup and a ham sandwich with Swiss cheese, which came with a small pile of homemade potato chips. Thus satiated, I paid the check and slipped into a public telephone booth for a person-to-person long-distance call to Colonel Dwight Beecher, my boss, at MID's western headquarters in San Francisco.

"Hello, Spicer. How did things go this morning?"

"Once I figured out what the hell you sent us down here for, things went well. I now know that damned thing from stem to stern. What's next?"

"You and Pierce have a meeting with the big boss here tomorrow at 1400 hours. He's flying in specifically to see you two, so don't be late. He said for you and Pierce to meet his plane at the airfield."

To quote Alice, this whole thing was getting curiouser and curiouser. The big boss, of course, was Chester Davis, and Major General Davis is a busy guy. For him to fly clear across the country and back just to see little ol' me meant we were butt-deep in something very big. Of course, I still had no idea what the very big something was, but that didn't seem to matter. We were in it and that was that.

"Yes sir, we'll be there."

"Good. After you meet with him, I hope you can tell me what this is all about."

Chuckling, I said, "Yes sir, but only if you have a need to know."

"Nobody likes a wise ass, Spicer. Anything else on your mind?"

I considered mentioning my feeling that something was out of whack down here, but Beecher wasn't the sort of guy to put much stock in hunches and feelings, so I asked a question I suspected might be related.

"Yes sir. Do you have anything new on the incident last night . . . the one I called you about?"

After a momentary pause, Beecher said, "Nothing that hasn't been in the papers, except that our Navy brethren are turning the whole damned Pacific Ocean upside down looking for that Jap sub."

"All right, sir, see you tomorrow."

"Don't forget, Major, 1400 hours. Don't be late."

I made a face at the telephone. "Yes, sir."

A woman passing by the booth saw me stick out my tongue at the phone and laughed. I restrained myself from sticking my tongue out at her, too.

Having gotten my chores out of the way, I had a couple of hours to kill, so I picked up an *LA Times* from a rack outside the coffee shop and caught up on the news. I also caught up on my sleep with a short nap to make up for my early departure from Santa Barbara. I hoped the need for a nap was not a sign of old age creeping in after only 32 years. Well, almost 33.

About quarter to five I splashed some cold water on my face and plunked my butt down on a metal lawn chair in a pleasant little garden area near the parking lot. While waiting for Sally and Russ, I wondered what kind of automobile California blondes might be driving these days. Surely it would be the ultimate in snazziness. Sally didn't disappoint me.

A bright red Mercury convertible with its top down drove into the lot and parked next to where I was sitting. Sally was still a kid at heart. The Mercury had a car radio and I could hear Artie Shaw just beginning the beguine when Russ shut off the engine. Yes, Russ was driving. That made me wonder who was enchanting whom. I stood up and walked over to the car.

Sally was grinning from ear to ear again, or still. "Good afternoon, Major Spicer."

"Hello, Sally. You're living dangerously letting Sergeant Pierce drive your Mercury. He's used to driving Jeeps."

She laughed. "Oh, Russ did a wonderful job of getting us here."

I looked at Russ and gave him a wink. He just grinned. Everybody was grinning but me. Maybe old age really was setting in.

Sally said, "Is that offer of a drink still good, Major?"

"Yes, but only if you call me Johnny for the rest of the day."

She laughed again. "Okay, Johnny. It's a deal. Hop in."

Sally started to open her door, but I put a hand on the window sill and vaulted into the back seat. That made me feel a lot younger.

Obviously surprised by my gymnastic prowess, Russ said, "Well done, sir!"

"I'm not dead yet, Sergeant."

Laughing, presumably at my childish behavior, Sally said, "Johnny, do you like South Seas bars? Trader Joe just opened a new one in Inglewood and I've been dying to see it. Would that be okay?"

Russ looked back over his shoulder to see if I was going to answer her question honestly or humor her. I humored her.

"Then Trader Joe's it is. Drive on, Sergeant Pierce."

Russ looked at Sally for directions. "Go back up to Imperial Highway and turn right toward the plant. Drive on past the plant and make a left turn on La Cienega. That will take us up to Manchester and Manchester intersects Market Street after a couple of blocks."

I hollered from the back seat, "You get all that, Sergeant Pierce?"

"Yes, sir. Easy as pie."

Sally turned around and winked at me. Then she slid over a little closer to Russ.

Trader Joe's Trade Winds bar was located in one of those oddly shaped triangular buildings they put up to take full advantage of the space available where two downtown streets meet at an acute angle. Inside, it was pure kitsch with wallpaper representing South Seas flora in gaudy hues, an overabundance of bamboo, and carved wooden Tiki gods scowling at us from all sides. The lighting was also something to behold. The local hardware store must have had a big sale on colored lightbulbs.

We seated ourselves in a U-shaped booth with Sally in the middle, and since the joint had jukebox gizmos at almost every table, Sally immediately set about providing some mood music. She chose Kay Kyser's recording of *Why Don't We Do This More Often*.

The cocktail waitress wasn't on duty yet, so the bartender, came over to take our drink orders. Of course, he was attired in a colorful green, yellow, and red Hawaiian style shirt. At least you couldn't miss him.

Sally enthusiastically ordered a Mai-Tai. Russ asked for Pabst Blue Ribbon and I ordered Scotch-rocks. Sally did not approve.

"You guys are a couple of party poopers. In a place like this you're supposed to order something exotic."

I said, "Fruit juice is for breakfast."

Sally glowered at me. "Oh, you!"

The next hour or so proceeded pretty much along the same lines, and then we decided to make a night of it by adding dinner to the evening's menu. This change in plans led to the chore of choosing an establishment at which to dine.

Sally said the best food in town was found at a hof brau up Main Street a block or so, but people stopped going there because of the war. I wasn't sure a declaration of war was sufficient reason for passing up decent schnitzel, but Sally resolved the issue by suggesting a nearby Chinese joint. Apparently Chinese food was all right because China was our ally.

Our evening on the town ended for me around nine when we pulled into Patmar's parking lot. After giving Russ the key to his room and telling him his duffel was already in the room, I said goodnight.

Sally, bless her soul, was still smiling. "Goodnight, Johnny. Thank you for a lovely evening."

Russ added, "Yes, thank you for the drinks and dinner, sir."

"You're welcome. Oh, by the way Russ, we're due back at the Presidio by 1400 hours tomorrow. That means we need to hit the road no later than 0500. See you then."

I noticed Sally's smile fade a little when she heard that piece of news. Oh well, war is hell.

My watch said it was about 2115 when I climbed into bed looking forward to some sleep. As it turned out, I was up again two hours later when every damned air raid siren in the county went off.

I was out of bed, into my pants, and out the door faster than you could say Jack Robinson. Russ's room was two doors down from mine and I only beat him outside by a few seconds. I noticed he came out with his sidearm on his belt. We were both looking skyward, but there was damned little happening up there.

"Any idea what's going on, sir?"

"Not for certain, but after Monday night's escapade up the coast, I would not be surprised if we were witnessing a jumping of the gun."

"Yes sir. Sally said folks around here are pretty edgy.'"

Leading Russ out into the parking lot so we could see the sky beyond Patmar's second story, I said, "I guess that's to be expected. Half of them are probably sleeping with BB guns under their pillows."

The patrons of Patmar's Motel, however, were not sleeping at all. Within a few minutes the parking lot was nearing its capacity to hold sky watchers. I recognized one of the folks out there as the office night man. He headed directly for us with a slip of paper in his hand.

"Sergeant Pierce, you just had a telephone call. Here's the number to call back."

Russ accepted the message slip and looked at it. I asked, "Sally?"

A little sheepishly he said, "I'm afraid so, sir."

"Poor kid's probably scared out of her wits. Go call her back if you want, Russ."

"Thank you, sir."

Russ jogged back to his room while I stood around with everyone else and looked up at nothing until the sirens abruptly stopped at about 0135 hours. As folks began returning to their rooms, I saw Russ come back out of his. I was standing next to the Army's Dodge when he caught up with me.

"She okay, Russ?"

"Yes, sir. You were right. She was scared. Sally said they just installed those sirens a few weeks ago. She never expected to hear them again except when they were tested."

"I trust you put her mind at ease?"

He nodded. "I'm sorry, sir. I never expected to . . . get involved with her, but that's sort of what's happening."

"What are you apologizing for, Sergeant? Sally's cute as a bug's ear, she's smart, and she's got a great personality. I don't know how you could do any better."

I thought Russ might be blushing a little as he said, "I noticed, sir."

Making sure nobody was watching, I unlocked the Dodge's trunk and said, "I thought maybe you had."

He watched me unlock the secret compartment below the trunk floor. From that compartment I extracted a web belt and sidearm holster along with the Colt .45 caliber semiautomatic pistol they were intended to carry. I slung the belt over my shoulder while I relocked the secret compartment and trunk.

With concern Russ asked, "You think you're going to need that before the night is over, sir?"

I laughed. "Hell no, but I can't have my ADC looking more

'Army' than I do."

It was Russ's turn to laugh. "No, sir. That would never do."

On that note, we said goodnight and returned to our rooms with only a few hours of our night left. As things turned out, we had even less time left for sleeping than we thought. At 0315 by my trusty Longines Czechoslovakian Air Force chronometer the sirens went off again, only this time when we went out to look there was something to see.

No, there were no Jap bombers over LA, at least that we could see. What we saw instead was about a hundred searchlights scanning the skies for intruders. It looked like the Hollywood premiere to end all premiers, but there was more. Anti-aircraft batteries from LA to Long Beach were firing everything they had at something, but what? I saw nothing in the searchlight beams to shoot at.

Standing next to me in the parking lot again, Russ said, "This is nuts, sir! What in blazes are they shooting at?"

I shook my head. "Lord only knows. It looks like the searchlights here near the coast are tracking something coming in our direction from the north, but I sure don't see it."

The lights kept tracking toward us, passed more or less overhead, and kept going in the direction of Long Beach to the south. All the while, the AA batteries at Mines Field were hurtling hundreds of rounds at whatever they thought the searchlights held in their beams. At that moment Los Angeles sounded like a full-fledged war zone. We stood there shaking our heads in amazement.

Eventually the anti-aircraft guns went silent and the sirens shut off. The searchlights continued searching, but things were considerably more peaceful. I looked at my watch again. It was nearly 0400 hours. So much for sleep.

Turning to Russ, I told him the time and said, "I suggest we get packed up and hit the road. It's earlier than I planned to leave, but with all this going on, we could encounter roadblocks and who knows what other problems. We can take turns napping on the way."

"Yes, sir. I'll meet you at the car in fifteen minutes."

Seeing Russ had left his room door open, I said, "Give me your room key. I'll turn it in when I check us out at the office."

As he handed me his key, I grinned and added, "Don't let any enemy aircraft get you on the way back to your room."

"I'll watch out for them, sir."

Back in my room I did a quick wash job, shaved, and slipped

into a fresh uniform shirt and underwear. I was about to slip into my uniform blouse when I decided to wear my leather flight jack at a hedge against a chill in the morning air. Finally, I put on my cap and walked out the door, B-4 bag in hand.

In the office, I settled our bill and handed over the keys to our rooms. Then I headed for the Dodge. Russ was already there, and not too surprisingly, he had a blonde in his arms. It was a good thing we were leaving town before that blonde kidnapped my ADC.

I threw our bags into the trunk and opened the driver's door. As I did that, Sally trotted over and gave me a hug, too.

"Please take good care of Russ, Major."

I laughed. "You've got that backwards, Sally. It's Russ's job to take good care of me."

She looked me in the eye, and with a good deal of authority in her voice, said, "Whichever it is, I want him back when you're through with him."

"Yes ma'am. I'll send him back special delivery."

That got me a smile. "Thank you, Johnny."

Russ and I were on Sepulveda heading north toward the pass when the sirens commenced again and the 40-milimeter anti-aircraft cannons opened up. The sky looked like a Fourth of July celebration.

Russ was leaning forward to see the show through the windshield and I said, "You, know, I believe there is a law of physics that says what goes up must come down."

"I was just thinking the same thing. With all the rounds they're firing tonight, there's bound to be a fair amount of damage on the ground from falling shrapnel."

I breathed a sigh of relief when we turned left on US 101 and headed up the coast while the Battle of Los Angeles raged on behind us. I thought about the uneasy feeling I'd had when I left North American Aviation and drove through the communities around Mines Field. I was fairly certain the fireworks over our head were a manifestation of what caused that feeling. The folks in America were scared as hell. For once, I thought, the people had gotten it right.

Four

Crissy Field, San Francisco

In my opinion Crissy Field's most outstanding feature is its view. The airfield is situated right on the San Francisco Bay shoreline at the south end of the Golden Gate Bridge offering an uninterrupted view from the bridge and Marin headlands all the way around past Alcatraz to Oakland on the bay's east shore.

To the Army, however, the little airfield is significant because it is the only place you can land an airplane in San Francisco. For that reason, the Army has hung on to Crissy Field since the Great War. Crissy is tiny as Army Air Corps fields go, and to make matters even more cramped, the Army shares their narrow strip of beach with a Coast Guard Station.

The aircraft parked alongside Crissy's runway are all fairly small, like the twin-engine Beech AT-7 Stu Irvin flies. At the moment it was the only twin on the field. The rest of the ships were single-engine transports of various types or little Piper Cub O-59 observation ships.

With a prevailing wind from the west, most landings at Crissy are made from east to west. I parked the Dodge at the west end of the strip because that was where General Davis' plane would most likely end up after it landed.

Russ and I were leaning on the Dodge's front fenders, and from the corner of my eye, I saw him stifle a yarn. That, in turn, made me yarn. We were both dog-tired after our eventful night in LA. I hoped we would have time for a little sack drill before leaving for wherever General Davis sent us next on our current assignment.

As for the assignment, itself, we still had no idea what it was.

Our only clues were it was big and had something to do with B-25s. Maybe.

I glanced at my wristwatch. General Davis was ten minutes late, but generals can get away with tardiness because there's nobody left in the chain of command to reprimand them. Then the drone of distant aircraft engines reached our ears. Russ and I both turned toward the sound. It was coming from the east, somewhere over Oakland.

Before long the familiar shape of a Douglas DC-3 banked slightly to the left over Treasure Island for a straight-in approach to Crissy. The pilot set his ship down smoothly at the east end of the field and rolled in our direction. It's considered bad form to bounce landings with a general aboard.

The sparkling silver ship carried the usual red and white horizontal stripes on its rudder and US star roundels on its wings. The passenger hatch on the port side at the rear of the fuselage was already open and an enlisted man inside the ship attached a ladder to the opening as soon as the DC-3 rolled to a stop.

Seconds later Major General Chester Davis stepped off the ladder and walked briskly in our direction. He carried himself in an erect posture that left no doubt about who was in charge. Russ and I met him halfway with smart salutes. The general returned the military courtesy and said, "Let's take a walk, gentlemen."

I expected that. From past experience I knew Davis was a firm believer in conferences that traveled on foot and were far from any walls that might have ears. He took off toward the beach and I fell in on his right with Russ in step to my right.

I also knew from past experience that Davis didn't waste much time on chitchat. He got right down to cases.

"Johnny, I assume you know who Hap Arnold is, right?"

"Yes, sir. General Arnold is chief of the United States Army Air Force."

"Correct. Now gentlemen, those are the last words any of us will say during this meeting that aren't classified at the highest secret level in the land. You are not to repeat a single word of what we talk about today to anyone, not even to Colonel Beecher. Got that?"

Russ and I answered in unison. "Yes, sir."

"All right, here's the story. The president has ordered Hap Arnold to conduct a retaliatory mission against Japan as payback for Pearl Harbor. FDR expects that retaliation mission to accomplish two objectives. First, American morale is at an all-time low right now, to say nothing of panic in the streets like they had in Los Angeles early this morning. A raid on Tokyo would do wonders for our drooping morale.

"FDR's second reason for insisting on this mission is to make clear to the Japanese people that their Emperor is full of beans when he says the US can't attack Japan. Apparently, we can and will attack Tokyo, and very soon.

"The way Arnold explained the mission to me is we are going to give the Japs a taste of their own medicine. The aerial bombing raid on Tokyo will be carried out by modified B-25Bs flown by specially trained crews from the deck of the aircraft carrier Hornet, which will be operating as part of a task force that also includes the carrier Enterprise and a several escort ships.

"The specific details of the raid are known only to the men who planned it, and the anticipated date of the attack is known only to the task force commander and the man directly in charge of the aircraft and crews. That man is Lieutenant Colonel Jimmy Doolittle. Obviously, this is a joint Army-Navy operation. Do you understand all that?"

Again, Russ and I answered in unison. "Yes, sir."

"Good. You now know enough to get yourselves shot if you repeat it to anyone."

I was getting tired of hearing how top secret this thing was. "You're made that quite clear General."

Davis stopped and gave me an angry look, and then he smiled. "You're right, Johnny. I forgot who I was talking to. I wouldn't have chosen you and Sergeant Pierce for this job if I had any doubts about your ability to keep secrets.

"Now we need to talk about what I expect you to be doing while you're keeping that secret. Hap Arnold gave me this job on the QT, and I'm not sure who else knows about his request for our involvement—quite possibly nobody. I have the feeling we are Arnold's private little insurance policy for guaranteeing the security of a very complicated mission.

"As you might imagine, the preparations for this mission are taking place in multiple locations. For that reason, I have established two counter-espionage teams who will work at opposite ends of the country. You two are my west coast team. At this point I see no reason for you to know who your opposite numbers are on the east coast. If that need arises, I will put you in the know.

"Now, your actual orders are a little vague, but I know you are used to that by now. What I expect you to do is nose around here and there keeping your eyes open for anything that doesn't seem right. Like I said, vague, but picking up on irregularities seems to be your specialty, Spicer. You know what I mean?"

"I think so. I'm very big on vague, sir."

General Davis chuckled. "It's your hunches that make you valuable to me, not your vagueness. Okay, here are some places for you to begin your nosing around: Pendleton Air Field in eastern Oregon, McClellan Field in Sacramento, and Alameda Naval Air Station over there across the bay.

"Pendleton because the crews for this mission are being selected from the 17th Bomber Group which was flying antisubmarine missions from there, McClellan Airfield because that's where the B-25s will receive their final preparations, and Alameda because that's where the aircraft and crews will board the Hornet. Just so you know, the 17th Bomber group is no longer at Pendleton. The entire group has been transferred to another airfield where they're already training for the raid on Japan."

I said, "Got it."

"Good. Now just a few more background details. Arnold and Doolittle are looking at this raid as something very close to a suicide mission. They'll be stretching the range of their B-25s to the limit. It's entirely possible some of the ships won't have the fuel necessary to reach their designated landing fields after dropping their bombs and could end up in Japanese occupied China. For that reason, the crew assignments are strictly voluntary.

"B-25s were chosen for this mission because they are the only bombers in the Army Air Force fleet that have the short field take off capability required for launching from an aircraft carrier with a capacity load of fuel and bombs. Also, because of the additional fuel required to reach the target, the bombers can only carry four five-hundred pound bombs. As a result, the damage caused by the raid will be relatively minor. As I said before, the expected benefits of this mission are more psychological than physical. Are you with me so far?"

I said, "Yes, sir," and Russ echoed my reply.

"Good. The timing for this mission is short, so yours is, too. Get moving as soon as I'm out of your hair here.

"You are to communicate with me directly and nobody else on this mission. Do so only when you have something I need to know about or you require special assistance of some kind. Needless to say, anything you need is yours. I've already made that clear to everyone here and at HQ in Washington. They don't know why, but you get anything you ask for short of a battleship.

"Sergeant Pierce, I have added you to the Priority Able list just in case you fellows need to reach me and Major Spicer can't make the call for some reason. Just tell the DC HQ operator you are placing a Priority Able call for General Davis and give them the six-digit number on your MID ID. They will put the call through to me even if I'm sitting on the crapper, but don't abuse the privilege.

"Sergeant Pierce, your primary job on this assignment is to watch Spicer's back so he can concentrate on sniffing out those irregularities we talked about. I want you both back from this operation in one piece. Any questions?"

I shook my head. "I'm pretty sure you've told us all you're going to, so we'll take it from here. Russ, do you have any questions for General Davis?"

"No, sir."

Davis nodded. "All right then, I'll say so long. I have to get back to Washington."

The props on his DC-3 were already turning when we got there. From the top of the boarding ladder, Davis looked back at us and hollered, "Good luck, gentlemen."

Russ and I saluted and the hatch slammed shut. We were on our own.

A few minutes later we were sitting in the Dodge. I'd started the engine, but I had no idea where to point the car. An assignment as complicated as this usually requires some planning, but we didn't seem to have much time for such niceties. Thinking of time made me look at my watch. It was 1515. Unfortunately, knowing the time did not cause any brilliant ideas to form in my mind.

Russ said, "This is a tough one, isn't it sir?"

"It is Russ. We are looking for a needle in a haystack without knowing which haystack it's in or even if there really is a needle. Say, you told me you came from Oregon originally, didn't you?"

"Yes, sir. I was born and raised in Corvallis, south of Portland."

"Where is Pendleton from there?"

"It's a little north and way east over by the Idaho border."

"That's just swell. Why the hell would they station an antisubmarine group that far inland? That's crazy."

"It seems that way to me, too, sir. Are you thinking we should start in Pendleton?"

"Pendleton is the coldest trail right now so if there's any intel to be had there we should probably get to it. Any idea how far

Pendleton is from here?"

Russ gave the question a moment of thought. "Well, sir, it has to be more than seven hundred miles by road. I think it's at least a sixteen-hour drive."

"That's no good. We can't waste more than 30 hours on the road getting to and from the hinterlands of Oregon on what could turn out to be a wild goose chase."

"What about Captain Irvin, sir?"

"Good idea, Russ. He must be here because his AT-7 is over there. Any idea where he hangs out when he's not up in the clouds?"

"I found him in the main hangar the other day when he flew me down to Los Angeles."

Pulling the Dodge's gearshift into low, I said, "Okay, that's where we'll look first."

I parked alongside Crissy's main hangar and we as we got out, I spotted a public telephone nearby. "Russ, see if you can find Irvin and tell him our problem. I'm going to use that payphone to check in with Colonel Beecher. He's been pretty much shut out of this assignment and he isn't going to be happy to hear that."

"Yes, sir."

I was less than a mile from MID's building at the Presidio, but I decided to call Colonel Beecher instead of going to his office. The excuse I gave myself was time. Seeing Beecher in person would use up too much of our valuable time. Sure it would.

"Beecher."

"Hello, Colonel. This is Spicer."

"Yeah, I figured it might be when I heard the DC-3 take off. You don't have to tell me about your meeting. I got the word straight from the horse's mouth. Good luck."

I opened my mouth to reply, but the phone clicked in my ear. Oh well, I didn't really want to talk to Beecher anyway. I hung up, and then dialed 0 for the operator to place a long-distance call to Casa Sobre El Mar, the private hospital in Santa Barbara where Susan works.

When I got Susan on the line, I said, "Hi, Angel. I'm just checking in to say hello."

The phrase "checking in" was code Susan and I agreed on to let her know I couldn't say much, but everything was okay. Susan said, "Thank you, Johnny. Mister Whiskers and I miss you."

"I miss you guys, too. I'll check in again as soon as I can."

"Be careful and hurry home."

"That's my plan. Take care of yourself, Angel."

"I will. Johnny?"

"Yes."

"I love you."

"I love you too, Angel. Bye."

"Goodbye, Johnny."

Hanging up the telephone, I noticed Russ standing a few feet away. Stepping out of the booth, I said, "What's the word?"

"Captain Irvin is available. He's checking the weather conditions up that way."

"Good. I talked briefly with Beecher, and I do mean briefly. He said he'd gotten the word about our mission from Davis. The Colonel did not sound happy. He wished us luck and hung up on me."

"Really, sir?"

"Yes, really. I gotta say I'm gettin' dang tired of the prima donnas in this outfit. Beecher's predecessor was no better. Here comes Stu."

Captain Stu Irvin, MID's unofficial pilot, is a casual sort of fellow who is a little on the husky side, smokes fat cigars, and always looks just a little rumpled around the edges. On the other hand, I've heard he's very good at what he does.

"Hello, Stu. What's the word?"

"Hiya, Spicer. The word is 'lousy.' There's a full-fledged blizzard up north that stretches from above Yakima, Washington clear down to the Oregon-California border, an area which just happens to include that little burg you want to go to."

"Well, hell. I guess I don't really want to go to Pendleton after all. How long before things clear up in that area?"

"Probably three or four days at least, allowing them time to dig out from under all that snow." He grinned and added, "I can get you to Palm Springs, though."

"You're a lot of help."

"Always in there tryin'. Anything else I can do for you?"

I was about to say no, but a thought occurred to me. "Yeah, maybe there is. You know anything about B-25s?"

"Sure. I got a left seat check out in a C model down at the factory where they make 'em. You got a Mitchell that needs flying?"

"Not at the moment, but I have some questions. You got time for a drink at the O-Club?"

Stu grinned. "If you're buyin', I got time."

I looked at Russ. "You want to go get some sack drill? I'm pretty sure we aren't going anywhere until tomorrow morning."

"Yes, sir. That sounds good."

"All right, come on. We'll drop you off on the way."

The three of us squeezed into the front seat of the Army's Dodge business coupe and I drove into the Presidio. Dropping Russ and his duffel off at the enlisted men's barracks, I said, "All right, meet me out in front of the VOQ with your duffel tomorrow morning at 0700."

"Yes, sir. See you then."

A few minutes later Stu Irvin and I were sitting at a table in the Presidio Officers' Club with a terrific view of the Golden Gate Bridge. Stu ordered a straight shot of rye and I asked for a cup of coffee.

"Okay, Major, what is it you want to know about B-25s?"

"What's the quickest, most efficient way to sabotage one so it can't get off the ground?"

Irvin laughed. "If anyone else asked me that question, I'd shoot 'em for a spy. You want this hypothetical B-25 completely out of commission or just temporarily grounded?"

"Something that would take at least several days to fix."

He relit his cigar and took a long pull on both the cigar and his rye. "There are several things that could cause that kind of damage, but the one I'd pick as the easiest and quickest would be to cross a couple of wires creating a direct short to ground on the upstream side of the circuit breaker panel.

"That way, when someone turned the master switch in the cockpit, there would be a big bright flash immediately followed by a hell of a lot of smoke while the insulation on the ship's primary wiring fried itself into ashes. I like that method because it happens on the ground with little chance of a crew member getting seriously injured."

Nodding, I said, "I'm not sure a Jap spy would be too awfully worried about that, but your idea sounds like something that would guarantee the ship wasn't going anywhere."

"It would definitely do that and replacing all the cooked wiring would take a couple of days, assuming the wiring harnesses and other parts to do it were available."

"How difficult would it be to pull that off? I mean, could someone with little or no technical knowledge be taught to cross those wires."

"Sure. The circuit breaker panels are easy to open. All you have to do is remove four screws and you're in. The wires are all color-coded, so the job could be summed up in a simple drawing on one page in a notebook."

"Okay, one more question."

Stu held up his nearly empty shot glass. "A second question gets a refill."

"Fair enough." I signaled the waiter for another round and wondered what the hell would happen if Stu was suddenly needed to fly somewhere.

"Okay, second question: how could the kind of sabotage you described be prevented?"

"Geez, Spicer. First you want to destroy the aircraft, and now you want to protect it. Make up your mind."

"If it's a Jap's business to destroy the aircraft, it's my business to protect it. In my war, the two go together."

Making an offhand gesture, Stu said, "Yeah, I guess that's the way it has to be. Well, sabotaging the circuit breaker panel would require the saboteur to be inside the ship, so the first thing to do is step up security so no unauthorized personnel have access to the ship's interior. That can be difficult, though, on a busy flight line.

"The next most surefire way I can think of to prevent the wires from being crossed is to make it more difficult to get into the circuit breaker panel, but that has a drawback, too. If the crew can't easily get to the circuit breakers, it defeats the purpose of having the damned things in the first place.

"There is another possibility. An electrical engineer could probably design a continuity checker of some kind that would spot the crossed wires before the master switch was thrown. Maybe it could be an extra step in the preflight checklist, but I'm not smart enough about electrical stuff to figure out how it could be done."

"I'm not either, but I know someone who knows someone who is."

Stu chuckled. "I hope you notice I'm not asking any questions. I don't want you to have to shoot me because I know too much about some cockamamie mission you've gotten yourself into."

"Smart man. I need to get going. You want a lift back to the field?"

Draining his glass, Stu said, "Yeah, that would be a good idea."

After dropping Captain Irvin back at Crissy Field's main hangar, I stopped at the officer's mess and chowed down on some pretty decent chicken croquettes. Then I went to my room at the Base Officer's Quarters and slept like a baby for about ten hours.

Five

Presidio, San Francisco

I was already in the Dodge with its engine idling and two cardboard cups of coffee a few minutes before 0700. Russ arrived precisely at the appointed hour. He tossed his duffel behind the seat and climbed in. I handed him one of the cardboard cups of coffee.

"Thanks for the coffee, sir. I'm still groggy from sleeping too long."

"You're welcome, Russ. Here, use this."

I handed him a funny looking thing consisting of a tin can soldered to a U-shaped bracket that fit over an automobile window sill. The U was upside down and the tin can was big enough to hold a cardboard cup of coffee securely.

Pointing to the U-shaped part, I said, "Slide the side of this farthest from the can between the side window glass over there and the window molding, and presto, you've got a place to put your coffee cup."

Following my instructions, Russ said, "Hey, that's pretty slick. Where did you get these, sir?"

"Our pal Stu Irvin had the mechanics in the hangar make up a bunch of them for use in cars, airplanes, and just about any other moving vehicle where you might need to set down a hot cup of coffee. He designed different versions for different applications. Stu is quite proud of these things."

"Captain Irvin is a clever fellow. I wonder if he could sell something like this to automobile manufacturers. All cars ought to have these things. What does he call it?"

"A cup holder. The name could use some spiffing up, but the

idea is a good one."

Pulling the Dodge's gearshift lever into low, I drove away from the curb and Russ asked, "May I ask where we're headed, sir?"

"Across the bay to Alameda Naval Air Station, mostly to take a look around so if we need to be there later, we'll know what to expect."

"The B-25s won't be there yet, will they?"

"I'm guessing the planes are wherever the crews are training, and from what Davis said, that is probably in the east somewhere. That's the tough part of this assignment. We're flying blind. How are we supposed to help insure the security of a bunch of airplanes if we don't even know where they are?"

"Yes, General Davis sure left a lot out of the information he gave us."

"He surely did. Like Davis said, he wants to see if we can figure things out for ourselves. If we can it's likely a Jap agent can do the same thing."

"But if everything is so hush-hush, how could we figure anything out, sir?"

"At least some of it by going back to see a cute blonde in Inglewood."

"But she said she didn't know about any ships being prepared for special missions."

"Russ, when you've been in the detective business as long as I have, you discover that most people don't know what they know until you ask the right questions. Now that I have some better questions to ask Miss Sally, we may find out she knows more than she thinks she does. Seeing her again won't make you too unhappy, will it, Sergeant?"

With a big grin plastered all over his face, Russ said, "No, sir, not at all."

"I didn't think so. We'll head south as soon as we finish up at Alameda NAS this morning. We should probably stop a little later and let her know we're coming. We are going to need a good deal more of her time because I have quite a few questions, including some that came out of my conversation with Stu yesterday."

As I zigzagged across San Francisco from northwest to southeast, I related what Stu Irvin told me about sabotaging a B-25. Eventually I got us onto the San Francisco-Oakland Bay Bridge in the eastbound direction.

They say it's the longest bridge in the world, or some such thing, and a zillion people drive over it every day, but crossing the Bay Bridge always gives me the heebeegeebees. The guard rails on the sides of the bridge are open and you can see all the way down to the water, making you wonder if the guy who put all those rivets in the bridge was having a bad day. Next time I have to cross the dang thing I'm putting in for hazardous duty pay.

Alameda is a small island on the eastern edge of the bay southwest of Oakland. What makes it an island is a long narrow body of water known as the Oakland Estuary that separates Alameda from Oakland. The Navy part of Alameda is mostly a huge airfield covering the upper end of the island. Besides the runways—five of them crisscrossing each other in all directions—the Naval Air Station also has a harbor for supply ships and a seaplane lagoon.

I'd been to that part of Alameda before. The China Clipper on which I'd returned from Hawaii last December landed in the Navy's lagoon.

Alameda Naval Air Station was protected by a high chain-link fence running the full width of the island. The curls of razor sharp concertina wire atop the fence were not there as decoration. At the west end of Atlantic Avenue, a major east-west thoroughfare through Alameda, there was a break in the fence. We had arrived at the main entrance to the Navy's airfield. In keeping with the concertina wire, the gate was well guarded by a contingent of sailors with Shore Patrol armbands. They had .45 Colt automatics on their belts and M1 carbines over their shoulders.

As I pulled to a stop next to the gate's guard shack, a Shore Patrolman with a Master Chief Petty Officer's chevron on his sleeve stepped out and said, "Good morning, sir. Please state your business at Alameda Naval Air Station today."

I handed him our MID IDs, saying, "Just having a look around, Chief."

My smart aleck answer earned me a who-the-hell-do-you-think-you-are glare, and then he looked at our IDs and found out who we thought we were. "Sir, forgive the delay, but I must report your presence on the base to the OD. Please stay where you are."

"Do your duty, Chief."

In a low voice Russ said, "I sure wouldn't want his job. It can't be fun standing here for hour on end with nothing to do except annoying a few officers who drive in now and then."

"Believe it or not, some enlisted men enjoy annoying officers, Sergeant."

"I suppose so, but there's no percentage in it. The officers always win. The rules are rigged in their favor."

"You know, you're right. We need to get rid of all those

danged officers."

Russ looked like he'd just stepped in something unpleasant. I quickly said, "Relax, Sergeant. I'm kidding you."

"Yes, sir."

The Chief returned to my window, handed me our ID cards, and said, "You and Sergeant Pierce are cleared onto the base. Do you need directions to anyplace in particular, sir?"

"No, thank you, Chief. I think we know the way."

'Very good, sir." With that, he snapped to attention and gave me a sharp salute.

I returned his salute and drove straight ahead from the gate, which put us on Second Street. I kept going until we came to water and could go no further. There I turned left on Avenue F which ran along the southern edge of the seaplane lagoon. Avenue F dead-ended at Fifth Street, where I turned right. Needless to say, the folks who name streets on naval bases are not big on imagination.

Fifth Street took us out to the harbor mooring area beyond the lagoon. I was negotiating a tight squeeze alongside a large truck when I heard Russ say, "Holy cow!"

Looking where Russ was looking I saw the reason for his exclamation. It was a very big reason. Fifty yards ahead on our right was the bow of the aircraft carrier Hornet. The dang thing was gigantic.

The pier alongside the Hornet was blocked by a lot of loading activity, so when we'd driven as close to the ship as we could, I pulled to the side of the road and we got out of the Dodge for a better look, but that close to the ship it was difficult to appreciate the Hornet's enormous size.

An officer with a single gold bar on each shoulder walked by and I stopped him. Offering my hand, I said, "Hello, Ensign. My name is Spicer."

He shook the hand I offered, saying, "Stephen Johnson, sir."

"Would you mind helping a couple of Army landlubbers out here? How long is that dang thing?

Ensign Johnson looked me over and he must have decided I wasn't good spy material. "It's about 825 feet, sir."

"Thank you, Ensign."

He should have stopped right there, but his curiosity got the better of him. "What's going on with you Army guys? Seems like I see you fellows hanging around the Hornet every time I come out here now."

"Well, Ensign, it's like this. We're thinking of buying the

Hornet and we're trying to figure out how much Army green paint it would take to cover it."

He laughed and said, "A lot, sir."

The young ensign tossed me a salute and went on his way. I jotted his name into my notebook. His big mouth was going to earn him a dressing down at the very least.

Russ said, "Did we just learn something there, sir, I mean besides how long the Hornet is?"

"Very good, Russ. If we were spies and we didn't already know the Hornet was scheduled to take part in a rare joint Army-Navy operation, we would now certainly have reason to wonder about the Army's interest in this great big boat."

Russ quoted a poster we were seeing frequently these days. "Loose lips might sink ships."

"Words of wisdom. Now let's do a little figuring here. Do you remember how long Sally told us a B-25 is?"

"I believe about 53 feet, sir."

"Okay, let's assume they're going to park them nose to tail in two rows of eight ships at the stern. That looks to be about the most compact grouping possible. Allowing for a little overlap, each ship takes, say, 40 feet of deck space. What's eight times 40?"

"Three-hundred-twenty, sir."

"So, 825 less 320 leaves us around five hundred and five feet for takeoff. I don't know what the typical takeoff run for a B-25 full of bombs and fuel is, but it has to be a lot further than that. So now we have an idea what kind of special training the crews are getting, plus a clue about what sort of modifications might be needed for Doolittle's mission. Those two pieces of the puzzle along with some nosing around could add up to where the ships and crews are."

"But why do we need to know those things if that location is in the east somewhere and General Davis has a team covering that end of the country?"

"It's not that we need to know those things, Russ, we need to know how someone else could know them and if they do."

"I never thought of it that way. There sure is an awful lot to think about in the counter-espionage business."

"And you just put your finger on the biggest part of our job, observing and thinking about the meaning of what we observe."

"I'm beginning to see that, sir."

"Good. I'd say this has been a productive visit to our Navy neighbors. Now, let's hit the road."

Once off NAS Alameda and their little island, I turned south on State Route 17, otherwise known Hesperian Boulevard in these parts. In the little community of San Leandro, I pulled into a Shell gasoline station and filled the tank. While I did that, Russ used a handy public telephone to place a long-distance call to Inglewood.

Before we resumed our trip south, I used the same public telephone to call the main hangar at Crissy Field to satisfy my curiosity. I asked for Captain Stu Irvin.

"Captain Irvin speaking."

"Hi Stu. Spicer here."

"Geez, Spicer, what the hell do you want now?"

"The answer to a hypothetical question."

"Shoot."

"If you were sitting in one of those ships we talked about last night and it was fully loaded, how much distance would you need to take off?"

"Well, they give you all kinds of numbers in the ship's operation manuals, but the plain and simple answer is you'd need around fifteen-hundred feet for a sea level takeoff with no wind. Is that what you need to know?"

"Yes, Stu. Thanks. I owe you another round."

I heard him laugh on his side of the bay. "And don't think for a minute I won't collect on that debt. Now here's a free tip, Spicer. If you are in contact with the manufacturer of that ship, talk them out of a pilot's manual. Based on the questions you've been asking, it seems to me you ought to have one in your back pocket."

"You've convinced me, Stu. I'll do it."

Sliding back behind the Dodge's steering wheel, I glanced at my watch. It was 0930.

"What do you think, Russ, about ten hours from here?"

"That sounds right."

"Then we should make Patmar's about 1930. I guess we should stop talking about it and do it."

"Yes, sir."

From San Leandro we followed State Route 17 down to where it meets US 101 in an area called Mission San Jose. Once on 101, it was a straight shot to Inglewood—a very long straight shot.

About 1330 hours we rolled into a little burg called King City, where we made a fuel stop. We could have gone further on the gasoline we had left, but we also needed people fuel. There was a walk-up hamburger stand with a public telephone booth next door to a Chevron station, so I sent Russ to run some errands while I got our tank topped up.

Included in those errands were two telephone calls. The first was to Patmar's Motel to make sure we would have rooms tonight. The second call was to Sally MacLure. I told Russ, if he was going to invite her to have dinner with him, he should ask her to bring along a B-25 pilot's manual. His third errand was to bring back a few burgers and a couple of Cokes. The drinks fit very nicely into Stu Irvin's cup holders.

We swapped seats and Russ drove the rest of the way down to Santa Barbara. We refueled there, and I was sorely tempted to make a quick stop at an apartment on State Street to visit Mister Whiskers and his pal, but I didn't want to make our trip any longer than necessary. I did step into a pay phone booth at the Seaside station where we refueled and made a local call.

"Hi, Angel."

"Johnny! It's so good to hear your voice, and you sound close by."

"I am, but Russ and I have been on the road all day and we still have some ground to cover, so I'm resisting the urge to stop by and say hello to Mister Whiskers."

"I understand darling. It's just that I always miss you more when we've seen each other recently. Oh, don't take that the wrong way. I want to spend every minute we can together. I just . . ."

"I know Angel. It works the same for me. Everything going well at work?"

"Yes. Everything is normal, except we got a request from the Army for nurse volunteers. We had a meeting about it and I said that was fine for big hospitals with large nursing staffs, but we don't have any nurses to spare. Everyone seemed to agree.

"I suppose that's not a very patriotic attitude, but we have to think about people on the homefront, too. Also, Doctor Rothenberg announced we'll be taking on some Army and Navy patients requiring special kinds of treatment they might not get at military hospitals. I was pleased to hear that."

"That's a good thing for him to do, although you'd sure look cute in Army nurse fatigues."

"Not in the ones I've seen."

"Well, we need to get back on the road. Take care of yourself, Angel. I call again as soon as I can."

"You take care, too, Johnny. Don't forget I love you."

"That ain't gonna happen. I love you, too."

It was my turn to drive, so Russ and I traded seats again. As I pulled back onto US 101 Russ said, "It's none of my business, sir, but did you get to talk to your girl?"

"Yeah. I called her. I have to introduce you two sometime. You'd like Angel."

"From what you've told me, I'm sure I would. She sounds like a very special lady."

"She certainly is to me."

We hit our arrival time estimate pretty closely, pulling into the Patmar Motel parking lot at 1915 hours. I'd made myself a bet there would be a red Mercury convertible waiting for us when we got there. I won that bet. I went into the office and filled out registration forms for our rooms while Russ filled his arms with a blonde.

After Russ and I stowed our gear in our rooms, Sally joined us for dinner at Patmar's coffee shop. We avoided talking business during dinner for obvious reasons, but I left with a copy of the official *Pilot's Manual for the North American Aviation B-25C and B-25D (Mitchell)* under my arm. For some strange reason I could not fathom, the manual wasn't classified. I wondered how many Jap and Nazi spies had well-worn copies in their libraries.

After dinner I retired to my room with the pilot's manual. Russ and Sally went for a drive. I'm pretty sure Russ had more fun. I have no romantic interest in Sally, but the idea of going for a drive with one's best girl had a lot of appeal.

Six

North American Aviation Plant, Inglewood

At quarter past eight Russ and I dutifully clipped our NAA plant security badges on and followed Sally out to North American's run-up line. I noted a wooden pallet with several rolls of camouflage netting had arrived since our last visit. I wondered why the netting wasn't installed yet. Go easy, Spicer, you're turning into a real pain in the butt.

Sally's Friday outfit was a pair of pleated black slacks with a simple white blouse. Her hair was up and held in place by a black and white checkered headband with a bow. I tried to remember the days when I actually had a choice about what clothes I put on in the morning. It wasn't really that long ago, but it seemed like it.

"All right, Major Spicer, what questions do you have for me this morning?"

I noted that I was "Major Spicer" again. She was all business at the plant. Sally had a good sense of decorum.

Pulling my notebook out of my pocket, I said, "Here's a good one. Let's say you wanted to increase the fuel capacity of a B-25 in the field. How would you go about it?"

Sally frowned. "The only way I can think of is to install a ferry tank in the bomb bay."

"That won't do. We need to carry a load of bombs in there."

"Oh. Well, I don't know if fuel tanks can be added anywhere else without major modifications. As I understand it, the 25C and D are already subject to weight and balance issues."

I smiled. "Don't limit your answer to C and D models. Let's go for an earlier variant, say the B model, if it makes a difference. And be imaginative, Sally. Come up with something innovative."

She laughed. "You mean like designing a trailer to pull behind us for the extra gas."

"That might be a little too innovative."

Sally turned toward the B-25C we boarded on our last visit. At least I think it was the same one. She walked around the ship, looking here and there.

Russ looked at me curiously. I winked at him and held up a finger to indicate he needed to be patient.

Suddenly Sally spun around and trotted back to where Russ and I were standing. "You stinker! You knew the answer to your question before you even asked it, didn't you?"

I smiled. "That's Major Stinker to you, and no, I do not know the answer to my question. I just know there has to be one. What did you come up with?"

Her expression said she still thought I was playing with her, but she told me what I needed to hear. "One of our engineers just figured this out and I happened to see his drawings. That's how I know about it. He designed a sort of funnel and hose system that is mounted just above the wing on each side of the aircraft near the dorsal turret gunner's position. The funnels have a standard latching fuel cap over them and the hoses go to the aft wing fuel tanks.

"The B-25 has two fuel tanks in each wing. Both tanks feed the engine on that wing. Fuel is drawn from the aft tank to the forward tank, and from there to the engine.

"With this system, extra fuel is brought aboard in those square metal cans and stowed wherever there is space. As the fuel in the aft tanks is consumed, a crew member refuels them through these funnel devices."

I said, "Very clever solution to the problem, and these funnel gizmos will work in a B-25B?"

"Yes, they should work in any variant we've made so far. They might not be necessary, though, because I understand a future model will include an additional fuel tank in each wing."

"But will these in-flight refueling systems be installed in all existing B-25s?"

Sally shook her head. "No. They have a major flaw that makes them dangerous. If an enemy tracer round goes through the fuselage and hits one of the fuel cans, the resulting explosion and fire could destroy the ship. Since one of every three rounds fired by a German fighter is a tracer, there is a very real danger of that happening."

"So, what's being done with this refueling device?"

"That is the strange part and why I didn't remember the in-flight refueling system at first. We are manufacturing a small number of them as kits to be installed in the field, just as you originally asked."

"And where are these kits being sent?"

Frowning again, she said, "I don't know, but it must be someplace where they are modifying 25s for a special kind of mission. I think I can find out if you want."

"Please do. It's critical that we have that information."

"Okay, sit tight here and I'll go call engineering. They should be able to tell us."

"Thanks, Sally."

As we watched her walk briskly toward the administration building, Russ said, "You were right, sir. Sally did know more than she thought she knew."

"Yup, and if you think about the circumstances, you can understand why she didn't think of the in-flight refueling gizmo until I asked the right question. It doesn't always work out as well as this situation did, but it looks like we got lucky. Now we have to hope the trail leads somewhere."

It took her about ten minutes, but Sally came back with the goods. "The Eighth Air Force ordered 24 in-flight refueling system field installation kits about ten days ago."

I was jotting the details into my notebook, but so far, they didn't help us much. The Eighth Air Force was only about a month old and was still getting organized. The Eighth is, however, a strategic bombing outfit, so it figured they would be interested in a gizmo that increased the range of a bomber.

I asked the next logical question. "Do you know where the refueling gizmos were shipped?"

"They haven't been shipped anywhere yet because they're still being assembled. According to requisition form—Sally consulted a note pad she brought out with her—128-4196-420219, however, the assembled kits are supposed to go to the Sacramento Signal Depot."

Russ and I grinned like a couple of kids getting to lick the cake batter out of the mixing bowl. I said, "Now we're getting somewhere. That detail fits with the McClellan Field information we have. They are two different facilities, but they're in the same town. Sally, can we find out who asked North American to design a gizmo for in-flight refueling in the first place?"

Sally thought about my question. "Maybe. It has to be someone up high in the Army Air Corps, but design Engineers don't always know exactly who they are designing parts for. We can ask Michael Wilkins, the engineer who designed the device, and see what he knows."

"Do you think it would be possible to get Michael out here where we can interview him without the entire plant knowing about it?"

She looked me square in the eye for several seconds, and then said, "Johnny, this is a big deal, isn't it? I mean a real big deal?"

"Yes, Sally, this is a big deal, and that's all I can say except your help could make a difference in the outcome of this war we're in."

Sally looked over her shoulder at Russ, and then back at me. "I don't mind telling you this scares the heck out of me. I do not like knowing things that are so important to this country's enemies. It makes me feel . . . I don't know . . . like I'm caught in the middle of something dark and sinister."

"That pretty well sums up our part of the war. Sally, you would be entirely within your rights to refuse further cooperation, and there isn't much we could do about it. That choice is yours."

"Johnny . . . I'm sorry . . . Major Spicer, would it be all right if I talked to Russ alone for a few minutes?"

I gave Russ a questioning look and he gave me a barely perceptible nod of his head. To Sally, I said, "Sure. I'll be over there counting rolls of camouflage netting."

Walking back toward the administration/assembly building, I lit a Lucky Strike and leaned against a light pole. Sally was a nice kid, a smart one, too. She didn't deserve to be under the dark and sinister cloud that seems to follow me around these days. For that matter, I'm not sure I deserve to be under it either. More than anything, I just want to marry an angel and live peacefully under the palm trees on a beach somewhere.

Sally and Russ were having quite a conversation. He was in a tight spot, torn between a woman he obviously liked and his duty. I had not the slightest doubt that, if push came to shove, Russ would put his duty first, and knowing that made me feel worse. The guy who said war is hell didn't know the half of it.

Then the conversation ended, and they were walking in my direction. I field-stripped the Lucky and met them half way. Sally stood as close to Russ as was possible without being in his arms. I looked at Russ and he gave another imperceptible nod.

Sally looked up at me again with determination in her bright blue eyes. "Major Spicer, I've decided to help you all I can. I'll go in and ask Michael to come out here and join us. His full name is

Michael Wilkins and his title is Senior Design Engineer."

Sally looked up at Russ and smiled. He smiled back, and she walked into the administration-assembly building. Russ and I strolled back to the run-up line.

"She's scared, sir, very scared."

"I can see that, Russ, but I don't think Sally is in any real danger. We have no indication that anyone has the slightest interest in our assignment."

"No, sir. I think it's more the general idea of enemy spies and espionage combined with the Japanese shelling of that Santa Barbara oilfield and all that fuss the last time we were down here."

"'The 'Battle of Los Angeles,' as the newspapers called it?"

"Yes, sir. All of that taken together is enough to scare anyone and working here puts her closer to the danger than most civilians. What you said to her about this being a big deal was certainly true, but it made her realize she's in the middle of something, as she put it, 'dark and sinister.'"

"All right, Russ. I see your point. How can we put Sally's mind at ease?"

"I don't have any ideas on that, sir. I wish I did."

"Well, there is one thing we could do that might help. Do you have civvies with you?"

"Yes, sir. I have a sport coat. Also, some shirts and regular slacks."

"Good. At lunch time we'll drive back to the motel and go under cover. Our uniforms and side arms can be intimidating. Also, we'll be a little less noticeable in civvies, at least around this place."

"I think that's a good idea, sir."

"See, Sergeant, I do get a good idea once in a rare while"

Risking insubordination, Russ rolled his eyes heavenward. "Yes, sir."

I couldn't imagine the young man Sally escorted out to the run-up area being a "senior" anything. He looked about 12 years old. Sally introduced us, and he gave me as weak a handshake I've ever experienced.

"Hello, Michael. Nice to meet you."

He stared at me through glasses with Coke bottle lenses and looked as though no one ever thought it was nice to meet him before. Maybe nobody had.

"Michael, our job is preventing enemy espionage and sabotage. At the moment we're working on a case that requires kind of a backward approach to find out who knows what. The thing we need to know is, who originally asked you to design an in-flight refueling system for the B-25?"

Wilkins' brow furrowed as though I'd just told him hypotenuses don't actually equal the square root of A-squared plus B-squared. By the time he came up with an answer most people would have forgotten the question.

"He was a soldier, like you. I remember he had two silver bars on each shoulder of his uniform."

"The bars make him a Captain. Do you remember his name?"

He shook his head. "No."

Getting information out of Michael Wilkins was not unlike pulling teeth. "Would his name be in any of your files?"

"No. I was instructed not to make any notes of our conversation, except what I absolutely had to have for the design work."

Whoever wanted the refueling gizmo was taking no chances. I pointed to the MID shoulder patch on my uniform. "Do you remember if he had a patch on his uniform sleeve?"

"Yes. I remember he had a patch."

"Can you describe it?"

"I think so. The patch had a yellow eight with something like bird wings on a blue background. The bottom loop of the eight had the same red, white, and blue star design they paint on the wings and fuselages of military aircraft."

He'd just given me a very accurate description of the Eighth Air Force patch. Unfortunately, the only thing he remembered was something we already knew. "Okay. Is there anything else you recall about this fellow?"

Wilkins gave my question some thought, and then said, "I remember he was rather husky. He made me nervous looking over my shoulder at my desk."

I nodded. "Anything else?"

"Well, he didn't seem to know much about B-25s. He specified that the in-flight refueling system had to work on the B variant. I told him the design would work on any of the variants built so far because the fuel systems were all the same." After a short pause, Michael added, "Oh, and the knot in his necktie was crooked. It was off to the left. I like things to be symmetrical and it bothered me. I kept wishing he would fix his necktie."

I almost laughed, but the little fellow was trying his best. "All right, Mister Wilkins. Thank you for your help. We're investigating a very secret matter here, so please do not mention our conversation to anyone, and if you happen to think of anything else about this captain that might help us identify him, please let Miss MacLure know. She'll pass it on to us."

"Okay."

He just stood there looking nervous for a few moments before Sally told him he could go back to his work. On hearing that news, Wilkins hurried off without a backward glance as if he was afraid I would change my mind about not needing him anymore.

Sally smiled. "Would you believe that little guy has a doctorate in engineering from MIT? I always feel sorry for Michael because he is at a complete loss in any situation that doesn't involve a slide rule."

"Thus proving it takes all types to win a war."

"I guess so. What is your next question for me?"

"Actually, it's not a question as much as a suggestion. Can we go aboard that B-25 again for a few minutes?"

She said, "Certainly," and we all headed toward the ship. Russ reached up and opened the hatch. At the top of the ladder we were directly behind the cockpit. I leaned forward and looked to my right. The circuit breaker panel was mounted to the fuselage wall behind the copilot's seat, right where the B25C/D pilot manual said it would be.

Pointing at the panel, I said, "Sally, you know what that is, right?"

She nodded. Sure, that's the master electrical panel."

"Right, and do you know what I could do if I took a standard screwdriver and removed the four screws holding that panel cover in place?"

"No, but I bet it's nothing good."

"Right again. I could cut and twist two wires together which would create a direct short to ground, causing the entire electrical system in this aircraft to go up in smoke when the pilot turns on the master electrical switch up there on his instrument panel."

"Oh, great."

"I got that from a B-25 pilot when I asked him what would be the easiest and most effective way to sabotage one of these ships."

Sally sighed. "I guess that's something the electrical engineers need to fix."

"The fellow I spoke with suggested installing a continuity tester in the master electrical switch circuit to prevent the switch from closing in the event a short to ground exists. Your engineers may come up with their own solution, but this panel presents a significant sabotage risk. An enemy agent who can get aboard a B-25 on the flight line with a screwdriver for ten minutes can pretty much guarantee that ship won't be going anywhere for quite a while."

Sally shook her head in what I took to be frustration. "As if designing aircraft to survive air combat wasn't hard enough, now they have to be built to survive just sitting on the ground, too."

Trying to lighten the mood a little, I smiled and said, "If your job was easy, even guys like me could do it."

She gave me a token smile and looked at her watch. "The engineer we need to tell about this will be going to lunch soon. It would probably better to see him this afternoon."

"Okay, unless you have lunch plans already, how 'bout joining Russ and me? We have to swing by the motel for a minute, so we could eat there."

That suggestion earned me a real smile. "That sounds awfully good. Your car or mine?"

"Let's use the Army's gas."

Twenty minutes later we were parked in Patmar's parking lot. As we climbed out of the Dodge, I said, "Sally, would you mind grabbing us a table in the coffee shop? We'll only be a few minutes."

"Sure, but you fellows better hurry. I'm hungry."

After opening the Dodge's secret trunk compartment to swap the Army's heavy Colt .45 for my trusty little Smith & Wesson Police Special and its shoulder holster, Russ and I went to our rooms to get civilianized. I changed into a white cotton shirt, tan slacks, and a brown tweed sport coat. After checking the bathroom mirror to make sure my jacket didn't bulge too conspicuously, I made tracks for the coffee shop.

Russ was already there when I arrived and so were a lot of other people. Patmar's Coffee Shop is popular with the local lunch bunch and the noise level was not quite a din, but it was close.

As I joined Sally and Russ at our table, she grinned. "Wow! You guys look really different in regular clothes. It's a big improvement."

I laughed at her honesty. Russ leaned toward her and said quietly so as not to be overheard at nearby tables, "This is what Major Spicer calls 'going under cover'. He says we don't look as intimidating in civvies."

Grinning, Sally said, "I don't know, Russ. If I was a nasty spy, I would still think twice about tangling with you two no matter what you're wearing."

I said, "Then becoming a nasty spy would not be a good career choice for you. Unfortunately, I haven't met one yet who had any qualms about tangling with me."

Sally looked at Russ with an expression of concern. "Your work is really dangerous, isn't it? I don't mean interviewing people, but what you have to do with the information you get from those interviews."

Russ looked at me for a second, and then said, "I guess it is a little dangerous sometimes, but that's only a small part of our job."

Sensing Russ was trying to downplay the danger, I said, "Sally, Russ is well trained to handle tough situations, and we try to be smart about how we do things. That keeps the risks to a minimum."

Sally looked at me. "I notice you didn't say you were well trained."

"Nope. I'm just lucky. I never would have survived to this old age without a lot of luck."

"What are you talking about? You aren't old."

"I just feel that way sometimes. Hey, I thought you said you were hungry. I sure am."

Because of the crowd at Patmar's coffee shop for lunch, it took a while for our lunches to be prepared. They were worth waiting for, but it was nearly 1330 hours when we got back to North American Aviation. After making sure Russ and I both had our plant security badges on, Sally told us to head for our regular meeting location out on the run-up line while she went to find the electrical engineer we needed to talk with about the circuit breaker panel security problem.

Once out of the building, Russ said, "Sally sure speaks her mind, doesn't she sir?"

"She surely does. It's one of her qualities I appreciate most. I'd much rather work with someone who doesn't pull any punches than someone who tries to feed me baloney all the time to get on my good side."

Russ laughed. "Yes, sir. No baloney with Sally, that's for darn sure."

This time the fellow Sally had in tow as she left the administration building looked more like an engineer. He was tall with a short beard and carried himself erectly. He was also as blonde as she was. She introduced him as Walter Schuster, another Senior Design Engineer.

He scowled at me as we shook hands. "What is so important that you must take me away from my work, Mister Spicer?"

I already didn't like the guy. "Mister Schuster, we have . . . ."

"Doctor Schuster, if you please."

"All right. Doctor Schuster, we have discovered a security risk in the B-25's circuit breaker panel. I simply want to bring it to your attention in the hope you can design a means of preventing would-be saboteurs from . . . ."

"Mister Spicer, security is not my . . . ."

'That's Major Spicer, if you don't mind, and the security of this airplane most certainly is your business. Now, you can either listen to what I have to say, or I'll call Dutch and have him fly out here. I think he would rather you listened instead of taking up his time, which really is valuable."

Red was not a good color for Doctor Schuster, especially the shade of red his face turned. "All right, all right. What is it you think is wrong with the circuit breaker panel?"

"The gist of the problem is it is too easy to sabotage while the aircraft is parked on a flight line. In less than ten minutes with a screwdriver and a pair of diagonal cutters, I can guarantee this aircraft will be on the ground for a long time while every inch of its wiring is replaced."

Schuster looked puzzled. "How do you think you could do that?"

"I would remove the panel cover with the screwdriver, and then I would cut the red wire to the power buss and the green wire to the ground buss. The last step is stripping those two wires of their insulation and twisting them together."

Now Schuster was nodding. "Yes, yes, I see. In that way closing the master electrical switch on the instrument console would send full voltage to ground, the wires would instantly become hot, and the insulation would quickly burn."

"Exactly right. How difficult would it be to design something to detect such a short to ground and prevent the master electrical switch from closing if there is such a short to ground?"

Schuster didn't even need to think about the question. "It could be done quite easily with a fuse I know of. This fuse responds instantly to a ground fault, in this case preventing the master switch from directing power to the breaker panel. It would perform the same function if enemy bullets were to damage circuit breakers through the fuselage, thus preventing an in-flight fire. We might even consider hinging the panel cover and holding it closed with a positive latch. That would make it possible to find a short quickly and repair it, possibly even in flight.'

He looked at me, nodded in a curt manner, and said, "Thank you for bringing the problem to my attention, Major Spicer. I will put one of my junior engineers to work on designing the solution immediately. Good day, sir."

We watched Schuster march back to the administration/assembly building, and when he was out of sight, Sally broke into uproarious laughter. Her laugh was contagious and soon Russ and I were soon laughing with her.

When she regained her composure enough to speak, Sally said, "That is a conversation I will never forget. You played him like a Stradivarius violin! I didn't even know you knew Mister Kindelberger."

I smiled at her. "I don't."

Sally looked shocked. "But you called him by his nickname and you knew he was at the Kansas City plant right now and . . . and everything!"

Russ looked down at Sally. "Let that be a lesson to you, never play poker with Major Spicer."

She stared at me with an incredulous expression. "You mean that was all a bluff?"

"I prefer to think of it as creative duplicity. Whatever you call it, though, trickery is part of our business and it pays to be good at it."

"You had me fooled. I will certainly be less gullible in the future. What else do you have for me?"

"Unless Russ can think of anything I've forgotten, that's it. We can let you get back to work."

Sally's expression seemed a little sad. "Oh. Okay, then. I hope we accomplished what you came down here for."

"We did. The link to the Sacramento Army Depot, alone, makes the trip worthwhile. Russ, I don't see any advantage to heading north this afternoon. Let's plan to leave tomorrow morning. Say 0700 hours. In the meantime, you're on your own, Sergeant."

Russ smiled at that and I noticed Sally sneak a glance at her wristwatch. "I have some work to do for about an hour or so. Can I treat you fellows to dinner later?"

I smiled. "You can treat Russ to dinner, but I have some work of my own to do this evening."

Sally looked hopefully at Russ. He said, "I never turn down a free meal."

Wearing a big smile, she said, "Can I pick you up at the motel about six?"

With a smile to match Sally's, Russ said, "That would be fine. I'll be ready."

Russ and I turned in our plant security badges and headed for

Patmar's. On the way, Russ said, "Are you sure you don't need me tonight, sir?"

"Positive. Go have a good time with Sally."

"Thank you, sir."

Seven

Patmar's Motel, El Segundo

The first thing I did when Russ and I got back to the motel was use a public telephone to check in at the Presidio. Neither Russ nor I had any messages, urgent or otherwise. With that chore out of the way, I retired to my room and went to work consolidating my notes on the day's activities.

Something we learned at North American was nagging at me, but I couldn't put my finger on it. I hoped reviewing my notes would jog the memory loose. It didn't, but the B-25C/D pilots' manual on the desk did.

What I remembered was Michael Wilkins mentioning the Eighth Air Force Captain who came to him with the in-flight refueling project specified the system had to work on the B-25 B variant. A quick review of my notes from the assignment briefing General Davis gave us confirmed the connection. He said the Japanese bombing mission would be flown by B-25Bs.

It was by no means a sure thing, but the connection strongly supported the idea that the in-flight refueling system was intended for the Doolittle raid, and more importantly, vice versa. A Jap who connected the refueling system with whatever was being planned could assume the secret mission involved as many as 24 B-25Bs because that's the number of field modification kits the Eighth Air Force ordered from North American. It was an intelligence jackpot.

WHUMP!

The explosion didn't quite rattle the windows, but it got my attention. I was still contemplating what might have just blown up when a siren wailed into my room. The vehicle attached to the siren was somewhere to the south in El Segundo but coming in my direction at high speed. A few seconds later the first siren was joined by three or four more. I stepped out of my room to see what I could see.

What I saw first was Russ standing in the parking lot looking at something in the distance. He saw me and pointed to the northeast, the direction he'd been looking. What I saw when I looked in that direction was a tall column of black smoke rising into the cloudless blue sky.

I was figuring out where that column of smoke was coming from when Russ saved me the effort. "It's coming from North American, sir, or very close to there."

"I'll lock up my room. Meet me at the Dodge."

With my shoulder holster and jacket on again, I locked my room door and hustled over to the Dodge. Unlocking the passenger door for Russ, I told him to give me one of the red lenses in the glove compartment.

The Dodge was equipped with dual spotlights and the Army had thoughtfully provided two threaded red lenses to fit those spotlights. I screwed a lens on the driver side spotlight and climbed behind the wheel. After backing out of our parking spot, I pulled a knob on the dashboard that lit up the spotlight.

Russ asked, "Siren?"

"Let's see if we need it."

Half a block north of the motel I turned right on Imperial Highway. As we ran along the southern border of Mines Field, it became increasingly apparent that Russ was right about the source of the smoke.

There was an edge of concern in his voice now. "It's the main building, sir."

A crowd of onlookers and their cars were already lined up along Imperial Highway next to the chain-link fence bordering North American's parking lot to watch the excitement. The parking lot, itself, was a three-ring circus. First, there were nearly twice as many cars in the lot as usual and it took me a moment to realize there were two shifts' worth of employee cars in the lot. The swing shift was just arriving when the explosion went off. According to my watch, it was 1601.

Besides employee cars, the parking areas in front of and alongside the building were full of firetrucks—at least five of them—and just about every other kind of emergency vehicle imaginable. Large diameter fire hoses snaked into the building from fire hydrants, and a pumper truck. Ambulances were lined up at the plant entrance like taxicabs in front of the Biltmore. One roared out of the lot with its siren going full blast as I pulled the Dodge to a stop on the southern edge of the employee parking lot.

Most of the smoke, which was now diminishing some, came from first floor windows blown out by the explosion. As we approached the building on foot, I recognized the security guard we'd met on our first visit to North American.

He recognized me, too. "How come you guys didn't prevent this? That's your job!"

"We aren't mind readers. We had no reason to expect anything like this. Exactly what happened?"

"A bomb or something exploded in one of the employee locker rooms near the assembly areas. It happened during the shift change, so the place was jammed with workers coming and going. You guys really dropped the ball this time!"

I was tempted to ask him why he let someone into the plant with a bomb but thought better of it. Instead I led Russ around to the west side of the building. From there we could see a lot more damage. In addition to more blown out windows, a hole about five feet in diameter gaped near the employee entrance. Through that hole we could see several bodies on the floor and firemen hurrying to rescue survivors.

Pointing to a window directly above the hole, Russ said, "That's Sally's office up there, and her car is in the parking lot, so she was still here. I hope she was somewhere else in the plant when it happened."

"Go find her, Russ. I'm going to take a look around and see if I can spot the guy who did this. He might be hanging around admiring his handiwork."

Russ hurried off to see if anyone knew where Sally was, and I turned around to study the crowds in the parking lot and along Imperial Highway. If the bomb was the work of a Jap espionage agent, he might well stick around so he could report the success of his mission to his superiors.

The biggest problem with spotting a Jap spy is they seldom look Japanese and they don't have "SPY" tattooed across their foreheads in big red letters. Of course, the saboteur didn't necessarily have to be working for the Japs. He, or she, could be in the employ of the Nazis or even Mussolini. Still, a Jap agent was more likely. Why should Germany send someone clear across the country when they have allies already here to do their dirty work?

No, the best way to spot a spy is to look for someone who

might be looking for someone who might be looking at them. I saw just such a person standing about twenty yards away on the other side of the chain link fence along Imperial Highway.

She was tall and slender with blonde hair, and the moment our eyes met, she looked away. That alone might mean nothing, but when I turned and began walking in her direction, the woman hurried to a recent model pale gray Chevy sedan parked a few feet away from where she was standing. She turned for another look in my direction, and then climbed into the Chevy and drove away, spinning her tires in the dirt shoulder as she took off east on Imperial Highway.

The woman might not be an enemy espionage agent, but whoever she was, she didn't want anything to do with me. Maybe she just didn't like the way I looked at her, but I jotted her information in my notebook anyway. The Chevrolet wore yellow on black California plate 39 T 147.

I was still watching her progress on Imperial Highway when Russ reached my side. "You have something, sir?"

"Probably not, just a woman who got nervous when I looked in her direction. I have her description and a license number. We can run it through the California Department of Motor Vehicles just for ducks. Did you find Sally?"

He nodded. "Yes, she was injured in the explosion. I don't know any details, but her injuries were serious enough for her to be taken away by ambulance. She's at Freeman Hospital in Inglewood. I have directions to the place."

"All right, Russ, let's go see how she's doing."

"Thank you, sir."

Freeman Hospital wasn't far from Mines Field, and we didn't really need Russ's directions. We easily found the place by following a continuous stream of ambulances going there and returning to the North American plant.

It was surprisingly calm inside the hospital's emergency ward, despite there being patients in every available corner. Their injuries ran the gamut from minor to what I would call life-threatening, but they all seemed to be getting the attention they required from the staff. Nobody was being ignored, and that included Russ and me when we stepped up to the nurses' station.

A blonde nurse with glasses in stylish red plastic frames immediately asked if she could help us. I showed her my MID ID and said we were looking for a patient named Sally MacLure from the North American plant.

The nurse consulted a clipboard and said, "Miss MacLure is in treatment room four, bed two. You'll find it down that hall, second door on your right. Please make your visit as short as possible."

"We will. Thank you."

I made an "after you" gesture and followed Russ to treatment room four. He peeked in the room and I heard Sally squeal, "Russ!" We were in the right place.

By the time I got through the door, Russ was already at her side and holding her left hand. He had to hold her left hand because her right arm was held immobile by a tightly wrapped wooden splint. Also, Sally had what looked to me like an entire roll of gauze wrapped around her head. Some blood had leaked through the gauze near her left temple.

While I was noticing her injuries, Sally looked up and noticed me. "And Johnny!"

"How are you, Sally?"

"Not bad. I managed to fall and break my arm trying to get down the stairs from my office. I think I was dizzy because I'd just gotten a solid whack on the side of my head from some kind of pipe that flew up out of the floor. Other than that, I'm ready to go out on the town."

"Then I'd suggest putting on the black and white headband you wore this morning. Gauze headbands are out this year."

"You noticed my headband this morning?"

"Yes, why?"

"I didn't know guys paid much attention to that kind of thing."

I chuckled. "Our Uncle Sam pays me to be observant. Listen, I've got to make a couple of telephone calls, so I'll leave you in Russ's capable hands. Can I call anyone for you to let them know where you are?"

"No. thank you. You guys already know I'm here."

She earned a full-fledged laugh for that comment. "I was thinking more of your folks or someone like that?"

"No, I'll call them later. I don't want to scare Mom and Dad out of their wits. They're clear up in Portland and I don't want them thinking they have to rush down here."

I noticed Russ's ears perk up when she mentioned her hometown, which I gathered was not far from his hometown of Corvallis. I said, "Okay, I'll be back. You two try to behave yourselves while I'm gone."

The last thing I heard as I walked out was Sally saying, "Spoil sport!"

Leaving the emergency ward, I walked to the hospital's lobby at the main entrance. There I found a long bank of wooden telephone booths with glass insets in their folding doors, about half of which were occupied. I stepped into an empty one and called Colonel Beecher in San Francisco. I picked Beecher to call as a sort of peace offering. He was out of the information chain on our assignment and not very happy about it. Since I couldn't see how the North American Aviation plant explosion was related to our mission, I figured I was on safe ground.

"Hello, Major Spicer. What can I do for you?"

There was a coolness in his voice that said his nose was still out of joint. I said, "I thought you ought to know that somebody blew a hell of a big hole in the North American Aviation plant at the Los Angeles airport a little while ago. It happened right at the shift change, so the final lists of casualties and deaths will be long,"

"That's not good. Any leads on who is responsible?"

"Maybe. It's a long shot, but I spotted someone acting strangely among the spectators after the bomb detonated. I have a California plate and a description of the vehicle. Would you please have someone run them through DMV to see what we can find out?"

I gave him the Chevy's description and the plate number. "Will do. Are you working on this also or is it part of your primary assignment?"

"I can't see how it is related to anything we're working on, so I'll leave it in your capable hands. I would like to find out what you get on that plate, though, just in case I encounter the car again."

"All right, I'll leave the information we get back for you to pick up when you check messages."

"Thank you, sir."

"And Spicer?"

"Yes, sir?"

"Thanks for calling this in. We'll get right on it."

"You're welcome, sir."

I walked back to the emergency ward and found Russ sitting in a small waiting area. I sat next to him. "What's up?"

"They're putting a plaster cast on her arm, and then a doctor is going to evaluate her head injury. Sally acts as if this is all some great adventure."

I chuckled. "That, Russ, is known as being a trooper."

"I guess so, sir. She's certainly handling it better than I am. All I can think of is how much worse things could be and getting my hands on whoever planted that bomb."

"Well, that could happen. I just gave Colonel Beecher the

description and California license plate number of that woman I saw out on Imperial Highway by the plant. He's going to run the plate number through DMV for us."

Russ sounded puzzled. "Colonel Beecher, sir? I thought we were supposed to work directly with Washington?"

"Yes, concerning our primary assignment. I don't see this being part of that."

"You may change your opinion on that, sir."

"Oh? What do you know that I don't?"

"It's something Sally told me just before they showed up to do her cast. She said two strange things happened right after you and I left the plant this afternoon. The first thing was a telephone call from a woman who claimed to be with the Eighth Air Force concerning a shipment of parts delivered to the Sacramento Army Depot."

"You're right, that is interesting, Did Sally tell you what she told the woman?"

"In Sally's words, she smelled a rat. She told the woman she didn't handle that sort of information and to call NAA's order processing department."

"I knew she was a smart gal. You said there were two strange things?"

"Yes, sir. The second thing happened just before the bomb detonated, if it was a bomb. Sally's office has inside windows that overlook the assembly lines and she was watching a problem area in the line when she noticed a woman she'd never seen before among the arriving swing-shift workers. Something about her caught Sally's eye."

"What's the strange part?"

"This woman was carrying a lunch pail, just like everyone else, and she went into the employee locker room below Sally's office with everyone else, but the woman came out of the locker room again after only a minute, and she was no longer carrying her lunch pail. The woman hurried straight for the employee side door, and on the way, Sally swears the woman took a furtive glance up at Sally's office, and quickly looked away when she saw Sally watching her."

"I see."

"Sally said she went to her desk thinking to call security. She no sooner sat down when the explosion happened."

"And what has Sally concluded from these two incidents?"

"I'm not sure she has drawn any conclusions, but I have, sir."

"All right, Russ, what conclusions have you drawn?"

"I think we should consider the possibility the bomb was something more than a simple act of sabotage. It might be somebody decided to kill a whole lot of birds with one stone, and Sally was supposed to be one of those birds."

"That's certainly possible. I've seen the true motive for an act hidden in another incident before, and the woman's behavior was certainly suspicious, especially if she really looked up at Sally's office. My question is why? What reason would someone have for killing Sally?"

"We could be the reason, sir."

"How do you figure that?"

"Supposing the Japs suspect or even know a raid on Tokyo is being planned and someone was following more or less the same trail we've been on. Then we suddenly show up the other day and begin spending a lot of time with Sally. You pointed out that people sometimes know more than they know they know. Suppose Sally knows something about this woman agent, if that's what she is, and they don't want Sally to tell us what she doesn't know she knows?"

I almost laughed at Russ's complex explanation of his conclusion. I did not laugh, though, because I want to encourage him to think, and because it was just possible he was right. I hoped not, though, because if he was, it meant Sally's life was suddenly worth about twenty-cents, the price of a .45 caliber bullet.

"All right, Russ, I'll buy your conclusion for the moment. What do you propose we do about it?"

He looked at me like the answer to my question was obvious. "We need to keep Sally safe, sir, especially if she knows something that could help us find a leak."

"I figured that much, Russ. What I meant is how do you propose we keep Sally safe?"

Now Russ looked a little sheepish. "I was hoping you would come up with the answer to that one, sir."

I smiled. "I see. You leave me the hard part."

Russ doesn't always know when I'm kidding him. Flustered, he said, "No, sir, I didn't mean to do that. I just thought you would know what options . . . ."

"Relax, Russ. I was kidding you."

"Oh. Sorry, sir."

"All right, let's look at some of those options. First and foremost, Sally has to go along with whatever solution we come up with if we want her cooperation. Keep that in mind."

"Yes, sir."

"One possibility would be to get an MID security team to follow her around every minute of the day."

Russ shook his head. "She wouldn't go for that, sir."

"I don't think she would, either. It's pretty clear, though, that we need to get her away from the plant until the coast is clear. We can't control the situation at the plant. Too many things can go wrong there."

"What about taking Sally up to her folks in Portland?"

"No good. If we are really dealing with a Jap agent, finding out where Sally's family is would be a piece of cake and the first thing an enemy agent would do if Sally disappears."

"Yes, sir. I didn't think of that."

"We could stash her someplace where MID controls the environment, like at the Presidio. Sally would be bored to tears, but she would be about as safe as she could be."

"I know she's not going to be happy about that idea, but short of babysitting her ourselves, it seems like the best solution."

"Russ, the only way we could babysit Sally would be to take her with us on this assignment. That might appeal to you, Sergeant, but I think it stinks. If you are right about why the North American plant was bombed, we can look forward to more such unpleasantness. I need you a hundred percent focused on what we're doing, and as much as I like Sally, she would be a distraction that reduces our effectiveness."

"Yes, sir. I understand that."

Despite his words, I thought I heard some disappointment in Russ's voice. All I needed were a couple of lovesick puppies following me around.

While Russ and I were discussing strategy, the emergency ward was gradually clearing out. We saw some patients leave on their own. Most, though, were moved somewhere else in the hospital on gurneys. A few were taken out through another door with sheets covering their faces.

Russ said, "A couple of doctors just left Sally's room. Maybe they're done with her."

"All right, let's go see what we can work out to keep your gal safe."

Sally now had a brand new white cast up to the elbow of her right arm. She also had a fresh wrapping of gauze around her head. She was, however, wearing the same bright smile for Russ and me.

Russ asked, "What do the doctors say?"

"They said I must have a hard noggin." She mimed knocking the left side of her head with her fist. "No permanent damage has been done."

Sally offered her left hand to Russ and he took it. I said, "That's good. How much longer are they going to keep you here?"

"They want me overnight just to make sure I don't start acting coo-coo or something."

I chose that moment to add a little levity to the proceedings. "How will they tell?"

"Oh! You're a meanie. Beat him up, Russ."

"I can't beat him up. He's my boss."

Sally put on a pouty expression. "Some boyfriend I picked. You won't even defend my honor."

Russ replied, "Sorry, but the Army has very strict rules about that sort of thing."

"Phooey!"

We talked a little about the chaotic scene at North American and the tragic loss of life. Then, looking glum for the first time since we arrived at the hospital, Sally quietly asked the sixty-four-dollar question.

"What now?"

Russ looked at me and I said, "Did the doctors say when you could go back to work?"

"I suppose I could go back tomorrow, but that depends on how things are at the plant. They might have to shut down production until the damage is repaired. I don't know how long that would take."

"Sally, Russ told me what you said about a couple of strange things that happened before the explosion. Can you describe the woman you saw just before the bomb detonated?"

"Yes. She was tall and slender with a narrow face and sharp features. Her hair was a dark shade of blonde and done sort of stylishly in rolls. She was wearing a dark blue dress with some sort of small white pattern in the material. Her shoes were black and white Saddles. Does that help?"

I thought how much simpler my life would be if all witnesses were as observant. More important, Sally's description of her mystery woman fit the gal I'd seen with the white Chevy to a T. I wondered if we might actually be on the trail of something worthwhile.

"Yes, Sally, that's a good description. It helps a lot because I saw the same woman when Russ and I got there. To answer your question about what happens now, tell me what you think ought to happen."

She looked up at Russ, and then over at me. "I don't know what to say, Johnny. All of this is very scary. I don't want to whine about it, but I also don't want any more bombs going off under my chair."

An idea had been percolating in the back of my mind as we talked. It wasn't a perfect solution to our problem of keeping Sally safe, and it wasn't exactly what Russ and I discussed, but I was pretty sure it would make everyone happy. Well, almost everybody. I decided to go with it.

In an authoritative voice I said, "Sally, as of this minute I am placing you in federal custody."

Russ looked surprised and Sally stared at me wide-eyed. Then the lightbulb went on over Sally's head and her shock turned into a smile as she realized what I meant by federal custody.

She held her left arm out in my direction. "Put the cuffs on me officer, I confess."

Then Russ got it and smiled along with Sally. I said, "This is no joke, Sally. From now until I say differently you go absolutely nowhere without Russ or me with you. I mean absolutely nowhere. Do you understand me?"

I could tell Sally was fighting to keep a straight face, but she lost the battle and broke into giggles. "Nowhere? That could be embarrassing."

"Better embarrassed than dead, don't you think?"

Sally nodded, but she was still fighting the giggles. I said, "Russ, you stick with Sally tonight. If you need me to spell you, I'll be at the motel later. In the morning I'll pick you up and we'll all go to North American where you can pick up Sally's car and I'll clear her absence with whatever powers that be I can find. While I do that, you take Sally home and help her pack a bag. Better pack well, Sally. You might be away for a while."

The gravity of her situation was beginning to dawn on Sally. "Am I being kidnapped?"

I nodded. "In a sense, yes. You are going to disappear for as long as it takes to make sure you live to a ripe old age."

"Yes, sir."

"And don't call me 'sir.' It's bad enough Russ has to do that all the time. You can call me Johnny or warden, whichever you like."

In a very respectful tone of voice, Sally said, "Yes, Johnny."

Russ asked, "Where do we go tomorrow, north?"

"Yes. Sally and I are going to look through a mug book when we get to the Presidio. I want to identify this mystery dame who likes to blow things up."

"Got it, sir."

"Okay, any questions? Sally?"

"No, Johnny, but thank you for rescuing me."

"We aren't rescuing you. We're making you an official spook, junior grade."

"Spook?"

"Yup. That's what they call us folks in the intelligence trade."

"Oh boy!"

I pulled a curtained partition on wheels into place so Sally's bed couldn't be seen from the hall when her room door was open. Then I pulled my Smith & Wesson and handed it to Russ along with a little leather gizmo that snapped onto my shoulder holster and held six spare rounds.

"You probably won't need this, but I'm tired of carrying it around. It's your turn until morning."

"Yes, sir."

I glanced at Sally. Her eyes were wide again. I said, "Don't worry. That's just in case any handsome doctors try to get fresh with you."

She gave me another "Yes, Johnny," and then gestured with her finger for me to come to her bedside. When I got there, Sally said, "Lean down here."

Thinking she wanted to whisper something to me, I leaned. Sally latched onto the lapel of my jacket and pulled me down for a kiss on the cheek. I gave her hand a squeeze and said, "Now, one more thing. Sally, in a little while Russ is going to take you out to the hospital main lobby where there are a bunch of public telephones. Use one of them to call your parents."

Sally frowned. "Can't that wait until . . . . "

"No, it can't. On the way out of here I'm going to close the book on Sally MacLure as far as this hospital is concerned. That means if your folks hear or read about an explosion at the North American Aviation plant in Inglewood and call to see what happened to you, the hospital is going to say they never heard of you. That will worry them a lot more than a telephone call from you tonight. Okay?"

Sally nodded. To Russ I said, "See you in the morning, about 0800 hours, unless you need me to come back earlier and spell you."

"Yes, sir. See you in the morning."

I waved goodbye to Russ and Sally and walked to the nurses' station. The same blonde woman with red glasses was still on

69

duty. This time I took note of her name badge. She was "Miss Gilbertson, RN."

She looked up and said, "I see you're still here. That isn't what I would call a short visit."

"I know, and I apologize, Nurse Gilbertson. It seems we have a security issue. We believe Sally MacLure's life is in danger."

The nurse gave me a stern look. "Now really, Major, our food isn't that bad."

I couldn't help laughing. "I'm sure your food perfectly safe and tasty, too. Our problem is of a different nature, and it's grave enough that I'm leaving Sergeant Pierce with Miss MacLure for protection tonight. I wanted to be sure you were aware of what we're up to."

"Thank you, Major Spicer. Is there a number where we can reach you if it should be necessary?"

I gave her the motel number and my room number. "Now, there is a favor I need to ask of you, Nurse Gilbertson."

"What would that be, Major Spicer?"

"We will be taking Miss MacLure to a more secure location tomorrow morning, but we would like you to make her do a disappearing act beginning tonight, at least as far as anyone outside the hospital is concerned. For example, if someone calls or comes in and inquires about her, you have no information about Sally MacLure. Even if the person claims to be a relative or a close friend. Can you arrange for that to happen?"

"I can and will. I'm sorry to hear she might be in danger. Miss MacLure has helped keep the entire emergency ward in good humor ever since she arrived. She is a model patient."

I smiled. "It doesn't surprise me at all to hear you say that. We've been working with her for a few days now, and she has the same effect on us." As an afterthought, I added, "You know, Nurse Gilbertson, I think it would do wonders for Sally's morale if you stopped by her room and told her what you just told me."

Nurse Gilbertson smiled back at me. "You know, Major Spicer, I am going to make it a point to do just that."

On that note we wished each other a pleasant evening and I walked out to the Army's Dodge. Everything was now peaceful in the hospital's parking lot. I wished it was that way around the world tonight.

Eight

Freeman Hospital, Inglewood

When she and Russ walked out of Freeman Hospital, Sally was about the happiest mess I've ever seen. Besides the gauze wrapped around her head, a sling had been added to help support the cast on her right arm. If that weren't enough, she was wearing the same black slacks and white blouse she wore to work Friday morning, which were torn and covered with dirt, blood, and soot. What's more Sally was favoring her right leg, but in spite of it all, she also wore a big smile. She was clearly happy to be out in the real world again.

Russ, too, looked a little bedraggled as he held the passenger door open for her. That was understandable since he'd been up all night keeping Sally safe from a danger we had yet to clearly identify.

Sally hopped right in and slid across to the center of the seat. "Good morning, Johnny!"

I said, "Hi, Sally. You're certainly looking bright-eyed and bushy-tailed this morning."

"Thank you, Johnny. It's wonderful to be out in the sunshine again."

"Looks like you wore Russ out, though."

"It wasn't me! I think he was chasing nurses while I was sleeping."

Russ just shook his head as he slipped onto the seat to Sally's right. I said, "Not Russ. He's all business when he's on duty."

With a pout on her face and in her voice, Sally said, "So I discovered."

"How did it go last night, Russ?"

71

"No problems, sir, and Sally called her folks as you instructed."

To Sally I said, "I imagine they were glad to hear from you."

"I suppose so." In an I-told-you-so tone of voice she added, "Mom and Dad had not heard about the explosion at the plant yet."

Ignoring her jab, I said, "Did you get anything to eat, Russ?"

"Yes, sir. That nurse we met when we first got to the hospital had two dinners delivered to Sally's room. The chow wasn't bad."

Sally made a face that said she didn't agree with Russ's opinion of the hospital's menu. I said, "Sally, you have to consider Russ's point of reference. There's a reason they call an Army chow hall a 'mess.'"

It was fifteen minutes past the hour of eight when I pulled into the North American Aviation parking lot and parked next to Sally's red Mercury. There was a lot less activity this morning than when I'd last seen the place. There were, however, several workmen busy patching broken windows with sheets of plywood, and almost as many men in suits were standing around gesturing toward the worst of the damage. There were also a few California National Guard troops doing sentry duty around the perimeter of the facility. They were, I presumed, an effort to close the barn door after the last horse departed for parts unknown.

Fortunately, Sally had the good sense to grab her purse as she escaped her burning office, so there would be no problem starting the Merc or getting into her house. It's surprising how important little things like a ring of keys become when you haven't got them.

Russ helped her down from the Dodge and up into the Mercury. "See you at Sally's house in an hour or so, sir?"

"See you then."

As Russ drove away, I checked my uniform blouse pocket—yeah, I was back in pinks and greens—to be sure I had the note Russ gave me with Sally's address on it, and then I pulled around to the front of the building and parked in an open slot. The lot was lousy with official-looking vehicles, including an olive drab Mack two-and-a-half-ton truck with Army markings stenciled all over it.

A National Guard corporal holding an M1 carbine with bayonet affixed stood at the entrance doors. I showed him my MID ID and he responded with the correct manual of arms salute. The corporal then directed me to the lobby reception counter, where I was to sign in. At the reception counter I asked for the fellow Sally told me was head of the plant's personnel department, Melvin Nordoff.

In addition to the other damage sustained by the plant, it seemed the in-house telephone system was out of service. The woman sent someone's teenage son to carry a message to Mister Nordoff.

The man was a walking definition of "nondescript." From the top of his very ordinary barber shop haircut to the tip of his unadorned black shoes, there was absolutely nothing distinct about Nordoff you could write down on a description form. He could have been the inspiration for those mannequins you see in department store windows.

He studied my MID ID for quite a while, and then asked the most intelligent question he could think of. "How can I help you, Major Spicer?"

"I'm here about a confidential matter. Is there somewhere less public where we can talk for a few minutes?"

Since no one ever asked him that question before, he had to think about his answer for a moment. "Well, there is my office, or we could go to the cafeteria and get a cup of coffee."

The coffee idea sounded good to me, so I followed him down a couple of hallways and ended up in the North American Aviation employee cafeteria. The room was deserted and that suited my needs perfectly.

It was the self-serve sort of cafeteria, so we simply walked up to a giant stainless steel urn with spigots and filled a couple of white ceramic mugs with a tepid brown liquid. From there we went to a table for four next to the back wall.

"Now what is the confidential matter the Army wishes to discuss with me?"

"It concerns an employee, Miss Sally MacLure. Do you know her?"

He shook his head vigorously as if admitting any knowledge of Sally MacLure might land him in Leavenworth. "No, what does she do here?"

"She is a production design engineer."

"Oh? What has she done?"

I was already growing weary of having a nondescript conversation with a nondescript man in a nondescript gray suit. "She has done nothing wrong, Mister Nordoff. I'm here to tell you we have taken her into protective custody and she won't be returning to work for a while. During her absence you are to tell no one about this conversation and you will answer no questions about Miss MacLure. Do you understand what I've said?"

"Yes, I understand, but I don't think I can promise to do what you are asking."

The man was trying my patience. Doing my darnedest to remain reasonable, I asked, "Why not, Mister Nordoff?"

"Well, supposing someone from the FBI wants to know about her? I would have to answer their questions."

"No, Mister Nordoff, you would not have to answer their questions." I held up my MID ID. "During wartime this trumps every badge in the country, including the one pinned to J. Edger Hoover's bloomers. Understand?"

"Well, I guess so."

"There's no guesswork about it. If you fail to follow my instructions, I will eventually know about it and you will end up being tried for treason. Now do you understand?"

"Yes, I understand. I will tell nobody about our conversation and I will answer no questions about Miss . . . ah . . . ."

"MacLure. Sally MacLure."

He nodded enthusiastically. "Yes, Miss MacLure."

"And you will also keep her position open for her return. Right?"

His expression became noncommittal. "I'll try."

"No, Mister Nordoff, you will keep her position open without fail. Miss MacLure is sacrificing a great deal for the war effort. In that sense she is an American hero. We treat our heroes right."

The last part of what I said might have been a slight exaggeration, but it got the job done. Nordoff nodded. "All right, her position will be open for her return."

I stood up. "Good. Mister Nordoff, thank you for your cooperation."

He was still sitting at the table when I glanced back leaving the cafeteria. I hoped the guy had some sort of defense worker draft deferment. I would hate to think the future of democracy depended on his ability to defend it.

The address Russ gave me for Sally was in a housing tract on Hillcrest Boulevard in Inglewood. It was only a couple of miles northeast of the plant, and not far from where we had South Seas drinks and Chinese food Tuesday night. Sally's home turned out to be a little California bungalow in a neighborhood full of little California bungalows.

When I got there, I spotted Russ locking a narrow garage at the end of a narrow driveway that ran down the right side of the house. He waved and disappeared from my view only to reappear a few moments later on the bungalow's porch with a suitcase in his hand and Sally at his side.

She locked the front door and he helped her down two steps to the walkway. I unlocked the Dodge's trunk, Russ tossed Sally's bag in, and we were off toward our final stop before heading out of town.

On our way to Patmar's Motel, I related my conversation with Melvin Nordoff at the plant. Sally laughed at my department store mannequin comparison.

"Johnny, thank you for making sure my job will be there when we're done with this. I worked hard for that position."

"No need to thank me, Sally. That's only fair. I hear congress is passing laws about returning GIs getting their civilian jobs back when the war is over. You are in the same position they are and deserve the same fair treatment."

"I know, but . . . well women don't always get the same benefits men do. Knowing you're looking out for me means a lot."

At Patmar's, Russ headed for his room to change and pack his gear while Sally accompanied me to the office, where I checked out and paid our bills. Then we met back at the Dodge and conducted what today's modern Army would call a "space utilization analysis."

Our problem was the Army didn't figure on me hauling a lot of folks and their luggage around in my car, so they gave me what Dodge calls a two-door business coupe. In practical terms that means there is no actual back seat. The space back there is intended for samples and whatever salesmen haul around with them. There is, however, an inward facing fold-down jump seat under each of the two rear side windows.

So far we'd all shared the front seat. It was wide enough to carry three comfortably for short distances, but it was going to get cramped on the long trip to San Francisco. Russ and I already knew from past experience that the jump seat solution wasn't at all comfortable for fellows our size.

We began the project by loading the trunk. The space was shallower than it was when the Dodge came from the factory because of the secure hidden storage compartment the Army installed. Still, we managed to fit my B-4 bag, Russ's duffel, and Sally's suitcase back there. So far, so good.

That left the space behind the front seat available for a passenger. Sally would fit the space better than Russ or me, but I couldn't see her climbing back there with only one arm for support. Sally, however, thought differently. While Russ and I were preparing to flip a coin or fight a duel at twenty paces to see who would stuff himself into the space, Sally nimbly hopped through the passenger-side door and settled into the jump seat on that side. She actually looked pretty comfortable.

Russ said, "Sally, you don't have to sit back there. I can do it."

"No you can't. You need some sleep and it's a cinch you won't get any back here. I'm fine, but this going to cost you guys."

Grinning, I said, "Oh, oh."

Sally proceeded to list her demands. "I get to ride up there with you guys part of the time, and you have to take me to that Fisherman's Wharf place while we're in San Francisco."

I turned to Russ. "What do you think, Sergeant? Does that sound like a good deal to you?"

With enthusiasm, he said, "Yes, sir, I definitively do."

"All right, Sally, you have a deal. Climb in, Russ, and we'll get on the road."

At precisely 1015 hours we headed out, jogging around the airport property and turning north on California Route One, also known as Lincoln Boulevard south of Santa Monica. North of Santa Monica California One becomes Pacific Coast Highway.

I figured the trip was going to take about 12 hours, putting us into the Presidio a little after 2200 hours. A glance to my right showed me that Russ was already catching up on his sleep. Behind him Sally was catching up on her reading with Hemingway's new novel, *For Whom the Bell Tolls*.

Nine

0800 Hours – Sunday – 1 MAR 42

Ocean Park Motel, San Francisco

San Francisco's Great Highway follows the surf and sand dunes along the western edge of the city. The extremely Art Deco Ocean Park Motel is three blocks east of the Great Highway and a block or so north of the city's new Fleishhacker Zoo. The Ocean Park Motel is also where we spent Saturday night after driving nearly five hundred miles from Inglewood.

Why, you may wonder, did I decide to put us up in a touristy motel when we could have slept four or five miles away at the Presidio for free? While it was true Russ and I had access to free accommodations at the Presidio, Sally was a different matter. Arranging a room for a female civilian, especially a room in which Russ and I could also stand guard, would involve a lot more fuss and bother than it was worth.

So, we stayed in two adjoining rooms at the Ocean Park Motel with Russ and I standing two-hour shifts in Sally's room while she slept. My clever scheme for keeping Sally safe was working just swell, but it was costing Russ and me a lot of sleep.

By 0800 hours Sunday morning, however, we were checked out of the Ocean Park and about three miles north on the Great Highway at an amusement park known as *Playland at the Beach*. We were there because *Playland* was the closest place with a restaurant that was open for breakfast early on Sunday morning. We sat around a table near the back of the Splendid Inn's dining room drinking coffee while we waited for our breakfasts.

Even with her gauze headband and plaster cast, Sally managed to look chipper in tan slacks and a short-sleeved mint green blouse on which the right sleeve was split at the seam to accommodate her cast. Russ and I, of course, were in uniform. I doubt if anyone thought we looked chipper.

While we were waiting, I figured it might be a good idea to prepare Sally for what was about to happen. "Sally, our next stop is the Presidio Army Post. It's just a few miles from here. When we get there, you need to be in the back of the car again and sitting as low as you can get so you aren't visible from outside the vehicle."

Sally looked puzzled. "You have to smuggle me in?"

"No, in fact I will be very careful to give the guard at the gate your name and show him your California Driver's License. I will also explain that you are in MID custody."

"Then why do I have to hide?"

"We don't want anyone else who happens to be watching the gate to know you're there. Once we're through the gate, it won't matter so much."

The waitress arrived with our breakfasts about then and we all dug in. The Splendid Inn was overpriced, but they did serve a pretty fair breakfast, or maybe I was just extra hungry.

Between bites of waffle, Sally asked, "Is there anything else special I have to know about this Presidio place? I've never been on an Army base before."

"Right now, the Military Police are very touchy about people who show interest in certain buildings and areas on a base, so just try to be oblivious to what is around us when we're driving or walking around, and whatever you do, don't get a camera out and start snapping pictures. That could get even Russ and me thrown in the stockade."

"Oh, oh. I packed my Brownie in the suitcase before we left."

"As long as the camera is in your suitcase it won't be a problem. In fact, I'm glad you brought it. When we leave, I'll take you to a couple of places where you can snap some pictures of San Francisco landmarks."

"Oh, good! I was hoping we could do that. Can you tell me what else we're going to do here?"

"Sure. Russ is going to take care of some business for us while you and I look at photographs of known female Japanese and Nazi spies. We need to identify that woman you and I saw at the plant. I hope you still remember what she looked like."

"Believe me, Johnny, I won't forget that woman for a long time. Oh, and that's another thing I was wondering about."

"What?"

"Is it okay to call you 'Johnny,' or should I call you 'Major

Spicer' in public?"

I gave that a moment of thought. "On military bases like the Presidio and the Sacramento Signal Depot, where we'll be tomorrow, 'Major Spicer' is probably more appropriate. Otherwise, 'Johnny' is fine."

"Okay. I'm sorry to ask so many questions. I just want to do everything right because this is so important to you and Russ."

I looked across the table at Russ. "What do you think, Russ? Will she do okay?"

"I'm certain Sally will do just fine, sir."

"I am, too. Let's get this show on the road."

With Sally back in her jump seat, I drove north past the point where the famous Cliff House restaurant hangs precariously from a precipice overlooking the Pacific Ocean and the appropriately named Seal Rocks. We passed the Sutro Baths next and the Great Highway turned east, where it became Point Lobos Avenue, and ultimately, Geary Boulevard. We stayed on Geary until we got to Arguello Boulevard. Turning north on Arguello took us to the Presidio gate at Pacific Avenue.

I gave the MP at the gate our IDs and Sally's driver's license with an explanation for what we were up to. He gave our IDs and us a thorough inspection. The young corporal was particularly interested in Sally. That was either because she was a civilian or a cute blonde. Then he gave me a snappy salute and gestured us through the gate.

Arguello Boulevard continued beyond the gate and wound around through the trees to what those who serve at the Presidio refer to as the quad, which consists of the parade grounds surrounded by a dozen or more large two-story red brick buildings remodeled in the mission revival style back in the late 1920s. More buildings were under construction to the south of the quad. War was bringing growth to the base.

I pulled to the curb and parked at our destination, Building 100, otherwise known as Army Military Intelligence Division—Western Headquarters. Russ helped Sally out of the Dodge and she got her first real look at the San Francisco Presidio.

"Wow, this place is really something!"

Russ said, "It is, but the Presidio is the exception to the rule for Army bases. You have to go a long way to find another one this nice. I've read that this site has been in use as a military installation since 1776. It belonged to the Spanish back then. They gave the fort up and the Mexicans took it over. We took it away from the Mexicans about a hundred years ago during the

Bear Flag revolution."

Sally grinned at him. "You sound just like a tour guide."

Russ shrugged. "I just like to know something about the places I'm stationed. If you have to be stuck on an Army base, you couldn't do much better than this."

I said, "All right, Russ can continue the tour later. Let's get on with our business. Russ, you have your shopping list?"

"Yes, sir. I also have Sally's driver's license." Turning to Sally, Russ added, "I'll give your license back when we're through here. Okay?"

With her usual smile in place, she said, "I'm in custody, so I guess it has to be."

Russ quickly said, "You aren't really . . . ."

"I was kidding, Russ. Everything is fine."

"Oh, okay."

With Sally at my side and Russ bringing up the rear, our little procession climbed the steps and entered Building 100. From there Russ went one direction and we went another. Sally and I were headed for MID's archive room, literally a library chock full of information intelligence agents find useful in the pursuit of intelligence. I asked the archivist, a civilian employee. to bring us the photo book containing known enemy spies.

The woman eyed Sally in her gauze headband suspiciously as if her picture might be in the book of spies. The photo book was a thick cloth-covered three-ring binder kept on a shelf behind the counter, but now there were two big binders full of pictures instead of one. The spy business was apparently a growing wartime industry.

I led Sally to a wooden library table and examined the books to see what we had. One of the books was labeled "Asian" and included mostly Japanese spies. The second book said "European" on the cover and included agents from Germany, Italy, and I guess anywhere else on the other side of the Atlantic where they don't like us at the moment.

Since I was betting on Japan as the employer of our mystery woman, I began with the Asian spy book. The book contained both male and female spies in alphabetical order by the name they most commonly used in the US. In addition, each photo was accompanied by a short dossier providing other aliases, notes on their activities, and an LKL, which stands for last known location.

As I turned pages scanning for photos of women, Sally said, "All of those people are spies?"

"Yes, but only spies who work for Japan. The Nazi and Italian spies are in the other book."

"Good heavens! There are hundreds of them."

"There are, and these are only those for whom we have photographs. There is also a file of index cards listing those we don't have pictures of yet."

Sally stared intently at the photos for a few moments, and then asked, "Johnny, are there books in Japan and Europe like this with your picture in them?"

Her question threw me for a moment because I'd never given the subject much thought. "I suppose so, but strictly speaking, Russ and I aren't spies. We don't sneak around pretending to be anyone we aren't. We are intelligence agents, which is something entirely different. Our specific job is keeping an eye on enemy activities here on the homefront. MID agents working overseas might be considered spies in some instances, but not us."

Sally listened carefully to what I said. "But there are still dangers in dealing with spies in this country, aren't there?"

I was trying to downplay the danger aspect, but I wasn't going to lie to her. "Yes. The people we look for don't want to be found, so they've been known to take drastic measures to avoid us on occasion."

"Like the woman who blew up the plant. I don't know how you stay so calm and collected knowing there are people out there who want to kill you. It scares the heck out of me."

"I would question your sanity if it didn't scare you, and I'm not so calm and collected all the time. I've had my share of close calls, but most of what I do is observe and analyze. The cases I work on are like jigsaw puzzles. I go around collecting pieces of the puzzle here and there, and then I try fitting the pieces together to see if they show me a picture that makes sense. When they do, I go where the picture tells me I need to look for the next puzzle piece.

"That's why we're here, to add an important piece of the puzzle. If we can identify Madam X, we'll have a much better idea of what and with whom we're dealing. Does any of that make some sort of sense to you?"

Sally gave me a toned-down version of her smile. "Yes, it makes sense. I'm beginning to understand more about the world you and Russ live in. It's very different from my world. I don't think I could ever adapt to your world."

I was pretty sure I knew what she was really trying to say. "Sally, Russ is here because he is a very good soldier. He's also smart. He and I have never talked about it, but I'm not sure he'll want to stay in the intelligence business after the war is over. Don't give up on him quite yet."

Her smile got a little bigger. "You read minds, too?"

"I wish I could. I said that because it is obvious to me the two of you are attracted to each other. Just remember, things are always out of whack during times of war. Russ is no different than thousands of other guys who feel they have a duty to their country. Give him a chance to fulfill that responsibility, and then see how things stand."

Sally nodded in a thoughtful way. "I will. It's none of my business, but what about you? Will you keep doing this when the war is over?"

"I don't think so. A special redheaded angel in Santa Barbara has captured my heart. We plan to get married soon. When this is over Susan gets a hundred percent of my attention, and somebody else can chase the bad guys for a while."

Now Sally's smile was up to full volume. "Russ told me a little about your angel. For what it's worth, I happen to think Susan is a very lucky gal."

I chuckled, mostly out of embarrassment. "I don't know if lucky is the right word. She is, however, very patient. Now, let's find Madam X. If you see anyone familiar in this book, holler."

"Okay, and Johnny?"

"Yes?"

"Thank you for the explanation. Things are clearer to me now."

We spent the next half hour turning pages and looking at bad guys and gals, and I was beginning to think we were on a wild goose chase. We were into the Y pictures without much alphabet left. I was pretty sure the woman wasn't going to be a Yamamoto or a Yoshida because she didn't look at all Japanese.

Then I flipped a page and Sally's voice echoed off of the room's high ceiling, "There! There she is!"

The archivist gave us an annoyed glare and I looked at the photo at which Sally was pointing. Sure enough, Madam X was recognizable even in the grainy out of focus photographic copy of a Kodak snapshot. She was seated on a bed or cot with her legs crossed and she held a cigarette in her right hand. "You're right that's her. No question about it."

Pulling my notebook out of my pocket, I copied the details accompanying the picture. Her name in the book was Marjorie Yount, but she also goes by the name Mary Adams on occasion. The ID number MID had assigned to her was 25-0039. In the notes section all it said was, "Caucasian." For an LKL the book had, "Oakland, California (22 Oct, 1940)."

"Sally, do either of those names—Marjorie Yount or Mary Adams—mean anything to you?"

"No, at least nothing I can think of right now. What does that part about Oakland, California mean?"

"It simply means that the last time an MID agent recognized her was in Oakland during October, 1940. We'll update the Last Known Location with our sightings of her on Friday. Come on, let's set some wheels in motion."

Sally followed me to the archivist's counter. I showed her the photo Sally and I found and said, "We need a photo copy of that image and I have an LKL update for you."

The woman nodded and pulled a notepad out of a drawer. "Where and when?"

"The North American Aviation plant in Inglewood, California on Friday. Twenty-Seven February, Forty-Two. She was seen there by two witnesses before and after a bomb was detonated inside the plant. The explosion killed quite a few employees and injured several more. I don't think there is a final count on the victims yet."

The woman gave me a surprised look. "That was only two days ago."

"That is correct. When can I have a copy of that photo?"

"I'll pull the copy negative out of our file right away and send it to the photo shop. They should have a print by tomorrow afternoon."

I shook my head. "Not soon enough. I need it today."

She shook her head. "That's not possible. This is Sunday. There isn't anybody at the photo shop on Sunday."

"Then call someone in. In case you haven't noticed, wars are open for business seven days a week. Check with Colonel Beecher if you need to authorize the request. He will also want a copy of the photo sent to him. Tell Beecher Major Spicer made the request on behalf of General Davis."

I could tell she was getting ready to say it still couldn't be done until she heard General Davis' name. "Yes, Major Spicer. We'll get right to it. I'll try to have the photo for you shortly after lunch."

"Please deliver my copy to Pauline Ashley in a sealed envelope with my name on it."

"Yes, sir."

We found Russ waiting for us out in the hall outside the archive room. He said, "Judging by the smiles, I'm guessing you found what you were looking for."

"Yup. Sally picked Madam X out as soon as she saw her. The woman's name is Marjorie Yount. They'll have a copy of her mug shot for us after lunch."

Russ looked at Sally. "Good work!"

She grinned at him. "See, I'm earning my keep already."

I said, "She sure is. Now, how did you do, Russ?"

"Not quite as well as you and Sally, but I was partially successful." Handing me an envelope, he said, "Here's the temporary ID you wanted."

I opened the envelope and looked at a typed card that carried all of the information on regular MID IDs except a photo. The card was signed by Colonel Beecher and laminated between two clear plastic sheets. I read the information on the card. "Blonde, blue, five-four, one-twenty-six, DOB Eighteen April, Seventeen. Yeah, that sounds like our gal."

Sally blushed a little. "Why don't you just put all that on a billboard, so everybody will know?"

I laughed. "Oh, don't be so sensitive. There's nothing wrong with those statistics, is there, Russ?"

"Nothing at all, sir."

I handed the envelope to Sally. "This is a temporary MID ID card. Your driver's license is in there, too."

She took the envelope and Russ said, "I hope you didn't lie about any of that stuff. I had to swear to it all."

"It would serve you right if I did. If I was a pound off, it would probably mean the firing squad for you. Now what am I supposed to do with this?"

I said, "It is a temporary civilian MID ID card. Keep it with your driver's license. The card identifies you as one of the good guys. It will get you onto any military base in the country, and a good deal more. An MID ID is a handy thing to have."

Sally did not look convinced. "If you say so."

"I say so. What else have you got for us, Russ?"

He handed me a much thicker envelope. "Two-hundred-and-fifty-dollars expense money, sir. I had to sign my life away for that, too."

I opened the envelope and counted out five twenty-dollar bills. "Here, keep this in case you need it and I'm not around."

Russ tucked the twenties into his wallet. "Thank you, sir."

"How 'bout the last item on your list, Russ?"

"That's where my luck ran out. The information on the license plate hasn't come back from DMV yet."

"We don't need to worry about that right now. We can get the license information over the telephone from Pauline tomorrow, or whenever it shows up."

"Yes, sir."

I looked at my watch. The time was a few minutes shy of eleven-hundred hours. "Okay, I need to see Beecher and explain a few things. I shouldn't be long, and then we can take Sally for a ride to see the sights and buy her the lunch we owe her at Fisherman's Wharf." With a wink, I added, "In the meantime temporary civilian agent MacLure is your problem."

With a grin growing on his mug, Russ said, "Yes, sir!"

Once again, we headed off in different directions. My destination was the office of Colonel Dwight Beecher, Director of MID's Western Operations. Beecher's domain was at the front of the building's second floor. He had a grand view of the quad.

He saw me walk into his outer office and yelled for me to come on in. "Good morning, Colonel Beecher. Sorry to show up unannounced, but there have been some new developments."

"All right, sit down and tell me what you can."

I sat in one of the guest chairs facing his desk. "The development has to do with the bombing of the North American plant the other day. Since I spoke with you, we have evidence that points to a connection with my other assignment."

"So, you want to handle the plant investigation differently?"

"No, sir. The changes in my plan specifically concern the woman I saw at the plant after the explosion—the one driving the car with the license plate number I gave you. Now it seems likely the plant bombing was intended to kill a witness who is key to my other investigation."

The Colonel frowned. "That's not a very efficient method of assassination."

"It is if you don't want it known that assassinating someone was your primary objective."

Beecher nodded his understanding. "And the witness; would she be the woman to whom we just gave a temporary civilian MID ID?"

"Yes, she would. My problem is we need to provide tight protection for her as well as have her help steering us through a maze of Army red tape. I decided the best way to do both of those things was to keep her with us. Giving her an ID leaves fewer questions to be answered when we go on a base. The fewer the questions, the less attention we draw."

The Colonel nodded again. "Makes sense, and you also need

the information on that license plate as soon as we get it, right?"

"Yes, sir."

"I assume you will also go through the mug books in the archive."

"Just came from there, sir. We made a positive identification. If you will hand me a piece of paper, I'll copy the information for you, so you'll know who we're dealing with."

He handed me a piece of notepaper from his desk drawer. "Good idea."

I copied the mug book information onto the notepaper and slid it back across his desk. Beecher looked at it and said, "I don't know her. You want a law enforcement all-points bulletin sent out for her?"

"We might at a future time, but I don't want to tip our hand yet. She may already be spooked because she saw me looking at her after the plant explosion when I got her automobile license the other day. If she knows I'm looking for she'll be harder to find."

"All right, Major. Will you be here at the Presidio long?"

"No, sir. I hope to be on the road again soon after lunch."

"Okay. I'll make sure the information from DMV is in the telephone message drop as soon as it arrives."

"Thank you, sir. I'll stay in touch as best I can."

"Thank you, Major. Good luck."

Ten

1130 Hours – Sunday – 1 MAR 42

San Francisco Landmarks

Leaving the Presidio, I retraced the route we took to get there until we reached Thirty-Fourth Avenue, where I turned north and drove through Lincoln Park to the Palace of the Legion of Honor, San Francisco's snazziest fine art museum. This edifice, a scaled-down replica of some historic joint in France, was built back in the 1920s by one of the city's zillionaires who apparently figured San Francisco just wouldn't be complete without such a magnificent monstrosity.

The Palace is impressive, complete with a huge reproduction of Rodin's *The Thinker* in its forecourt, but the real reason I brought Sally up to its perch on the low cliffs overlooking the entrance to San Francisco Bay is a few hundred yards away along a road that skirts the edge of those cliffs. If you know where to go, you can snap a terrific photo of the Golden Gate Bridge from its seldom photographed ocean side.

I pulled off to the shoulder of the road and we all bailed out of the Dodge for a look at the view. The sun had burned off the morning fog by then and the brilliant orange bridge stood out in Technicolor contrast against a deep blue sky while dazzlingly white seagulls put on flying demonstrations overhead. Sally was impressed.

"Oh my! This is like a picture postcard!"

Russ agreed. "It surely is."

I walked back to the car while they enjoyed the view and Sally made her photograph. I was more interested in the passing cars. I saw no pale gray Chevrolet sedans, no Marjorie Yount, or anyone else who paid the slightest interest in a couple of tourists ogling the view.

That could be a good thing or a bad thing. My problem at the moment was I needed to find Miss Yount and I had no idea where to look for her. That meant I had to rely on her finding us, but if she did, I had to know about it before she took another swing at Sally.

In a sense, I was using Sally as bait. I suppose I felt sort of guilty about that, but I was also now convinced having Sally with us was still the best way to protect her from an enemy we knew pitifully little about.

San Francisco is lousy with palaces and our next stop was another one, the Palace of Fine Arts in the Marina district just east of the Presidio. This palace is a holdover from the 1915 Panama Pacific Exposition and you have to see it to believe it. The structure is an octagonal rotunda covered with more gewgaws than I've ever seen in one place before. This monument to the classical arts is reddish tan with a white dome topping it off. The rotunda and a backdrop of columns and arches are impressively mirrored in a large reflecting pool. Aside from housing some tennis courts, the primary function of the place seems to be purely ornamental.

Fortunately, Sally didn't require that a landmark make sense or be practical to enjoy it. She snapped her Kodak at the thing a couple of times and I watched the traffic again. Neither her cast nor her head injury slowed Sally down. She accomplished more than I did.

Next, we stopped at what's known locally as the Marina Green, a large patch of lawn right on the bay where the big attractions are views of the federal penitentiary on Alcatraz Island and more scenes of the Golden Gate Bridge. If you turn around and look south from the Green, you will see some of the most expensive mansions in San Francisco. They're jammed together cheek to jowl, but the views from their front windows are spectacular, and if all that wasn't enough to make a tourist's heart go pitter-pat, the San Francisco yacht harbor is right next door to the Marina Green. Sally found enough photogenic scenery to finish off one of the two rolls of film she brought on the trip.

By this time my stomach was telling me it wanted lunch. Since we were only a stone's throw from Fisherman's Wharf, we loaded up and drove the short distance to Taylor Street, which dead ends at the wharf. There are two attractions at Fisherman's Wharf. First, there are the quaint little fishing boats crewed by the descendants of Italian immigrants. The second attraction is the tasty seafood served by restaurants owned by more descendants of Italian immigrants.

Back in 1939 I worked a case requiring me to spend a fair amount of time in the City by the Bay. During that visit I was told by locals, including a tough San Francisco homicide cop by the unlikely name of Horatio Bailey, that the best seafood to be had at the wharf was at a joint called Number Nine Fisherman's Grotto. With that recommendation in mind, I parked as close as I could get to the place and we wandered in.

We were seated in a second floor dining room with windows overlooking the fishing boats tied up out back. By that time Sally had loaded her second roll of film and she was getting snap-happy again.

After studying an extensive hand-printed menu listing every seafood dish I ever heard of and a few I hadn't heard of, we gave our orders to a fellow with a thick Italian accent and a threadbare tuxedo. Our lunches, accompanied by thick-crusted sourdough bread, were well prepared, and best of all, the seafood was fresh. In fact, our waiter swore up and down that the Dungeness Crab in my crab cakes was caught that morning.

Sally clearly enjoyed her lunch right down to the last bite. As she laid her fork on her empty plate, I said, "Well, Miss MacLure, I'd say we can mark our debt for sticking you in the jump seat paid in full."

"And then some! Thank you. That was a wonderful lunch. And thank you for chauffeuring me around to take pictures." Sally paused, put her hand on Russ's arm. "This was a wonderful morning."

Russ smiled at her and I said, "Yes, especially finding our mystery woman in the mug book. Now, we need to finish our business at the Presidio and get on the road."

I paid the tab at Fisherman's Grotto and hoped that General Davis didn't go over the expense report too carefully. Fisherman's Wharf is easily one of the most expensive places to eat in the entire state of California.

Back at Building 100 Sally and Russ waited in the Dodge while I picked up the photo copy of Marjorie Yount and checked to see if we had any messages. We didn't, so I pointed the Dodge east through town to the San Francisco-Oakland Bay Bridge for another death defying ride across that span.

Sally seemed to be having the time of her life crossing the bridge. She even told us about a ship she spotted passing under the bridge way, way down below us. It was just what I needed to hear.

After cheating death yet again, I turned north on US Highway 40, or San Pablo Avenue as the route is known in Alameda County. It is also officially known as the Lincoln Transcontinental Highway. Whatever you call it, we followed the road through Oakland, Berkeley, Richmond, and several smaller towns as the route more or less followed the eastern shore of San Francisco Bay.

Then, at the dinky burg of Crockett we had to pony up thirty-cents to cross yet another damned bridge. This one, the Carquinez Bridge, was a bargain. The San Francisco-Oakland Bay Bridge cost forty-cents.

The bridge dumped us in the tiny burg of Vallejo. Vallejo is a Spanish surname pronounced vah-LĀY-hoe. Now you know everything I know about Vallejo, except they build submarines on an island somewhere nearby and you can buy Flying A gasoline for 20.9-cents per gallon there. I learned that last detail because we stopped at the Flying A station to fill up the Dodge.

As we left the outskirts of Vallejo we also left what is usually referred to as the San Francisco Bay Area. The countryside became a boring vista of rolling hills studded with oak trees. As we passed a highway sign showing the distance to Sacramento as 55 miles, Sally took note of the fact.

"Fifty-five miles? Where is this Sacramento place, in Nevada?"

When I didn't answer her right away, I saw Russ look in my direction, and then into the mirror on his side of the car. He said, "Problem?"

"Maybe. Black Plymouth back there. It pulled in and parked on the apron of that Flying A station while we were getting gas."

"Got it."

"I'll slow down and see if it catches up or hangs back."

I eased up on the accelerator pedal a little and Sally asked, "Is something wrong?"

I answered her question this time. "Probably not. Don't turn and look, but there's a car behind us that aroused my curiosity."

"Oh."

I'd been rolling along at about fifty. I let our speed drop below forty-five and a moment later the Plymouth did the same. The gap between us remained at about two hundred yards. That was not the response I was hoping for.

I saw a small road sign coming up on the left and said, "Hang on, we're going to make a turn."

Braking only as much as was necessary to get the Dodge through the left turn without losing control, we left US 40 for Lynch Road.

It's called a road, but it isn't much more than a narrow gravel track. It is also thickly lined with large oak trees, which is exactly what I needed. I increased my speed and hurried along to a gap in the trees that couldn't be seen from the highway behind us. I braked hard and pointed the Dodge through the gap. We bounced around a little, but we were instantly out of sight.

I eased the Dodge around, so we could see the road through the trees and we waited. There was a fork in Lynch Road two hundred feet or so beyond where we left it. I hoped the Plymouth would speed right by us trying to figure out which fork we took, giving me an opportunity to get behind him. If, that is, the Plymouth was actually following us.

While all this was going on Sally sat quietly in her jump seat. I saw Russ turn and give her a look of assurance after our bumpy escape into the trees. She had to be scared out of her wits.

"Russ, if that Plymouth goes by, you and Sally bail out. I'm going to see who's so interested in us."

"Yes, sir. We'll wait here in the trees for you."

The words were barely out of his mouth when we heard the sound of a six-cylinder engine whining its heart out. By the time the black sedan flashed by, Russ was already helping Sally out of the back. He slammed the door and I shot out of our hidey hole just in time to see the Plymouth take the left fork in the road.

I mashed the foot feed to the floorboard and gave chase. I figured our cars were evenly matched in weight and horsepower, so to catch the Plymouth I had to drive better and faster than the guy—or gal—up ahead.

It took a while for the driver of the Plymouth to glance in his rearview mirror and realize he was no longer the hunter, but the hunted. By the time he—and I could see through the rear window that the driver was definitely male—realized what was happening I was nearly on his rear bumper.

He had three choices available. His best option was to slam on the brakes and confront me, indignantly demanding to know why the hell I was chasing him. If he'd done that, the advantage would have been his because I had no legitimate reason to pursue him other than he might have been following us. Fortunately, he wasn't that smart.

The second choice was only available to him if he was armed. If he had a gun, he could try taking a shot at me through a side window when we rounded one of the road's switchback curves. This option had the least chance of success because hitting a moving vehicle from another moving vehicle, especially when both vehicles are bouncing along a rough road, depends much more on luck than marksmanship.

His third choice and the one he picked was to simply try outrunning me. With luck and superior driving skills he would have a fair chance of success with this option. He had neither.

The road was climbing along a narrow shelf cut out of a hillside with a steep gorge on our left. Seeing the Plymouth fishtail every time he took a turn too wide and his tires got off the gravel and into the dirt, I decided to back off a little, so he didn't end up taking us both over the edge.

That was when I finally remembered that the red spotlight lens Russ and I used on our way to the North American plant after the bombing was still attached to the driver-side spotlight. Just for ducks, I pulled the knob out and pointed the light straight ahead. If nothing else, it sort of identified me as a law enforcement officer.

The red light must have flashed in his rearview just as he came to a narrow spot where runoff from a spring had carried a fair-sized piece of the road down into the gorge. The road was still passable, but you had to hug the hillside to make it. He didn't, and the result was startling.

Standing on the brake pedal, so I didn't go where the Plymouth went, I watched his left front tire slip off the gravel and catch on the sheer edge of the washout. The driver instinctively jerked his steering wheel to the right in an attempt to force the tire back onto the roadway, but the washout was too deep for the tire to turn back, so his attempt to change the direction of the car levered the rear wheels left, causing them to slew through the gravel toward the drop-off. Two seconds later the Plymouth sedan was bouncing ass over tea kettle down the wall of the gorge.

Shedding parts like a molting chicken, the sedan bounced and rolled downward faster and faster. At the halfway point the top collapsed. When it finally stopped at the bottom of the gorge, the Plymouth was little more than a crumpled ball of sheet metal. I thought about hiking down there to see what shape the driver was in, but it was damned unlikely anyone could live through that ride. Also, the wreckage ended up no more than a hundred yards from the highway, so it was bound to attract the attention of passersby. So, unless I wanted to spend the afternoon explaining how the Plymouth got there to a bunch of California Highway Patrolmen, it was time to leave.

I cautiously backed down the road to a wide spot where I could turn around, and then I hotfooted it back to where Sally and Russ were waiting for me. Russ spotted me coming down the road. I saw him holster his forty-five before he led Sally out to meet me.

Cradling her right arm, Sally climbed into the front seat to sit between Russ and me. She wasn't smiling.

As I got us back on US 40 in the eastbound direction I described what happened to the Plymouth. Russ showed no particular reaction to the story, but Sally seemed shocked at the outcome.

"That man in the other car is dead and you're just leaving him there?"

My adrenalin level wasn't quite back to normal, so my response to her was a bit testy. "What in blazes would you have me do?"

"I don't know. Call someone. You can't just leave him there."

"The hell I can't. There's nothing anyone can do for him and the wreck is in plain sight from the highway. Someone will report it sooner or later."

Her voice rose in volume and shrillness. "But you killed him!"

"Sally, I did not kill that guy. He did that to himself, and if he hadn't there's a good possibility I'd be dead now, or worse, you'd be dead. Russ, explain this to her, will you please?"

"Don't you dare patronize me!"

Russ said, "Sally, Major Spicer did what he had to do, which at the moment includes protecting you. Don't forget, a couple of days ago these people killed several North American Aviation employees, and darn near killed you, too."

Sally folded her arms as best she could with the cast and stared ahead through the windshield without another word. I looked at Russ. He gave me a little shrug. I felt like saying something about the country being at war and American soldiers being killed in places like Pearl Harbor and the Philippines, but I kept my mouth shut.

It was about 1600 hours when we rolled into West Sacramento, just across the river from downtown Sacramento. I had a nodding acquaintance with the area because I was there a couple of years ago trying to recover a rare African elephant statuette misplaced by Jack Warner's biggest star.

What I learned then was that, aside from a couple of stodgy downtown hotels catering to politicians, all of the lodging for

Sacramento is either to the west or the south along the most common routes into town. For simplicity's sake, I chose the same motel Susan and I stayed in on that trip.

I spotted the El Rancho Motel's giant neon windmill alongside Route 40 and pulled up to the office. I checked us into adjoining rooms and we carried our bags in. When Russ opened the connecting door, I saw Sally sitting on the edge of the bed in the other room. Her mood had not improved. I decided her morale was Russ's problem.

Looking around the room, I was reminded of the night Susan and I spent in a similar room a few doors away. The memory made me miss her, although as I recalled, she wasn't overjoyed with me either when we were here.

I hollered through the open connecting door, "Russ, I'm going to take a look around and make a couple of telephone calls."

He hollered back, "Yes, sir."

Donning my uniform cap, I strolled around the parking lot looking for anything that didn't seem kosher. I saw nothing that fit that description. I ended up back at the office, where there was a bank of public telephone booths next to the motel's gift shop. I stepped into one and dialed 0 for an operator. While I waited for my call to be placed, I admired the collection of chintzy pot metal models of the hotel's windmill symbol in the gift shop window across the hall. No tourist should be without such a wonderful souvenir.

My first call was to Building 100 at the Presidio to check for messages. There were none for me, but I left a message of my own for Colonel Beecher, asking him to run the license plate number of the black Plymouth through DMV.

My second call was to Major General Chester Davis in Washington DC. I didn't really expect him to be in his office at this hour on a Sunday. It was early evening back there, but he was in his office.

"Hello, Spicer. I hear you've had a busy couple of days."

"You could say that. I gather you heard about the explosion at the plant in Inglewood?"

"I sure did. We didn't see that one coming, did we?"

"No, sir, and I'm thinking there was an ulterior motive hidden in the incident."

"Oh? Tell me."

I gave Davis a complete report of just about every move I'd made since seeing him on Wednesday, beginning with what we learned about the B-25 refueling gizmo and ending with the

Plymouth incident out on Route 40. I sensed he was making notes from what I was telling him, especially about Marjorie Yount and the Plymouth.

When I finished, the General asked, "Any witnesses to the Plymouth incident?"

"No, sir. We're in the clear on that one; however, the wreckage ended up in view of Highway 40. Someone is bound to report it."

"That should not be a problem, but I'll tell Beecher to have someone keep an eye on the local newspapers to see what they say about it. What's the name of that town again?"

"Vallejo, V-A-L-L-E-J-O."

"That's a strange way to spell it. Must be Indian or something."

"Spanish, sir. Also, I left a message for Colonel Beecher with the car's license number and asked him to run it through DMV."

"Good. Now, what about this MacLure woman? Do we really need her slowing things down?"

"She isn't slowing us down, sir. In fact, she's been a big help so far. She also attracts Jap spies for some reason. I'd sure like to know what they think she knows that they don't want me to know."

Davis laughed. "Trolling for Jap spies with live bait, huh?"

"I guess you could say that is a secondary benefit of having Miss MacLure with us."

"Okay, Spicer, you're running this show and it seems like you're making progress, so keep doing what you think needs to be done."

"Thank you, sir."

"Anything you need from me?"

"No, sir, at least not at the moment."

"All right, stay in touch."

"Will do, sir."

I hung up wondering how much of what I'd just told him he already knew. Davis handed me a lousy assignment. I understood what he hoped to gain by keeping me in the dark and sending me on a wild goose chase, but I didn't have to like it.

Dialing 0 for the operator again, I made a collect call to Santa Barbara. Susan's enthusiasm at hearing from me always cheered me up.

"Hello, darling! I hope you know you just made my day."

"Made mine, too. How are you doing?"

"I'm doing well. Mister Whiskers and I spent a lazy Sunday

doing a little housework and catching up on our reading."

I laughed. "I didn't know Mister Whiskers could read."

"Sure, he can! Sometimes he even plunks himself down in my lap right on top of the book." After a pause, Susan asked, "Is everything okay with you?"

"Everything is fine, Angel, except I miss you like crazy."

"I miss you, too, Johnny . . . more than I can possibly tell you."

I sighed and changed the subject. "Hear anything new from Jack?"

"Not much, except big brother is coming over for dinner tonight. I made a tuna-noodle casserole."

"Well, say hi and eat some of that casserole for me."

"I will. Jack always asks about you."

"Well, I guess I'd better get off here before we end up owning Pacific Telephone and Telegraph."

"All right, darling. Please take good care of yourself and hurry home when you can."

"You can count on both of those. You take care of my Angel. Oh, and Mister Whiskers, too."

Susan laughed. "If you asked him, Mister Whiskers would tell you he takes care of me. Goodbye, darling."

I hung the handset on its hook and sighed again. To hell with the war, to hell with the Japs, Nazis, and all generals.

Back in our room, Russ said quietly, "Sir, I think Sally has thought things through and she feels badly about the way she talked to you. Would you mind talking with her so she can apologize?"

I sighed for a third time. "All right. While I do that, find a room service menu. I'm hungry."

"Yes, sir."

Sally stood up when I walked into her room. "Hello, Johnny. I'm sorry for the way I spoke to you before. I'm afraid I let things upset me again. I'm just not used to all this . . . violence and hatred."

I gave her a small smile. "Apology accepted, but you're wrong about the hatred part. I don't hate our enemies. That would make what I have to do too personal. I feel the same way about that Jap spy in the Plymouth, if that's what he was, as you feel about a problem on one of your assembly lines. He was just part of the job."

Sally stared at me for a moment and I expected another tirade, but she simply nodded. "I understand. I will try to look at things the same way."

"It works for me. Now let's see about some food." Turning toward the connecting door, I hollered, "Sergeant, get in here with that room service menu on the double!"

He rushed through the door with a folder in his hand. "Here it is, sir."

"Good. I can vouch for the food in this motel's Round Up Room. Susan and I had an excellent dinner here. I recommend the roast beef."

Eleven

Sacramento Signal Depot, Sacramento

I'm a little embarrassed to admit it, but I learned everything I know about the Army's Signal Depots from a civilian. Things are happening so quickly in preparation for the war we entered less than three months ago it's impossible for any one person to keep track of it all. Fortunately, Sally was one of the enlightened few because North American Aviation sent out a paper about the Army's depot system to its employees who might encounter it.

She explained that the Sacramento Depot was one of a dozen such facilities scattered across the country for the purposes of receiving equipment and supplies from manufacturers and shipping them all over the globe to where they are needed by Army personnel. Sally said the Navy had a similar setup. Heaven forbid we make do with one system for both services when we can spend twice as much of the taxpayers' money by having two separate systems. Of course, nobody's heard the communities in which the depots are located complaining because the government employs civilians from the local work force to do the work under the direction of Army officers.

Most important at the moment, however, was that Sally knew the Army's Sacramento Signal Depot was temporarily housed at the California State Fairgrounds located southeast of town until they finish an entirely new facility, hopefully before the war ends. The El Rancho's desk clerk provided me with driving instructions to the corner of Broadway and Stockton Boulevard, from which point, he claimed, one could not miss the fairgrounds. He was right, they would be damned hard to miss.

Apparently, the Army rented the portion of the fairgrounds it needed from the state, and it was a big portion, consisting mostly of livestock exhibit buildings and hastily erected temporary storage structures, some still under construction. Surprisingly, the depot was only a month old and it appeared far more organized than I expected it to be, but we were about to put that observation to the test.

After showing our IDs to a civilian security guard at the gate, we drove to what we were told was the central administration building and parked. Russ chose that moment to ask the sixty-four-dollar question.

"How do we handle this, sir?"

"Darned if I know. Sally?"

"Do you still have the notes you made when we found out the in-flight refueling system kits were being shipped here?"

"Yes, they're in my notebook."

"Did you write down the requisition number I gave you?"

Opening my notebook to the appropriate page, I said, "Yes. You said it was one-two-eight-dash-four-one-nine-six-dash-four-two-zero-two-one-nine."

"Good. That's the same number they should be using in their filing system here. That means we can identify the specific order we are interested in. All you have to do is get them to tell you whose signature is on the order, or just get them to let us look at the order. I can probably translate most of it for you."

"All right, but I'm afraid what you suggest sounds a lot easier than it will turn out to be. I imagine I will have to bully some poor civilian ribbon clerk. Russ, put on your 'we mean business' face."

"Yes, sir."

"Okay, let's go in and see what we can get away with."

Just inside the building's entrance doors an ancient wooden easel supported a large hand-lettered cardboard sign with arrows directing visitors to the locations of various offices. Sally pointed to one called CENTRAL RECORDS, and said, "I think that's where we need to go."

How she figured that out, I have no idea, but we marched off down the hallway to which the sign pointed. There were several doors on both sides of the hall, each with a small card thumbtacked to the wall beside it identifying what activities took place within. The door we were looking for was about halfway down the hall on our left.

Central Records was a large windowless room with gloomy gray walls and a floor of cracked brown linoleum. The occupants of the room were ten or twelve women seated at beat-up gray metal desks banging away on typewriters. The wall to our right was papered with notices of one sort or another and the requisite "loose lips might sink ships" poster.

The left wall was home to at least a dozen dark green four-drawer metal filing cabinets I thought might be veterans of the Great War. In front of all this was a temporary counter of half-inch unfinished sheets of plywood supported by stacks of large cardboard boxes containing, according to their labels, commercial grade toilet paper.

Sally and I walked up to the makeshift counter and Russ assumed a semi-military posture near the door. He looked quite businesslike.

I held my MID ID card up for a young woman to view and said, "We are here to inspect an order requisition submitted by the Eighth Air Force."

With only a brief glance at my ID, the woman said, "Yes, sir." She slid a wooden clipboard with a sign-in form clipped to it in my general direction. In a tone that sounded as if she said the same thing a hundred times a day, she said, "Please print your name and the organization you represent, and then sign your name. Print the number of the requisition you need in the request column."

I printed my name and rank in the NAME column. In the ORG column I printed Army MID and signed in the SIGNATURE column. In the REQUEST column I printed 128-4196-420219 and slid the clipboard back to the woman. She wrote the requisition number down on a slip of paper and walked to the row of filing cabinets on the left wall. The woman stopped at the third cabinet from our end and opened the second drawer from the top.

After looking through the folders in the drawer, she got a worried expression on her face and went through all the folders again. Then, still looking worried, she closed the drawer and searched through several folders in a wire in-basket atop the filing cabinet. Suddenly her worried look was replaced by her happy face and she headed back in our direction carrying one of the manila folders.

"Here you are, sir. It took me longer to find it because someone else requested the file recently and it had not been refiled yet."

Opening the folder, I glanced at it to be sure we had the right one and handed it to Sally. After only a moment of study, Sally said, "The kits were ordered by Captain Frank Ellis of the McClellan Air Service Command. The kits are to be sent directly to his attention at McClellan Army Airfield as soon as they arrive.

Those are the only significant details you don't already have."

I hardly heard what she said because something else grabbed my attention. I handed Sally my notebook. "Write all that down, will you please?"

No sooner had I handed her my notebook than I realized copying the information would be difficult with the cast on her right hand. I turned to say I would do it, but she was already at work, holding the notebook with her left hand and carefully printing the information in it by holding my pencil in the fingers of her right hand while resting her cast on the makeshift counter. It was awkward for her, but Sally was determined to get the job done.

The clipboard with the sign-in sheets was still on the counter and I picked it up. Fortunately, the women in Central Records were also behind on filing old sign-in sheets. I found what I was looking for on the third page down. Requisition number 128-4196-420219 was requested on 28 February by one Mary Adams of the Air Service Command.

Just to make sure of my facts, I took the copy photograph from the Jap spy mug book out of my pocket and gestured to the young woman who retrieved the requisition form for us. I held the photo up and said, "Do you recognize this woman?"

After staring at the photo for a moment, she said, "Yes, I think she was in here a few days ago requesting a file."

Holding the file folder up, I said, "To be specific, your sign-in sheet says she asked for requisition number 128-4196-420219 on Saturday 28 February."

The young woman had her worried look on again. I added to her worries. "Mary Adams is a known Japanese spy. I don't know how she got into the Depot or why someone here simply handed her this file, but I will make certain it never happens again."

We trooped out of Central Records leaving a very worried clerk standing behind her commercial grade toilet paper counter. Outside, I looked around for a public telephone. Finding none, we piled into the Dodge and drove back toward town until I found a Raley's market with a public telephone in its parking lot. I parked and stepped into the telephone booth.

I dialed 0 for an operator and placed a collect call to Washington DC. A woman at a desk three-thousand miles to the east accepted the charges from Major Johnathon Spicer, and then said, "Yes, Major Spicer?"

I said exactly what I was taught to say in such situations. "ID three-three-eight-seven-two-one requesting a Priority Able call to

General Davis."

It only took her a moment to match my name to her master list of ID numbers and then to verify I have the authority to make a Priority Able request, after which she said, "Please hold on the line, sir."

That response told me Davis was in his office. No more than ten seconds later Davis said, "What's up, Spicer?"

"Sorry to bother you, sir, but I just uncovered one hell of a hole in Army security."

"Tell me."

"I was just at the Sacramento Signal Depot to take a look at the requisition information for the gizmos I told you about yesterday. They showed me the forms, all right, but I discovered one Miss Mary Adams also came in to look at them. She saw them last Saturday. Mary Adams is Marjorie Yount, our Jap spy. The woman in Central Records also identified her from our mug shot. You understand the significance of this situation better than I."

Davis said, "Trust me, it's significant. I can't believe this."

"The problem is the place is staffed by civilians and they need something more than a 'loose lips might sink ships' poster to understand what's at stake and why security is so important."

"I've got the picture. That facility is in Colonel Beecher's bailiwick. I'll get him on this today. Anything else?"

"Only if you have any special instructions for dealing with Marjorie Yount. It's seeming more and more likely we will encounter her before too long."

"Nothing special, just SOP. If you can take her alive, we have some questions for her, but the most important thing is to remove her and those she's working with from the picture ASAP."

"Understood, sir. Talk with you soon."

I ended the call and jiggled the handset hook a couple of times to get the operator back on the line. My next call went to Building 100 at the Presidio. The only message for us was the information from the Department of Motor Vehicles on the license number of the gray Chevrolet. California license number 39 T 147 was registered to a Mary Adams who resided at 1697 12th Street in Oakland. It was probably the address of a vacant lot, but I jotted the information in my notebook anyway. The choice of an Oakland address might be telling us something. The auto registration on the black Plymouth was not in yet.

Back in the Dodge, I rolled down the window and lit a Lucky. "General Davis is telling Beecher to roll some heads at the Sacramento Signal Depot as we speak. Also, we have an address for Marjorie Yount's Chevrolet. It's in Oakland, although I'd bet money it's a vacant lot."

Sally said, "I feel a little sorry for that clerk we talked to back there. She hardly looked old enough to be out of high school, let alone to be handling classified files."

"It's hard to say who's at fault in this case. Technically, the file we requested is not a classified document. On the other hand, we're at war, so everything the military does is sensitive right down to instructional films on how not to catch VD. I'm guessing that point has not been stressed enough to the civilian employees, especially to the civilian security guards at the gate who let Marjorie Yount into the depot in the first place."

I picked McClellan Army Airfield as our next stop, mainly because it was the only stop left on my list. Getting there, however, proved a challenge to my patience. Having no idea where the field was, I asked a Chinese gentleman leaving the Raley's market for directions. His English was excellent, and he gave me very precise driving directions.

Essentially what he told me was that we were down at the southeast corner of the city and the airfield was up north of town. The difficulty was the American River ran between us and our destination and there were only two points where the river can be crossed by automobiles between where we were and where we needed to be.

I won't bore you with the details, but it took more than half an hour to cover a distance of about ten miles. I cursed whoever laid out the roads in Sacramento at every arterial stop and traffic light we encountered. I almost ran out of expletives.

Security was much tighter at McClellan Army Airfield. The MP at the gate gave us and our IDs a thorough going over. When he was satisfied we were who we said we were, I asked him where to find McClellan Air Service Command HQ. He gave me clear directions and a snappy salute. The building we were looking for was one block east of the flight line. While I went in search of the man I was there to see, Russ took Sally over to watch the airplanes take off and land.

What I know about the Army Air Force Air Services Commands is only slightly more than I know about the Army's signal depots. There are four ASCs, each serving a geographic area of the country. They were created to manage the signal depots' acquisition and distribution of aircraft parts, along with overseeing the AAF's aircraft maintenance programs, or something like that.

Inside McClellan Air Service Command headquarters, a corporal behind a real counter asked how he could help me. He got a funny look on his face when I asked for Captain Frank Ellis.

"I'm sorry, sir. Captain Ellis isn't here."

Judging by the corporal's expression, there was more to the story, a lot more. "Where is Captain Ellis, Corporal?"

"Ah, sir, I'll get his assistant. I'm sure he can help you."

I was beginning to get a bad feeling about Captain Ellis. "All right, Corporal, that sounds like an excellent idea."

He dialed a telephone on a desk behind the counter. When he spoke into the handset he spoke softly and turned away from me so I couldn't hear what he was saying, all of which made that much more determined to find out what was going on at McClellan ASC.

While waiting for Captain Ellis' assistant I looked at a large US map on the wall. It showed the twelve signal depots and the four Air Service Command headquarters. In addition to the one I was in, there were ASCs in San Antonio, Texas; Fairfield, Ohio; and Middletown, Pennsylvania. I had plenty of time to study the map because Ellis' assistant took his sweet time about coming to talk with me, or possibly someone else took his sweet time telling the guy what he should say to the spook from MID.

The fellow who finally showed up was a First Sergeant who introduced himself as Joe Richards. He invited me to follow him down the hall to a conference room. Inside with the door closed, Richards said, "Now what is it you need to know, Major?"

Sergeant Richards was off to a bad start. I showed him my MID ID and said, "Sergeant the first thing you need to know about dealing with an MID officer is I ask the questions and you answer them. Understood?"

First Sergeants think they're almost as important as officers, and they are, but it's not a good idea to encourage such thinking. "Yes, sir. I'm sorry, sir."

"The burning questions of the moment are where the hell is Captain Ellis, and why is everybody around here so afraid of that question?"

Richards took a few moments to decide how best to answer my question. "Frankly, sir, we do not know the whereabouts of Captain Ellis. It seems he has disappeared."

Now we were getting somewhere, but I didn't like where we were going. "And Captain Ellis is well liked here so you fellows are trying to cover for him, right?"

Again, Richards gave his response a moment of thought. "Sir, I wouldn't use the word 'cover,' but, yes, Captain Ellis is a good officer and none of us would like to see him in trouble."

"And, Sergeant, what makes you think Captain Ellis is likely to be in trouble?"

"Well, sir, technically he's A-W-O-L. The Army Air Force does not treat that sort of thing lightly."

I shook my head. "Sergeant, do you know what the road to hell is paved with?"

He looked confused. "Good intentions, sir?"

"That's correct, Sergeant. Has it occurred to any of you that Captain Ellis' absence might be due to something beyond his control?"

"I don't know what that could be, sir. He was fine when he left here Friday afternoon."

I was still missing something. "Sergeant, what aren't you telling me about Captain Ellis? For example, does he have a drinking problem?"

Sergeant Richards' expression told me I'd hit the ball out of the park with my first swing. "Well, sir, I guess he has been known to enjoy a cocktail now and then."

"And he has also been known to show up for work on Monday morning with a hangover?"

With an expression I thought might be similar to the one Judas Iscariot had on his face when he sold Jesus out for 30 pieces of silver, Sergeant Richards said softly, "Yes, sir."

"Okay, Sergeant, now that we have a few facts on the table, let's see if we can find out what's happened to Captain Ellis." I showed him Marjorie Yount's mug book photo. "Do you recognize this woman?"

He shook his head. "No, sir. I don't think I've ever seen her before."

I looked him in the eye. "Be straight with me, Sergeant."

"I am, sir. If I've seen that woman before, I don't remember her."

"All right, Sergeant. Call everyone in here who handles Captain Ellis' calls or sees his visitors."

"Yes, sir."

He left the room for about five minutes. When the Sergeant returned he had three enlisted men in tow. When everyone was inside and the door was closed again, I said, "Gentlemen, I'm Spicer with MID, and I'm trying to locate your Captain Ellis. I have reason to believe something may have happened to him. I can't go into details, but if you know anything about MID, you probably know some of us deal with espionage on the homefront.

That's my bailiwick.

"I'm going to show you a photograph. I want you each to look at it and tell me if you have ever seen the woman in it. Also, I want to know if the names Marjorie Yount or Mary Adams mean anything to you. This is a matter of national security, so be on the level with me."

I set the photograph of Marjorie Yount on the conference room table and said, "All right, take a look."

One by one the men studied the photo. I saw no signs of recognition in their faces. The last fellow, the corporal who manned the reception counter, did have something to contribute, though.

"Sir, I don't recognize this woman, but I recognize one of the names you said earlier, Mary Adams."

"Good, Corporal. Where have you heard that name before?"

"Actually, sir, I spoke with her. A Mary Adams called a little before noon last Friday. She said she was with the Sac Signal Depot and needed to speak with Captain Ellis."

"And did she?"

"Yes, sir. Of course, I didn't hear their conversation, but they were on the line together for several minutes."

"Thank you, Corporal. Anyone else have something to add?"

I got head shakes in response, so I tried a different direction. "Can anyone tell me what Captain Ellis' schedule was on Friday from late morning on?"

Sergeant Rogers nodded. "Yes, sir. He left the base at lunch time and was gone for about ninety minutes. He got back around 1330 and we spent the rest of the day straightening out a batch of duplicate requisition orders. Captain Ellis left the office about 1630 hours."

"All right. Sergeant Rogers, I have a few more questions for you. Everyone else can return to your duties. Thanks for your help."

When Rogers and I were alone again, I asked, "Sergeant, is Captain Ellis married?"

"No, sir. He has no family in the area that I'm aware of."

"When Ellis returned from lunch, did you have any indication that he had been drinking?"

"No, sir. Captain Ellis controls his drinking to the extent that he only drinks after work."

"That's unusual for an alcoholic."

"Sir, may I speak freely?"

"Please do, Sergeant."

"I would not describe Captain Ellis as an alcoholic. He may be borderline, but I think his problem is that booze . . . alcohol . . . affects him more than it does most people."

"Your observation is noted, Sergeant. Now, going back to Friday afternoon, would you say Captain Ellis' schedule was normal for a Friday?"

"No, sir. He seldom leaves the base during lunch hour and is never gone more than an hour unless he has a luncheon meeting. Also, it is unlike him to leave work before seventeen-hundred hours, and he often works later than that when we're swamped."

I reviewed the notes I'd taken during my conversation with Sergeant Rogers. Sometimes an interview clearly points in a definite direction. The new puzzle pieces I had were a telephone call from a known Jap spy, a long lunch hour off base, and an early departure from work, and they were more than enough to suspect foul play.

"Sergeant, have you tried to reach Captain Ellis this morning?"

"Yes, sir. I tried calling him on the telephone around oh-nine-thirty when we began wondering where he was."

"I take it there was no answer?"

"Correct, sir."

"Does Captain Ellis live at the BOQ or in base housing?"

"Neither, sir. Base housing is only available to married officers and the Base Officers Quarters are limited. He rents a small house off base."

"Do you have the address? I'd like to take a look."

"I have the address in my book. I can get it if you'd like."

"Yes, I think we're done here for now, so I'll go with you. I'd also like to see Captain Ellis' office."

Rogers gave me a slip of paper on which he'd written Captain Ellis' address, along with a few words of direction for finding the place. Then we walked into the captain's office. It was a typical military office with typical furnishings and typical photos on the wall, including one of our Commander-In-Chief looking slightly bewildered. The only thing I found meaningful was that his desk calendar had no entry for noon on Friday. That might mean one of two things. If he had a lunch appointment, it was last minute and he didn't bother to write it on his calendar, or it was something he didn't want on his calendar where anyone could see it.

I thanked Sergeant Rogers for his cooperation. Looking very concerned, he said, "I certainly hope Captain Ellis is all right."

"I do, too, Sergeant. I'll let you know what, if anything, I find at his home."

"Thank you, sir."

I walked out of the McClellan Air Service Command building into bright sunshine. I put on my dark glasses and looked around for Sergeant Pierce and Sally. I spotted them sitting in the Dodge. Apparently, they got tired of watching airplanes go up and down.

We left Sally in the car while Russ and I walked close by and I related my conversations with the ASC staff. When I was done, he said, "That doesn't sound good, sir."

"It sure doesn't. I'm going to drive over to Ellis' house and take a look around. While I do that, try to find Sally some lunch here on the base. I don't suppose they'll let her into the enlisted man's mess, but they probably have a snack bar or something around here."

"Yes, sir. I spotted a little civilian-run café a block or so from here for personnel arriving by air, but . . . ."

"But what, Russ?"

"Sir, General Davis said I was to be your back-up. I should be with you when you go to this missing captain's house in case there's trouble."

"For the time being you have a new assignment. Your job is keeping our number one witness alive. Besides, I don't think taking her off base right now is a good idea, and we sure can't leave her here alone."

With a resigned expression that clearly indicated he wasn't happy, Russ just said, "Yes sir."

Twelve

1200 Hours – Monday – 2 MAR 42

McClellan Army Airfield, Sacramento

The same guys I cursed for their idiotic design of Sacramento's roads also had an odd preoccupation with inventors. Several of the main streets in the northern part of the county are named for them—Edison, Whitney, Marconi, Fulton, Bell, and so on. That point was brought to mind because the main drag in front of McClellan Army Airfield was named for a Scot known as James Watt who, if I recall my Fifth grade lessons correctly, cobbled together some sort of new and improved steam engine and came up with a measurement of power, appropriately called a watt.

My destination as I turned off Mister Watt's Avenue was another cunningly named street called Wings Way, which intersected Watt a few blocks north of the gate I used to exit McClellan Airfield. It was on Wings that Captain Frank Ellis rented a tiny bungalow in a neighborhood I suspect might have already seen its best days by the time Clara Bow appeared in a silent picture by the same name.

Ellis' rented front yard was thick with trees—five big ones, all taller than the house they hid from passersby. I parked across the street and studied the situation for a while. Wings Way was only about three blocks long and I was at its eastern end, so I could see the entire street. Absolutely nothing moved anywhere along its length. It occurred to me that Wings Way was the perfect locale for a graveyard.

The house, itself, seemed to be a one-bedroom design with that room being at the front on the left. There was a swamp cooler in the bedroom window and, judging by the racket coming from that direction, it was running. If there was nobody home, Ellis was wasting a lot of Mister Watt's watts, especially since the outside temperature was only in the mid-60s.

Okay, Spicer, sitting at the curb in front of Ellis' home contemplating his electrical usage is getting you nowhere. Get out and knock on the damned door. I walked through the forest across a patchy lawn and arrived at the front door. The concrete walkway from the driveway on my right was bordered by a gravel planting area, home to a disintegrating wicker chair and two dead shrubs.

In addition to the front door, there was also a screen door, but no doorbell button. The screen door was warped and didn't close right, so when I rapped it with my knuckles, it made a racket loud enough to be heard over the roar and rattle of the swamp cooler. Nothing happened. I knocked again. Still nothing. After a third attempt, I was satisfied that I wouldn't be disturbing anyone if I walked in.

Before contemplating which window I would break to gain entry, I tried the obvious. Pulling the screen door open, I turned the front door's knob and gave it a little push. It swung open on hinges that were badly in need of 3-In-One oil. When the squeaking from the hinges stopped I was left with the swamp cooler racket again. I hollered "hello" a couple of times, and still getting no response, I cautiously entered a house full of very chilly air.

I was in a tidy little living room furnished with a threadbare couch and chair. There was also a scratched coffee table and one end table. The end table was home to a telephone. Using my handkerchief so I didn't add my fingerprints to any that might matter, I picked up the handset and listened. The dial tone was loud and clear. Topping off the living room décor was a cheap print in a cardboard frame depicting what I imagined was meant to be a scene in the Sierra Nevada Mountains.

A small kitchen with a breakfast nook was located directly behind the living room. The kitchen cabinets were about as well stocked as you would expect the larder of a bachelor to be stocked. The kitchen also housed a small refrigerator and a narrow gas stove, complete with an oven and even a broiler.

I headed back through the living room to a short hallway that connected the bathroom on my right and the bedroom to my left. I stepped into the hall and stopped dead in my tracks. I could see part of the bed from where I stood, and someone was on it.

I never met Captain Frank Ellis, but it's possible that even someone who knew him well might not recognize the battered, bruised, and bloodied thing on the bed. Rigor mortis generally relaxes about 70 hours after death, but the condition lasts longer in cold temperatures. I tried moving an arm and found it still somewhat stiff, so Ellis could have died as long ago as, say, Friday night. The rest of it was up to the coroner, but now the swamp cooler's racket made sense. Without it, the odor of decomposition might easily become strong enough to smell clear out on Wings Way.

It was abundantly clear that someone tried very hard to make Captain Ellis—assuming I was looking at the remains of Captain Ellis—tell them something he did not know or want to tell them. He'd been tortured unmercifully and there was no way to know whether or not his tormenters were successful.

My next chore was to positively identify the body. A uniform blouse on the bedroom floor bore Captain's bars and a wallet I found on the dresser contained a driver's license that said the thumbprint on it belonged to Franklin L. Ellis, but that wasn't enough. I needed an actual physical ID of the body.

I walked back to the living room and used the telephone to call McClellan Air Services Command. When I got Sergeant Richards on the line I told him to drop what he was doing and get over to Ellis' home on the double, and to tell nobody where he was going, only that he was meeting me.

I went out in the front yard and smoked a couple of cigarettes while I waited for Richards. He got there within fifteen minutes and I could see the question on his face from twenty feet away.

"Thanks for getting here quickly, Sergeant Richards."

"Sir, I take it the news about Captain Ellis is not good?"

"You take it right, Sergeant. I hate to ask, but I need someone who knew Ellis to make an identification."

Richards looked startled. "Identification, sir? Captain Ellis is dead?"

"At this point all I know is that someone in the bedroom is very dead. I need to know for sure whether or not it's Ellis."

"All right, sir. I'll take a look."

As I led him into the house, I said, "I have to warn you, this isn't pretty."

Richards looked into the bedroom and gulped. "You weren't kidding, sir."

He walked closer to the bed and looked at what was left of the dead man's face. Then Richards turned away and nodded. "Yes, sir. That's Captain Ellis."

"Thank you, Sergeant. Let's go back out front."

Standing under the trees where the world seemed like a better place, I said, "Sergeant, we have to handle this situation very carefully because we've got a serious matter of national security to consider. If news of Captain Ellis' death or a picture of that bedroom should end up in the papers, our situation is going to go from very bad to a whole lot worse."

"I understand, sir."

"Good. I need your help for a few more minutes. Will you stand by out here to make sure nobody wanders in there while I make a telephone call to Washington?"

His eyes widened a little when I said Washington. "Yes, sir. I'll be right here."

"Thanks, Sergeant."

I went inside and made my second Priority Able call of the day to General Davis. The General made note of that fact when he came on the line. "What's going on, Spicer? Two Priority Ables in one day must be a record of some sort, even for you."

"We've got a bad situation on our hands and we need to move quickly."

"What's going on?"

I explained Captain Ellis' connection with my mission and what happened to him, including the telephone call he received from Marjorie Yount as Mary Adams. I finished my explanation by saying, "I'm keeping a lid on it here, but I need someone to get this mess cleaned up while I find Dragon Lady."

"Dragon Lady? That's very funny, Spicer. If a team has to come from San Francisco, how long will it take them?"

"The travel time is three hours, give or take."

"Can you keep things quiet there that long?"

I glanced at my wristwatch. It was nearly 1400. "I can if you will approve the use of a couple of MPs from McClellan. For one thing, I need to get Miss MacLure out of here and back into hiding. I'm not sure her life is worth a plug nickel until that happens."

"Give me ten minutes and then call McClellan's Military Police."

"Will do, sir."

"One more thing, Spicer. I want you to get settled someplace safe for the night, and then call me. I don't care what time. I need you to fill in some holes in all of this for me."

"Yes, sir."

I hung up the handset and walked back out to the front yard. Richards was standing next one of the larger trees watching the street.

"I need you here for another fifteen minutes, Sergeant, and then you can take off."

"Yes, sir. I know you can't tell me what's going on, but if you have any suggestions about how to keep someone else from ending up . . . like that," he gestured toward the bedroom, "I would certainly like to hear them."

"Besides stationing a couple of MPs at your building, I think the best thing we can do at this point is circulate that picture I showed you earlier and for you to be sure you keep an ear out for those names I mentioned. I'll have a copy of the picture sent to you from San Francisco tomorrow."

Sergeant Richards looked surprised. "Sir? A woman did that?"

Nodding, I said, "If she didn't do the actual torture, she certainly set Captain Ellis up for it to happen."

"Damn! Who would do a thing like that?"

Turning to go back into the house, I said, "Japs. I'll be right back, Sergeant."

I called McClellan's public number and asked to be connected to the base Military Police headquarters. A few seconds later a voice said, "Military Police, Corporal Baker speaking."

"Corporal Baker, this is Major Spicer with MID. I think you just had a call from my boss in Washington, General Davis?

"Yes, sir. I understand we are to give you whatever help you need, no questions asked."

"Thank you, Corporal. What I need right now are two experienced MPs who can follow orders and keep their mouths shut. I'll need them for about four hours."

"Yes, sir. Where do you need them, sir?"

"The residence at 3664 Wings Way. It's across Watt from the base."

"We'll find it, sir. We'll have two men there in a few minutes. Will you be at that address to give them their orders, Major Spicer?"

"I will, and side arms should be sufficient."

"Yes, sir."

Every time I left the house and went back out to the trees in the front yard, they seemed more welcoming. Richards turned as I closed the front door.

"Okay, Sergeant. You can take off."

He looked relieved. I didn't have the heart to tell him the mental images of what he'd seen in the bedroom of that house would take a long time to go away, if they ever went away.

"Thank you, sir. Any special instructions about this?"

"Just keep it to yourself. I would rather nobody heard about Captain Ellis' death just yet, and we certainly don't want anyone to know how he died. Our people will handle whatever notifications need to be made."

"Yes, sir."

As he turned to leave, I said, "Sergeant Richards, what happened here is tragic, but it is not uncommon. Anyone who tells you this war isn't being fought on US soil doesn't know the facts, and maybe that's the best way for things to be. You, however, have now seen the truth and what our enemies are capable of. I hope you'll keep what you've seen in mind. Thanks for your help."

He saluted and said, "I will, sir, and you're welcome. And, sir?"

"Yes, Sergeant?"

"I surely do not envy you your job."

Smiling the friendliest smile I could muster, I said, "I don't envy me, either, Sergeant."

Richards was hardly out of sight when a Jeep with two hefty Army Air Force MPs in it pulled up to the curb. I greeted the fellows and gave them their marching orders: one at the front of the house and one at the back of the house, do not enter the house for any reason, be as inconspicuous as possible, and remain on guard until relieved by an MID security detail in about three hours, possibly sooner.

When I returned to the base, I found Sally and Russ sitting on a bench outside the ASC building. "Sorry to be so long. I ran into a situation that required some time to resolve."

Russ knew something was up. "Everything okay, sir?"

I shook my head. "No. At this particular moment I would say nothing is okay. I want you to find a public telephone and call the Presidio. Tell them to get three copies of Marjorie Yount's mug shot made and sent to the attention of First Sergeant Joe Russell, care of McClellan ASC on the double."

"Yes, sir."

"We'll meet you at that café you found earlier."

"Yes, sir."

The Feathered Prop, a small flight line café, was a block south of the ASC offices. The place had both indoor and outdoor tables, and the outdoor tables were all empty, so I steered Sally to one of them. This was one conversation I definitely did not want overheard.

We ordered a Coke for Sally and a cheese sandwich with coffee for me, and then I began explaining what had happened and what I hoped would happen next. "Russ already knows some of this, Sally, but you should hear it, too."

Sally looked tired, but she rested her right arm with its cast on the table and gave me a half-smile. "From the look on your face, I'm not sure I want to hear it. Are we in trouble?"

"Not at the moment, but we're not far from it. It turned out the guy I came here to see, Captain Frank Ellis, didn't come in to work today. I had a problem getting the facts out of his staff because they all liked Ellis and were trying to cover for him.

"What I finally dragged out of them were three interesting facts. First, Ellis received a telephone call from a Mary Adams who claimed to be with the Sacramento Signal Depot a little before noon on Friday. Mary Adams, if you recall, is one of Marjorie Yount's aliases. Second, Ellis was gone longer than usual for lunch on Friday, but there was no indication on his calendar that he had a reason to be gone longer than usual. Third, Ellis left work early Friday afternoon, and that was the last time anyone we know of saw him.

"First Sergeant Joe Richards, Ellis' assistant, finally told me a few more facts about Ellis, including that he tended to drink heavily after work. That was the reason his staff wasn't talking. They figured Ellis didn't come in because he was hungover. The other thing Richards gave me was Ellis' home address. He lived off-base in a rental house."

Our orders and Russ arrived at the same time. I took a bite of cheese sandwich before returning to my story.

"Russ, I just briefed Sally on what I told you about Captain Ellis earlier. I'll pick up the story from there."

"Yes, sir."

"I went to Ellis' house. He was there, all right, but he was also dead, and somebody did a bang up torture job on him before he died."

Sally said, "Oh, God! They killed him?"

I nodded. "Yes, eventually. He was so beat up and bloody his own assistant barely recognized him."

Sally had tears in her eyes. "And they want to do that to me, too, don't they?"

"No, Sally, they don't. They already know what they think you know. They just want you dead, so you don't tell us what they think you know. That may not sound like much of an improvement, but it is.

"Anyway, I called the situation in to General Davis and he's sending a security team from San Francisco or someplace to clean things up at Ellis' house. I left a couple of MPs guarding the place until the security team arrives."

I handed Sally my handkerchief and she dabbed at the tears rolling down both cheeks. "I don't want to die for my country or for any other reason. I really don't."

Russ looked at me with a helpless expression. I said, "That's good, Sally, because we aren't going to let you die, even if you wanted to. The next to last order General Davis gave me over the phone a little while ago was get you to somewhere safe and dig in."

Sally's curiosity got the best of her. With a sniff, she said, "What was his last order to you?"

"To call him and explain what the blazes is going on with Dragon Lady and how we're going to make her and her pals into good little Jap spies."

Sally looked puzzled and Russ filled in the blank for her. "The expression goes 'the only good Jap spy is a dead Jap spy.'"

"And who is Dragon Lady?"

I grinned. "She's the femme fatale in the *Terry and the Pirates* comic strip. It seemed like a good code name for Marjorie Yount."

For some reason, that gave Sally the giggles. "A comic strip character? You guys are nuts!"

I said, "Yeah, but we're loveable nuts." Pointing to Russ, I added, "At least he is."

"You are, too, Johnny. You really are."

I shoved the last bite of cheese sandwich into my mouth and washed it down with a swallow of coffee. "Okay, folks we need to get this show on the road. The question is which road and in which direction?

"There are lots of places we can go to ground and not be found, but going too far to ground won't find Dragon Lady for us. I hate to keep splitting us up, but we've got two missions here and they're taking us in opposite directions."

In a sense we were discussing Sally's fate and she wanted some say in the matter. "Listen, I don't want to be the reason that woman gets away with more killing and other bad things. How would it be it I hid out by myself for a few days? That way you guys can go find your Dragon Lady without worrying about me."

Russ and I both shook our heads at that plan. I said, "That won't work, Sally. We're up against some real pros here. Look at how slickly they put that black Plymouth on our tail. I even expected someone to follow us, but they trailed us all the way from San Francisco to Vallejo before I spotted the guy."

Sally looked disappointed. "Oh."

"Cheer up, we'll figure this out. We've got one more lead to follow up, maybe two, if HQ has the information on that Plymouth from DMV. I think we'll spend tonight in the exciting city of Oakland and follow up on Marjorie Yount's address. It's probably a vacant lot, but there might still be a clue in there somewhere. We'll figure out our next step in the morning."

With light traffic on Route 40 and a full tank of gasoline, we made the trip west to Oakland in about two-and-a-half hours. We pulled into the circular drive of the Claremont Hotel around 1600 hours. I dropped Russ and Sally at the entrance with our bags and went off to park the Dodge nearby. Before I locked it up I swapped the Colt .45 I'd been lugging around all day for my Smith & Wesson revolver and its shoulder holster.

When I turned around to head for the lobby, I got a good overall view of the Claremont. It was something to behold. Sitting atop a rise, the Claremont sprawled outward from a central tower that stood at least a dozen stories. I have no idea what the architectural style is called, but the lines seemed very formal to my eye, with tall peaked roofs rising above buildings that were four or five floors. Without a doubt though, the hotel's best features were its fabulous views of the bay and San Francisco. This is where the rich folks came to play, which is exactly why I picked it. The Claremont is not the sort of hotel where you would go looking for people with a reason to stay out of sight.

In keeping with our standard procedure these days, I checked us into two adjoining rooms with a connecting door. The rooms at the Claremont are what you'd expect from a quality hotel. The furnishings, carpets, and draperies are top quality and the rooms also have telephones. It was to that instrument I turned my attention. My first collect call was to the Presidio on the other side of San Francisco Bay—a location I could actually see from the windows in our rooms.

There were two messages waiting for me. The first was information on the black Plymouth from DMV. It was registered to a Harada Daisuke, who lived at 1697 12th Street in Oakland, the same address as Dragon Lady. Imagine that.

My second message was from a staff investigator Colonel Beecher ordered to check out 1697 12th Street in Oakland. Of course, that house number does not exist on 12th Street.

I left a message for Colonel Beecher, telling him I'd be back at the Presidio in the morning and asking if he could round up a fast sedan equipped with the same accessories as my Dodge business couple. The Dodge was becoming too well known and we could use a little extra room for passenger comfort.

Hanging up the telephone receiver, I told Russ what I'd learned, or more accurately, what I had not learned from the Chevrolet and Plymouth license numbers. He said, "I guess we wasted a trip to Oakland."

"I don't think so. The Plymouth DMV address is the third reference to Oakland we've encountered since Sally and I identified Dragon Lady as Marjorie Yount. This burg has some connection to her."

Smiling, Russ said, "Technically, sir, we are not in Oakland at the moment. It is, however, right outside our window. According to the bellman, the hotel is actually in Berkeley, but the tennis courts and parking lot are in Oakland. The dividing line is right in front of the hotel."

"Oh, swell. Run out there and see if Dragon Lady is lounging around the courts somewhere."

"Yes, sir. I'll do that right after dinner."

My next collect long-distance call was to Washington DC. They connected me to General Davis. He wasn't in his office. It sounded as if he was in a bathtub. Well, I guess generals need baths, too.

"Okay, Spicer, I want you to lay this all out for me again from the top. I need a solid handle on what you've learned and where you learned it."

I started with learning about the B-25 in-flight refueling gizmo, and continued through the NAA plant explosion, Sally's and my spotting of Marjorie Yount at the plant, and our identification of Yount as a Jap spy. I refreshed his memory about the black Plymouth tail we picked up on our way to Sacramento and its connection with Yount I'd just learned about.

From there I reminded General Davis of the security breech at the Sacramento Signal Depot and our discovery that Marjorie Yount, using her Mary Adams alias, had seen the requisition form that led us and probably her to Captain Frank Ellis at McClellan Air Services Command, the man who placed the order for the in-flight refueling installation kits. I concluded my summary of the investigation with my discovery of Ellis in his bedroom and Marjorie Yount's connections with that discovery.

"Okay, thanks, Spicer. I think I've got it now. That's an almost textbook investigative trail. The next questions we need to answer are what did Captain Ellis know about the mission beyond placing the order for the in-flight refueling kits and did he tell Marjorie Yount what he knows?"

"It's just a hunch, but I don't think he told her or whoever was questioning him a damned thing. It would help if we knew what actually killed him. If he died of injuries sustained during the torture, it would be a strong indication they didn't break him. How soon can we get a coroner's report?"

"Ellis is at the Mather Army Airfield hospital morgue in Sacramento. I'll ask them to rush the autopsy."

"That would help, sir. Another way to answer your question is to talk to your contact planning the mission and find out what Ellis actually knew. I know that's not in the game rules, but the enemy seems to be getting desperate. It might be time to change our approach to this thing so nobody else gets dead."

Davis was quiet for a few moments. I thought he might be thinking about my suggestion. I was right about that, but not right enough.

"All right, Spicer, I'll go along with you far enough to find out what Ellis might have known. I'll do that first thing in the morning and leave you a message at the Presidio . . . 'the barn door is open' will tell you he knew enough for us to be concerned. 'The barn door is closed' means we don't have anything to worry about."

I sighed. Davis heard me. "Spicer, I know I've tied your hands on this one. I'm sorry about that, but I figure if my sharpest guy can't figure out what's going on, the Japs can't either. If you don't buy that, get a couple of stars on your shoulders and you can tell me to go to hell."

"Don't hold your breath waiting for that to happen. I'll check messages first thing in the morning. Anything else, sir?"

"Just this. Regardless of your opinion, I'm pleased with what you've accomplished, very pleased."

Thirteen

0800 Hours – Tuesday – 3 MAR 42

Presidio Building 100, San Francisco

I started Tuesday off about 0500 with a drive along Oakland's Twelfth Street to take a look at the nonexistent address Harada Daisuke, the Plymouth driver, and Dragon Lady gave the California Department of Motor Vehicles as their residence. It was an older neighborhood with narrow two-story 1920s houses jammed together so tightly you couldn't slide a dollar bill between them without ruffling the eagle's feathers, and after nearly twenty years, the neighborhood was beginning to look a little dingy and worn around the edges.

I drove around a few blocks looking for some clue as to why Dragon Lady picked this particular neighborhood for her phony address. I found no such clue and concluded she might have simply opened a telephone book at random and picked whichever address caught her eye first.

Having accomplished little on my early morning quest, I met Sally and Russ in the Claremont's coffee shop for breakfast at 0700. The uniform of the day was civvies, which pleased me no end. Sally wore a skirt for the first time since I met her. It was a pleated black number worn with a white blouse. She looked very cute and girlish, even with her gauze headband and her arm in a sling. After breakfast, I checked us out of the hotel and we loaded our bags into the Dodge.

By 0930 we were across the dreaded San Francisco-Oakland Bay Bridge and in downtown San Francisco. Traffic was heavy with people driving to work at that hour, so we didn't pull up in front of Building 100 until about 1000 hours.

Pauline Ashley had two messages for me. One was from

General Davis. It said, "The barn door is open. Call me."

The second message was from Colonel Beecher. It had a shiny new automobile key attached to it and said, "This is a loan from the motor pool. Bring it back in one piece."

"Russ, I have to make a call. While I do that, please go down the hall to the archive room and hunt up the Jap spy book photo for Harada Daisuke. Have them rush a copy photo. I need it before we leave here in a couple of hours. When they tell you it can't be done, tell 'em the photo is for General Davis. That worked last time. With a grin and a wink at Sally, I added, "Sally knows the way so you won't get lost."

I found an empty office with a telephone and called Davis. What he told me was short and not very sweet.

"Your Captain did not know the overall mission plan, but he did know that a large number of aircraft were going to arrive at his location for modifications, and he knew roughly when they were scheduled to arrive—not the exact date, but close enough."

Knowing that was all I was going to get, I simply said, "Thank you, sir. Goodbye."

What I now knew that I didn't know before was Ellis had knowledge of value to Dragon Lady. Did she get that knowledge from him? We would know how likely that was when we got Ellis' coroner report back later today, but even then, we wouldn't know for sure.

I walked out of Building 100 for a smoke and found Sally and Russ waiting for me by the Dodge. Russ spotted me and said, "The photo will be ready around 1130."

"Okay, that gives us time to pick up our new car."

Sally put on a happy face. "We get a new car? Maybe one with an actual back seat?"

"Could be. It's at the motor pool around the corner." I tossed Russ the Dodge keys. "Drive the Dodge over there, will you? I need to stretch my legs some. I'll walk."

Sally said, "I'll walk, too."

Russ shrugged, slid into the driver's seat, and drove off. Sally and I started walking. I set an easy pace because she was still limping a little, but nothing like when we left the hospital in Inglewood four days ago.

"Johnny, I'm sorry for being such a baby yesterday. I'm scared, and I have trouble hiding that."

I was getting a little irritated with Sally's apologies. "Oh, stop apologizing. I realize you're scared, and believe it or not, I know what that's like. I've been scared on quite a few occasions."

"You? Scared? I don't believe that. You're always so calm and cool. Nothing phases you."

"Just between you and me, that's all an act to fool enemy agents."

"Really?"

"Yes, really. I've been scared many a time. I remember once looking straight down the barrel of a big antique revolver as the guy holding the thing fired at me from twenty feet away."

I took my hat off and pulled the hair out of the way above my left temple. "There's the proof."

Sally stared at the quarter-sized white scar. "Wow."

"Yeah, and that guy wasn't even a spy, just a two-bit hack writer."

"Gosh, you're the bravest man I've ever met."

"Hey, don't sell Russ short. I know for a fact he's been there, too."

Sally chuckled, and I asked, "What's so funny?"

"You are. Every time I pay you a compliment or admire something you've accomplished, you immediately downplay yourself and wave Russ's banner."

"No, I . . . ."

"Johnny, relax. I'm not flirting with you. I know you're taken and I'm not foolish enough to think I stand a chance against your Susan. It's obvious she's the light of your life. Okay?"

Suddenly I was knee-deep in a conversation I did not want to have, so I changed the subject. Pointing across the street, I said, "There's the motor pool garage. Let's cross the street."

Sally laughed at me but said no more about things I didn't care to discuss. In fact, she spotted Russ waiting for us and trotted over to grab his arm. Good for him.

I found the captain in charge of the motor pool and showed him the key Beecher left for me. "I'm Spicer. I understand Colonel Beecher arranged for me to swap cars with you for a while."

"Oh, yes, Major." He offered his hand, "I'm Cooper. The Colonel said to give you the fastest sedan we've got, and that's it right there."

I looked where he was pointing and saw a highly polished dark blue Buick Roadmaster four-door sedan with whitewall tires and Buick's signature Cruise-a-Line Vent-a-Ports above its front fenders. "Damn! You could bolt a turret on that thing and use it for a tank!"

"Don't let its size fool you, Major. That beauty has a 320 cubic inch in-line eight-cylinder engine that makes 165 horsepower. She moves right out."

"Okay, Captain, I'll take your word for it. Does it have the lockable false bottom in its trunk?"

"Yup, and with more room in it than you've got in your Dodge. It's also got GM's police suspension option, a siren, and red lenses for the spotlights. Everything you need."

"You've sold me. Okay if we pull the Dodge in and swap our gear over?"

"Sure, Major. Just pull your Dodge right up next to the Buick here. And while you've got the Buick, we'll tune up your Dodge and do some maintenance on it."

I gestured instructions to Russ and a minute later he slipped our Dodge into the motor pool garage bay next to the Buick. As he got out, I said, "Open the trunk and we'll transfer our gear over."

Even with its false bottom, the Buick's trunk was so large I could have rented it out to a family of four. It was nice, though, not to have to squeeze our bags in, and then slam the trunk quick before they popped back out. While Russ and I transferred our firearms and other unmentionables to the Buick's hidden trunk compartment, Sally hopped into the front seat.

"Wow! This is really snazzy!"

I looked through the open door. She was right, in fact snazzy barely described the dashboard's opulence. The three-spoke steering wheel had a full-circle chrome horn ring with a stylish Buick emblem at its center. A huge chrome waterfall of radio speaker grille filled the entire center of the dashboard, and the right side was taken up by a giant glove compartment that seemed darn near as big as the Dodge's trunk. What's more, the glove compartment door had a clock in it, and the clock was big enough to read from the back seat. Everything on the dashboard that wasn't chrome was painted a glossy dark blue to match the exterior paint.

The seats and door panels were upholstered in a soft tan leather worthy of quality living room furniture. The carpeting looked thick and well padded. The headliner was made of that stuff they call mohair and perfectly matched the color of the upholstery. There was enough room in the backseat to easily hold three adults with plenty of legroom. What's more, the interior of the Buick smelled like a new car. I wondered if that was an option.

Sally sat back on the front seat and crossed a pair of shapely legs. "Yes, I think this will do quite nicely. The only thing it needs is a bar."

Russ laughed, and I handed Captain Cooper my Dodge keys. He was smiling at Sally's enthusiasm for our new transportation. "Now don't forget, Major Spicer, this is a loan. We want our Buick back when you're done with it."

"Have no fear, Captain Cooper. We'll bring your Buick back with most of its paint and parts still on it."

I tossed the Buick's keys to Russ. "You're drivin', Sergeant, and don't spare the horses."

Russ chauffeured us back to Building 100. It was about the smoothest two block ride I ever experienced. When we got there, I hopped out.

"You two sit tight. I'll see if our photo is ready."

Pauline Ashley had our photo in a manila envelope with my name on it. There were no other messages. I said, "I'm waiting for a coroner's report from the hospital at Mather Army Airfield in Sacramento. Please keep an eye out for it, Pauline."

"I will, Major Spicer. Anything else?"

"No, I can't think of anything. Thanks, Pauline."

She smiled. "You're welcome, Major."

I felt honored. Pauline's smiles were reserved for MID personnel who treated her with respect. Pauline also had ways of getting even with those who didn't.

Walking back out to our Buick, I realized I didn't have the slightest idea what to do next. Aside from going back to Oakland and wandering around in hopes of stumbling across Dragon Lady, we didn't have a single lead to follow.

When I climbed into the back seat I heard Maxine, LaVerne, and Patty, singing their little hearts out about the Boogie Woogie Bugle Boy. "I see you figured out how the radio works."

"Yes, sir. Will it bother you?"

"Not at all. Your choice of music seems quite appropriate to our circumstances."

"Yes, sir. Where to next?"

"Sergeant, I haven't the foggiest notion."

Sally laughed. "All dressed up with a new car and no place to go."

"That's about the size of it. Tell you what, Russ, drive over to Crissy Field and park someplace with a good view. I need some think time."

I saw him glance at Sally. They were both wearing grave expressions now. The Major was losing his touch. Maybe I was. I was certainly missing something somewhere.

Russ parked the Buick near the Coast Guard Station beyond

the runway and I said, "If you guys want to wander around, go ahead. I'm not going to be very good company for a while."

"Yes, sir." My two cohorts in the front seat exchanged looks again. The situation was getting serious now. They got out and were having an earnest conversation as they strolled toward the beach. Good. They needed to understand that being a clever MID agent wasn't all fun and games.

I decided to go back through the case notes in my notebook. That would not take long because there weren't many of them, but something might trigger an idea.

The first couple of pages were notes I took on our first trip to North American Aviation—mostly facts and figures about the B-25C. The next pages were a summary of our assignment as General Davis gave it to us about a hundred yards from where I was currently sitting. The Davis notes were deliberately vague— more reminder words than details.

My next notes referred to our Alameda Naval Air Station visit and were mostly figures and calculations concerning the length of the Hornet's flight deck and such. Here there was a name: Ensign Stephen Johnson. He was the fellow who spoke so freely about the Army's interest in the Hornet. It would serve him right if the Japs got their hands on my notebook and sought him out.

Then came a few more pages of B-25 notes from our second trip to NAA and a few reminder words about the in-flight refueling gizmo Sally finally remembered. After that I'd made notes about Marjorie Yount from the MID archives and the license number of the black Plymouth.

The next pages threw me a curve for a moment. They were not in my handwriting. Then I remembered Sally painstakingly copying the information from requisition form number 128-4196-420219 for me. I never really looked at the information, so I was correcting that oversight when a name jumped out at me. Along with Captain Frank Ellis, the notes mentioned Michael Wilkins. Who the hell was Michael Wilkins? In front of his name Sally had written "dsgnr." Designer? Yes! He was the little fellow with the Coke bottle lenses in his glasses who designed the in-flight refueling gizmo.

My brain suddenly shifted gears. Damn! Young Mister Wilkins not only designed the gizmo, he actually saw the person who requested it, which definitely made him a person of interest to Dragon Lady, and she saw the same information on the requisition form we saw. I tucked the notebook back in my jacket pocket and bailed out of the Buick's backseat.

I hopped back in behind the steering wheel, started the engine, and blew a couple of toots with the snazzy chrome horn ring. I saw Russ look back, I flashed the headlights, and then he and Sally came running.

Leaning across the seat, I opened the passenger front door. "Get in. We've got work to do!"

As I pointed the Buick toward the main Crissy Field hangar, Russ asked, "You figured something out, sir?"

"I sure did. A big something I missed until now. That guy who designed the refueling gizmo, Wilkins. His name was in the requisition form and Dragon Lady would not have been so careless as to miss something like that."

Sally said, "Oh! I didn't think about that either! Do you think he is in danger?"

"Unless he was killed in the plant explosion, he is definitely in danger. Sally, there's a public telephone alongside the hangar over here. We're going to call the North American plant and find out what's become of Mister Wilkins. Russ, while we do that, see if Stu Irvin is here and available for a flight to Mines Field."

"Yes, sir."

I pulled up next to the telephone booth and Russ headed into the hangar. I stepped into the telephone booth. "Sally, after I place the call, I'd like you to do the talking. I seem to scare that little guy."

"Okay, Johnny. Who are you calling at the plant?"

"I think I'll call person-to-person and try to get Wilkins on the line directly. I'll hand the phone to you as soon as the call is being placed. If he isn't there, get someone on the line who will know where he is or what's happened to him. Okay?"

"Okay."

After going through the process of placing the call and charging it to MID, I stepped out of the booth and Sally took my place, holding the handset in her left hand. Then we waited.

While we were waiting, Russ came out of the hangar shaking his head. "Captain Irvin is somewhere over Nevada on his way to Denver."

At the same time, I heard Sally ask for Melvin Nordoff, the NAA personnel guy I talked to on my last trip to the plant. Apparently, Wilkins wasn't at the plant. When she got Nordoff on the line they had a long conversation. Finally, she seemed to be getting answers, so Sally was doing better with Mister Nondescript than I did.

Then Sally gestured to me. "Johnny, write this down . . .

orchard-three-one-seven-eight . . . seven-two-four-four Brynhurst Avenue."

I jotted what sounded like a telephone number and an address into my notebook while Sally continued her conversation with Nordoff. Finally finishing the conversation, she hung up the telephone and glared at it. "Grrrr! I hate that man!"

"Nordoff?"

"Yes! I swear I could have gotten the information faster talking to a brick wall. At first he told me he couldn't talk to me because you told him he couldn't discuss Sally MacLure with anyone."

I laughed. "At least he remembered what I told him. So what information did we just record for posterity in my trusty notebook?"

She looked at me as the answer to that question should have been obvious. "Why, Michael Wilkins' address and telephone number. Isn't that who you want to find?"

"Yes, that's who I want to find, but I only heard half of the conversation."

"Well, some of the engineering offices were damaged in the explosion, so a few of the engineers are working at home while repairs are completed, including Michael."

"Do you know when he was sent home to work?"

"Mister Nordoff said they were still trying to make space for them there until yesterday. Having the engineers at home is a nuisance because they can't work on any classified information outside the plant."

"All right. We need to see Colonel Beecher again for a minute."

Back at Building 100 Beecher's secretary, a bright young woman named Helen-something, sent me straight into his office. "Hello again, Major. Did you get your Buick all right?"

"Yes, sir, thank you. I hate to bother you again, but we've got a North American Aviation engineer down in Inglewood who is almost surely a target for the Japs. Do we have a security team available in LA that can provide some undercover protection until we get there?"

"Undercover?"

"Yes. I don't want troops standing around in front of his house or anything that will spook Dragon Lady if she's got him staked out, assuming she hasn't already gotten to him."

"We have two men down there who just finished an assignment. They're waiting at Los Angeles Municipal Airport for a lift back up here. I can assign them to your engineer."

"Good. I'll give this guy a call to make sure he's still among the living, and then we can get in touch with the guys at Mines Field. That all right with you, sir?"

He nodded. "Do it. We don't need to carry off any more mutilated bodies like that one General Davis sent us to recover in Sacramento."

"Okay, sir. I'll borrow your secretary's telephone, if that's okay."

"No, use mine. I'll get Helen started on tracking our men down at the airport military hangar."

I got the long-distance operator on the line and gave her Wilkins' number in Inglewood. Wilkins got around to answering his telephone after four or five rings.

A young voice with a tentative tone about it said, "Hello?"

"Hello, Michael. This is Major Spicer with Army intelligence. I met you at the plant last week with Sally MacLure. Do you remember?"

There was no response for a moment as if he were trying to remember me. "Oh, with Miss MacLure. Yes, I remember now. You were asking about the . . . ."

"Don't say it over the telephone, Michael."

"Oh. Yes, you're right. What can I do for you now, Major Spicer?"

"I don't want to alarm you, but we have good reason to believe the same people who blew up the plant may have an interest in you personally."

"Oh, my. That isn't good, is it?"

"No, Michael, that is definitely not good. We have a couple of MID men down in Los Angeles who will be showing up at your house in a short time to keep you safe. Until they arrive, please stay inside your house with the doors locked and the shades or curtains pulled. Do not let anyone in unless they give you a password . . . ah . . . oh, I've got it. Something about the man who brought you the project we discussed bothered you—something that wasn't symmetrical, something that was crooked. Do you remember what it was? Don't say it, just tell me if you remember it."

He thought for a long moment, and then said excitedly, "Oh yes! I remember!"

"Good. Don't let anyone in until they say that word. Got it?"

"I have it. Are you coming to see me, too?"

"Yes, but it will be a while—maybe late tonight, but I'll get there as fast as I can. Sally will be with me."

"Oh, good. She's a nice girl."

Wilkins is one of those guys who always make me wonder if they understand what I'm saying, or even if they are on the same planet. "Yes, she is. Now, remember the code word and my instructions. Stay inside, lock your doors, close your curtains or shades, and do not open your door for anyone who doesn't know the password. Okay?"

"Yes, Major. I will remember. Thank you."

I hung up and stepped into Beecher's outer office. When Helen saw me, she spoke into the telephone. "Here comes Major Spicer now. I'll give him the telephone."

I accepted the handset from Helen and said, "Spicer here."

"Hello, Major. This is Lieutenant Herb Long. Nice to meet you, so to speak."

"You, too, Lieutenant. Here's the deal. We have a witness whose life is in danger from a group of Jap spies. They just killed an Air Service Command Captain in Sacramento after torturing him for several hours, so we know they're real bad hombres.

"What I need you and your cohort to do is get to this guy's house and keep him alive until I can get down there from San Francisco. We'll be leaving by automobile as soon as you and I finish this conversation."

"Got it, sir. What's the address?"

"Seven-four-two-two Brynhurst Avenue, Los Angeles. His telephone number is O-R-three-one-seven-eight. That address is right on the border between Inglewood and LA."

"Seven-four-two-two Brynhurst Avenue and O-R-three-one-seven-eight. Got it."

"I've told him to expect you and to stay inside and locked up until you arrive. I gave him a password . . . he strikes me as the kind of fellow who goes for that sort of super spook stuff. The password is 'necktie.'"

"Yes, sir, necktie. We have access to a car here, so we'll get instructions or a map and head over there right away."

"These Japs—one of them is a woman who does not look Japanese—are killers, so don't fool around with them. Anything suspicious happens around that house, shoot to kill. You can always apologize to the neighbor for shooting his wife later."

Long laughed. "We'll try to avoid that. See you after midnight sometime?"

"That sounds about right. Thanks, Long. I owe you a favor."

"It's all part of the job, sir. See you later."

I hung up the telephone and thanked Helen for loaning it to me. Beecher was back in his office. I stuck my head in and said, "All set, sir. Thanks for your help today, Colonel."

He smiled at me. "You're welcome, Spicer. Just bring that Buick back in one piece or the motor pool will have my hide."

"Will do, sir."

On the way out of Building 100 I checked with Pauline Ashley for messages. The coroner's report from Sacramento still wasn't in. I told Pauline I would check with her in the morning.

Outside, Russ and Sally were enjoying the Buick's radio again. Miller's band was playing *Tuxedo Junction*.

As I walked up to the driver's door, I said, "Okay, hep cats, we're on our way."

Sally grinned. "Hey, big daddy, hep cat is strictly off the cob. We jive it eight to the bar!"

Fourteen

0030 Hours – Wednesday – 4 MAR 42

Michael Wilkins Residence, Los Angeles

I had a twelve-hour drive to contemplate what I ought to do about Michael Wilkins, and when we arrived in Inglewood, I wasn't any closer to a good solution than I'd been in San Francisco. Ultimately, it was a question of ethics. Was it ethical to use Wilkins, a highly educated engineer, as bait to catch Dragon Lady and prevent Japan from sabotaging what could be one of the most important missions of the war?

The answer to that question depended on who you asked, but I was running the show and I couldn't bring myself to put a little guy at risk who could barely function away from his drawing board. It just wasn't right. Besides, his skills were valuable to the war effort.

I knew all that before we left the Presidio, so what I'd really been doing for the past twelve hours was rationalizing a decision I knew could be questioned by some. Phooey on 'em.

According to Sally, Wilkins lived northeast of Inglewood near the community cemetery. According to my trusty Thomas Brothers LA Street Guide, the address supplied by Mister Nondescript was technically in the City of Los Angeles, not Inglewood. The brothers Thomas also informed me the short section of Brynhurst Avenue on which Michael's address was located is a north/south residential street beginning at a major east/west thoroughfare called Florence Avenue. Brynhurst ran south from Florence for two blocks, where it made a 90-degree turn to the east and became 74th Street. The only street crossing that extension of Brynhurst Avenue was an east/west alley about a third of the way along the distance between Florence and 74th.

Wilkins' house was located on the east side of Brynhurst halfway between Florence and 74th Street. The pros and cons of that location depended on how smart Dragon Lady was. There was no parking on Florence, so to stake out the house she had three choices: park on the street, park in the mouth of the alley, or park around the corner on 74th Street.

Parking on the street was the only practical choice, otherwise she couldn't see cars coming from both directions. If she parked on Brynhurst, however, we could see her, and she could see us coming. That might create a situation requiring us to get in and out fast and to be ready for an encounter with Dragon Lady and/or her goons.

To prepare for such an encounter, I pulled into an all-night Chevron Station at the corner of Florence Avenue and West Boulevard. I used the station's public telephone to call Wilkins' number and alert his bodyguards we were about to drop in for a visit—or to make sure Dragon Lady hadn't beat us to the punch, depending on how you wanted to look at it. While I did that, Russ removed the Winchester Model 1912 and a pocket full of extra shells from our secret trunk compartment.

The Model 1912, or M12 as it was more popularly known in military circles, is a pump action shotgun. Ours was the 12-gauge short-barrel model. One reason the Army likes the M12 is it can be slam-fired. That means if you hold the trigger back, it fires every time you pump the slide. An expert can fire the six rounds the M12 holds in a matter of seconds, making it as effective as a Thompson in close quarters. I knew, however, if I tried to use the damned thing, I was likely to shoot my foot off. Russ handles the M12 like a pro.

What I learned from talking to Herb Long on the telephone was things had been quiet at Wilkins' house since they arrived yesterday afternoon. I also found out the Army sedan he and his partner borrowed was parked facing the street in a narrow driveway on the north side of the house. That mattered because if Dragon Lady saw an Army vehicle on the street she'd know something was up. The car was far less noticeable parked in the driveway.

Sally was in the back seat, and as we neared Wilkins' neighborhood, Russ explained what was about to happen and that she needed to get down on the floorboards and stay put no matter what happened. Sally said she understood, but she didn't sound happy about any of it. I wouldn't have been happy about it either.

Since our fastest escape path from Wilkins' house would be

north to Florence, and to save us greater exposure while making a U-turn in the middle of the street, I turned off Florence on the next street east of Brynhurst. I also switched the Buick's lights off, and then made right turns on 74th Street and Brynhurst, which left us pointing north toward Florence. Russ and I kept our eyes open for gray Chevys but saw none. Of course, Dragon Lady might be driving something different these days.

We pulled up in front of Wilkins' house and it only took a few seconds to get the lay of the land. It was a 1920s bungalow with a small half-walled front porch area, a narrow driveway on our left, and a large tree with a wide trunk on the right. Best of all, the distance from the curb to the front door was short, not more than fifteen feet. There were no lights on in the house.

There were also no streetlights on Brynhurst, which made it a small miracle that I spotted a large sedan that, by its silhouette against the white house behind it, looked to be a Caddy—a Cadillac that seemed out of place in an older low-rent neighborhood. What gave the car away were its large white sidewall tires, which reminded me our Buick also had whitewalls. That was something I would mention to the motor pool guys.

The Cadillac was about two houses away on the west side of Brynhurst and facing our direction. I couldn't tell if there was anyone inside it. I pointed at the sedan and said, "Does that look like a Caddy to you, Russ?"

He stared into the darkness for a moment, and then said, "It sure does. Good catch, sir."

"It might have a perfectly legit reason for being here, but it would be a good idea to keep it in mind. You ready to do this?"

"Let's go."

Over my shoulder, I said, "Hang on, Sally. We're going to get your pal, Michael."

From the backseat I heard, "I crossed him off my pal list."

We bailed out, locked the doors, and dashed for the front of the house. Russ got there first and took up a position on the porch from which he could see the street. I knocked on the door and said, "necktie," loud enough to be heard inside the house.

Two seconds later the front door opened. Through the opening I saw Michael behind a fellow in a suit. The fellow in the suit said, "Herb Long, you Spicer?"

"I am. Hello, Michael."

Michael Wilkins opened his mouth to answer me, but the voice I heard was Russ's. He said one word loud and clear. "Cadillac!"

As if he'd said a magic word, all hell suddenly broke loose on Brynhurst Avenue. Russ fired a round at two barely visible shapes—one large and one smaller—running across the street toward us, the front door slammed shut behind us, and a muzzle flashed back at us from the street. I reached for my Smith & Wesson and a slug hit the house a foot to the right of my head, causing a small explosion of stucco. That shot was fired by the larger of the two shapes. Russ's first shot put the guy down in the middle of the street. I couldn't say if Russ actually hit him or he went down to present a smaller target. Either way he was definitely still in the fight.

I fired a round at the smaller shape just before it disappeared behind a parked car to my right on our side of the street. By this time, I had the second shape pegged as female. She ran like a woman in shoes designed more for fashion than running.

Then another country was heard from. A medium caliber handgun popped, and a muzzle flashed in the Caddy's driver side window. It was turning into quite a party out there on Brynhurst Avenue. At nearly the same instant, Russ fired another round at the larger shape in the street but hitting a prone figure from our position was an all but impossible shot.

The door behind us opened far enough for us to hear Herb Lang say, "I'm going out the back and down the driveway to see if I can get a shot from there."

I said, "Be careful. We have another witness in our car. She's on the floor in the backseat."

"Got it."

The large guy in the street was moving, but he was crawling toward cover behind our Buick. That was a no-no I couldn't allow for Sally's sake, and Russ still had no shot. I said, "Dragon Lady is behind a car to our right and there's a guy with a gun in the Caddy's driver-side front window. Try to keep their heads down while I go after the guy in the street."

With that, I jumped down from the porch and ran for the large tree on our left. I heard a shot from somewhere behind me. I don't know who fired it, but since it wasn't a shotgun round, it figured to be Dragon Lady or her pal in the Caddy. Herb Long couldn't be in the driveway yet.

Making the tree trunk in one piece, I took a deep breath in preparation for a ten-foot sprint to the rear of the Buick. As I darted out, I heard several more shots from three different guns, including Russ's M12. There was a real battle going on behind me and I hoped it stayed back there. A slug ricocheting off the sidewalk as I crossed it told me that was too much to hope for.

With what I suspected was far more luck than I deserved, I arrived at the back bumper of the Buick without getting myself shot. From there I peeked into the street around the Buick's left rear fender. The big guy was at the Buick's left front fender next to the tire, and since his attention was focused on the front porch, I figured he had not seen me dash out to the street.

Kneeling on one knee, he was aiming a big caliber revolver toward the porch for another shot when I fired two rounds at him. The first one hit him in the head. The second shot missed because he was already down and dead by the time it got there.

Staying low, I moved alongside the Buick to check on the big guy. A temple shot is generally fatal. This one was no exception.

I was congratulating myself on some pretty fair shooting when I was suddenly lit up like Bette Davis on a Warner sound stage. I heard the Caddy engine start and I was about to take a shot at one of its headlights, but Russ beat me to it. From the clatter of metal pieces on the pavement, it sounded like he shot the whole damned fender off. With one headlight still lighting the way, the Caddy swerved sharply across the street and Dragon Lady's silhouette jumped into the backseat.

The next thing I knew everybody but me was banging away at the Caddy. I was busy diving under the Buick to get out of the Cadillac's path. I made it, but the dead Jap spy in the street didn't. The Caddy's big tires bounced over his body. Some folks just have no respect for the dearly departed.

As the Cadillac disappeared around the corner onto 74th Street, I stood up and hollered toward the house. "Get Wilkins out here!"

I unlocked the driver's door and looked behind the seat. Sally looked back at me wide-eyed. "Are you okay, Sally?"

There was a quiver in her voice. "Yes. Is it over?"

"I think so. They're bringing Michael out now."

Sally threw the backdoor open and jumped out. She went straight into my arms. I held her while Long got Wilkins into the back seat on the other side.

I heard the passenger side rear door close and Long came around to my side while Russ climbed in the front seat. Long said, "Hell, Spicer, that was easy. Next time give us something to do that's challenging."

Sally turned around to see who was talking and promptly stuck her tongue out at him. Long laughed and I helped Sally into the Buick's front seat.

To Herb Long, I said, "Can you wrap things up with the cops here? I want to get Wilkins far away from here."

"Sure. You gonna call this in to HQ?"

"Yes. We're going over to the military hangar at Mines Field. I'll make my calls from there."

"All right. We'll be over there as soon as we can get rid of the local cops here."

"Good. We'll wait for you there. Remember, identify yourselves as MID to the cops and tell them who the bad guy out here in the street is, but say nothing about Wilkins or our mission."

"Don't worry, Spicer, I have no idea what the hell just happened here."

"Thanks for your help, Long."

"Sure thing. It's been a pleasure working with you."

I smiled at him. "Sure, it has. See you in a while."

As we left Brynhurst, the street was no longer dark. Lights were on in every house we passed, and the sidewalks were crowded with neighbors wondering what all the shooting and excitement was about. That was okay. It gave them something to talk about at work tomorrow morning, or more accurately, to talk about at work this morning. According to my watch, Wednesday had been in effect for more than two hours.

I'd been hearing sirens for several minutes, and as I turned west on Florence, a cop car with a flashing red light made the turn onto Brynhurst. It gave me an idea. Back at the Presidio Russ and I threaded the red lenses on our spotlights in case we needed them on the way down. I pulled the switch on and we aimed the spotlights straight ahead. Then Russ flipped the siren switch and we were instantly on the side of law and order. We made it to Mines Field without delay.

I stopped the Buick outside the military hangar on the south side of the field and Russ changed seats with me. The idea was for him to keep Wilkins and Sally company while I made certain the coast was clear inside but it didn't work out quite that way. Sally insisted on going in with me. I looked at Russ and he gave one of his shrugs. After what we'd just been through, arguing with Sally seemed like more work than it was worth, so we just went in.

The military hangar isn't really a hangar. It was a hangar at one time, but now it was just a large building surrounded by a concrete apron with plenty of room for parking transport ships. The interior of the building is mostly a big waiting room for servicemen leaving Los Angeles by military aircraft.

A counter occupies one end of the room. It is manned by an Army Air Force First Lieutenant whose knack for creating order out of chaos keeps arriving and departing servicemen arriving and departing. The rest of the room is home to an odd assortment of mismatched chairs and benches; a long row of public telephone booths; and a collection of vending machines offering snacks, cold drinks, and coffee or watery soup. I'd made a meal out of the contents of those machines on more than one occasion.

At that moment, though, I was more interested in the telephone booths. I needed to let General Davis know what was going on and get him busy taking care of a mess back on Brynhurst Avenue. I was about to step into one of the booths when I realized Sally had a firm grip on my right hand. I looked into her eyes and saw yet another crisis brewing.

"Sally, I need to borrow my hand back for a few minutes to make a telephone call. You can have it again when I'm done. Promise."

She nodded and let go of my hand. I stepped into the booth and closed the folding door. Sally turned around and watched the waiting room, but she remained next to the telephone booth. I looked at my watch. It was about 0530 hours in Washington. Too bad.

I went through the rigmarole of placing my third Priority Able call to Davis in three days. Despite the hour he did not sound groggy like most folks would if awakened in the wee small hours. It was possible he never slept.

An exasperated general said, "What is it now, Spicer?"

"Another dead Jap agent, a damned close call, and a life saved."

Davis sighed loudly enough for me to hear him clearly three thousand miles away. "Tell me, Major Spicer."

I gave him the whole story from the point I realized that Michael Wilkins' name was on the requisition form Dragon Lady saw at the Sacramento Signal Depot to the gunfight at the Brynhurst corral. I finished up by mentioning that, now we had him out of harm's way, we needed to stash Wilkins somewhere.

"Geez, Spicer, you gotta stop killing off Jap spies. You're gonna shoot us all out of a job."

"Don't worry, General, you can still hunt Nazis."

"Sure, we can. Okay, I'm going to call Beecher and have him provide quarters for your engineer with 24-hour security. Can you get this guy up to San Francisco?"

"I think so. The two MID agents who baby sat Wilkins while

Russ and I were getting down here are heading up there from the military hangar at LA airport. They can escort him safely to the Presidio."

"Good. I'll also have someone call the cops in . . . tell me again where the hell you and Pierce shot up the neighborhood and killed this Jap?"

"The incident occurred at 7244 Brynhurst Avenue, Los Angeles"

"That's B-R-Y-N-H-U-R-S-T?"

"Yes, sir."

All right, I'll make sure the LA cops know this is one of ours. I'll also get the coroner down there to ID the guy for our records. Anything else I can do to help you in your crusade to singlehandedly snuff out the entire Japanese espionage service?"

"We might need a little more ammo."

"Spicer!"

"No, sir, I think we've covered it all."

Throughout the telephone call I'd been watching Sally. She hadn't moved a muscle. Okay, on to the next crisis.

I opened the telephone booth and Sally turned around. I said, "Let's find a place to talk for a minute." I gestured toward a quiet corner. "Over there."

The waiting area was nearly deserted, but a half dozen pairs of eyes followed the cute blonde and the Major to a quiet corner. Majors were common there, but not majors with cute blondes hanging onto their arms.

We arrived at our quiet corner and I said, "How are you holding up?"

That question blew the lid off the last of her composure. Panic filled her eyes. "I feel like I'm living in a nightmare! You saved my life back there, didn't you? Where was Russ? How come he's not my hero?"

"Russ was making it possible for me to get to you because he was the only one with the weapon and the skill it took to do that."

The panic in her eyes was replaced with sadness. Softly, Sally said, "You always have an answer for him, don't you? Well, here's my answer to that."

Sally wrapped her good arm around my neck and pulled my face down to hers. The kiss that followed was not at all sisterly. I won't say I didn't enjoy it, but they were the wrong lips. They didn't fit mine the way Susan's did.

When the kiss ended she cuddled her head to my chest and I half expected the guys in the waiting room to cheer, but they had the decency to keep their applause to themselves. I put my hands on her shoulders and held her at arm's length.

Now her expression was sheepish. I said, "Sally, I'll accept that kiss as a token of your appreciation. Just be sure you show Russ the same appreciation."

"Johnny, I don't love him. I thought I did, but I don't."

Before she got any further, I said, "Stop right there. Your feelings for Russ are your business, but what you said at the Presidio yesterday still goes. There's only room in my life for one woman, and that woman is Susan. You can count on me for anything else, but not for that. Do you understand?"

She nodded with what seemed to me sadness. "I know, Johnny. I'm not sorry for what I just did, but it won't happen again."

"Thank you. Now let's get the rest of this motley crew in here before they think we've . . . ."

At that moment I saw Russ and Michael Wilkins with Herb Long, and his partner trooping across the waiting area in our direction. Russ had a concerned look on his face.

As he got there, I said, "Sorry to be so long, Russ. Sally needed to let off some steam. I think she's okay now." I turned to her and added, "Am I right?"

Without looking at either of us, Sally nodded. "Yes. I'm better now."

"Good. We've got some work to do. Herb, would you mind escorting Michael up to the Presidio? Colonel Beecher is expecting him."

Herb smiled. "Not at all, Major. We're getting to be old friends."

"Great. First, though, I need to ask Michael a couple of questions. While I do that, please square things with the first louie in charge of operations here. Russ, keep Sally company for a few minutes. Michael, come with me."

Michael Wilkins, his eyes big as saucers behind his Coke bottle glasses, and I walked to a couple of chairs next to a beat-up end table. We sat, and I said, "Michael, when we met at the plant you said you didn't recall the name of the man who gave you the assignment to create an in-flight refueling system for the B-25. Now that man's name has become even more important to our investigation. Is there any chance you're remembered his name in the meantime?"

Wilkins shook his head in the negative. "No, Major Spicer. I've thought about it, but I still don't remember. I'm not even certain I ever knew his name."

"All right, Michael, let's try something. I want you to close your eyes and picture yourself in your office where you were when the hefty captain came in to talk with you about the in-flight refueling system design. Picture it as if you were there right now. Okay?"

His response sounded dubious. "Okay."

"Did the captain come into your office by himself or was he with someone?"

After a moment's hesitation, Michael said, "He came in by himself. He didn't even knock. He just walked right in. That annoyed me a little."

"I can understand that. It would annoy me, too. Did he sit down or stand up while he described what he wanted you to design?"

This time Michael's answer came more quickly. "He stood up. I remember he was carrying a briefcase. He set it on the floor and stood next to my drawing board."

"Good work, Michael. Now take a look at his uniform. Do you see a name tag?"

There was another moment of hesitation. "No. He didn't have a name tag. His uniform looked very plain. He did have a row of those little colored bars over his jacket pocket, but I don't recall any of them specifically, just that they were there."

"Okay, do you recall anything unusual about his voice or the way he spoke?"

Again, a quick response. "He was from somewhere in the south. He spoke real fast and sounded like one of the fellows in purchasing who is from Tennessee."

"That's good to know. What about his cap. Did it have a bill on it or was it a narrow cap, the kind we call an overseas cap?"

"It had a bill on it. I remember the hat was kind of floppy on the sides, like it was almost worn out."

What Michael was describing was called a "fifty mission crush." Pilots took the shaping rings out of their caps, supposedly so they could wear earphones over them. I always figured the real reason they did it was it gave them a bold, daring look and identified them as pilots.

"By any chance did the man have a pair of wings above the campaign ribbons you mentioned?"

Michael almost jumped up. "Yes! Now that you mention it, he did have wings. They were silver."

"Great work, Michael!"

That piece of information might have been the most helpful tidbit I was going to get out of Michael. So, what I had now was a hefty fast-talking captain with a single row of campaign ribbons, pilot's wings, and a cap with a fifty-mission crush who might be from the south. I was about to thank him for his help when Michael opened his eyes wide.

"I just remembered something else, Major Spicer!"

"What did you remember, Michael?"

"His briefcase. It had gold initial letters on it near the top where it closed."

"And?"

He grinned for the first time since I'd known him. "They were a V and a C in that order."

"Terrific, Michael! Thank you. I think we might be able to track the man down from what you remembered."

I wasn't really so sure about tracking the guy down from what Michael told me, but he was so pleased with himself for remembering more details, I thought he deserved a pat on the back. He was still wearing his smile when we joined Sally, Russ, and the two MID agents.

Thanking Michael and the two agents for their help again, we parted company. Sally, Russ, and I went back out to the Buick and climbed in. Sally sat quietly in the back and Russ sat quietly in the front. That made me wonder exactly when he came into the military hangar and what he might have seen. I decided then and there I was going to unload the excess baggage and finish this mission on my own. To hell with the former lovebirds. At least there wouldn't be a lot of idle chat to distract me from my driving.

I contemplated our next step. All that happened in the past 24 hours, plus an hour of excess adrenalin left me exhausted.

I thought about checking into Patmar's Motel for some sleep, but that didn't seem like a good idea with Sally along. Russ and I were regulars at Patmar's. If anyone was searching for us, that was a place they would be likely to check.

Then I got an idea that might even kill a couple of birds with one stone. I circumnavigated Mines Field and turned north on Lincoln Boulevard, otherwise known as California Route One. I didn't announce my plans, but we were going to Santa Barbara.

Fifteen

Biltmore Hotel, Santa Barbara

Including a fuel stop, I covered the 90-some miles between Inglewood and the Santa Barbara Biltmore Hotel in just under three hours. We arrived at the Biltmore a few minutes before 0930 hours. I went in, rented two connecting rooms, and went back out to the Buick.

I handed Russ the room keys and told him to slide over and drive. Sally was watching the drama playing out in the front seat with a great show of indifference. Next, I directed Russ over to State Street, Santa Barbara's main drag, and up State to the small apartment complex at number 3412. When we got there, I pulled my B4 bag out of the trunk, got the Army's Colt .45 out of the secure trunk compartment along with spare ammo for the .45 and my Smith & Wesson .38, and stowed it all in my bag.

Finally, I went to the Buick's driver-side window and gave Russ his orders. "Stay at the Biltmore tonight and drive up to the Presidio tomorrow."

Russ looked puzzled. "Without you, sir?"

"Yes, without me. When you get back to San Francisco, trade this damned tank for my Dodge and move the stuff in the trunk compartment back to the Dodge. Then see Beecher and tell him I asked that he park Sally somewhere you can keep an eye on her. Keeping Sally safe is your full-time assignment until you hear differently from me. Understood, Sergeant?"

"Well, yes sir, but . . . ."

"I'll see you up north when Dragon Lady has gone to meet her honorable ancestors. As for Sally, if she gives you any trouble, shoot her."

Russ knew I was kidding, but I heard a surprised, "What?" from the back seat.

"Goodbye, Sergeant."

"But, sir . . . ."

"Goodbye, Sergeant."

I turned and climbed a stairway to the second floor balcony of the four-apartment complex and knocked on the door with a metal "3" screwed to it. I was fairly certain there would be no answer to my knock. The time was almost ten-hundred hours and Susan Jackson, at whose apartment door I stood, was almost certainly at the private clinic where she holds the lofty position of head nurse. That meant the only occupant of the apartment at the moment was Mister Whiskers, who firmly believes his place in life demands that people open doors for him, not vice-versa.

When it became apparent that nobody was going to open the door for me, I opened it myself with a key Susan gave me for just such emergencies. Inside, Mister Whiskers welcomed me enthusiastically and received ear-scratches as a reward.

After carrying my bag to the bedroom, I used the telephone in the kitchen to call Susan at work. She was delighted. "Johnny! Gosh, it's so good to hear your voice!"

"I'm glad because you're going to hear it a lot during the next twenty-four hours."

"I am? Where are you?"

"In your kitchen."

"Really? That's swell, but what are you doing there?"

"I don't have transportation at the moment and I'm in serious need of some sleep—it's been a long night."

I heard concern in her voice. "Are you okay?"

"Yes, Angel. I just need a few hours sack-drill and I'll be hunky-dory."

"Do you want me to come home?"

"No, thanks. You've got an important job to do at the clinic, but could you take a late lunch around one-thirty and take me to pick up my personal car at the garage where we stashed it?"

"Sure, if the offer includes lunch. Should I call Elton and ask him to get your car ready for you?"

"That's a good idea, and the offer definitely includes lunch."

"It's a deal. Now go get some sleep."

About the next thing I knew Mister Whiskers was leading a parade of one up and down my back and Susan's bedside clock was reporting one o'clock. I spent a few minutes in the shower and put on fresh civvies. Then, I took a cup of warmed-up coffee out on the second-floor porch, watched the traffic on State Street, and made a few decisions.

My first decision was that the decision I made on the way up from Inglewood was a good one. Matters were getting far too complicated with Sally as part of the mission. She was now a major distraction, pun intended, and distractions get guys in my business killed.

My next decision was that my first step after retrieving my car was to call the Presidio and find out if the coroner's report on Captain Ellis ever showed up. Hopefully, it would contain an indication of whether Ellis died from injuries sustained during torture or if he was killed at some point after the torture. If he died during the torture it would be a strong indication he did not tell Dragon Lady what he knew.

That mattered because, according to General Davis, what Ellis knew was significant. He knew that a large number of B-25s, perhaps 24 based on the quantity of in-flight refueling installation kits ordered, were going to show up at McClellan Airfield on an approximate date for the installation of a device that would extend their range. We knew Dragon Lady had the requisition form information, but if she knew the rest of the details, she had ninety percent of the mission.

That she staked out Michael Wilkins' house was a positive sign. It likely meant she was still missing crucial pieces of the puzzle. There was more good news in what Michael remembered about the fellow who brought him the in-flight refueling project. Finding that fellow would likely lead to significant intelligence about the raid on Japan. I had the clues to his identity and Dragon Lady did not. If I could find the guy and keep him out of her grasp, I would be ahead of the game.

Discovering his identity and locating him required translating what Michael told me into a name and location. That task would be much easier if I could simply call General Davis and have him locate the guy through personnel records. Hell, Davis might already know who Captain V. C. is, but I had the same chance of getting that kind of cooperation from him as Dragon Lady. He was insisting on playing this game through to its natural conclusion, regardless of how many people got dead in the process.

That's what hacked me off about this cockamamie mission. We were beyond the game now. We needed to concentrate on preventing Dragon Lady from finding people like Michael Wilkins and the man who gave him the assignment, thus depriving her of the information they had and keeping them alive, but I couldn't protect those people if I didn't know who the hell they were.

It was possible the Army Air Force was already taking steps to protect their people involved in the raid, but Captain Ellis' death told me they weren't doing a very good job of it. Besides, if they didn't know Dragon Lady, they had no idea who they were dealing with. I'd encountered her and her pals on four different occasions and knew from firsthand experience what to expect from them. They didn't play by anybody's rules.

Then there was the question of Russ. I apparently overestimated his ability to remain professional regardless of what Sally pulled. That relegated him to the role of errand boy in all this and that meant I was on my own. Hell, I'd always worked alone as a private investigator. I could do it again.

That's when I saw Susan pull up on the street below in her Pontiac convertible. Time to end my wool gathering and get to work. I had two jobs to do. One was finding Dragon Lady and the second was finding Captain V. C. I decided to tackle finding Captain V. C. first because I thought I knew someone who might be able to identify him. Talking to that person would require another trip up to Sacramento because I couldn't count on their telephone lines being secure, but Davis promised me whatever I needed short of a battleship on this assignment. I was about to find out if he really meant it.

Susan gave me a hug and a kiss, along with further raising my spirits by telling me I needed to get more rest because I was looking haggard. My Angel definitely has way with words.

She drove me out State in the direction of Goleta to Bishoff's Garage, just west of San Roque. Elton Bishoff, the proprietor, was a childhood friend of Jack Jackson, Susan's big brother.

As we pulled up I saw my baby parked out front of his shop. She was all shined up and her dark green paint gleamed in the midday sun.

Bishoff came out to greet us. Wiping his hands on a faded red shop rag, Elton called out, "Hiya, Suzy! Hello, Mister Spicer."

Susan cheerfully returned his greeting. I waved and walked over to my Buick Century Sedanette. It was a dumb name for one of the fastest production cars made in the US. Elton joined me and wiped at an invisible dirty spot on the fender with his rag. Bishoff was one of those lanky guys who give the impression of being all knees and elbows. Elton Bishoff was also a damned fine mechanic with a craftsman's touch.

"You know, Mister Spicer, my offer is still good. Anytime you want to sell this beauty here, I'll give you a hundred more than you paid for it."

"Elton, please call me Johnny, and if I was going to sell it to anyone, you'd get first dibs, but I'm not through having fun with it yet."

Elton laughed. "You can have a lot of fun with eight cylinders, 250 cubic inches, and 125 horses in a light weight coupe like this, that's for sure."

"That's why I bought it."

Actually, I'd purchased the little Buick on sort of a whim when a wealthy client rewarded me with a handsome bonus for recovering a stolen object d' art. I'd hardly gotten the quick little coupe broken in when my Uncle Sam called me back to service with Army Intelligence.

Elton spent five minutes listing all the details he'd taken care of so the Buick would be ready to go when I showed up. I thanked him and said I expected to be placing it back in his able care before long.

Leaving Elton Bishoff's garage in separate cars, Susan and I met at Joe's Café down State Street toward the beach. Joe's had become a favorite of ours and the food was always tasty. I hadn't eaten anything since grabbing a candy bar at the military hangar at some absurd hour that morning, so I was hungry. Susan and I split a dinner platter of spaghetti with two meatballs as big as my fist.

Then Susan needed to get back to work, so it was time for her to ask the inevitable question. "When do you have to go, Johnny?"

"I think I can stay until tomorrow morning. I need to make some travel arrangements, but I think that will work."

Susan smiled. "That's better than I hoped for. Is it okay for me to ask where your helper or whatever he's called is?"

"Sergeant Pierce is at the Biltmore."

"The Biltmore? Those are pretty snazzy quarters for a Sergeant."

"He's not alone."

She nodded. "Oh, I see."

Even though I was pretty sure the situation wasn't exactly what Susan was picturing, I let the matter drop. It wasn't that I wanted to keep anything from her, I simply didn't feel like going through the saga of Sally just then.

"And is it okay to tell Jack you're in town? I know he'll want to see you if he can."

"Sure. How about setting us up for dinner with big brother somewhere?"

"That would be lovely, darling. About seven? That would give me time to get home and change before we go out."

"Seven is fine, Angel. I'll see you at home about five-thirty?"

"I might be a little later. I need to stop at the market."

"What do you need? I have time to make a stop."

"Okay. After all, it's for your pal, Mister Whiskers. He's almost out of canned cat food."

Putting on as serious an expression as I could muster, I said, "That's almost a national emergency! What kind does he like?"

"His favorite is Puss N' Boots fish flavor, but he'll settle for Strongheart or one of the other popular brands."

"My friend, Mister Whiskers, will not have to 'settle' for anything less than his favorite. Puss N' Boots fish flavor it shall be!"

Susan rolled her eyes and muttered, "Oh, brother." After that I received a rather nice kiss and she headed back to work.

I went to work, too, only the work I had in mind required a public telephone. I found one next to a Chevron station at State and Cota. My first call was collect to Building 100 at the Presidio and I hit the jackpot right off the bat.

Pauline Ashley said, "You have a letter from the Pathology Department at Mather Army Airfield Hospital in Sacramento. Could it be the autopsy report you've been waiting for?"

"If it is, they sent it by pony express. Would you please open it?"

"Opening it now." I heard an envelope tearing and some paper rattling. "That's what it is, Major Spicer."

"Good. Please see if you can find what is entered in the 'Cause of Death' blank."

After a moment Pauline said, "Here it is. 'Cause of Death: Cumulative damage to the deceased's primary motor cortex from repeated severe traumatic brain injury caused failure of reflexive motor functions.' Is that what you need?"

I jotted the doctor mumbo jumbo into my notebook. "Yes. Now I need an interpreter, but I think I know someone at this end who can do that. I won't need that autopsy report any longer, so no sense leaving it laying around. Please destroy the paperwork and envelope. Anything else, Pauline?"

"No, sir, that's it."

I jiggled the receiver hook and got the long-distance operator back on the line. She connected me with Crissy Field operations and when the call was answered, I asked for Captain Stu Irvin.

"Captain Irvin speaking."

"Hi Stu, Spicer here."

"Hello, Major. What's up?"

"You and your AT-7. I need you at Santa Barbara Municipal Field at 0800 hours tomorrow."

"Sorry, Spicer. No can do. I have to pick up some brass hats at Boeing Field in Seattle."

"Forget the brass hats, Stu. As of right now, you're working for me."

"Oh? That's news to me. By whose authority am I working for you?"

"Major General Chester Davis. You can verify that with Davis or with Colonel Beecher."

"I will, Major. Assuming this is legit, where are we going from Santa Barbara?"

"McClellan Army Airfield in Sacramento, From there, I'm not sure yet."

"Say, you're serious about this, aren't you?"

"You'd better believe I am, and wherever we go and whatever we do is top secret at the highest level. Remind me to give you your cyanide capsule in case you're captured by the enemy."

"Sure, pal. Where can I reach you if I need to?"

"Montecito-four-nine-five-six in Santa Barbara, but I probably won't be there until after dinner tonight, so I'll check with Pauline Ashley late this afternoon. Okay?"

"Okay, Spicer. Unless I find out you're tryin' to pull a fast one, I'll see you at Santa Barbara Municipal's parking ramp tomorrow at 0800."

My telephone business completed for the moment, I turned my attention to my next important assignment. It was carried out in the pet food section of the A & P on Chapala Street where I loaded up a shopping basket with six big cans of Puss N' Boots fish flavor cat food. Nothin's too good for my pal, Mister Whiskers.

From the A & P I took my speedy little Buick down to the ritzy enclave at the southeast corner of Santa Barbara known as Montecito. There, I pulled into the parking lot of the Casa Sobre El Mar Clinic. The name means "House on the Sea" and it fits the rustic buildings nestled in the pines above the Pacific Ocean perfectly. The place is a little larger now than it was when I was a patient four years ago, but despite its size the clinic still has the charm of a country seaside cottage.

I walked into the lobby and the receptionist recognized me immediately. Everybody at Casa Sobre El Mar knows Susan's guy. "Hello, Mister Spicer! I bet you want to see Miss Jackson."

"Now how did you know that? Mary, you must be a mind reader."

Mary giggled. "Miss Jackson is in a meeting with Doctor Rothenberg, but they shouldn't be much longer."

"Thank you, Mary. I'll just admire the view while I wait."

"I know, Mister Spicer. It is perfectly lovely here."

I had no sooner gotten to one of the big picture windows that flank the lobby entrance doors when I heard an office door behind me open and Susan said, "Thank you, Doctor. I'm sure we can resolve this now."

Another voice I recognized said, "Wait just a moment, Nurse Jackson. I believe I see someone I know. If I'm not mistaken, he is a former patient of ours."

I turned around and Susan smiled a greeting. Doctor Ham Rothenberg said, "I was right! I do know that fellow. Hello, Mister Spicer."

We shook hands and he automatically reached up and pushed my hair out of the way so he could see the scar a large caliber bullet made just above my left temple. Smiling, Rothenberg said, "Yes, I'd recognize that scar anywhere, but I still don't know if it was my surgical skills or Nurse Jackson's charms that healed you."

Susan's grin widened, and she gave me a wink as I said, "I'm pretty sure it was a combination of the two. How have you been, Doctor?"

"Oh, getting along. As you probably noticed, we have expanded some since you were here. It turned out we finished the new wing just in time to accommodate some of our brave boys who suffered severe and complex injuries at Pearl Harbor."

"Susan told me about that program. It's darn good of you, Doctor."

"It's the least I can do for them and for my country."

"Speaking of your country, Doctor, do you have a minute to explain something to me?"

"Certainly. What is it you want to know?"

I took my notebook out of my jacket pocket and opened it to the last page of notes. "Please translate, 'cumulative damage to the primary motor cortex from repeated severe traumatic brain injury caused failure of reflexive motor functions.'"

"My goodness, that is a mouthful. In the most basic terms it means the patient was hit on the head hard enough and often enough to cause his brain to stop sending the muscle impulses required for breathing, heartbeat, and the other automatic functions necessary for life to continue. The patient would have lost consciousness and died within a minute or two."

I nodded. "Thank you, Doctor Rothenberg. I kind of figured that's what it meant, but I needed to be sure."

"I suspect what you just read to me is the cause of death from an autopsy report. Coroners like big words. Glad I could help. Now I have some patients to visit. Very good to see you again, Mister Spicer!"

"And good to see you, too, Doctor."

Rothenberg stuck his hands into the pockets of his white doctor coat and hurried off down the corridor. Watching him, Susan said, "Doctor is such a nice guy. I'm glad you got a chance to see him. I think he was honored you asked him that question. He knows you are with Army Intelligence."

That surprised me a little. That I work for MID is no great secret, but we generally don't advertise the fact, either. "He does?"

"Yes, but I didn't tell him, so I don't know how he knows."

"Knowing MID, they probably sent someone down here to make sure all my marbles hadn't leaked out the hole in my head before they recalled me. Anyway, I came to ask you the question I asked him, so I guess I should get out of your hair."

In a quiet voice so Mary wouldn't overhear her at the reception desk, Susan said, "I like having you in my hair, and everywhere else . . . oops! I shouldn't say things like that. Shame on me!"

"Oh my! All this time I thought you were the picture of innocence and now I learn the awful truth!"

"Mister, if you hadn't figured that out by now, you aren't much of an intelligence agent."

"Well, I might have had a few small indications. I have to go, anyway. I have an important delivery to make, six big cans of Puss N' Boots fish flavor. Mister Whiskers will have his favorite chow for dinner."

"Six cans? My goodness! Oh, speaking of dinner, I talked with Jack. He said dinner tonight would be great."

"Good. Where are we meeting him?"

"Jack suggested that new seafood place out on the wharf. I told him I thought that would okay with you."

"Looks like everybody gets fish for dinner tonight."

Sixteen

0755 Hours – Thursday – 5 MAR 42

Santa Barbara Municipal Airport, Goleta

After Susan dropped me at Santa Barbara's municipal airport, I stood in the brisk morning air sorting out a few thoughts while waiting for Stu Irvin to arrive. At the top of the list was the cause of death in Captain Frank Ellis' autopsy report.

If it is possible for such a document to contain good news, this one did. The indication was that Ellis died while still being tortured. Unless you're dealing with a very sick individual, inquisitors do not generally continue torture once they find out what they're after, so it is most likely Captain Ellis took his secrets to the grave. For that he deserved recognition and the appreciation of his country.

Also on my list was the day's mission for which I was again in uniform. Depending on how thorough the veil of security over Doolittle's upcoming bombing raid on Tokyo really is, it's possible the man who worked with engineer Michael Wilkins on designing the in-flight refueling system was also known to the man who placed the order for the installation kits. That man was Frank Ellis and he was beyond answering questions, but he had an assistant who seemed to be an observant fellow. Maybe Sergeant Joe Richards saw a briefcase with the initials V. C. on it and knows what those initials stand for.

At exactly 0755 hours, the distinctive drone of two Pratt & Whitney radial engines floated down from the heavens. I didn't even have to look because I knew without a doubt I was hearing Stu's A-T7 on a straight-in approach from the north.

For the curious, Stu explains that the AT-7 is a variant of the Beechcraft B-18 light twin. The Army Air Force has a bunch of B-

18s they use for everything from passenger transport to navigator, bombardier, and gunnery training. In AAF lingo AT stands for Advanced Trainer, and since the ship Stu generally flies started life as a navigation trainer, he still refers to it by the ship's original designation.

If you've never seen a B-18, they are tail-draggers with two engines and twin rudders. Most AAF versions are unpainted and fly around in their sliver birthday suits. The interior is somewhat cramped, but still manages to carry eight or nine passengers, plus a two-man crew. The Navy also flies B-18s. The sailor boys call their AT-7s SNB1s.

Stu taxied up to the terminal building and spun the ship around smartly before he shut down his engines. A moment later the hatch on the ship's port side popped open and Stu hopped out.

Around the ever-present cigar stub in his mouth, Stu said, "Hiya, Spicer."

"Good morning, Stu. I gather you decided I was on the level."

Stu pulled the cigar out of his mouth, looked at it, and said, "Never doubted you for a moment, Johnny boy, I just like to have all my T's dotted and my I's crossed. You ready to go?"

Picking up my B-4 bag, I said, "All set."

After we climbed aboard, Stu said, "Just toss your B-4 back here somewhere. You can ride up front with me if you want. View's better up there."

Five minutes later we were beginning our climb over the southwest end of the coastal mountains separating California's coast from its central valley. I glanced at my watch. It was 0810.

Stu saw me check the time. "McClellan is about 300 miles from Santa Barbara and we'll be cruising about 190 knots—that's a little better than 200 miles per hour—so our ETA is around ten-hundred, give or take."

My eyes automatically went to the fuel gauges on Stu's instrument panel. He didn't miss that, either. "Don't worry about fuel, Johnny boy. We've got plenty. I didn't fuel up in Santa Barbara because municipal airports charge us for fuel. We get it for free at AAF fields."

"Beats syphoning it out of a Ford when nobody's lookin'."

"Sure does. Say, I've been meaning to ask you, was that B-25 information I gave you useful?"

"It was. In fact, I talked to one of the electrical engineers at North American about the circuit breaker panel sabotage point you described. He is now designing a new master switch circuit that includes a short-to-ground detector that will eliminate the problem."

"I trust they're going to call it the Stu Irvin Master Circuit."

"I wouldn't count on that. You'll probably just have to be content in the knowledge that you made a significant contribution to the fight for liberty."

"Ha!"

By 0830 we were cresting the coastal range and could see the central valley spreading out in front of us with Bakersfield off to our right. Further up the valley we passed over tiny communities named in some cases by the early Spanish explorers in recognition of their characteristics, like Fresno, which refers to the ash trees of the area. In other instances, little farming towns bore the family names of the people who first settled them, like Atwater, Livingston, and Turlock.

About an hour later Sacramento began to take shape on the horizon ahead of us and the ground became a patchwork quilt of farms and orchards. Off to our right the dazzling snowcapped peaks of the Sierra-Nevada Mountains towered above us. Beyond our left wing were the much lower coastal mountains, and just beyond them was Francisco Bay, but we were beginning our descent into Sacramento and were soon too low to see the bay itself.

Stu talked with the folks at McClellan Army Airfield's control tower on the radio and learned the wind was blowing at 15 knots out of the northeast and that the barometric pressure was twenty-nine-point-nine-nine. He dialed this number into a small window on his altimeter so as to improve its accuracy. McClellan tower also cleared us for a straight-in approach to runway three-four-zero. Irvin explained that runway numbers referred to their compass headings, so three-four-zero, or runway thirty-four, pointed twenty degrees west of due north.

Stu made a slight right turn after passing over the American River five or six miles south of the field and we were lined up perfectly with runway three-four-zero. The next thing I knew we were rolling along that runway with hardly a bump to know we'd landed.

Even though I knew better, I congratulated Stu on a smooth landing. He looked insulted. "All of my landings are smooth, Johnny boy."

Stu parked the AT-7 in a location on the east side of the runway as instructed by the tower and asked, "Got any idea how long you're going to be?"

"I shouldn't be more than an hour, assuming the guy I have to see is there."

Irvin looked surprised. "You didn't find that out before we flew all the way up here?"

"Stu, you're the smartest guy I know when it comes to driving airplanes around the sky, but you've got a lot to learn about the intelligence business. Forewarned is forearmed. It's almost always better to show up unannounced and catch the people you want to question before they can dream up answers that have no relation to the truth."

"I'll remember that, Spicer. Is there someplace nearby a guy can get a late breakfast?"

"Yeah. There's a café on the road that parallels the runway on the other side of these hangars. Turn right and walk about a block and you'll hit the place."

"Okay, Spicer. I'll meet you back here in about an hour. By that time, we'll be refueled and ready to hit the wild blue yonder again."

"See you then. If I'm delayed, I'll try to send word. Have a good breakfast."

Approaching the McClellan Air Service Command building, I immediately observed something new had been added. An AAF MP was stationed at the entrance and the shiny bayonet attached to the business end of his M1 rifle looked sharp enough for shaving. He said, "Sir, this is a restricted area. May I see your identification, please?"

I showed him my MID ID and it made him so happy he gave me a snappy salute. His twin was standing in the corner of the ASC lobby, but he didn't have a bayonet. The barrel of the Colt Tommy Gun he cradled in his arms was not designed to accommodate such accessories. It didn't need them. His eyes never left me the entire time I was at the lobby counter. My MID shoulder patch apparently didn't cut me any slack in his view. It was good to see the Army actually taking security seriously, albeit one Captain too late.

First Sergeant Joe Richards was summoned and appeared from somewhere in the back. He recognized me because he had good reason to remember my last visit.

"Hello, Major Spicer. How can I help you?"

"You can take a short walk with me. I know you're busy, but we need to have another conversation."

"Yes, sir." He turned to the corporal manning the counter. "I'll be out of the building with Major Spicer of Army MID for a while."

As Richards and I strolled along the street that paralleled the flight line, I said, "First of all, I want to set your mind at ease about something. If you'll recall, I had some concerns as to whether or not Captain Ellis was forced to tell what he knew about B-25s that might be coming here for accessory installation. According to the autopsy report, it is very likely that he died without giving his torturer any information."

Sergeant Richards nodded. "I would have bet money that was the case, but thank you for confirming it, sir."

"You're welcome. Now we come to the reason I'm here today. I will describe a man to you and I'd like you to tell me if you recognize the fellow from my description. Okay?"

"Yes, sir."

"The guy I'm looking for is an AAF Captain. He wears one of the new Eighth Air Force patches on his shoulder, pilots' wings on his chest, and his cap has a fifty-mission crush, which means nothing more than he discovered how to remove its shape ring. He's a hefty guy and may have a southern accent. Does that description match anyone you recall?"

I'd deliberately left the part about the briefcase initials out, so I would have something to verify any names Richards might come up with. If the names didn't match the initials V and C, I would know we were talking about the wrong guy.

Sergeant Richards gave my question some thought, and then said, "Sir, can you give me a point of reference? I see a lot of Captains who might fit that description. Can you help me narrow it down by telling me in what context I might had encountered him?"

"It might have been concerning something very hush hush Captain Ellis was working on. Also, I suspect the fellow is from the east coast, or perhaps the south, although that's only a guess."

Richards gave the matter more thought, and then asked, "Would this have anything to do with those North American Aviation accessory installation kits for B-25s, sir?"

I nodded. "It could have, Sergeant."

"Then I think you might be talking about Captain Vern Carlson."

"What can you tell me about Captain Carlson?"

"Very little, sir. I only saw the man once, and that was only for a few minutes when he was here to meet with Captain Ellis. The only reason I know their meeting was about the B-25 installation kits is Captain Ellis called me into his office while Captain Carlson was with him and showed me a copy of the requisition form for the installation kits. He wanted me to follow-up on the parts to make sure they got here no later than Twenty-Six March."

"Do you happen to know what Captain Carlson's job is? Is he part of Air Service Command?"

Shaking his head, Sergeant Richards said, "I can't say for sure, but I think he's further up the pecking order. If I had to guess, I'd say he was some sort of liaison officer between the AAF and aircraft manufacturers. My impression is that he's a freelancer, sir."

"Freelancer?"

"Yes, sir. Sort of like you, someone who is given a problem to solve and is at liberty to solve it anyway he can, except in his case, he solves problems with aircraft manufacturers."

"I see. Actually, that's a pretty good description, Sergeant."

"Thank you, sir."

"One thing about this confuses me a little. The Eighth is a bomber command, and yet it sounds as if Captain Carlson's purview is larger in scope, involving other types of aircraft besides bombers. So why would this fellow be attached to the Eighth?"

Sergeant Richards smiled. "Sir, the general impression in the ranks is that the Eighth is something of a catchall outfit. I'm sure its mission will be refined with time, but it seems to have started out as a response to the notion that everybody has to be somewhere, if you get my meaning."

I matched his smile. "Got it."

"Yes, sir."

"All right, Sergeant, I'll let you get back to more important duties. Thank you for your help. You solved a mystery for me."

"Glad to help, Major Spicer. By the way, sir, did you notice our increased security since Captain Ellis was killed?"

"I did, and I'm glad to see it. We're dealing with some very bad actors with few scruples. I hope you can drive that home to your people. They need to be looking over their shoulders constantly. We're not used to living that way in America, but it has become necessary."

"I understand, sir. I'm thinking about starting a weekly security meeting for the ASC enlisted staff to discuss that very subject. It might not be absolutely necessary, but it can't hurt."

"Agreed, Sergeant. Your meeting idea could save some lives, to say nothing of making life more difficult for Jap espionage agents."

Sergeant Richards and I parted company at the ASC building

and I headed on down the flight line to find Stu Irvin or a public telephone, whichever came first. I found a bank of payphones outside the hangar near where Stu parked his AT-7, so I stepped into one and got a long-distance operator on the line to place a collect call to Washington DC.

When the MID operator, in turn, put me through to General Davis, he answered in his usual gruff manner. "Whatcha got, Spicer?"

"A new player has joined our game, one Captain Vern Carlson."

"Hell, Spicer, how did you turn him up so fast?"

"Just a little rudimentary detective work, sir. I take it you know who Carlson is."

"I do, but I'm not happy that you do."

"Well, if you know where he is, I suggest you get a hold of him and tell him to keep his head down. I know Dragon Lady hasn't come up with his name from the same sources I used, but that is no guarantee she doesn't have it."

"Damn it, Spicer, don't you ever have any good news?"

"I didn't know giving you good news was in my job description, General."

"Careful with that stuff, Spicer. You're damned close to insubordination."

"Good. Fire me."

General Davis was silent for a long time. I guessed he was calming down. He knew how to work with me, and threats weren't part of that process.

Finally, his voice came across the wires again. "All right, Johnny. Point taken. Do you think you can find Carlson from what you know?"

"If that's what you want me to do, I think so, but it could take some time. Can you narrow it down to which half of the country he might be in?"

"What would your guess be?"

"Where the preponderance of aircraft manufacturers are, the Midwest or the West coast, which means either Seattle, Los Angeles, or San Diego."

"Hang on the line a few minutes."

I hung for about five minutes before the General got back to me. "I can save you a little time. Start in the City of Angels."

He'd tossed me a clue, but not a very good one. I knew of at least three major aircraft manufacturers with half a dozen plants in the Los Angeles area, and that didn't include the lesser manufacturers, like Hughes, Vultee, and Northrop.

I sighed. "All right, General. Please have someone arrange a car for me at the Los Angeles military hangar."

Surprised, he said, "What the hell happened to the car you got from Colonel Beecher?"

"Sergeant Pierce has it. We've temporarily split up the mission."

"Oh yeah? Who the hell is watching your back then?"

"The same guy who's been watching it for thirty-two years."

"Damn it, Spicer, I can't afford to lose you."

"Don't worry, sir, Stu Irvin is with me."

"Oh, swell. He's a damned pilot, not a soldier."

"Don't sell Captain Irvin short, sir. He's a good man."

"I hope so. All right, Spicer, I've already passed the word for Captain Carlson to be aware he could be a target, but I'm counting on you to find him and deliver that message personally."

"And hopefully catch up with Dragon Lady in the process."

Unenthusiastically, Davis said, "Yeah, that, too. Take care of yourself and keep me informed."

I hung the handset back on its hook and took a moment to absorb my conversation with Davis. I concluded none of it was good, but as General Davis noted, there's not much good news going around these days.

I set off in search of Stu Irvin. We agreed to meet back at the plane, so that's where I headed next, and that's where he was. I found him leaning against the fuselage near the hatch chewing on his cigar butt.

"You're late, spook."

"Yeah, I'm late, so let's get going."

"Where to?"

"Mines Field."

He mumbled something like "Back and forth, back and forth," as we climbed into the cockpit. After he fired up the engines and conferred with McClellan tower, we taxied out to the south end of Runway 34. It was 1115 hours when the AT-7's tires lifted off the asphalt.

Stu's calculation of our arrival at Mines Field came out to just about 1300 hours. That gave me four or five hours to find Vern Carlson before I'd have to call it a day. The three major aircraft manufacturers where I would be most likely to find Captain Carlson were Douglas, with plants in Long Beach and Santa Monica; Lockheed, headquartered in Burbank; and North American in Inglewood. That was a lot of ground to cover and still left the smaller manufacturers. The logical place to start looking for the needle in the haystack was North American since we would already be in Inglewood.

As we taxied up to the military hangar at Mines, Stu asked, "How long you gonna be this time, Spicer?"

"We're lookin' for a guy and we have a lot of bases to cover, so I'm thinking we'll be here over night."

"Maybe I should go back up to San Francisco and come back to pick you up tomorrow."

"I've got a better idea. You got a sidearm stashed somewhere in this crate?"

"Sure, My Colt is in my bag. Why?"

"Good, strap it on. It's time you earned that MID patch on your shoulder."

"I figure puttin' up with you guys entitles me to the patch with a few medals for valor thrown in."

"Not even close. Come on, you're my back-up on this one."

Stu didn't look happy. "All right, but you have to tell me who to shoot."

"I'm pretty sure you won't be shooting anyone. The sidearm is window dressing. All you have to do is stand around and look mean. Besides, we're visiting some places you'll find interesting."

"I can hardly wait."

Seventeen

Los Angeles Municipal Airport, Inglewood

The First Lieutenant in charge of operations at the military hangar began apologizing even before handing me the keys to the car he had for our use. It was a '39 Plymouth sedan staff car that would have been on a scrap heap somewhere if there wasn't war on. Still, I'm a Chrysler guy and appreciated the sedan's finer qualities that were lost on Captain Irvin. When Stu first saw it, he unholstered his .45 intending, he said, to shoot the Plymouth and put it out of its misery.

The Plymouth was mechanically sound, though, and that was all that mattered. It got us to our first stop, the North American plant, in good order. The plant was in considerably better shape than when I'd last seen it. In the week since Dragon Lady set off a bomb in an employee locker room, most of the exterior damage was repaired.

Stu waited for me at the car while I showed my ID to the National Guard corporal at NAA's lobby entrance. The woman behind the reception counter reported the assembly lines were running again despite continuing repairs to some interior areas.

When I asked if Captain Vern Carlson was by any chance around the plant today, she knew who I was asking about, but said she had not seen him for a few weeks. Encouraged by the fact she at least recognized Carlson's name, I thanked her and checked the first of three primary manufacturers off my list.

For no particular reason other than I frequently drove by it in civilian life, I picked the Lockheed plant and airfield in Burbank for our next stop, but I got quite a surprise when we arrived. The modern streamline style administration building I was used to seeing had disappeared. In place of the plant's buildings, runways, and rows of P-38 fighters were rolling hills, trees, alfalfa fields, and houses. At least that's what Lockheed's extensive camouflage netting would look like to a Jap bomber crew looking for an aircraft plant to bomb. Even Stu Irvin was impressed.

Before entering Lockheed's lobby, I showed Stu Marjorie Yount's photo from MID's Jap spy mug book and told him to wait outside and keep an eye open for her or anyone else he thought was acting suspiciously. It would not have surprised me to learn Dragon Lady knew we were in town and was following me around in the hope I would lead her to someone useful. I had no idea how she would know where I was, but her organization had already proven its resourcefulness.

Inside, I showed Lockheed's receptionist my MID ID and asked if Captain Carlson happened to be around the plant today. I got my second big surprise of the day when the woman said she thought he was and set to work tracking him down.

I didn't have to wait long. Not more than five minutes later a hefty Captain carrying a briefcase strolled into the lobby. The briefcase had two brass initials on it, a V and a C.

Since I was the only one in the lobby, he walked in my direction, asking, "You Spicer?"

"I am."

He offered his hand. "Vern Carlson. What can I do for you?"

I shook the hand he offered and showed him my MID ID, saying, "More to the point, I might be able to do something for you, like keep you alive. Got a minute to take a short walk with me?"

He grinned. "For a cause like that, I'll follow you anywhere."

Outside I looked around for Stu and spotted him leaning against a wall twenty feet away. He gave me a small nod of his head to indicate the coast was clear. I gave him a nod in return, and then Carlson said, "Hey, there's an old friend. I gotta say hi."

When he walked straight up to Stu and they greeted each other like long lost cousins, I shook my head. After flying all the way up to Sacramento searching for the mysterious Captain V. C., he turns out to be an old pal of the guy flyin' the damned airplane.

Stu read the expression on my face and put two and two together. "This is the guy you been lookin' for all over hell and gone? All you had to do was ask me."

I glared at Irvin and changed the subject. "Come on, Carlson, let's keep movin'. Irvin, you're watching' for Dragon Lady and her pals."

As we followed a walkway under the camouflage netting, Carlson asked, "Who the hell is Dragon Lady?"

I handed him the copy photograph from MID's mug book. "She's a Jap spy by the name of Marjorie Yount. She and her pals killed Frank Ellis and . . . ."

Carlson stopped abruptly in mid-stride. "Frank Ellis is dead?"

"He's as dead as they get, but before he died the Japs beat the crap out of him trying to find out what he knew about some Army Air Force B-25s." Now the expression painted on Carlson's face was shock. It looked genuine, and I gave him more to be shocked about.

"They also damned near got the North American engineer who designed your B-25 in-flight refueling system, but we were a step ahead of them on that one. The Japs know something's up, but we haven't figured out how much they know. I'm pretty sure Ellis didn't tell 'em anything, if that's any consolation."

The Captain stood there for several seconds, apparently entranced by Marjorie Yount's photograph. Then he shook his head as if to clear it. Handing the photo back to me, he asked, "Why the hell am I just hearing about all this now? When did Ellis die?"

"We're guessing it was last weekend, right after Dragon Lady blew the hell out of the North American plant in Inglewood."

Carlson nodded. "Yeah, I heard about that." He paused a moment. "Say, you don't happen to know what happened to one of North American's production engineers, a young woman named Sally MacLure?"

An already small world suddenly got way too small for comfort. "What's your interest in Sally MacLure?"

His expression suddenly turned to caution. Well, Sally and I . . . well, we . . . ."

My anger level at everyone involved in this fouled up assignment was rapidly approaching the boiling point. "Come on, Carlson, now's the time to get real honest with me. What about you and the MacLure dame?"

"I guess you could say we dated off and on."

"You guess? Just exactly how close were you two?"

He looked down at the walkway. "Pretty close. We sort of ended it a few weeks ago, though."

Perhaps Russ's wholesome little girl next door wasn't quite as innocent as she appeared. "Well, if it still makes any difference to you, Sally is fine. She sustained a few injuries in the explosion, but nothing permanent. We have her stashed at HQ as a witness."

Carlson looked up at me. "A witness to what?"

That's when it happened . . . one of those moments when a tone of voice, an expression, or who knows what, caused a bunch of the puzzle pieces stored in my head to spin around and fall into place. In that moment a bunch of stuff that made little sense to me became perfectly clear.

I looked the Captain square in the eye. "When did Marjorie Yount turn you, Carlson?"

He tried his surprised act again, but he couldn't pull it off this time. "What are you talking about, Spicer?"

Stu was standing about thirty feet away and I gestured to him as I said, "Give it up, Carlson. You're the damned inside guy who's been feeding Dragon Lady . . . ."

I'd miscalculated Carlson. Oh, I had him figured right about his connection to Dragon Lady, but I didn't figure on him pulling any rough stuff, especially in broad daylight with Lockheed employees all around us. I thought about that miscalculation all the way to the ground after he threw short uppercut to the point of my chin that sent me sprawling.

A small crowd was forming around me, including Stu Irvin, as I got back on my feet. We were at the junction of three walkways leading off to unknown areas of the plant and, of course, Vern Carlson had disappeared into thin air.

I looked around and asked nobody in particular if anyone had seen which way the captain went. Apparently, everyone was watching the silly major get knocked on his butt and failed to notice which way the captain went. I didn't even consider trying to find him on the sprawling Lockheed plant grounds.

Irvin said, "What the hell happened. It looked like Vern slugged you."

"Your eyesight is a lot better than your choice in friends."

"Why did he slug you?"

The show was over and the crowd was going about its business, so I answered Irvin in a quiet voice so as not to attract anymore unwanted attention. "Your old pal Captain Carlson sold out to the Japs. He's feeding them secrets while doing business as usual for the Army Air Force with aircraft manufacturers."

"You're kidding!"

"Yeah, Stu, this is all a big joke. I need to find a pay phone."

I found a public telephone booth at a Seaside service station on San Fernando Boulevard a few blocks south of Lockheed. I pulled in and told Stu to stay put.

I rubbed my aching jaw while waiting for General Davis to get on the line. When he did, I said, "I just blew the lid off this cockamamie assignment."

"Yeah? What have you got?"

"The Jap agents working on the mission we're interested in have an inside man and I just found him."

"Who?"

"Captain Vernon Carlson. The same guy they sent to North American for a means of increasing the B-25's range."

The long-distance lines between Burbank and Washington hummed and buzzed for quite a while before I heard the General's voice again. His tone was as sober as I have ever heard it.

"What is your confidence level in what you just told me?"

"One hundred percent. When I confronted Carlson twenty minutes ago he sucker punched me and took off like a scalded dog. By the time I got after him, he'd vanished. That was my fault. I misjudged the guy. It won't happen again. Do we know how much he knew about the mission?"

"I'll find out. I've got to talk to some people and alert them to what's going on. Notices must go out to aviation plants that Carlson is no longer authorized to do business for the AAF. Call me back in an hour without fail."

I opened my mouth to reply, but there was nobody left on the line but me. I climbed into the Army Air Force's Plymouth and pointed it back to Mines Field.

Irvin said, "Listen, Spicer, I'm sorry about this. I had no idea what Carlson was up to. Hell, I haven't seen him in a couple of years."

"Don't worry about it, Stu. I'm not blaming you for any of this."

"Where are we going now?"

"Back to Mines Field. I need to do some thinking on the way, so make yourself useful by keeping an eye out behind us to make sure we don't pick up a tail."

We were on my home turf, so I engaged my mental autopilot and put on my thinking cap. Something had been nagging at me since Dragon Lady redecorated the North American Aviation plant with a lunch pail full of explosives. I still had confidence in my conclusion she intended to kill two birds with that stone, one of them being Sally, but I never figured out exactly why Dragon Lady wanted Sally dead.

Since the attacks on Sally coincided with Russ and me arriving at the plant to question her, I correctly concluded Sally knew something Dragon Lady did not want me to know, but what? After my encounter with Captain Carlson, however, a bunch of puzzle pieces spun around into their proper positions and I now knew exactly why Dragon Lady needed Sally dead. Simply put, Sally was a dangerous loose end because of her affair with Captain Carlson.

Vern Carlson romanced Sally, pumped her for information, and dumped her. Apparently, Sally did not tumble to Carlson's objective because she was in love with the louse, but I suffered from no such affliction. Conclusion: Dragon Lady didn't want Carlson's name to come up in my conversations with Sally because I was likely to figure out why he was so interested in Sally and, from that, I could make the connection between Carlson and Marjorie Yount.

Next question: What would Dragon Lady do when Carlson told her about me accusing him of being a turncoat? While thinking about the answer to that question, another more important question occurred to me. Would Carlson even tell Marjorie Yount I'd discovered his involvement with her?

She would figure it out on her own eventually because Carlson could no longer function in his Army Air Force role as aircraft manufacturer liaison—General Davis was already making damned sure of that. Losing his job made Carlson worthless to Dragon Lady and he became just another loose end to be dealt with, but if Carlson succeeded in killing Sally after all of Dragon Lady's attempts failed, the Captain might be thinking he could make up for his blunder and stay on Marjorie Yount's good side, thus avoiding certain death at the hands of a venomous Jap spy or her minions.

To make matters much worse, I'd practically told Carlson where Sally was because he sounded sincerely concerned about her welfare. He was sincerely concerned, all right, but for a much different reason than I thought when I opened my big mouth and told Vern Carlson we were holding Sally as a witness at MID Headquarters. That wasn't true yet, but it would be in a few hours.

I looked at my wristwatch. It was nearly 1600. Even if Russ and Sally left Santa Barbara by 0700 this morning, they were still four hours from the Presidio. I needed to let Russ know the situation had changed, but by the time he arrived in San Francisco and I got a message to him, Dragon Lady or one of her thugs, or even Carlson could already have Sally in their sights, or worse. I could only think of one possible solution.

"Stu, we're thirty minutes from Mines Field. Could you get us to Crissy before twenty-hundred hours?"

He looked at his watch. "Depending on weather, we should

make it."

"Good. This flight is a matter of life or death."

"Okay, we'll give it our best shot."

"I have to make one telephone call from the military hangar. You get the AT-7 fired up while I do that. I'll make it fast."

"Roger."

We hit more slow traffic but making use of some short cuts I knew about from years of dodging LA traffic, we rolled up to the military hangar at 1630 on the dot. I tossed the Plymouth sedan's keys to the lieutenant behind the counter and made a beeline for the nearest payphone. It took a few minutes to get General Davis on the line and every one of those minutes seemed like an hour.

"Okay, Spicer. I just put all of our asses on line by telling Doolittle's people Carlson is a turncoat."

At that point I expected him to say he hoped to hell I was right. He did not. Instead Davis said, "The only thing about this in our favor is Carlson's knowledge of the mission was limited to the need for increasing the range of the B-25s and the associated details, like where the work would be done and roughly when. They're sure he was in the dark about the mission's target and other specifics."

"That assumes he hasn't turned up clues to that information from other sources along the way, like the Sacramento Signal Depot, Air Service Command, and North American Aviation."

Davis said, "That's true, but we know what those people know, and it isn't enough to help the Japs out. We have to proceed on that assumption until we learn otherwise. Now, what's your next move?"

"Correcting another blunder on my part. Before I realized Carlson was with the opposition, he asked what happened to Sally MacLure after the North American plant bombing. Carlson apparently had an affair with the girl while he pumped her for information, but he sounded genuinely concerned about her, so I told him she was all right and stashed at HQ as a witness."

Davis sounded puzzled. "So?"

"So, it finally dawned on me that Dragon Lady is trying to kill the MacLure dame because she might mention Carlson to me and give us the connection between him and the Japs, which in turn would make Carlson useless to them and might lead us back to Marjorie Yount. Now that cat is out of the bag and Carlson is in big trouble with his Jap employers. Since I told him where to find Miss MacLure, I think there's a good chance he'll try to make things right with Dragon Lady by killing Sally himself."

"Oh, swell."

"Fortunately, I exaggerated slightly. Sally MacLure isn't at the Presidio yet, but she will be in a few hours. Stu Irvin and I are about to try getting there before she and Sergeant Pierce do and alert Pierce to the increased danger."

"Then get going."

"One thing first, please have someone call the Presidio and leave a message at the gates for Pierce. That's the back-up plan in case Irvin and I are delayed getting up there somehow."

"Okay, Spicer. I'll have someone get on it."

Two minutes later I was pulling the hatch cover closed on the AT-7 while Stu taxied us out to the active runway. Our wheels cleared runway Two-Five-Right at 1705 hours. With an estimated flight time of just under two hours, I figured we would make Crissy with time to spare.

That's when Stu chose to tell me the bad news. "Keep your fingers crossed, Spicer. According to the weather prognosticators there's a large weather front moving into San Francisco and they say it's a wet one."

"How is that likely to affect us?"

"Crissy is a tiny postage stamp surrounded by big obstacles like tall buildings and the Golden Gate Bridge, so visibility is essential to making a night landing there. Low storm clouds dumping buckets of water aren't going to make that landing any easier."

"Yeah, but I'm riding with the best pilot in the Army, just ask him."

"Let's just hope he's as good as he thinks he is."

For the first time since I'd known him, Stu Irvin was sweating. Even his cigar was drooping at a less than jaunty angle. None of that seemed like a positive sign for the success of our mission.

"Stu, up here you're the boss. Do what you can. Whatever that turns out to be, I'll make the best of it."

Our route to San Francisco took us right along the mountain range that separates coastal California from the central valley. In order to clear the peaks in that range, Stu took us up to six thousand feet. Meanwhile, the sun was sinking rapidly into the Pacific Ocean off to the left. By 1730 the only light on the ground came from small towns on either side of our flight path, and before long, even they disappeared, which I presumed meant there were clouds between us and the rest of humanity.

According to the compass mounted above the AT-7's windshield, we were flying a course of 315 degrees, which translates into a heading of northwest. Then, about 1800 hours, Stu swung us north and began descending. Fifteen minutes later, he turned back forty-five degrees to the west and continued our descent on his original northwest heading.

Explaining these maneuvers, he said, "If my seat-of-the-pants navigation is close, we should be just about over San Jose at the bottom of San Francisco Bay. From here we fly up the middle of the bay, but this is where things get tricky. We have to stay above 800 feet until we're north of the San Francisco-Oakland Bay Bridge to avoid bridge towers and stuff like that.

"The Bay Bridge is also about where we have to turn west and begin our descent to Crissy. The tricky part is knowing when it's safe to make that turn. Everything hinges on being able to pick out a landmark or two through the clouds from 800 feet so we know where the hell we are and when to make our turn. I'll need your help for that."

Watching the AT-7's altimeter unwind, I said, "What about other aircraft flying through the area?"

Stu gave me a sarcastic laugh. "Hell, Spicer, no pilot in his right mind would be flying around in this muck!"

"I see."

"Just sing out if you see anything down there you recognize. Sing out even if you see something you don't recognize."

As I searched the thick swirling mass of cloud ahead and on the right for anything that might be a landmark, Stu called Mills Field, San Francisco's municipal airport, on the radio. He asked for a condition report and we learned that the barometric pressure was two-nine-point-eight-four and falling; the ceiling was between six and seven hundred feet; the wind was out of the northwest at twenty knots; and Mills field was closed to arriving and departing traffic due to poor visibility.

Stu dialed the new barometric pressure into the altimeter, chomped down on his cigar, and mumbled, "Hell, they close Mills down at the first sign of a cloud."

I glanced at Stu. In the dim glow from the instrument panel lights he was all business, regularly alternating his attention between the instrument panel and the muck outside. I told myself he knew what he was doing and things couldn't get any worse. Then, just to prove me wrong, somebody began throwing buckets of water at our windshield.

Stu reached up and turned a switch that started a couple of barely adequate windshield wipers in motion. I renewed my efforts at landmark searching and was almost immediately rewarded by four blinking red lights coming up below us, one to the west and three more to the east.

I called the lights out to Stu, and he said, "I've got 'em. Those lights are on top of the power poles that run along the south side of the Dumbarton Bridge. That means we're right where I thought we were. Keep looking."

Stu got credit for the next landmark sighting. "Look left. What do you see?"

I looked. "I see a light flashing white . . . green . . . white again."

"That combination of lights means a civilian airfield. It has to be the beacon at Mills and it means we're about three-quarters of the way up the bay to our turn toward Crissy. The thing we want to see next is some indication that we're over the San Francisco-Oakland bridge. Right after that we make our turn to the west."

I was glad to hear a little more confidence in Stu's voice after he spotted the Mills Field beacon, but staring into the gloom, I found it hard to believe we were flying between two of California's largest cities. There wasn't a light to be seen anywhere. I hoped if the Japs ever showed up to bomb San Francisco, it was a night like this.

Then a flash appeared briefly in my peripheral vision. It was off to the right and I looked that way hoping to see it again. I did. It was another rotating airfield beacon, but it was flashing green-green-white.

"Military airfield on our right. Maybe Alameda Naval Air Station?"

"It has to be. That puts us about three miles from our turn. At our current speed of ninety miles per hour we should cover three miles in about two minutes." He looked at the faintly illuminated clock in the instrument panel and added, "We'll use that as our turn reference in case we can't see the bridge."

We never did spot the bridge. The clock hands were pointing at 1921 hours when the AT-7 banked left and Stu brought us to a compass heading of 260 degrees, just a little south of west. At the same time, he began another descent.

When the altimeter said 500 feet, Stu began working his way through the AT-7's landing checklist. Mostly to himself, he said, "Fuel boost on . . . landing lights . . . props to 2100 . . . gear down . . . . airspeed eighty . . . ."

While he was pulling levers and turning switches, I was looking out the windshield with no small amount of concern. We were all set to land, but there was no runway out there and Stu was still descending.

"Hang on, Spicer, next few hundred feet or so will tell the tale."

I hung on and was rewarded as the altimeter passed 300 feet. Directly ahead was the hook-shaped pier and breakwater of Aquatic Park. Stu banked hard left, and after a few seconds, hard right. That pair of maneuvers put us directly over the brilliantly-lit Palace of Fine Arts and in line with the runway lights of the Crissy Field. Faster than I can tell it, we covered the remaining distance, there was a slight bump, and I felt the wheels rolling along the tarmac. We had arrived. The instrument panel clock showed 1939.

After parking the AT-7 in front of Crissy's main hangar, Stu took a deep breath, removed a soggy cigar stump from his mouth, and said, "You may now congratulate your pilot on an amazing job of navigation and seat of the pants flying."

"I do so congratulate you, Captain Irvin. Now it's my turn to do something heroic. Do you have a car here?"

"Sure, but you don't expect me to drive an automobile in this godawful weather, do you?"

Eighteen

2000 Hours – Thursday – 5 MAR 42

Presidio Building 100, San Francisco

I took the steps up to Building 100's entrance two at a time. I was anxious to find out if there was any word from Russ. Also, it was still raining cats and dogs, and I didn't particularly want to spend the rest of the night in a soggy wool overcoat.

Pauline Ashley went home for the day hours before I got there, but her nightshift counterpart, a young corporal known to those of us who kept late hours as Ken was on duty. He checked the message stack and shook his head. "Nothing for you, Major Spicer."

"Thanks for checking. By any chance is Colonel Beecher still here?"

"Yes, sir. I believe he's up in his office."

"All right, Ken, if anything comes in for me during the next few minutes, I'll be in Beecher's office."

"Yes, sir."

I walked into Beecher's empty outer office and he saw me through the connecting doorway. "Spicer, come on in here."

"Good evening, Colonel."

"Major, I don't know what you're up to, and I don't want to know, but whatever it is, you've sure got General Davis in a snit."

"I seem to be doing that a lot lately."

Gesturing to one of the guest chairs in his office, Beecher said, "Quoting the General, 'Sometimes I wish Spicer wasn't so damned good at his job.'"

Sitting in the specified chair, I laughed. "Gee whiz! Here I'm trying to be a good little soldier and he's complaining. I just can't win."

"Well, if that was you coming into Crissy with Stu Irvin a few minutes ago, I'd say your win/loss percentage is pretty damned good. The odds down on the field were a hundred to one against you fellows. They figured you two for goners."

"Frankly, so did I. I'll you this, Colonel, if I ever hear anyone say anything bad about Stu Irvin's flying skill, they'll have me to contend with."

"You'll get no argument from me on that score, but I'd be a lot happier with Captain Irvin if you could get him to stop chewing on those stinking stogies."

"I'm not sure anyone would recognize him without one of those stinking stogies sticking out of his face. On another subject, sir, have you heard anything from Sergeant Pierce recently?"

"Davis asked me the same question . . . told me to be on the lookout for him. You lose your ADC?"

"No, sir. I'm just expecting him to show up here any minute. Did he talk with you yesterday about secure temporary quarters for Sally MacLure?"

"Yes, he called this morning about that, and I just got through finding a place to park some aircraft engineer Herb Long brought back with him. Herb said the engineer belongs to you, too. Hell, Spicer, I'm not running a damned shelter for displaced witnesses here."

"I know, sir, but they keep following me home like lost puppies."

He gave me a glare that was mostly for show. "Sure, they do."

Removing a piece of notepaper from a pad on his desk, Beecher scribbled a few lines of what looked from my upside-down point of view like driving instructions. He pushed the note across his desk and said, "I've set you up with a little safe house over in Fort Scott. It's a small two-story building with a clear field of fire all the way around it and you'll have 24-hour outside security there. Please make Miss MacLure's stay there as brief as possible so I can free-up the security team for real work."

Several responses occurred to me, but I kept them to myself and simply said, "Yes. sir."

At that opportune moment, Corporal Ken knocked on the door to report Sergeant Pierce's arrival in the lobby. I excused myself and walked down to meet Russ.

I found him creating a fair-sized puddle just inside Building 100's entrance. "Hello, sir. I understand things are happening.'"

"They are, Russ. First, how's Sally?"

"She's fine, sir, although she's not very happy with either of us at the moment. I temporarily handed her off to the security detachment watching that engineer we sent up from Inglewood. They're at the VOQ."

"All right, Russ. Let's go talk in the car for a few minutes before we take Sally off their hands."

With my B-4 bag in one hand and holding my cap on against the wind with the other, I sloshed out to the Buick sedan with Russ right behind me. In the car, we lit a couple of Lucky Strikes and I filled Russ in on my discovery that Vernon Carlson was working for the Japs. I also gave him some of the background I had on Carlson, including that the Captain and Sally were an item not long ago.

Russ had no comment on Sally's involvement with Vern Carlson, but he did have something to say about Carlson knocking me on my butt and escaping. "I wish I'd been with you, sir. Between the two of us we might have hung on to Captain Carlson."

"That may be so, Russ, but the job you were doing is just as crucial. What's important now is we've solved the mystery of why Dragon Lady wants Sally dead."

"We have?"

"I think so. When Carlson figured he had everything he needed from what Sally knew about the B-25s rolling off the North American assembly line—none of which pertained to Doolittle's mission—she had outlived her usefulness. Then, when you and I started nosing around the North American plant and spending time with Sally, she became a liability.

"You put that bee in my bonnet after Dragon Lady blew up the NAA plant. The Japs certainly knew who we were and they sure as hell didn't want Sally mentioning her fling with Carlson and pointing us in his direction."

In the glow from Buick's instrument panel I saw understanding arrive on Russ's face. "I see, sir, but now that the Japs know you're onto Captain Carlson, do you think they still want to kill Sally? I mean, the damage is done."

"It is, and I'd like to think she's no longer at risk, but we can't count on that. We don't even know if Carlson will tell Dragon Lady we're on to him. She'll figure that out soon enough on her own, but she won't know exactly what Carlson told me, which makes him another liability to Miss Yount. In fact, if I were Carlson, I'd get myself lost in a big hurry. Crossing the Japs will get him dead just as quickly as being convicted of treason."

Russ frowned. "Aren't we a liability to them, too, sir?"

"I sure hope we are, but the tables are turned now. Dragon

Lady doesn't gain anything by killing us. She knows more MID agents with the same information we have about her would replace us and stay on her trail. No, I'm more concerned that she also may have outlived her own usefulness and, one way or another, will disappear on us."

"She might want revenge, sir."

I knew Russ was serious, but I almost laughed. "The bad guys only kill people out of revenge in comic books and movies. There's no profit in revenge, so I'm the last guy Dragon Lady or Carlson want to see right now."

"If you say so, sir."

"I do. Now let's go pick up Miss MacLure and take her somewhere safe where I can ask her a few questions. She's got some serious explaining to do, like why she made a big mystery out of some guy from the Eighth Air Force who met with Michael Wilkins about the in-flight refueling device when she knew all along it was Captain Vernon Carlson. If you think she's unhappy with us now, just wait a bit."

While Russ went into the Visiting Officer's Quarters to retrieve Sally, I stood watch at the car. A moment later Sally and Russ appeared on the VOQ's covered porch. Russ offered his arm to help Sally down the steps, but it was clear even from where I was standing, Sally wanted no help, especially Russ's. Pulling her jacket over the cast on her right arm to protect it from the downpour, she made it down the steps quite nicely on her own, thank you very much.

I expected her to just slide onto the front seat when they got to the Buick. Sally, however, played her martyr role to the hilt, opening the rear passenger-side door and climbing into the back seat. I almost laughed out loud at the childishness of her behavior.

Holding the driving instructions Colonel Beecher gave me up to the light from the Buick's dashboard, I checked the location of the safe house. Our destination wasn't more than a mile or two away.

Fort Winfield Scott is generally considered part of the Presidio, although it is technically a separate installation. Fort Scott was established a few years before the Great War as a coastal artillery post and became the HQ for San Francisco Harbor defenses during the '20s.

What all that means in plain language is Fort Scott is home to some damned big guns intended to defend San Francisco Bay in the event an enemy's ships show up on our doorstep. The guns and their concrete mounting platforms, called emplacements, are well hidden in the forests covering the western half of the Presidio grounds. The exact locations of the guns and their sizes are classified, but I can tell you there are a bunch of them and some are big enough to lob shells the size of refrigerators nearly twenty miles.

The safe house was among a scattering of offices and quarters west of the National Cemetery, which more or less separates Fort Scot from the main Presidio post. The structure, at least as much of it as I could make out through the deluge, was a tiny two-story office building that apparently was no longer needed for offices. It could not have housed many offices, though, because the entire structure only measured about 20-feet wide by 50-feet deep. Nestled between a couple of large trees, the building sits on a slope and was built atop a raised wooden foundation to make things level.

The entrance faced Ruckman Avenue on the building's north side and there was another porch with a door overlooking a paved parking lot on the east side. The second floor was equipped with a couple of windows in each of its side and back walls, and three more windows across the front. The entire building was painted white and given a red Spanish tile roof to fit in with the general style of Presidio architecture.

Our safe house's closest neighbors were a small storage building of some sort to the west at the corner of Ruckman and Upton, a warehouse and parking lot behind it to the south, and a row of duplexes for housing lower ranking base officers to the east on Ruckman. I could see nothing across the street but a large area thick with trees and shrubbery—a likely location for a big gun emplacement.

Colonel Beecher promised me security for the safe house and it showed up in force as I pulled to a stop in front of the house. A pair of Jeeps equipped with canvas convertible tops to keep the occupants from drowning immediately surrounded us. The headlights on the Jeep in front of the Buick were aimed directly into our windshield and damn near blinded us. I sensed Russ unholstering his forty-five.

"Hang on, Russ. I think these fellows are on our side."

I opened my door and stepped out, keeping both hands in clear view as I did. A sergeant appeared in front of me with his sidearm in hand. "Hold it right there, sir. Please identify yourself."

"Spicer, Major Jonathon, Military Intelligence Division. My ID is in my inside jacket pocket."

The sergeant holstered his pistol. "That's all right, sir. I recognize you."

"Thanks, Sergeant. Sorry to drag you guys out in this mess."

"It's all part of the job, sir. Do you have any special instructions for us?"

"No, just help us get through the night. I haven't figured out our plan for tomorrow yet."

"Yes, sir. Here's the key to the house. It fits both doors. We have two observation spots staked out that allow us to cover the entire building. If you need us inside, just flash any light we can see through a window several times. We'll come running."

"Okay, Sergeant. Thanks. See you in the morning."

"Yes, sir."

A few minutes later Russ, Sally, and I, plus our bags, were in the center of the main ground floor room. Russ checked the other rooms while I made sure both outside doors were secured by their deadbolts as well as the standard key locks.

Judging by its hand-me-down furnishings, the room we were in was intended to serve as a living room. A well-worn couch, two occasional chairs, and a couple of scratched wooden end tables left a lot of unused space in the room. Sally settled at one end of the couch and was still making a show of not being happy about being there or anywhere else with Russ and me.

The living room had three windows in the front wall, including one in the door, and all were equipped with pull-down shades. I pulled them down. When Russ returned, he reported all was well and that he'd found a coffee pot and a can of Folgers in the kitchen, which was apparently the room next to the living room on the east side of the building—the one with the second exterior door.

"Sounds good, Russ. You want a cup, Sally?"

"No, thank you, Major."

"All right, suit yourself. I'll have a cup, Russ. Thanks."

Knowing Russ could hear us in the kitchen, I saw no reason for prolonging the inevitable. I sat on an overstuffed chair arm and said, "Sally, I take it you aren't very happy with me or Russ, or both of us."

With a glare that might have melted a polar ice cap, Sally said, "You take it right, Major."

It was time to put an end to her childishness. "Well, that makes us even, because I'm not very happy with you, either, Miss MacLure. If fact, I'm downright annoyed with you."

That wasn't what she was expecting to hear. "Why? All I did

was be honest with you about my feelings."

"That may be, but you were not honest about some other things, like your intimate relationship with Captain Vernon Carlson."

I'd surprised her again. "That . . . that is none of your business!"

"It is as long as Captain Carlson is working for the Japs."

"No! No, he isn't. He's a kind, caring . . . ."

Completing her sentence for her, I said, "Traitor."

"That's ridiculous! He is not!"

I stood abruptly and said angrily, "Shut up and listen!"

Sally shrank back into the couch cushions with an expression of fear on her face she couldn't have faked. I almost felt guilty about the inquisition techniques I was using, but not enough to cut her any slack.

In a loud accusing tone, I said, "The fact of the matter is you are within inches of a treason charge all your own. You've got one chance of avoiding a firing squad, and that chance is to convince us you didn't know Carlson is a Jap turncoat."

Russ stuck his head out of the kitchen as Sally yelled back at me. "I didn't know any such thing. I still don't. Why are you doing this to me, Johnny?"

Expecting the tears to start flowing any moment, I said, "You know damned well why I'm doing this. You lied to us about Carlson from the very beginning, claiming you didn't know the identity of the Eighth Air Force officer who brought the B-25 refueling system project to Michael Wilkins. That dishonesty cost an Army Air Force officer his life. If we'd known who we were looking for, we might have prevented Captain Frank Ellis from being tortured to death."

Sally stood. Gesturing widely with her one good arm, she said, "Johnny, please stop! I don't understand any of this. Yes, I went out with Vern . . . Captain Carlson for a while, but we never talked about business. Why do you think he's a traitor?"

That was the point at which I decided Sally was on the level. I know a little about acting and Sally just wasn't that good an actress. She still owed us an explanation or two, but I was convinced she did not know Vern Carlson was Dragon Lady's inside guy.

That was also the point at which Russ brought two steaming off-white ceramic mugs of coffee from the kitchen. I took the one he handed me and said, "Okay, Sally. Relax. We'll back up a little, but I want your solemn promise you won't leave out any further details. Do I have it?"

Sally nodded. "Yes. Maybe I was wrong not to tell you about Vern Carlson and me, but I didn't know it mattered then. No more secrets."

I looked at Russ. Sounding relieved, he said, "You sure you don't want some coffee, Sally?"

She looked at the mug in his hand. "It does smell awfully good."

Russ handed his coffee to her, saying, "Here. take mine. I'll get another."

Sally thanked him, and I said, "All right, Sally. Sit down and let's see if we can keep you out of Leavenworth."

She sat on the sofa again, and I could tell by her expression I still had a hundred percent of her attention. "Almost from the very beginning one thing in particular about this assignment has nagged at me. You don't seem to know anything about the mission Russ and I are interested in, so why is Dragon Lady going to such great lengths to eliminate you?"

I glanced at my wristwatch for effect. "About ten hours ago I figured out the answer to that question. That's when I finally caught up with the mysterious Captain Carlson at the Lockheed Plant in Burbank. I intended to question him about his role in the B-25 in-flight refueling gizmo to see if I could figure out Dragon Lady's next move, but Carlson inadvertently spilled the beans about the two of you. Specifically, he asked about you in regard to the North American plant bombing. Carlson acted concerned about you, but his real concern was finding out if you'd been killed in the explosion, so he could put Dragon Lady's mind at ease on that score.

"I asked him how he knew you and he admitted you two had been a hot item a couple of months back. Suddenly I had a damned good reason for Dragon Lady wanting you dead. She didn't want you pointing me in Carlson's direction. Why? There is only one possible answer to that question; Carlson is, or was, in cahoots with her. He was in the perfect job to be her inside man.

"I confronted Carlson with that answer and he panicked, slugged me, and took off running for all he was worth. That is how I know Vernon Carlson is a traitor."

Russ returned to the living room with his coffee and sat in a chair strategically placed between Sally and the front door. Sally sat for several moments thinking about what I'd just told her. Finally, she said, "May I ask a question?"

I nodded. "All right."

"Vern . . . Captain Carlson brought us the request for an in-flight B-25 refueling system, so he must be involved with this mysterious mission you keep referring to. If that's true, why would he need me or anyone else to tell him about that mission. He should already know all the details, shouldn't he?"

"That's the only saving grace in this fiasco. I can't tell you how or why, but Carlson's information about the mission, if there is a mission, is limited to the knowledge that there is a need for increasing the B-25's range. The security around all this is that tight."

"Oh."

"Now, let's see if we can finish getting your neck out of the noose."

Her expression reflected hurt feelings mixed with fear. "Is my neck in a noose?"

"I'm afraid so, Sally. Let me explain how things stand. Right now, Russ and I, along with our boss, are the only people at MID who know you were romantically involved with Captain Carlson. At this point Russ and I are convinced you were an innocent victim of the Japs in that role."

I looked at Russ for confirmation. He nodded.

"Our boss, however, doesn't know you and he will want some evidence to clear you. Unfortunately, proving someone did not do something can be harder than proving they did do something. In this case, our best bet is being able to tell our boss we have questioned you about your relationship with Carlson and we see no indications you knew you were doing anything wrong. The snafu is you didn't tell us about Carlson to begin with. That is extremely suspicious. I need to be able to give our boss some good answers about why you kept that a secret."

Sally looked from Russ to me. "I suppose you know embarrassing doesn't begin to describe talking to the two of you about my relationship with another man."

"I can see that, but you could have saved most of that embarrassment by telling us you knew Carlson, rather than making us find the guy ourselves."

Standing, Russ said, "Sir, I could leave for a while, if that would make matters any easier. I don't suppose we both need to hear all of this."

I studied Russ for a moment and figured some part of his heart still belonged to Sally. Then I looked at Sally. The tears were finally making their appearance.

"I'm going to leave that up to you, Sally. Without another

witness to your statements, I effectively become your judge and jury in this matter." Looking her straight in the eye, I asked, "How do you feel about that?"

She sniffed once and said, "I trust you to be fair, Johnny."

With that, Russ headed for the stairs to get some rest after a long day of driving. I removed my notebook from my inside jacket pocket and got ready to write down Sally's answers to the questions I intended to ask her. I can't see that repeating those answers verbatim here serves any purpose, so I'll just summarize what went into my report. Sally and Carlson dated regularly for a about two and a half months beginning the week following Pearl Harbor and ending just before Valentine's Day. Sally particularly remembered those dates.

For the first few weeks their dating consisted of dinner and a show once or twice a week, and then they spent Christmas together at Sally's house. After that they began spending weekends together when they could. She remembered that happening four times. Then Carlson suddenly turned cold toward her and called things off.

It was clear Carlson hurt Sally badly. She fell for him hard only to have him lose interest, something I imagined had not happened often to Sally MacLure. Most guys would figure her for quite a catch.

Sally's answer to the sixty-four-dollar question rang true. She told me she did not mention knowing Carlson because he told her he could be in trouble for conflict of interest if the Army found out he was dating an employee of a defense contractor. He was supposed to remain impartial about all of the aircraft manufacturers he worked with.

It was just after midnight that I recorded her answer to that question and closed my notebook. Sally was watching me closely. When I didn't say anything, she asked, "How did I do? Is my neck still in the noose?"

I answered her question with a question of my own. "Did you tell me the truth?"

"Yes!"

"Then you're in the clear. To begin with, Carlson first approached you before the mission we would be concerned about—if there is such a mission—was conceived. That doesn't mean he didn't intend to use you as a source of information, but it rules out this specific situation as his original interest.

"Beyond that, I can see no holes in your story, and you've helped us in several ways that did not specifically concern Carlson, indicating your willingness to cooperate, even though you have no idea what you are cooperating about. I'll write my report with that general conclusion and I think we've heard the last of all this."

"Johnny?"

"Yes, Sally?"

"Do you think Vernon ever had any real feelings for me or was it all an act?"

"I can't answer that. It could have even been both and he was finding it difficult to keep things strictly business. I know that would be a problem for me in his shoes."

Sally gave me just a hint of a smile. "Thank you for that, Johnny, even if you're just saying it to spare my feelings."

"I wasn't. Believe me, that kiss you laid on me at Mines field a couple of nights ago was a definite temptation, but . . . ."

She interrupted me. "But Susan is your gal for life. I know. I wish I could hate her, but if I ever meet her I'm gonna give her a hug and tell her I think she's the luckiest girl in all the world."

Nineteen

Fort Winfield Scott/Presidio, San Francisco

I dressed in civvies and my shoulder holster just because I wanted to. Then I poured a cup of coffee and went out onto the front porch to see how the day was shaping up.

It seemed as if Friday might be okay. The storm finally moved on to leave everything sparkling and fresh, if a trifle damp. I heard drops of water spattering onto the ground from the safe house eaves and all the foliage within earshot.

I also noted with some satisfaction that my guess about the thicket across the street being a likely gun emplacement location seemed even more likely in the light of day. I couldn't actually see any of the block-shaped concrete structures usually associated with gun positions, but there was definitely something big back there in the shadows. I imagined the little safe house jumping right off its foundation when they fired that monster off.

One of my reasons for stepping out on the porch was to offer the security team some coffee, but their Jeeps were parked out of sight somewhere. Well, if they wanted Java, they knew where to find it. So did Russ. He stepped out to join me on the porch with a steaming mug in his hand.

"Good morning, sir. Anything going on out here?"

"Just a lot of dripping. How's Sally this morning? Or is she up yet?"

"I think she's up, although I didn't actually see her. I heard water running in the bathroom as I went by."

"Then I guess she survived last night's interrogation."

"It seems so, sir. I'm not sure I would have. You were pretty tough on her."

I glanced at him. His face gave no indication of how he felt about me giving Sally a rough time, one way or the other. "Sometimes you have to be tough if you want the truth. If anyone was tough on her, it was Vern Carlson, not me."

We stood out there watching the trees and shrubs drip and enjoying our coffee a while longer before the door behind us opened and Sally stuck her head out into the world. "Is this coffee klatch strictly for guys or can a gal join in?"

Russ answered her. "Sure. Come on out."

Sally, dressed in her brown slacks and a warm jacket with sleeves loose enough to fit over the cast on her arm, stepped out between us and said, "I love the way the air smells so fresh after a big storm."

I said, "It's even more noticeable down south. I think LA is dirtier to begin with, so a good scrubbing really helps."

Sally said, "I think you're . . . ."

It was one of those moments in time when so many things happen simultaneously, it wasn't until I thought things through later that I was certain about the sequence of events. It went like this: Sally stopped speaking in mid-sentence and took a jerky step toward me, I heard a distinct "pop" from the thick foliage across the street, and Sally's coffee mug bounced off the wooden porch boards and into the grass. I lowered Sally to the porch and vaulted the low porch railing with my Smith & Wesson already in hand. To Russ I shouted, "Across the street. Get Sally out of the line of fire."

I'd no sooner hit the ground when I heard two automobile engines start, one from the warehouse parking lot behind me and the other from somewhere off to my left. They both sounded like Jeeps. No more than a second or two later I saw the Jeeps. Our security team had arrived, albeit a tad late.

Pointing toward the thicket, I hollered at the Jeep coming from the west, "One shot . . . high powered rifle . . . back there."

That Jeep wasted no time turning into the foliage and stopping just off the road. The two MID corporals in it bailed out with their Thompsons and took up positions behind cover. The other Jeep pulled alongside the porch where I was crouched.

I glanced toward the porch. It was now empty, but the door was open a few inches. There was also a splatter of red about chest high to the right of the doorframe. I yelled to Russ, "You two okay?"

"Sally took a round in the chest. She's alive, but we need to get her to a medic fast."

I turned to the Jeep beside me. The first sergeant I spoke with the night before looked down at me from the driver's seat. I said, "We've got one down. Take her to Letterman Hospital as fast as you can get there."

The private who'd been in the passenger seat was already jogging toward the porch. The sergeant said, "Yes, sir," and squealed the tires pulling around in front of the safe house. I didn't think it was possible to squeal tires with a Jeep.

Seconds later Russ and the private hurried out the door carrying Sally. As they loaded her limp body into the back of the Jeep, I gave the Sergeant his marching orders. "You stay with this woman until I show up. She's not to be left alone for even a second. Got that?"

He already had the Jeep in motion when he said, "Yes, sir! Understood, sir."

Then Russ and I jogged across the street and crouched next to the Jeep on the edge of the thicket. The corporal who drove the Jeep was standing with us and his partner, another corporal, was a few steps away behind a large tree trunk. Russ and I still had our pistols in our hands, although I was pretty sure were absolutely useless at that point. Dragon Lady, or whoever did the shooting, had no reason to be hanging around.

"Corporal, find a telephone and tell base security we have an MID witness down from sniper fire. Tell 'em to look for civilians or anyone else who doesn't look like they belong here . . . possibly a woman . . . add armed and dangerous. We'll start a search in our car. Go!"

The Jeep bounced off and, as Russ and I ran for the Buick, I tossed him the keys. "You know this place a lot better than me. You drive."

He deftly caught the keys on the fly and asked, "Where are we going?"

Sliding onto the passenger end of the front seat, I gave him the best answer I could think of. "Unless he or she has a damned good fake ID, they must have snuck onto the base by some route other than one of the manned gates. It would be a good idea to find that route because they may be leaving the same way."

Russ nodded as he turned the ignition key in its slot. "That's one of the big difficulties of this place. Securing it takes a lot of manpower. If you want a suggestion, sir, we should follow Lincoln down along Baker Beach. There are a bunch of gun batteries out there. It's pretty desolate with lots of cover and there are roads going every which way. If I wanted to get lost on this post, that's where I'd head."

"Let's go."

Russ swung the sedan around and turned left on Upton, which took us in a loop around Fort Scott's main administration buildings to Kobbe Avenue, which in turn took us west to Lincoln Boulevard, a main drag both on and off the base.

While Russ negotiated the route to Lincoln, I went over what had just happened in my mind. Judging by the blood spatter I'd seen on the safe house's front wall and the limp state of Sally's body as she was carried out to security's Jeep, it would not surprise me to learn she was pronounced dead on arrival at Letterman Hospital. If she lived long enough to make it to Letterman, Sally might have a chance. I'd never had the pleasure of being a patient there, but the word was Letterman's medical staff knew their onions.

Turning to Russ, I asked, "Do you know that Top Kick who took Sally to Letterman?"

"Yes, sir. His name is Tiner. I've worked with him on security details before."

"Can we trust him to stick with Sally? That is, assuming she's still alive."

"Yes, sir. Tiner is a good man. Your orders were clear and he'll follow them to the letter."

"Good. We . . . or I . . . owe Sally that much, anyway."

Sounding just a little too sincere for my liking, Russ said, "Sir, you aren't to blame for what happened back there. You had every reason to believe the area was secure."

"Hogwash. Letting her stand around out there in the open was a stupid amateur mistake."

The stretch of Lincoln Boulevard where we joined it runs along the bluff forming the southern side of the entrance to San Francisco Bay. The Pacific Ocean was on our right and we saw concrete gun batteries through the trees to our left.

It wasn't long before Lincoln began to run out of bluff and we were descending to beach level. Near the bottom of the hill Russ made a right turn onto a dirt road. A small white sign with an arrow in the direction we were headed spelled out, "Chamberlin."

Russ said, "This access road will take us down to Battery Chamberlin. From there we should have a pretty good view of everything from the bridge to China Beach up by the Palace of the Legion of Honor."

Two post security MPs were stationed just off Lincoln Boulevard. As the corporal on my side of the car studied my ID, he said, "Gosh, I can't believe they sent MID down here to look for Lieutenant Winters' car. The Lieutenant must have some real pull."

I glanced at Russ, and then back at the corporal. "He doesn't have that much pull. Tell me about Lieutenant Winters and his car, Corporal."

With the nervous expression even tough guys get on their faces when they are questioned by MID, the corporal said, "Well, sir, Lieutenant Winters is the commander of this battery, and his car was stolen sometime last night . . . right out of the parking area down there. He called it in to post security and, well, I thought that might be why you were here."

"You could turn out to be right about that, Corporal. What kind of car does the lieutenant drive?"

Now he was wearing a curious expression. "It's a Ford station wagon . . . practically brand new. He got the fancy model with the wood paneling on it."

"What color is the part that isn't wood?"

"Pale green, sir. Sort of like the color of pea soup."

It sounded as if he was describing the color of my Dodge. Finding it hard to believe both Dodge and Ford both managed to end up with the same ugly green paint on their option list, I thanked the corporal for his help and gave Russ a "move on" gesture.

"That's sort of an interesting coincidence, sir. I mean a vehicle disappearing out here the night before someone shoots at us."

"It is that, Russ. It surely is."

Battery Chamberlin mounted two six-inch guns pointed out across the Golden Gate, which is the name given the entrance to San Francisco Bay long before there was any thought of building the bridge of the same name across it. The guns were mounted in a concrete pit at beach level and positioned to fire in a nearly straight-line trajectory at any enemy ships that wandered by. There were two additional mounts without guns in the battery, indicating there might have been four guns at one time.

We drove across the unpaved parking area just south of the guns and found a road that appeared to complete a loop back to Lincoln Boulevard. Just as we left the parking area, something flashed at me from a clump of pine trees just ahead to the right of the access road.

"Russ, pull up next to those trees over there."

"Yes, sir."

As Russ pulled into the pine tree grove, I saw the flash again, only this time I also saw what was flashing. It was the sun reflecting off window glass on the passenger side of a nearly new ugly green Ford Super Deluxe station wagon with wood paneling.

Russ also saw the Ford. "Well, will you look at that. It seems as if we just found Lieutenant Winters' missing station wagon."

"It surely does. Let's look it over."

Smith & Wesson in hand, I cautiously stepped down from the Dodge's passenger-side door. The grove was deathly quiet. The only sound came from breakers hitting the beach sixty or seventy feet behind us. Moving carefully so as not to disturb any evidence that might be laying around, we gave the Ford a going over.

The only things worth noting were inside the car: three wires hanging down from the dashboard below the ignition key and a small red, yellow, and white cardboard box that was now empty, but which once held twenty Winchester point-three-oh-eight, one-eighty grain Super Speed cartridges. They were high-powered rounds intended to take down game like deer, but they were also effective on blondes.

The little pine tree grove we were in covered a low hill, or maybe it was a sand dune. The terrain rose to a rounded crest about thirty feet beyond the Ford. A gentle breeze rustled the pine needles over our heads as I said, "Now, what do you suppose this estate wagon is doing here?"

As I spoke, I gestured to Russ, indicating he should circle around the hill to see what might be lurking on the other side. Russ nodded, and before he trotted off, he said, "I'd say someone wanted to put it where it wouldn't be found quickly."

For a big man, Russ moved about a quietly as anyone I ever met. Without making a sound he disappeared among the trees while I carried on our conversation.

"Well, that's something a parking valet might do, but I think shore battery parking is mostly self-service, so we probably need to find another explanation. Maybe . . . ."

Large caliber revolvers fired at close range sometimes make a "crack" sound. This one was easily within thirty-feet and it cracked. I was halfway to the crest of the hill by the time I heard the more familiar "pop" of a Colt semi-auto forty-five. That was Russ shooting back at whoever fired the first shot.

As I topped the crest, a commotion to my right immediately grabbed my attention. I spun that way and Vern Carlson crashed out of the brush a dozen feet away, spotting me at the same instant I saw him. The big Colt Army revolver in his hand swung in my direction. I was off balance from turning on the uneven ground and I was squarely in his sights. Carlson had me cold . . . but he hesitated.

I'll never know why he decided not to fire in that split-second, but it was the last decision Vernon Carlson ever made. The round from my thirty-eight caught him squarely in the chest. He got that bewildered look on his face folks often have when they know they've been shot but can't believe such an awful thing could happen to them, and then the Colt slipped from his hand and he collapsed in the underbrush.

Unnecessarily keeping an eye on him, I hollered, "One down over here, Russ." My voice sounded a little higher-pitched to me than usual.

Russ was working his way around lower down the hill to head Carlson off, but when I called to him, he headed straight for the sound of my voice. It didn't take him more than two seconds to size up the situation when he popped into the little clearing where I was standing.

Holstering my revolver, I said, "Sergeant Pierce, meet Captain Vernon Carlson. Please forgive the Captain for not getting up."

"Nice shooting, sir."

"Lucky shooting. He had me, but he hesitated. Learn from that, Russ."

"Yes, sir."

Despite a chill in the air, I wiped sweat from my forehead. "I still have no idea what the hell he was doing in this grove, though."

"I do, sir. Step over here."

Looking down the slope where Russ was pointing, I could see something black at the bottom of a tree trunk. When I got a few steps closer, it all became clear. I was looking at a small inflatable rubber life raft. In it were a paddle and what appeared as if it might be a Winchester Model 70 bolt-action hunting rifle poking out of an oilskin sack.

Russ said, "That's how he got onto the post without being seen. He must have come back here after shooting Sally to wait for night, so he could paddle back out to a boat that's supposed to pick him up."

"Looks that way. We gotta remember to alert our Coast Guard friends. They might find some interesting characters out here tonight."

"Yes, sir. I wonder why Carlson decided to sneak on base like a commando rather than just using his Army ID at the gate. It probably would have worked. It takes time for alerts to get out where they're needed."

I shrugged. "Who knows? But it doesn't matter. Russ, take the car and find a telephone so you can send for base security. I'll wait here."

"Yes, sir.

A moment later I heard the Buick drive up the access road and I walked over to Carlson. I was a little disappointed to find he was still there. I guess he didn't know he wasn't welcome at this party.

I was angry at the captain for a couple of reasons. For one thing, he made me shoot him by hesitating to shoot me. He also led a sweet little blonde down the garden path for nefarious purposes, and I owed him for knocking me on my butt in front of all those people at the Lockheed plant. It's not good practice to embarrass MID agents. We get even.

But now there was no longer anything to be angry at. Carlson paid for his transgressions with his life and I was almost feeling sorry for the jerk when the mental image of a shot down B-25 smashing into the Pacific Ocean appeared in my imagination. To hell with him.

I walked down the slope the way I'd come up and leaned against a rough pine trunk alongside the access road. It occurred to me that there were pine trees just like this in Santa Barbara. No, Santa Barbara pine trees were much friendlier.

Twenty

1200 Hours – Friday – 6 MAR 42

Letterman Army Hospital/Presidio, San Francisco

So much had happened since I stepped out onto the porch at the Fort Scott safe house Friday morning, I had trouble believing my trusty Czech Air Force watch when it tried to tell me the time was only noon. Five hours can seem like a lifetime, or the end of one.

When Russ returned to the little pine grove near Battery Chamberlin with the MID posse in tow, we set about cleaning up the site and taking the evidence into custody. Actually, the station wagon, rubber dinghy, rifle, and other items were not evidence in the sense they would ever see the inside of a courtroom. This was a wartime MID operation and General Chester Davis was the sole judge and jury in the matter of whether or not our actions were fairly in line with the organization's purposes of protecting democracy and the American way.

I planned to call Davis with my report when we arrived at Building 100, but first, I wanted to make a quick call to Letterman Army Hospital. If she survived long enough to make the hospital, Sally had certainly been there long enough that someone could tell me how she was doing.

While I called Letterman, Russ used another telephone to call the Coast Guard Station down by Crissy Field. He alerted them to keep a sharp eye out off the coast opposite Battery Chamberlain tonight because we expected a Jap vessel to extricate an agent hiding at Fort Scott. Russ also explained the Jap agent would not be attending the party.

My call to Letterman took longer than I expected because the nurse I spoke with in the emergency ward had no idea who I was talking about when I asked about the condition of Miss Sally MacLure.

"I'm sorry, sir, we have no patient by that name."

I was becoming increasingly convinced Sally did not make it to Letterman alive when it dawned on me that the MID Sergeant who brought her to the hospital didn't know Sally's name. When I mentioned the MID connection, the lights blinked on in the Emergency ward. Actually, the nurse was quite relieved to finally have Sally's name. Hospitals like to keep their paperwork in order.

Doctor O'Brian, a Letterman surgeon with an overly authoritative air about him was summoned to the telephone. "Yes, Major Spicer, the young woman is still among the living, but only barely. You fellows really need to take better care of your witnesses, if that's what she really is."

I experienced a momentary flash of anger at that comment, but I let it pass without comment. "What is her prognosis, Doctor O'Brian?"

"Fair. We have her stabilized and I've repaired the most serious damage done by the bullet, but she has some major healing to do and at least one more surgery to survive before I can upgrade her prognosis to good."

"When can we visit her?"

"Possibly this evening. In the meantime, kindly instruct your damned sergeant to stay the hell out of my way! I nearly had to forcibly eject him from the operating room because you ordered him not to leave the patient for any reason."

"That's correct, Doctor, and if you value your life, you'll humor him. Despite what you seem to think, MID does take care of its witnesses, which is exactly what Sally MacLure is. I will be by later tonight to make sure you are doing the same for her. Good day, sir."

Mouthing off to the surgeon is probably not the best way to engender cooperation, but I was growing weary of being treated like a subhuman goon. Next, I gave Russ a report on Sally's condition. He seemed pleased she wasn't dead.

Killing Captain Vernon Carlson earned me a "well done" from General Davis. The rest of our conversation concerned Dragon Lady.

The General agreed with my opinion that Miss Yount might have outlived her usefulness where her current assignment was concerned. On the other hand, the subject of her current assignment was still six or seven weeks away, so we couldn't count on the Japs just giving up, and since Dragon Lady probably knew more about the Doolittle mission than any of their other agents, she could still be in the game.

The problem was I had no leads to follow until Dragon Lady showed up again, and by that time we could be too late. When I expressed that thought to Davis, his reply irritated the hell out of me. "You still have that MacLure woman. If we make it known she survived an attempt on her life, Marjorie Yount might feel it necessary to take care of the problem personally."

"Why should she? She only wanted Sally MacLure out of the picture because Sally might point us at Carlson. Now Carlson is dead and the MacLure woman is no longer a threat to the Japs."

"You're getting tunnel vision, Spicer. That's only your opinion of why the enemy wanted MacLure out of the picture. It might be way off base. You aren't getting attached to that woman, are you?"

That was the final straw. In the past few hours I'd watched a young woman for whom I was responsible take a bullet that should have ended her life, I'd been squarely in the sights of a Jap agent who had no good reason not to shoot, and I'd killed a man. Now Davis wanted me to use a badly injured civilian we allowed to be shot in the first place as bait. I was a breath away from telling him to go straight to hell.

Fortunately, I realized telling Davis to go to hell could be Sally's death warrant and kept my mouth shut. If Davis replaced me on this assignment, the next guy might think using Sally as bait was a dandy idea. As long as she was part of my assignment, I had access to Sally and options for keeping her alive.

"No, sir, I have no attachment to the MacLure woman."

"Good. I'll have somebody here plant a story in the San Francisco and Los Angeles papers about a Jap spy's failed attempt to kill a defense plant engineer as part of an espionage plan. I'll have them include enough detail so finding the MacLure woman won't be too difficult. Then all you have to do is stake out the hospital and wait. I'll bet you dollars to donuts your Dragon Lady will take the bait within a day or two."

I said, "Yes, sir," but my mind was running at top speed developing ways to undermine Davis' lousy plan.

"All right, Spicer. Set things up on your end and good luck."

Russ was in the room the entire time I was talking to General Davis, so it seemed a pretty safe bet he was curious about the conversation. On the other hand, I needed some time to think before I let anyone else in on what I was up to. For that matter, I needed to figure out what I was up to before I let anyone else in on what I was up to.

"Russ, I have to think about a few things before we go much further. While I do that, I'd like you to pick up our gear at the safe house. Also take that damned Buick tank back to the motor pool and get my Dodge. When you return we'll have some lunch and a talk."

"Yes, sir."

If I said thirty minutes of concentrated thought gave me a clear vision of how to proceed with my assignment, I'd be a damned liar. I had a rough plan for protecting Sally, but I was missing some information I needed to finalize it. Hopefully, I could learn what I needed to know before the day was over.

The biggest question, though, was who to take into my confidence about the daring scheme I was concocting. Daring? No, "damned foolish" and "dangerous" were better words to describe my plan.

I felt I could trust Russ but telling him what I planned to do would put him in a tough spot if things went wrong. He was a good man and he didn't deserve to end his military career in a stockade for getting involved in my cockamamie scheme. I decided the solution to that dilemma was to hint I was up to something without being specific. That would alert Russ without putting him on the spot.

It was about 1330 when we parked in the tiny lot next to Eddie's Soup & Sandwich Shop at the intersection of Lombard & Broderick. Eddie's was popular with civilian employees at the Presidio because it was within walking distance for lunch and they served the best soup in town. The little café offered counter service, plus three small tables at the very back. Russ and I grabbed one of the tables.

We ordered the soup and sandwich combination. The soup of the day was Eddie's Creamery Tomato, which went well with my toasted cheese sandwich. We dug into our lunches and I told Russ what General Davis had in mind for catching Dragon Lady.

When I finished my tale, Russ shook his head. "I'm sorry, sir, but that just doesn't seem right. Sally has already had a tough go of it, and putting her at further risk is . . . well, it's wrong."

It was time to choose my words carefully. "Russ, a big part of this assignment we've been working on has become the elimination of Marjorie Yount. General Davis has ordered us to pursue that objective in a particular way. My job is to choose the most effective means of carrying out his order. Our personal feelings about that order are of no consequence. Understood?"

I watched Russ's facial expression change as he thought about what I said. It went from something like anger to what looked to me like curiosity. "Yes, sir. That is understood."

"Good. I am formulating a plan to comply with the General's order, but I need more information to finalize that plan. I hope to have that information by tonight. The scheme I have in mind is necessarily complex and it is possible you will not completely understand how it will accomplish our objective. Despite that, I expect you to follow my orders precisely and without question. Is that understood?"

Now Russ was watching me closely. There was a message within the instructions I gave him, and I could tell by his expression he was receiving it loud and clear. "Understood, sir."

It was time for the finale. "Good. Lastly, you may find it informative to pay closer attention to my actions than my words from here on out. Keep your eyes open."

Russ was almost smiling. "Yes, sir."

Back at the Presidio I aimed the Dodge straight for Crissy Field. There, I instructed Russ to take the Dodge to Letterman Hospital and relieve Sergeant Tiner at Sally's bedside. Tiner had to be falling asleep on his feet by now. As Russ drove off to carry out his orders, I went into the main hangar and hunted Stu Irvin down.

Irvin was studying an aircraft manual of some sort when he looked up and saw me coming. "Geez, Spicer, you back for more? I figured I scared you off for good last night."

"Hell, Stu, you made it look so easy, you convinced me flying these kites is the softest job in this man's army. I'm back for flying lessons."

Stu chomped down harder on his cigar and shook his head. "Mother of God, what did I do to deserve this?"

Gesturing my head toward the open hangar door, I said, "Come on, Captain Hotshot, let's take a hike."

Outside and well beyond earshot of guys in the hangar, I said, "Okay, Stu, everything I say from this point on is so damned classified the only ones who have clearance for it are you, me, and God."

Irvin looked at me dubiously. "Lucky me. Do I get a secret decoder ring?"

Ignoring his lack of appreciation, I said, "Your orders are to rig the AT-7 for carrying a litter. After that, fuel it up and standby to fly me and the person on the litter out of here with less than a moment's notice, day or night. Can do?"

I had Irvin's attention. "Sure. Do I get to know where we're going, or do we just fly around and hope we end up where you want to be by chance?"

"I'll give you our destination once we're in the air."

Irvin nodded knowingly. "Got it. You don't know where the hell we're going, do you?"

"Not precisely."

Stu shook his head. "Swell. When does all this fun begin?"

"We probably won't be leaving before tomorrow morning, but the way things are, almost anything can happen. We'll have to take this thing hour by hour."

"Listen, Spicer, sittin' around here will cut into my drinkin' and carousing time, so make it soon."

"Believe me, Stu, I want to get this out of our hair as much as you do, but to a large degree the timing is out of my hands."

"Okay, Major Spook, I'll be ready to go."

"Thanks, Stu. See you as soon as I can."

My next stop was the public telephone alongside Crissy's main hangar. I dialed 0 for an operator and told her I wanted FAirway two-two-seven-one in Santa Barbara, California. I also told her to charge the call to MOntecito four-nine-five-six in the same city. Susan would find the call on her bill, but she also had my checkbook to pay for it.

After the requisite clicks and buzzes required to make a long-distance telephone connection, a familiar female voice said, "Good afternoon, Casa Sobre El Mar."

"Hello, Mary, this is Johnny Spicer. Is my favorite nurse around?"

"She sure is, Mister Spicer. Hang on the line for just a minute while I locate her."

"Thanks, kiddo."

Mary giggled. "You're welcome, Mister Spicer."

It took about 60 seconds of long-distance time for Mary to track Susan down. "Hello, Johnny! Gosh, I'm glad to hear from you!"

"Good. That means I can talk you out of some free medical advice."

"Sure, darling. What do you need to know?"

"The name and location of the best cardiopulmonary surgeon in Los Angeles."

"Oh, oh! You didn't get shot again did you?"

"No, I'm not the patient this time."

"Can you tell me a little more? I'll ask Doctor Rothenberg for a recommendation, but I want to give him as much information as

I can."

"Okay. The patient is a female, about twenty-five, otherwise healthy except for a broken arm. She was wounded in the chest by a large caliber round from a hunting rifle. She is currently at a military hospital and the surgeon there told me he performed emergency surgery to keep her alive this morning, but she'll need at least one more operation and, in his words, she has a lot of healing to do.

"The problem is this woman is being hunted by Jap espionage agents. This is the third attempt they've made on her life, and they damn near got her. I have to stash her somewhere off the beaten path, so she'll live long enough to do all that healing.

"That's about all I know at this point. If you have specific questions, I might be able to get them answered later today."

With a smile in her voice, Susan said, "I have to say you have heaps of nerve asking your future wife to help you save some young cutie."

"How do you know she's cute?"

Susan laughed. "If she has your attention, she must be."

"Actually, she's an engineer at an aviation plant and uglier than sin."

"Oh, sure she is. Johnny, I'll take this in to Doctor Rothenberg and see what he suggests. Do you want to call me back later?"

"What time do you get off work tonight, Angel?"

"Five."

"How 'bout I call you at home sometime after that?"

"Okay, but if Mister Whiskers answers, just leave a message. I might be out with some Navy general."

"Admiral, darling. The Navy has admirals, not generals."

"Well, maybe they should get some."

On that note we finished our conversation and I set out walking toward Letterman Army Hospital. The twenty-minute hike from Crissy gave me time to contemplate the flaws in my plan. There were plenty to contemplate.

The biggest of those flaws was my scheme hinged on convincing Doctor O'Brian Sally needed to be elsewhere as soon as possible. I was pretty sure selling US War Bonds to Tojo would be easier. I could try to take her out of the hospital without his approval, but that was sure to cause a commotion, and if my plan had any chance of working, that chance depended upon secrecy. On top of that, I sure as hell didn't want to do Dragon Lady's job for her by killing Sally in the process of trying to save her.

By the time I got to Letterman I was close to giving up on the whole scheme, but then I witnessed the complete lack of security at the hospital. I found out Sally's room number simply by asking the exceptionally helpful woman at the lobby reception desk. I was in civvies, so she had no idea who the hell I was, but she happily told me what room Miss MacLure was in on the second floor and gave me detailed instructions for finding it. I would not have been surprised if she'd gone along to personally show me the way. What's more, she failed to mention that Miss MacLure is not allowed visitors.

When I got to Sally's room, I found Russ standing by the door and a sign next to the room number that said, "No Visitors."

Russ said, "Hello, sir. Everything is quiet here."

"Have you spoken with Sally?"

"Actually, yes. I wasn't supposed to, but I went in to keep an eye on a nurse and Sally was sort of awake. She saw me and said, 'Hello, Russ.' She was very groggy, but at least she knew me."

"I guess that's a good sign. I don't know if you've had a chance to check things out at this damned hospital, but security here is literally nonexistent. In fact, you're it."

"I got that impression, sir."

"I think we'd better set up something more effective. Figure out a manpower schedule and tell Colonel Beecher I asked that it be implemented immediately. I'll spell you here while you do that."

"Yes, sir. Do you think we should have more than one man outside her room?"

"I'm not sure that's necessary. I think we'd do better by putting a man or two on each of the entrances to this building. That way we head the bad guys off at the pass before they ever get up here. If we leave it at one man on this door, though, he needs to be relieved for five minutes or so every hour."

"Got it, sir."

Russ hurried off down the corridor to complete his assignment, and I turned around to peek through the small window in Sally's door. She was alone in the single bed room and appeared to be asleep. I went in to take a closer look.

Closing the door behind me, I quietly walked across the room to her bedside and she opened her eyes. She saw me and actually smiled. "Johnny."

"Hiya, kiddo. How are you feeling?"

Sally looked around the room as if that might give her the answer to my question. Finally, she said, "I don't know . . . I think they give me a lot of pain pills or . . . or something . . . ."

"I think you're right. I also think you are supposed to be sleeping. I just came in to see . . . ."

There was a touch of panic in her voice. "Oh, don't go away."

"I won't be far. Russ or I will be right outside the door. Can I get you anything before I go?"

Answering simple questions were a chore for her, but she pointed to an empty glass with a straw in it on her bedside table. I took that to mean she wanted some water, so I picked up the glass and took it to a sink in the corner of the room behind the door.

I was being careful to put no more than a few sips in the glass in case she wasn't supposed to be drinking a lot of water when I heard Sally's shaky voice say, "Johnny." I turned to look and saw her staring wide-eyed at the door.

Twenty-One

Letterman Army Hospital/Presidio, San Francisco

Spinning toward the door, I immediately saw why Sally was scared out of her wits. An arm was poking into the room and the hand on that arm was holding a revolver.

I flew at the door, hitting it hard with my left shoulder—the revolver fired, and the arm made a very satisfying crunch. That was followed by an earsplitting shriek from the guy on the other side of the door. Grabbing his now limp arm, I took the revolver from his hand and jerked the rest of him into the room.

He was a young Japanese fellow in a white orderly's jacket a couple of sizes too large. By this time, he'd passed out, which was fine with me. His screaming was getting on my nerves. I let go of his arm and his body flopped to the floor.

While all this was happening, the ruckus attracted a crowd out in the hall. A pushy nurse screeched at me hysterically, demanding to know what I thought I was doing. I told her to shut the hell up and call security.

Walking quickly toward Sally, I noted a small hole in the wall above her bed. The hole indicated where the assassin's bullet went when I ruined his aim by crushing his arm in the door. I'd gotten lucky yet again, or Sally had, depending on how you wanted to look at it.

Sally reached across the bed with her left arm and grabbed my hand. I said, "Relax, kiddo. Everything is okay now."

There were tears on her cheeks. "I'm scared. Johnny, please . . . "

Russ and an older fellow with a stethoscope around his neck shouldered their way into the room almost simultaneously. Without me saying a word, Russ took charge of the unconscious

Jap on the floor in the doorway, slapping handcuffs on him and dragging him out of the room. The guy with the stethoscope, presumably a doctor, stood beside the bed looking at Sally.

Then the doctor looked at me. My adrenalin was still rushing, and I guess my maniacal expression scared him. He backed away a step and looked back at Sally, and then hollered, "Nurse, we need a 150 milligrams of Nembutal sodium solution here."

I looked down at Sally. She looked back at me and mouthed the word "no."

I'm certainly no medical expert, but I know Nembutal is a barbiturate used to knock patients out. I figured the last thing Sally needed was more knocking out. She was trying to make sense of the world around her and Nembutal sure as hell wasn't going to contribute anything to that effort. On the other hand, it was possible the doctor intended the Mickey Finn for me.

A few seconds later, a nurse ran in with a syringe. I stepped in front of her, gently took her wrist in my hand, and removed the hypodermic from her grip. "Nurse, kindly wait out in the hallway."

Her mouth flapped open and shut a few times like a fish out of water before she followed my suggestion. By this time the doctor was nearly apoplectic. "Who the hell do you think you are? I'm this woman's physician. You are interfering with her care!"

I looked back over my shoulder toward the door. I could see Russ had some help now. "Sergeant clear that doorway and close the door. Now!"

Turning back to the doctor, I handed him my MID ID. "This is who I think I am, and this woman's safety and wellbeing are ultimately my responsibility. Now, before you pump anymore drugs into Miss MacLure, you and I are going to have a heart to heart conversation."

Making sure the syringe had a cap over the sharp end, I slipped it into my jacket pocket. The doctor was still looking at my ID. "Spicer? I know you! We talked on the telephone earlier." Waving my ID at me he added, "This does not give you the authority to interfere in the treatment of my patient!"

In a tone of voice that was a hell of a lot calmer than I was, I said, "Doctor O'Brian, perhaps it has escaped your notice, but had I not interfered, that bullet lodged in the wall over there would be in your patient. Now, I suggest you get down off your high horse and work with me here. Otherwise, I'm on my own and I'm pretty sure you will find that even less to your liking."

O'Brian handed me my ID and walked over to Sally's bedside. As he looked down at her, Sally nodded her head twice before her eyelids drooped shut again.

The doctor turned back toward me in a somewhat more relaxed mood. "All right, Major Spicer, say what have to say."

"How 'bout I start by telling you who Miss MacLure is?" I told him just enough of Sally's story to make him understand what she'd been through and why she was important to MID. I finished by saying, "The moral of this story is the Japanese obviously know Miss MacLure is here and that makes Letterman Army Hospital the last place she should be."

Doctor O'Brian said, "All right, Major Spicer, exactly where to do you think she should be?"

"It isn't so much the location that makes a place safe in this situation as it is the circumstances of her getting there." Then I threw him a curve, "By any chance do you know a Doctor Hamilton Rothenberg?"

O'Brian looked startled. "Ham Rothenberg? You bet I know him. What does Ham have to do with this?"

"Your pal Ham is also a pretty good friend of mine. If he recommended a cardiopulmonary surgeon to care for Miss MacLure, would you find that acceptable?"

Looking skeptical, he said, "I suppose so, but first, I insist on knowing how you know Ham Rothenberg."

I took a step forward and pulled the hair behind my left temple back to expose the scar Doctor Rothenberg left behind when he removed a bullet from my head. I leaned forward and let O'Brian take a look.

"Oh, I see."

"I was a guest in his home when that wound occurred, so he felt obligated to patch me up. I thought he did a pretty good job, so we've stayed in touch."

"All right, but why bother Ham? Why don't I just suggest a specialist in another locale for Miss MacLure?"

"It would be a hell of a lot safer for all concerned if he made the recommendation and you didn't know who he recommended. Four days ago, I had the misfortune of finding an Army Air Force Captain who knew something the Japs wanted to know. The coroner's best guess was that he died of head injuries after enduring several hours of agonizing torture."

It was difficult to read O'Brian's expression, but he made it clear he'd just heard a good reason for doing things my way. "I see your point. Would it work if I called Ham and briefed him on the patient, and then turned the telephone over to you for his recommendation?"

"That's fine." I glanced at my watch. It was a few minutes before five. "We'd better get a move on, though, before he leaves the clinic for the day."

Doctor O'Brian nodded and I handed him the hypo from my pocket. "I think this is yours."

I gave Sally's hand a squeeze and winked at her. I think she tried to smile back at me.

Leaving the room, I told Russ to watch Sally's room and turned left toward the stairway. O'Brian stopped and said, "No, my office is this way."

"We're not going to your office. We're going to the lobby for a pay telephone. If the Japs got curious enough, they could easily get a record of the calls made from and to your office telephone. That could put both Sally and Ham Rothenberg in danger."

"Damn, you think of everything."

"Not everything. The bullet hole in the wall over Miss MacLure's bed proves that. We're up against some pretty smart folks and staying ahead of them isn't easy. I never know what they'll come up with next."

I picked a public telephone booth at random from the row of six in Letterman's lobby and asked the operator for FAirway two-two-seven-one in Santa Barbara, California. I charged the call to an MID exchange. That I knew Rothenberg's telephone number without looking it up surprised O'Brian. I didn't let him in on the fact that I had more than one friend at Casa Sobre El Mar.

Mary had not left for the day yet. "Hi, Mary, Johnny Spicer again."

"Hello, Mister Spicer. Do you want to talk to Susan again? I think she's still here."

"Yes, but first, I'm with a gentleman who needs to speak with Doctor Rothenberg. Would you please tell him that Doctor Paul O'Brian is on the line?"

"Yes, and then I'll catch Susan before she leaves."

"Thanks, Mary."

Stepping out of the telephone booth, I offered the handset to O'Brian. He stepped in and held the receiver to his ear. I strolled a few paces from the booth to give O'Brian a little privacy. The doctors conferred for several minutes. Finally, I heard the doctor at this end call my name.

We swapped places and he handed me the receiver. "Doctor Rothenberg?"

"Yes, Major Spicer, it's me. You seem to have something of a dilemma on your hands."

I chuckled. "You could say that, yes. I'm sorry to change the plan and bother you again instead of just getting your recommendation from Susan."

"You aren't bothering me, Major Spicer. Besides, we're colleagues. We are both in the business of saving lives."

"I suppose so, but your methods are a bit more sophisticated than mine. I doubt if you even own a thirty-eight-caliber scalpel."

It was Rothenberg's turn to chuckle. "That is true, but I do own a pair of gum-soled shoes. Now, let's get down to business. After talking to Paul, I'm going to suggest we proceed a little differently."

"All right, what do you have in mind?"

"It so happens one of the best cardiopulmonary surgeons on the west coast is a neighbor of mine. He is retiring from his practice, but I believe I can convince him to take on one more patient. What I'm suggesting is that you bring the patient here to my clinic and we have Doctor Feigenbaum take over her care. We have private rooms available in the new wing and our operating theater is more up-to-date than you'll find in most hospitals. How does that sound?"

"Sounds fine, Doctor Rothenberg, but I have to pay for this out of a nearly non-existent budget. I'm pretty sure Uncle Sam won't go along with a private clinic."

"Our Uncle Sam is a cheapskate. From what Susan tells me, this woman is as deserving of care as any of our boys wounded in combat. There will be no charge."

"That's two I owe you, Doctor."

"Major Spicer, you owe me nothing but your friendship. The next issue we need to address is transporting the patient. Have you any ideas on that?"

"Yes, I have a plane that's set-up to carry a litter standing by."

"Good. How long would such a flight take?"

"Barring bad weather or some other delay, about three hours."

Rothenberg was silent for a moment. I asked, "Problem?"

"Not an insurmountable one. I'm concerned about the patient making a trip like that without medical care close at hand. Is there some way to send a qualified nurse up there to accompany the patient without delaying things a lot?"

"Yes. I can send the same aircraft down there in about four hours to transport your nurse up here for the trip back."

"Perfect, but let's make it five hours. I want to give Susan time to pack some supplies and make a few arrangements."

"Susan?"

"Yes, Major Spicer, Susan. Nurse Jackson is the best choice for this job. Do you have an objection?"

"None at all, Doctor."

I'm sure he heard the smile in my voice. "I didn't think so. If we proceed along the lines we've discussed, how soon would the patient be here?"

"We can have her there late tomorrow morning. Will that work?"

"It will. I'll arrange to have an ambulance at the airport to transport her here. Now, unless you have other questions or concerns for me, I'll let you speak with Susan to finalize your plans for her flight up there."

"All right. And Doctor Rothenberg, thank you."

"You're quite welcome, Major. Here's Miss Jackson."

"Johnny?"

"Hi, Angel."

"What's going on?   It sounds like I'm taking a trip somewhere."

"You are. I'm afraid your Navy General will have to do without the pleasure of your company tonight. You'll have to make do with an Army Major."

I heard excitement in Susan's voice. "Really? Tell me!"

"I'm sending a plane down to pick you up so you can escort the patient we discussed to the clinic tomorrow morning. She's going to be Doctor Rothenberg's guest for a while."

"Wonderful! When do I need to be where?"

"I think you'll need to be at the Santa Barbara Municipal Airport about ten o'clock tonight, but I'll call you after I've made arrangements with the pilot to make sure of the timing. Hang around home until you hear from me, okay?"

"All right, darling. I'll need a little time to get supplies together here. I should be home by six."

"Deal. See you in a few hours, Angel."

"I can't wait!"

I needed to finalize things with Doctor O'Brian for moving Sally, but he returned to the second floor during my conversations with Doctor Rothenberg and Susan. He could wait while I got a few other arrangements made.

Stepping into a fresh telephone booth, and hoping Stu was still there, I dialed Crissy Field.

"Captain Irvin."

"Hi, Stu, Spicer here."

"Major, anyone ever tell you you're a pest?"

"Several times a day. Listen, we've got a small change in plans. I need you to pick up a passenger where you picked me up Friday morning and bring her back here tonight."

"Her?"

"Yeah, her. She's a nurse, and she'll be going with us on the litter trip tomorrow morning."

"A nurse? Swell. Is she pretty?"

"A real dish, but you'll keep your mind on flying that crate of yours unless you want an MID major using you for target practice."

"Oh, it's like that, is it?"

"It surely is. Can you be down there by twenty-two-hundred?"

"Hang on, I'll check the weather."

I heard Stu yell, "Anyone seen a recent met report for southern California?"

In the distance someone replied, "Scattered at fifteen thousand over Mines, otherwise clear all the way down to Dago and up the central coast."

Stu yelled, "Thanks." Into the telephone, he said, "Yeah, weather's clear. I'll be on the ground up there by twenty-two-hundred. Do I need to give this doll a password or something, so she'll know I'm legit?"

"Irvin, it would take a hell of lot more than a password to make you legit. I'll be looking for you back here around oh-one-hundred."

On my way up to O'Brian's office I passed Sally's room. Russ was in the hallway standing guard. "Hello, sir. Everything under control now?"

"Yeah, at least as under control as things ever get in this business. How's Sally?"

"She was sleeping when I looked in a few minutes ago. That Jap scared the hell out of her."

"He scared the hell out of me, too. What did you do with him?"

"He's downstairs with an MID security team getting his arm set. You broke him up pretty good, sir. After that, he'll be transported to the maximum-security area for military prisoners on Alcatraz Island to await criminal proceedings, but that could take a while."

"Good. Maybe they will just leave him there to rot."

"Yes, sir. Does this change your plans for Sally?"

I nodded. "Somewhat." After looking up and down the corridor for eavesdroppers, I said, "Here's the new schedule. You and I will take turns watching out for Sally until about oh-nine-hundred tomorrow. After that she won't be here."

"Oh?"

"Yup. We're moving her to a new location. Also, I'll need you to spell me here for a little while around oh-one-hundred. We'll move Sally to Crissy at oh-eight-thirty and I'll travel with her to the new location. While I do that, you get some sleep. Then I want you to fuel up the Dodge and drive it to Sally's new location so we'll have wheels. Once there, you can help me make sure she isn't bothered. I'll give you her new location at Crissy. Got it?"

"Yes, sir." Russ' disposition seemed to have improved on hearing the news that in a few hours Sally would no longer be bait for Dragon Lady.

"All right. I need to see that Doctor O'Brien for a few minutes to finalize some things. After that I'll spell you for a while."

"Yes, sir. Just so you know, there are a couple of nurses on this floor who'd just as soon shoot you as look at you. You shook 'em up pretty good before, so watch your step."

I smiled. "Thanks, but I'm not worried. I've got you to watch my back."

He nodded dubiously. "Yes, sir."

Heading for O'Brian's office it occurred to me I should be grateful to the little Jap assassin down in the emergency ward. By showing up when he did, he gave me something in the way of a reason for moving Sally out of Letterman instead of leaving her here as bait. Well, Davis might not think it's as legitimate a reason as I did, but by that time the deed would be done.

Doctor O'Brian was anxious to hear what was going on with his patient. "First, you'll be happy to know Doctor Rothenberg is flying a qualified nurse up to accompany Miss MacLure to her new location."

"Good. I was concerned about that. When will you be moving her?"

"I would like to leave at oh-eight-thirty tomorrow. Can you make whatever preparations are necessary for the move by then and have an ambulance ready at the rear entrance of this building to transport Miss MacLure to Crissy as inconspicuously as possible?"

O'Brian nodded. "I want to make it clear, Major Spicer, that I do not endorse this move. I understand, however, why you believe it is necessary, so I'll cooperate as fully as I can."

"Your concern for your patient is duly noted. Thank you, Doctor O'Brian."

A few minutes after 1800 hours I was in yet another of Letterman Army Hospital's telephone booths. Susan answered after the first ring.

"Hiya, Angel. How are you doing?"

"Everything's fine, here, Johnny. What about up there?"

"We're all set here. The arrangements for your flight are all made. An Army Air Force transport will pick you up at the municipal field there at ten o'clock tonight, give or take. So you'll recognize it, the aircraft is silver with military markings, two engines, and twin tails. Your pilot's name is Captain Stu Irvin. He's a little rough around the edges, but Stu is damned fine pilot. I can vouch for that personally."

"Good. Thanks for making sure I'll have a safe flight."

"I should warn you, though, Stu is a kidder and he fancies himself a lady's man. He also knows he's transporting the Major's Lady and is expected to behave himself or I will personally shoot him."

Susan thought that was cute. "The Major's Lady appreciates you looking out for her honor. What's the weather like up there?"

"Clear and cool. You should have a smooth flight, but bring a jacket. Oh, and please use my car for your drive to the airport tonight. Doctor Rothenberg said he would arrange for an ambulance to transport Sally to the clinic, but I'll need transportation."

"Okay, darling. I take it Sally is our patient?"

"Yes, Sally MacLure." I sighed. It was time to clarify some things. "Susan, you ought to know that Sally has sort of a crush on me."

"Oh?"

"Yes, it's more of an attachment resulting from the fact that I've been her protector for several days. It doesn't help matters that she was once in love with the man who shot her this morning. He was an enemy agent. He used Sally as an information source, and then dropped her.

"He shot her? That's awful!"

"Fortunately, she doesn't know that part yet, but she does know I love you and there's no room in my life for anyone else. I wanted you to be aware of all that in case Sally says something to you."

"Thank you for telling me, darling, but I'm not worried about it in the least." Tactfully changing the subject, Susan asked, "Will you be at the field when I land up there?"

"You bet I will! Be prepared for a passionate welcome."

"Oh, my! I will be sure to wear my favorite shade of Kissproof lipstick."

On my way upstairs, I thought about the conversation I just completed. My "confession" to Susan went well. It should have because I had nothing to confess. I told her about Sally because the situation was a lot easier to explain now than it would have been if Sally said something about me to Susan, which I was certain was going to happen at some point.

I relieved Russ, and when he went off to catch a few hours' rest in the nurse's lounge, I checked on Sally. Even though I walked from the door to her bedside quietly, she sensed me there and opened her eyes. Her expression was a little panicky at first.

"It's okay, Sally. I'm just checkin' on you to be sure you aren't having any wild parties in here."

She had to think about that for a moment or two. Then she said, "No, I don't think sho."

Sally was still doped to the eyeballs. I hated seeing her that way, but when she coughed a moment later and I saw the pain on her face, I decided the medications were a necessary evil.

"Can I get you anything, Sally?"

She looked at me blankly for what seemed like a long time before saying, "You're Johnny."

"That's right. Russ and I are here keeping watch to make sure nobody bothers you."

"Rush?" She looked around the room without moving her head. "Is he here too?"

Her slurred speech was new. It made me suspect that the contents of the hypo I'd returned to O'Brian ended up in Sally after all.

"Yes. Russ is taking a short nap, but he'll be back in a while. A nap would be a good thing for you, too. Why don't you close your eyes and get some sleep until Russ gets back?"

Sally looked up at me. "You're shweet. I love you."

Her voice trailed off as she said the last part and her blue eyes disappeared behind drooping eyelids. I left Sally's room to stand guard out in the hallway and contemplate how and when I was going to explain our change in plans to General Davis.

Twenty-Two

0100 Hours – Saturday – 7 MAR 42

Crissy Army Airfield, San Francisco

I leaned on the Dodge's left front fender and waited. The Dodge was parked next to Crissy Army Airfield's main hangar and I was waiting for Stu Irvin to deliver the love of my life.

As I awaited the familiar drone of the AT-7's twin Wright Whirlwind engines, I thought about how different the field looked now from the way it looked when Stu and I flew in nearly blind Friday night. Tonight, the sky was mostly clear and there was a half-moon throwing nearly enough light on the field to cast a shadow.

The crisp, cold air sent me digging for my overcoat in the trunk when I first got out of the Dodge, but a little chill in the air was preferable to buckets of water, particularly if you're, as Stu described it, "making a night landing on a postage stamp surrounded by obstacles."

As always, I heard Stu coming long before I saw his AT-7, and when I did see it, the only visible parts were a bright landing light inboard of the engine on each wing. Stu was already lined up with the runway and descending smoothly. He let the ship sink slowly until the wheels made gentle contact with the ground and the ship's weight settled onto the main landing gear. No bounce, no fuss. It was a perfect landing. Stu was showing off.

He taxied to a stop in front of the hangar and shut down his engines. Next, the hatch popped open near the rear of the fuselage and I saw Stu hanging the rudimentary three-step boarding ladder from the opening. Stu didn't bother with the ladder for us, but Susan was getting the royal treatment.

By the time Susan appeared in the hatch opening, I was below it and ready to help her down. She gave me a smile and stepped onto the ladder. When she reached the second step I put my hands on her waist and swung her around and to the ground.

"Whee! That was almost as much fun as flying."

We kissed like two lovers who hadn't seen each other in years. I noticed Stu standing next to the AT-7's tail with a look of impatience on his mug. I figured a little praise might improve his mood, so I asked Susan a question I knew would get the right sort of response.

"Did Captain Irvin give you a nice smooth trip up?"

"Oh Yes! He even let me sit next to him in the front so I could watch him fly the airplane."

Grinning, I said, "Stu's a ham. He likes an audience."

"Hey, spook, I got your lady here in one piece and on time. I don't want to hear any complaints."

"You, won't, Stu. Thanks."

"You have a time for the litter flight yet?"

"Yes." I glanced at my wristwatch. "In about eight hours. The patient should be here before oh-nine-hundred."

Stu shook his head. "No rest for the wicked. I'd better have the ship fueled now so I can get some sleep. Goodnight, Miss Jackson."

"Goodnight, Captain Irvin, and thank you again for a very pleasant flight."

"My pleasure, ma'am. G'night, spook."

"Goodnight, hotshot."

I carried Susan's bags, an overnight case and a black doctor's bag, to the Dodge, where we shared another kiss. Then I pointed us toward Letterman. "I'm afraid you'll have to get what sleep you can at the hospital. Sergeant Pierce has been watching over the patient and it's my turn to do a shift."

"That's okay, Johnny. Will you tell me something?"

"Sure."

"Why did Captain Irvin call you 'spook?' Is that like a nickname or something?"

"Not exactly. Spook is Army slang term for spy. He knows I'm not a spy, but he calls me that to get my goat."

"Oh. Another question?"

"Okay."

"Is someone really trying to kill my patient?"

"I'm afraid so. They've tried three times so far. The last attempt was about nine hours ago."

That detail surprised her. "Gracious! How is she holding up emotionally under that strain?"

"Better than she probably has any right to. Sally's scared out of her wits, but she's not giving up. Of course, they have her drugged to the eyeballs right now, which results in a lot of confusion for her."

"I see. Doctor Rothenberg will want me to look into that. He advocates only using enough pain medication to keep the patient comfortable. Any idea what they're giving her?"

"The only medication I know about for sure is Nembutal. When a Jap agent took a shot at her last night, the first thing Doctor O'Brian wanted to do was shoot her with 150 milligrams of the stuff."

"On the surface, that doesn't seem appropriate, but I don't want to say that for certain without knowing more about her condition."

"I stopped the nurse from giving the injection and caught hell from O'Brian. I'm pretty sure, though, all I did was delay the shot."

Susan laughed. "Who do you think you are, Doctor Kildare?"

"Yeah, all I need is a white coat and a stethoscope hanging around my neck."

"You'd look cute in a doctor outfit."

"Sure, I would."

"If we are going to the hospital, there may be some questions about me from the nurses there, so I should explain a couple of things I don't think you and I have ever talked about."

"All right, shoot."

"I am what is technically known as a Registered Nurse." With a note of pride in her voice, she continued, "That's the highest level in the nursing field. In my case, it means I earned a Bachelor of Science degree in healthcare from an accredited university and I've passed California's strictest licensing tests for nurses."

"What school did you go to?"

"UCLA. This little gold pin below the red cross on my apron is from there. It's sort of a prestige thing, but it means something to other nurses. I'm telling you all this because nurses at any hospital tend to be a little touchy about strangers coming in. If anything is said, I just want you to know I have legitimate credentials."

"Plus, you have earned the Johnny Spicer seal of approval."

Susan laughed. "Gee, do I get a pin for that?"

"Nope, you get a ring, the one you're wearing on your left hand."

Susan held her left hand up so light from the streetlamps made my mother's engagement ring sparkle. "And your approval means more to me than any degree or license."

At Letterman, I led Susan upstairs. We stopped at the nurses' station in Sally's ward. I asked for Nurse Martinez. The nurse on duty gave Susan an appraising look, and then went off to find her boss. From her expression I got a pretty clear idea about what Susan explained to me in the car.

Nurse Martinez is the head nurse on the swing shift. In addition to that, she's head of the "Let's Lynch Spicer" movement. I guess I couldn't blame her too much for that since she was also the hysterical nurse I told to shut the hell up after the Jap took a shot at Sally. Nurse Martinez came to the counter, looked at Susan, and said to me, "What do you want, Major Spicer?"

"I want to introduce you to Susan Jackson. She will be responsible for Sally MacLure's care after oh-eight-thirty today. Until then she will be observing the patient."

Martinez took another look at Susan, paying particular attention to the tiny gold UCLA pin. She said, "University of California, Los Angeles, huh? I heard they were starting a nursing school there, but you're the only alumna I've encountered."

Susan smiled. "Then I will do my best to uphold the honor of my school."

"Where are you working, Jackson?"

I held my hand up. "That's enough of the third degree, Miss Martinez. I only intended this to be a courtesy call, not an inquisition."

"That's Missus Martinez, Major."

Slowly looking her up and down, I said, "Now there's a surprise for you."

Nurse Martinez gave me a glare that would have put a lesser man in his grave. As she stomped off, I smiled and Susan said quietly, "Johnny, be nice."

"I'll work on that. Let's go relieve Russ."

In the hall outside Sally's room I introduced Susan to Russ. "Susan, meet Staff Sergeant Russ Pierce. Russ, this is Susan Jackson."

Russ smiled. "Good evening, Miss Jackson. It is a real pleasure to finally meet you after all the good things Major Spicer says about you."

Susan smiled back at Russ. "Why, thank you, Sergeant, but you shouldn't believe everything Major Spicer says about me. He tends to exaggerate sometimes."

"Not that I can see, Ma'am."

Susan looked at me. "You didn't tell me Sergeant Pierce is a charmer."

"That's because he doesn't spend much time trying to charm me. Russ, you are relieved. Go get some rest and come back in, say, three hours."

"Yes, sir. Nice to meet you, Miss Jackson."

"And to meet you, too, Russ."

As Russ walked down the hall toward the nurse's lounge, Susan said, "He seems like a nice fellow."

"He is, but more important, he's a damned good soldier."

Susan acknowledged that comment with a nod, and then said, "May I see my patient now?"

Holding the door to Sally's room open, I said, "Might as well."

Sally's eyes were open as we walked toward her bed. She looked at Susan with curiosity.

"Hello, Sally. I'm glad you're awake. I brought someone for you to meet."

Before I got any further with the introductions, Sally said slowly, but with less difficulty than earlier in the evening, "You're Susan, aren't you?"

With a friendly smile, Susan said, "Guilty as charged."

By way of explanation to Sally, I said, "The three of us are going on an airplane trip in a few hours. Susan is here to make sure your flight is comfortable. When we get to our destination, she will be taking care of you."

Sally looked excited. "An airplane trip? Where are we going?"

"That's a secret for now, but I promise you will like being there."

Sally's eyes went back to Susan. "You're beautiful."

Susan took that unexpected comment perfectly in stride. "Thank you, Sally. We'll have to share beauty secrets sometime because, even in here, you're radiant." Then Susan turned to me and said, "Would you mind waiting out in the hall, Johnny? I'd like to give Sally a quick examination, preferably without interruption from the nursing staff."

"You've got it. I'll just shoot any Letterman nurses who want in."

Setting her doctor bag in the edge of the bed, Susan opened it and said, "You do that."

Everything was deathly quiet out in the hall. Hospitals can be spooky places in the wee small hours. It's one of the few times of the day when the hallways aren't busy with nurses, orderlies, and doctors running hither and yon on life and death missions.

Fifteen or twenty minutes later Susan joined me in the hall. "Sally's quite a gal."

"You two getting along all right?"

"We are, and stop worrying, Sally didn't declare her love for the dashing Major while I was with her."

"I'm not exactly worried, but you have to admit it's an awkward situation."

"Maybe, but it happens all the time. People form attachments to those who help them, like male patients falling in love with their nurses."

"Oh, swell."

Susan grinned. "What's eating you? That worked out pretty well for us."

"I'm sorry, Angel. I'm just on edge. In the past thirty hours or so I've killed one man, put another in this hospital, and damn near lost the woman I'm supposed to be protecting . . . twice. My disposition will improve when we're aboard Stu's AT-7 and leaving San Francisco behind us."

Susan linked her arm through mine. "I understand, darling, even though I can't imagine the risks you take. I think you could use a vacation."

I laughed. "I agree. Now all we have to do is convince a general in Washington of that."

She shook her fist in the air. "Let me at him. I'll give him what for!"

Things got moving a little after 0700 hours. Doctor O'Brian showed up and conferred with Susan for most of an hour. They came out of his office laughing like the best of friends. I don't know how she does it, but Susan has a knack for winning folks over. Whatever it is probably engenders a higher level of cooperation than my approach of threatening to shoot 'em if they don't do what I say.

A few minutes after 0800 hours an orderly informed me there was an ambulance at the rear entrance to the hospital to transport Miss MacLure. He and another fellow lifted Sally onto a gurney, attached her IV bottle to a carrier, and, with Russ, Susan, and I in close attendance, wheeled Sally down to the waiting transportation.

By 0830 the ambulance, along with my Dodge, was parked alongside Stu's AT-7. It took some jockeying around to get Sally's stretcher through the ship's narrow hatch, but it was accomplished without dumping the patient on the ground. In addition to Sally, there was also a stack of folders, X-ray films, and other documents having to do with Sally's condition. With the paperwork aboard, Susan climbed in with her doctor bag and sat in a seat across the aisle from Sally. To that load Stu and I added my B-4 bag and Susan's overnight case.

When the loading was completed, and the ambulance was pulling away, Russ and I held a quick conference. I said, "Your destination is Santa Barbara." I handed him a card on which I'd printed the clinic's telephone number and Sally's home number. "Memorize these numbers and destroy the card. Call me at the first number when you get into town and I'll give you directions to your final destination. The second number is Susan's. It's not likely I'll be there, but just in case."

"Got it, sir. I'll be on my way in a couple of hours."

"No need to rush, Russ. Get yourself some rest before you hit the road."

"I'm fine, sir. I could leave right now."

"Rest. That's an order, Sergeant."

"Yes, sir."

From the AT-7's hatch Stu yelled, "You comin', spook?"

"Yeah, keep your shirt on, hotshot."

Russ offered me his hand. "Good luck, sir."

I shook his hand. "Same to you, Russ. See you soon."

Stu pulled the hatch closed while I sidled by Susan and Sally. Stu said, "You gals ready to do some flyin'?"

Susan nodded, but her eyes were on Sally, who said, "Won't somebody please tell me where we're going?"

Stu chimed in, "Yeah, spook, it might be a good idea if you let me in on that particular secret, too."

I said, "Geez, you guys are pests. Stu, we're going back to Santa Barbara Municipal. Susan, you can fill Sally in from there."

She threw me a mock salute, and I followed Stu up the narrow aisle to the cockpit. Stu slid into the pilot's seat, and as he put his headphones on, I said, "Okay, if I join you?"

"Up to you, but you look like you've been rode hard and put away wet. You need some sleep."

"Maybe when we're on our way, assuming you can find our destination without me."

"Hell, Spicer, I just found it without your help a few hours ago. I think I can do it again."

"We'll see. Let's go."

Our route took us down the west side of the coast mountain range, so we could see the surf rolling over the beaches to our right. The compass on top of the instrument panel indicated a magnetic heading of 150 degrees during most of our flight, or at least the part of it I stayed awake for.

When I found myself drifting off for the third time, I told Stu he was on his own and worked my way back down the narrow aisle to find a comfortable sleeping position in the passenger cabin. First, though, I walked back to Susan's seat and said, "How's the patient?"

Susan said, "Ask her yourself. We're keeping the medications to a minimum and it's making a big difference."

I stepped past Susan's seat, so Sally could see me. "How's it going, Sally?"

"Good, thank you, Johnny. The air bumps hurt a little, but I'd rather have a little pain now and then than that constant confusion about where I am and what's happening to me."

"I understand. I'm not a big fan of pain, and when I was Susan's patient a few years ago, I was lucid—or as lucid as I ever get—most of the time, but I don't recall being uncomfortable. Besides that, the clinic is in a beautiful location with lots of pine trees and swell views of the ocean. Being able to enjoy the setting was a big incentive for me to drag myself out of bed and be more active."

"It sounds wonderful. Johnny, thank you for getting me out of that Army hospital and into Susan's clinic."

"You're welcome, but there were several people involved in making it possible for you to be at Casa Sobre El Mar, particularly Doctor Rothenberg, who owns the place. I also suspect Susan might have had a little to do with it. The point is, you've got a bunch of good folks on your side, so concentrate on healing so you can go walking in the pines."

"Thank you, Johnny. Or should I call you Major Spicer now?"

I looked at Susan. "I don't know. Let's ask the boss. Angel, what should she call me?"

Susan chuckled. "I don't see anything wrong with 'Johnny.' As I remember, that is your name. Right now, though, I'd call you dead on your feet. We'll have plenty of time for chats later; go sit down and get some sleep."

I leaned over and kissed her forehead. "Yes, boss."

Twenty-Three

Santa Barbara Municipal Airport, Goleta

It's a darned good thing no in-flight emergencies requiring my attention occurred before we got to Santa Barbara. I was out like a busted light bulb and didn't rejoin the living until Susan shook my shoulder, saying, "Wake up, darling, I think we're about to land."

The ambulance Doctor Rothenberg promised was not only there, but they drove it right out to the AT-7 on the aircraft parking ramp to simplify loading. I hated to leave Sally unguarded while I found my car, but it couldn't be helped. Carrying Susan's overnight case and my B-4 bag I hurried to the spot where she parked my Buick Sedanette.

After giving the speedy little coupé a quick going over to make sure nobody left me any surprises, I hurried to catch up with the ambulance, which was just pulling out of the terminal area. Susan was sitting in the back with her patient and waved to me through the rear window.

Santa Barbara Municipal Field is actually in the community of Goleta, north of town and Rothenberg's clinic is in Montecito at the south end of Santa Barbara, which is a distance of about fifteen miles. Under normal circumstances the trip takes about half an hour, but we arrived during the lunch hour and, judging by the traffic, everyone in town had lunch dates. It was 1320 by the time I followed the ambulance around the service road to one of Casa Sobre El Mar's rear entrances.

I parked nearby and made a thorough inspection inside and outside the clinic. When I was satisfied there were no immediate threats, I found Sally's room. She was in the new wing, which has the same outdoor ambiance as the rest of the clinic. Rustic wood paneling on the walls and skylights helped large windows let the outside in. The place has a tranquil feeling about it that must certainly contribute to healing.

The door to Sally's room was closed, so I leaned against the hallway wall to wait. A male nurse, Roger, who remembered me from when I was there as a patient stopped to say hello and tell me Doctor Rothenberg and Nurse Jackson were giving the new patient a brief physical exam preparatory to beginning her treatment.

I thanked him, and Roger asked if I'd had lunch. I said I had not, and he promised to send me a sandwich from the kitchen. I thanked him again. No more than five minutes later an orderly arrived with a chicken salad sandwich, which I washed down with a small bottle of milk.

Around 1415 Sally's door opened, and Doctor Rothenberg followed Susan out into the hall. Susan waved at me as she rushed off to take care of business. Rothenberg, however, stopped to chat.

"Welcome, Major Spicer. It looks as if you made the trip without difficulty."

"We did, Doctor. How's your patient?"

"Tired, but that's to be expected. She's weak and she's had a lot of excitement during the past day or two. Nurse Jackson is setting up a meal schedule and ordering a few tests. Also, I have a few questions I hope you can answer."

"I'll do my best, but please understand Sally is at the center of a very hush-hush operation and there may be some subjects I can't address directly."

"Understood, Major Spicer. I would like Nurse Jackson to sit in on our discussion, if that's all right with you."

"It's fine with me. My only concern is I want to be able to see Miss MacLure's room at all times. I have some help coming, but he won't be here until tonight, so until then, I've got the duty."

A look of concern landed on his face. "Are you expecting there to be trouble here, too?"

"No. The main idea for moving Sally here is to conceal her from the enemy, but her safety is my responsibility and I'm taking no more chances."

He nodded, but I could tell I had not entirely alleviated his concern. "All right. The room next to Miss MacLure's is empty at the moment and there is a connecting door between the rooms we can open. Will that work?"

"That should be fine. May I take a look inside Miss MacLure's room while we're waiting for Susan?"

Rothenberg nodded. "Certainly. I think Miss MacLure would benefit from knowing you're here."

I walked into Sally's room and found her in the bed with the blankets pulled up around her neck. "Hi, Sally. How are you doing?"

"Hi, Johnny. I'm fine, except they stole my hospital gown. I haven't got a stitch on under these covers, so no peeking."

"You have my word. What do you think of Doctor Rothenberg?"

Nodding enthusiastically, Sally said, "I like him very much. Best of all, he speaks English, not doctor-talk so I can understand what he's telling me."

"I've always liked that about him."

While we were talking, I gave the room a thorough inspection. The head of her bed was against the wall to my left as I entered. The connecting door Rothenberg mentioned was in the opposite wall. The wall across from the hall door was partially covered by a pair of large curtains. I looked behind the curtains and found they concealed two picture windows overlooking a grove of pine trees and the Pacific Ocean beyond an access road that completely circled the clinic. I remembered taking my first walk outside among those pine trees along the bluff when I was a patient at Casa Sobre El Mar.

I held the curtains open. "Here you go, Sally, the view I promised you."

"Wow! It is really beautiful here."

"It is. Unfortunately, we'll need to keep these curtains closed most of the time, especially after dark. Just tell Russ or me when you need a scenery break and we'll open the drapes."

Leaning forward for a better look, Sally said, "I understand, Johnny. I didn't see Russ on the plane."

As I closed the curtains, I said, "Russ is driving down so we'll have the Army's Dodge in case you want to go joyriding. He should be here sometime tonight."

"I'm afraid joyriding in that Dodge is out for a while. I doubt if I could manage the front seat right now, let alone those little seats in the back."

"Okay, scratch joyriding off the list for now."

"I sure am a pain in the neck to you fellows."

"True, but you're a cute pain in the neck, so we put up with you."

Sally stuck her tongue out at me. At the same time there as a knock on the connecting door and a nurse followed by an orderly carrying linens poked their heads into the room from the hallway. Sally's room was suddenly a busy place.

I opened the connecting door and found Susan on the other side. "Ready to meet with Doctor?"

"I am. I was just making sure there were no bad guys hiding in the closet."

She grinned. "Sure, you were." To Sally she said, "If Major Nuisance, here, bothers you, just ring your bell. Nurse Roger knows how to deal with him."

Leaving the room, I heard Sally say, "Thank you, Susan. I'll remember that."

The room next to Sally's was laid out just the reverse of her room. To give us a little more space for a table, the bed was turned ninety-degrees and pushed up against the wall opposite the connecting door.

A small round pedestal table was now standing close to the open connecting door with three wooden chairs arranged around it. Doctor Rothenberg already occupied the chair facing the hall. I sat opposite the connecting door and Susan took the remaining seat across from Rothenberg. There were a few sheets of blank paper, some printed forms, and a pencil in front of Susan.

Rothenberg started things off. "Major Spicer, the questions I want to ask concern the patient's injuries. Can you give me an idea how they happened?"

As soon as I began speaking, Susan started taking notes. Attempting to be thorough, I spoke in the same manner I'd used on many occasions when giving testimony in court. "Yes. I'll begin by repeating the patient's account of the first incident since I did not witness it personally.

"Miss MacLure is a production engineer at a Los Angeles aircraft plant. Her office there is on the second floor with windows overlooking the assembly lines. Late in the afternoon on Friday, 27 February, a bomb was detonated in the room directly below her office.

"While several employees were injured in the explosion, Miss MacLure received nothing worse than a bump on the head. However, in her haste to leave the building, she tripped going down the stairs. That's when she broke her right arm. The fall also resulted in a gash on the side of her head and apparently did some minor damage to her right knee. She was treated at Freeman Hospital in Inglewood and released the following morning."

Doctor Rothenberg said, "Yes, from talking with her, I believe she broke her radius and possibly her ulna as well. Susan please make note of the date Miss MacLure injured her arm and order an X-ray, so we can see how those breaks are mending."

"Yes, Doctor."

To me Rothenberg said, "Now, when and how did Miss MacLure sustain the chest wound?"

My eyes were on Sally through the connecting door. I looked away when the nurse helped her into a fresh gown. Even so, I got a quick peek at the dressing on her chest. There seemed to be an awful lot of gauze and tape there.

"The wound in her chest was caused by a round from a high-powered hunting rifle around oh-eight-hundred hours, or eight in the morning, last Friday, 7 March. She was shot from a distance of between twenty and thirty yards."

Susan flinched when she heard that, and Doctor Rothenberg shook his head. They were hearing stories from an entirely different world than the one in which they lived.

"Miss MacLure was immediately rushed to Letterman Army Hospital, which was close by. Her emergency surgeon was Doctor Paul O'Brian, with whom you have already spoken. He described her condition as fair after performing surgery to repair the most critical damage. I believe you have the X-rays and his report."

Rothenberg nodded. "Yes, I've seen them, but I want to spend more time studying the films and reports. Can you add anything else that might help us determine the best plan for Miss MacLure's recovery?"

Sally noticed me looking at her and gave me a little wave. I nodded in reply.

To Rothenberg, I said, "Perhaps. There was a third attempt on Miss MacLure's life yesterday afternoon. This one occurred in her room at Letterman Army Hospital. A Jap . . . an assassin attempted to shoot her with a large caliber revolver from the doorway. Fortunately, I was in the room at the time and was able to prevent the assassin from completing his mission. He got off a shot, but it went into the wall above Miss MacLure's bed.

"I'm telling you about this incident because it may help explain Miss MacLure's mental state. She has a lot of what I call spunk and covers her fear well, but under it all I know damned well she's terrified. Who wouldn't be after all that?"

Rothenberg nodded again. "Your point is well taken, Major Spicer. We will do everything we can to make her feel secure here, but I'm afraid we must all depend on you for her safety from the outside world. Based on my personal experience, however, I can think of no one I would rather have watching out for me, were I in her shoes."

I noticed Susan nodding when he said that. "Thank you for your confidence, Doctor, but in all fairness, I have to say we are up against a very capable enemy. I would be lying if I told you I'm not concerned."

"Well, do not hesitate to tell us if there is anything we can do here to make your job easier."

"Thank you, Doctor. Some help will arrive tonight—a fellow in whom I have a lot of confidence."

"Anything that relieves some of the pressure you are feeling right now is a positive thing. I think I know you well enough to appreciate your state of mind. I do not envy you, Major Spicer."

With that, Doctor Rothenberg excused himself and left the room. Susan put her hand on my arm, softly saying, "After hearing all of that, I can easily see why Sally formed an attachment to you. You have been her anchor in a terrifying storm. That poor woman has been through hell."

"Yes, she has, and that's a shame because Sally's a good kid."

Chuckling, Susan said, "And I knew she'd be cute."

Feigning surprise, I said, "Is she? I hadn't noticed."

Now Susan was laughing. "You, sir, are a lousy liar. Go take care of your cute blonde. I have work to do."

She stood up and kissed me on the cheek. With that fortification, I walked through the connecting doorway.

As I entered her room, Sally asked, "Is everything okay, I mean between you and Susan?"

Looking out into the hallway to be certain there were no Jap killers lurking out there, I said, "Everything's fine. She thinks you're cute."

"Did she say that?"

"She did."

"Is Susan angry at me?"

"No. There is no reason for her to be angry with you."

As I moved the curtain out of the way for a look outside, Sally said, "Johnny, Susan is an angel, just like you said. I want to be her friend."

"Good. I think she feels the same way. Did that nurse who was in here tell you what they have in mind for you next?"

Finally taking the hint, Sally said, "She promised they would bring me some lunch in a few minutes. That sounds good because I'm actually a little hungry."

"Great! The kitchen here is first class, not at all like the usual hospital fare. It helps if you can look forward to meals."

As promised, an orderly arrived carrying a tray with lunch for Sally. While she ate her soup and some lightly buttered toast, I stayed on my feet trying to look in all directions at once. After lunch, Susan showed up with the same orderly to wheel Sally to the X-ray laboratory. I followed along, and Susan introduced me to the X-ray technician. That done, I gave his lab a good look before stepping outside to wait.

Back in Sally's room, Susan drew three vials of blood, attached labels identifying whose blood was in the vials, and gave them to the orderly for delivery to a blood laboratory somewhere nearby. That, more or less, is how we passed the afternoon—testing, measuring, and putting numbers on charts.

By 1700 hours I began to relax a little, but only a little. Sally relaxed a lot and fell asleep. Susan and I stepped out into the hall. Shaking my head, I said, "You know, I'd forgotten how much there is to all this."

Susan smiled. "That's not surprising. You slept through a lot of the work we did in your case, but Doctor is known for his thoroughness. He says every little piece of information makes a difference, and in Sally's case we need every advantage we can get."

"Not good?"

Cocking her head slightly, Susan lowered her voice and said, "I think 'tricky' is the best word for it. I was looking over Doctor's shoulder when he studied the X-rays from Letterman and the ones we got this afternoon. If that bullet had gone half an inch to the right, Sally never would have survived the trip to the hospital. We'll have to wait for Doctor Feigenbaum to look at the films, but Doctor Rothenberg thinks some of what he calls 'plumbing'—blood vessels—will have to be replaced because they were weakened by the bullet and the temporary repairs made by Doctor O'Brian during emergency surgery."

That surprised me. "Can they do such a thing?"

"Yes, cardiovascular surgeons have been experimenting on blood vessel repair since the Great War, and the rate of success is getting better. At first, they used donated human blood vessels, but more often than not human tissue was rejected by the recipient's immune system. Now they are using tubes made of a synthetic fabric the recipient is not as likely to reject. That happens to be Doctor Feigenbaum's specialty, so he's Sally's best chance of survival."

"How soon would an operation like that be performed?"

"Very soon. There's no telling when one of Sally's major blood vessels might fail. We have to constantly watch for signs of internal hemorrhaging."

"No wonder Doctor O'Brian wasn't in favor of moving Sally."

"And that's why Doctor insisted on me escorting Sally down here. If she had hemorrhaged on the flight, her life would have depended on whatever I could do while getting her to a hospital for surgery. That could have had a very bad outcome."

"I see. Now I wonder if I should have left well enough alone and let Letterman care for her."

"For what it's worth, Doctor thinks you made the right choice, and I agree. At least here she stands a fair chance of getting through this. Another gunshot or some other trauma of this magnitude would mean the end of Sally."

Looking through the doorway at Sally sleeping, I said, "Thanks for the support, Angel. It helps. When is this Doctor Feigenbaum going to look at her?"

"Tomorrow morning. Doctor Rothenberg spoke with him by telephone a little while ago. I wouldn't be surprised if they scheduled the surgery for tomorrow afternoon. The only things that might delay things any longer are the availability of the synthetic blood vessel material and Doctor Feigenbaum's nurses. He has a team of surgical nurses he works with and they have to get here from Los Angeles."

Nodding, I said, "I don't know how you stand the pressure of this life or death world where you hold the fate of patients in your hands."

Susan thought for a moment, and then said, "I think it's a lot like you and Sergeant Pierce. You said you have confidence in him. That means you can depend on him. I have confidence in Doctor Rothenberg and the other nurses here. We depend on each other for help making good decisions and for coping when our decisions don't work out the way we hoped. Yes, it hurts to lose a patient, but when that happens, I have to remember the ones like you who made it because we did the right things. Does that make sense?"

"It does. Say, isn't it time for you to go home and get some rest? Mister Whiskers is probably hungry."

"I put out some extra kibble for him when I left last night. He won't starve to death. I was thinking of waiting until Sergeant Pierce gets here so we can go home together."

"I'd like that, but Russ may not be here until late. I told him to get some rest before he left San Francisco."

"I think I'll take my chances. Should I order up some dinner for us and we can dine with Sally?"

"Dine? Gosh, don't forget the candles."

"Careful there, Major. You're askin' for trouble."

"The oath says you are to do no harm."

"Doctors take that oath, not nurses."

With that she gave me a playful punch in the arm and headed off down the hallway. I walked into Sally's room and took a peek out through the windows. It was nearly dark, but I saw nothing in the shadows to worry about. When I turned around, Sally was watching me.

"Hi, Sally. Sorry if I woke you."

In a voice so quiet I almost didn't hear her she said, "You didn't."

Her eyes were red and puffy. "Are you feeling okay? You need something for pain?"

"No, I'm okay."

"Well, something's upsetting you. If you want to talk about it, I'll listen."

"I'm just afraid. I heard Doctor Rothenberg tell one of the nurses to watch for signs of hemorrhaging because one of my blood vessels could rupture. He was telling the nurse what to do if that happened. It didn't sound good. Now I'm afraid to move. Johnny, I'm not going to make it, am I?"

I had to tell her something and I hoped what I was going to say was the right thing. "Sally, I'm not going to lie to you. Susan says your situation is tricky, but she also says the doctor coming in to see you tomorrow is the best in the blood vessel business. He can perform an operation to replace those weak blood vessels. You are in good hands and you're going to make it just fine."

That started the tears. "No, I'm not. You're just trying to cheer me up."

"Hey, Sally, think about it. Would I be wasting my time keeping you safe if you weren't going to make it?"

Sally gave me a glare that startled me. In an angry voice she said, "You would if I'm bait to catch your Dragon Lady!"

Susan came into the room just in time to hear that comment. Sounding just as angry as Sally, Susan said, "I happen to know Johnny risked a court martial by moving you here. His boss is the one who wants to use you as bait. Sister, Johnny is the best friend you've got. You need to get straight on that."

Sally looked from Susan to me. "Is that true, Johnny?"

"Yes, it's true."

Sally said, "Oh, Johnny, I'm sorry. I'm so confused."

Susan spoke up again. "That's partly a side effect of the pain medication. Some food will help, and your dinner is on the way. Johnny and I are going to have dinner with you tonight. Is that okay with you?"

Sally nodded, and Susan said, "Good. Johnny, will you please move that table from the adjoining room in here with a couple of chairs so we don't have to eat standing up?"

Grateful to be off the spot, I did as requested. I'd no sooner gotten the table and chairs moved when an orderly showed up pushing a cart with three dinner trays on it. Dinner was hardly a gala event, but Susan got Sally to eat and I needed no prompting to gobble up the meatloaf, a small baked potato, and even the pile of string beans on my plate.

After dinner, Susan consulted the chart hanging on a hook at the foot of Sally's bed. She left and came back in carrying a hypodermic syringe.

"Sally, I'm going to add a little pain medicine to your intravenous line. It will make you feel better and a little sleepy. Don't fight it. Some sleep will do you some good. Johnny and I will be right here. Okay?"

Sally nodded. As Susan injected the medication into the IV tube, Sally said, "Johnny, I am really very sorry for talking to you the way I did. Will you forgive me?"

I put on a smile I didn't feel. "You've done nothing to be forgiven for. In fact, you're doing a lot better with all this than I did under similar circumstances."

She looked a little less glum. "Really?"

I looked at Susan. "Tell her, Angel."

"Oh yes. The brave Johnny Spicer was a really pain in the neck when he was here." Gesturing toward the windows, she added, "For two cents I would have pushed him off that cliff out there."

Sally actually managed a little smile. "I'm glad you didn't."

Susan returned her smile. "Me, too."

I spent the next hour or so pacing the room to stay awake. Another long day was catching up with me. Susan was in and out of the room taking care of chores, but she kept a close eye on Sally. Each time she checked on her patient she looked at me with a small nod to let me know all was okay.

Around 1930 hours Susan was checking on Sally again when an orderly stopped at the hallway door. "Major Spicer, you have a telephone call. It's a Sergeant Pierce."

I thanked the orderly and Susan said, "If you don't want to leave Sally, I can take Russ's call for you."

"That might be a good idea I told Russ to call when he got to town for instructions on how to get here. It's early, but knowing Russ, he might have left the Presidio sooner than I expected."

"Sure, Johnny. If he's calling for some other reason, I can take a message for you."

"Thanks, Angel."

Susan came back a few moments later. "You were right. Russ is in town. I gave him directions, and in a few minutes, I'll go out to the lobby to meet him and bring him back here."

"Thanks. It might also be a good idea if you showed him around the clinic a little, so he gets the lay of the land. And please introduce him to anyone you think he needs to know."

"Will do."

It was about 2015 when Russ walked into Sally's room with Susan. "Good evening, sir."

"Good evening, Russ. Everything is under control here, how about where you came from?"

"As far as I know everything's quiet up there, too. Sir, it might not be any of my business, but are you planning to tell General Davis what's going on?"

"Yes. I'm not planning to tell him where we are, but things might go a little easier if I gave him some kind of report."

"That's what I was thinking, sir."

"All right, I'll be back in about six hours. Will that work for you? If you need me, I'll be at the second number I gave you."

"That will be fine, sir."

With Susan snuggled up next to me in my little Buick coupé, I made my way across town to State Street. There, I pulled up to a pay telephone at a Chevron service station.

Susan said, "I was wondering if you needed to make a telephone call."

"Yes. I've put it off as long as I can."

"It's not going to be an easy call, is it?"

"Right again."

She leaned over and kissed me on the cheek. "Good luck, darling."

Before stepping into the telephone booth, I went into the station office and got several dollars' worth of change. A direct long-distance call from a public telephone can sometimes be traced, but it's a slow process. Hoping for the best, I got the operator on the line and placed my call.

When the MID telephone operator in Washington answered my call, I identified myself and asked for General Davis. She said he left for the day. I said, "Then make this a Priority Able call."

The time it took to get Davis on the line cost me about a buck. "Spicer what the hell are you trying to pull? I've had people looking all over Letterman and not only can they not find you, they cannot find Miss MacLure. Am I to understand you deliberately disobeyed an order?"

"General, the only way I would ever disobey an order would be deliberately and with good reason. I moved Miss MacLure out of Letterman for two important reasons. First, less than eight hours after her admission, the Japs already knew she was there. To make matters worse, one of them tried to kill her right there in her damned hospital room. Thankfully I was there and stopped the guy before he shot her, but it was damned close.

"Secondly, there are too many entrances to Letterman and so much traffic through them, it is impossible to effectively secure them. The place just doesn't work as a trap."

"Seems to me it worked just fine. You caught a Jap agent, didn't you?"

"That was pure luck."

"So where is our bait now?"

"Damned close to death from the last time she was shot, and scared out of her wits."

Davis was quiet for several seconds. "Not going to tell me, huh?"

"No, sir, I'm not. You've told me on several occasions I should go with my hunches because they are usually right. I'm following that advice to the letter now."

"What if I order you to tell me where she is, Spicer?"

"You can try that, sir, but this long-distance telephone connection is so noisy, I doubt very much I could understand what you said."

"And you know this tomfoolery puts you at the front of the line for a General Court Martial, right?"

"It does that only if you have lost faith in my ability to size up a dangerous situation and act in the best interests of our country."

That seemed to give him pause for more thought. Finally, Davis said, "Major Spicer, it's against my better judgement, but I'm going to give you 48 hours to resolve this issue. If you have not called me by this time Monday night with answers to my questions, consider yourself relieved of duty and you can expect an arrest warrant to be issued in your name. Got that?"

"I've got it, General Davis."

The next thing I heard was a distant click and the line went dead. I tapped the receiver hook a couple of time to signal the operator I was through with my call. She came on the line and told me to deposit another two dollars and forty cents. I made it with fifteen cents to spare.

On the way to Susan's apartment I gave her a blow-by-blow account of my conversation with Davis. She sighed. "Johnny tell me one thing. Why are you putting your neck on the line for Sally MacLure?"

"Because I'm responsible for the mess she's in. If I'd been smarter about all this, she'd be back at North American counting B-25s as they rolled off her assembly line and Dragon Lady would be pushing up lotus blossoms."

She shook her head. "Of all the men in the world, I had to pick one with a conscience."

"I'm sorry to be a disappointment, Angel."

Susan kissed me. "You aren't a disappointment, Johnny. In fact, seeing this side of you, it's entirely possible I love you more than before, and I think lotus blossoms are Chinese, not Japanese."

Twenty-Four

0230 Hours – Sunday – 8 MAR 42

Casa Sobre El Mar, Santa Barbara

When I got up around 0130, I insisted Susan stay in bed and get more sleep. After a shower and donning fresh civvies, I was ready to go. Actually, where I was ready to go was back to bed.

The first thing I did when I got to the clinic was hunt down a cup of coffee. After a few swallows of Java, I went in search of Russ. He was right where he was supposed to be.

"Good morning, sir."

"If you say so, Pierce. Personally, I haven't had enough coffee to see anything good about it yet."

"You could have gotten more sleep, sir. I'm doing fine here."

"I don't doubt that, but we can't afford to cut corners. You've done more than your share for one day. Go get yourself some rest."

"Yes, sir. Ah, where should I go?"

I fished some of our expense money out of my wallet. "The Biltmore where you and Sally stayed last time you were in Santa Barbara is just up the road a little bit. Get yourself a room for a few nights."

Russ handed the money back to me. "I still have most of what you gave me a couple of weeks ago."

Shoving the bills back into my wallet, I said, "Hell, I forgot to ask the most important question. How's our patient?"

"Sally seems fine. The nurses checked on her about every thirty minutes all night. I don't think she woke up more than once."

"Good. Before you leave, let's step out in the hall for minute."

Sally looked as if she was asleep, but I didn't want to take a chance on her hearing what I needed to tell Russ. When we were out of earshot, I said, "I have a couple of pieces of information to pass along. First, Susan briefed me on Sally's condition earlier. She described it as 'tricky'. Some of Sally's blood vessels are damaged and they need to be repaired or replaced.

"A specialist is supposed to be here this morning to examine Sally and look over her X-rays. Susan said if they decide to operate, it could be as soon as this afternoon. In the meantime, there is a constant danger that a blood vessel will fail. That's why they're watching her so closely."

"That doesn't sound good. I guess we took a hell of a chance flying her down here."

"Yeah, I thought that, too, but Susan told me Doctor Rothenberg says it was the right thing to do."

"Good. That makes me feel a little better."

"Also, I called Davis after I left here last night. He already knew I took Sally out of Letterman. Needless to say, he was not a happy general."

Russ frowned. "Oh, oh."

"He wanted to know where she is, and I didn't tell him. That ticked him off even more, so I now have 48 hours from last night to resolve all this with him or I'm relieved of duty and up for a general court martial."

"Holy cow! Do you think he'd actually do that?"

"He expects loyalty from his troops and I'm not being a loyal little soldier, so yeah, I think he's mad enough to actually toss me in the stockade and throw the key away, at least for a while."

"What can we do, sir?"

"Start by forgetting that 'we' stuff. The only thing you're guilty of is following my orders. I've made sure of that from the start and you'll want to keep it that way. This is my problem and I'll figure something out. Meanwhile we have to keep our priorities straight and that means keeping Sally alive."

Russ said, "Yes, sir," but his expression told me he saw my problem with General Davis as his, too.

"All right, Russ, that's all I've got for now. Get some rest and come back around oh-eight-hundred. We might have a busy morning."

"Yes, sir. See you at oh-eight-hundred."

I killed the next four hours or so pacing around Sally's room. At roughly 0630 the clinic woke up and got to work. A nurse came in and helped Sally wash up. I stepped out into the hall for that activity. After a spit bath, the nurse drew fresh blood from Sally's arm for another round of tests.

Next on the agenda was a breakfast of toast and chicken broth. I was sorry I told Sally how good the food was because she sure wasn't getting any of the good stuff. I, on the other hand, received a plate of scrambled eggs, a small slice of ham, and buttered toast.

With breakfast taken care of, Sally's nurse told her to relax for a while. An orderly would be in to take her for X-rays of her arm soon.

When we were alone again, I walked over to the bed and said, "Good morning, Sally. How are you doing?"

"Hi, Johnny. Have you been here all night?"

"Nope. Russ got here and took over, so I could get some sleep."

"Oh, good. I don't remember seeing Russ."

"He said you slept right through the night. That's a good thing."

Sally shrugged. "I guess so. All this waiting around is aggravating."

"I understand, but things should pick up before too long. Your specialist is due in this morning sometime. I'm not sure when."

I'd heard Susan's footsteps in the hall, so I wasn't surprised when she walked in and said, "Doctor Feigenbaum is expected at nine. Happy morning, Sally."

Sally said, "Good morning," while I got a kiss on the cheek from Susan.

To me, Susan said, "Mister Whiskers tells me I should instruct you on proper feeding protocol. He expects breakfast when his humans get up, either of them."

Puzzled, Sally asked, "Who in heaven's name is Mister Whiskers?"

I laughed. "Mister Whiskers is a big orange tomcat who rules the roost at Susan's apartment."

With a smile, Sally said, "Oh, you have a kitty? I've been thinking about getting one when I get back home." After a short pause, she added, "If I get back home."

I said, "You will get back home, and when you do, get yourself a cat who knows you're the boss. I don't think Susan trained Mister Whiskers properly."

Susan said, "Darling, you have a lot to learn. You don't train cats. They train you."

"Phooey!"

Sally said, "I think she's right, Johnny. And they're pretty clever about it, too."

"I repeat, phooey."

Doctor Rothenberg walked in and said, "Good morning all. What are we 'phooeying' about?"

I muttered, "Cats. Good morning Doctor."

Rothenberg nodded. "I see. Would I be correct if I were to guess a certain Mister Whiskers prompted that comment?"

Sally looked surprised. "Do you know Mister Whiskers, too, Doctor?"

Stepping closer to Sally's bed so he could apply his stethoscope, the doctor said, "My dear, everyone who is anyone in Santa Barbara knows Mister Whiskers. Take a deep breath please."

Susan winked at me and I stepped out into the hall where I could keep an eye on things without being in the way. Before long Doctor Rothenberg left and an orderly showed up to take Sally back to X-ray for more picture-taking. I followed along behind Sally's gurney.

The X-ray technician was the same fellow I met yesterday. Again, I waited out in the hall while X-ray pictures of Sally's arm were made. Then we trooped back to Sally's room, where I found Russ waiting for us. Russ was wearing his uniform. That seemed like a good idea. It gave him an air of authority and allowed me to hang out around the edges of things without being especially noticeable.

While Sally and Russ chatted, I followed Susan out into the hallway. "How is our patient this morning?"

"Well, I think between us we managed to raise her spirits a little."

"Yeah, she was pretty glum earlier."

Susan nodded. "It may be that keeping her spirits up is the best thing we can do for her right now."

"If worst comes to worst, I'll call Mister Whiskers, so she can talk with him. I bet he'd make her smile."

That earned me a laugh. "I bet you're right."

"On that note, I think I'll take a look around outside. Would you please tell Russ where I've gone?"

"Sure. Have a nice walk."

I left the new wing by way of its backdoor and strolled along the access road surrounding the entire facility. I was looking for anything out of the ordinary—something that didn't seem to belong where it was—and I was coming up empty.

The only excitement outside was some gardening taking place out in front. Two follows in coveralls and floppy straw hats were on their knees weeding a narrow strip along the perimeter of the parking lot, apparently preparatory to doing some planting. I concluded this because there were a couple of wooden flats of white flowers with yellow centers on the ground nearby. I remembered my mother planting something similar and calling them daisies.

They were hard workers. In the short time I watched them they cleared about four feet of their planting area and began industriously poking daisies into the ground. I decided detective work fit my temperament much better than anything requiring that much manual labor.

After completing my circumnavigation of the clinic, I stood on the front porch puffing a Lucky Strike and watching a black Cadillac limo that looked to be about a block long pull up to the main entrance. The driver jumped out and quickly came around to open the rear passenger-side door. The fellow who climbed out was short, bald, and a trifle portly, but the creases in his charcoal gray suit pants were sharp enough to slice butter and a pair of wire-rimmed specs gave him an intellectual presence.

To his driver, the new arrival said, "I expect to be here quite a while, so make yourself comfortable."

Closing the door behind the man, the driver said, "Yes sir, Doctor Feigenbaum."

The learned doctor walked briskly past, giving me only a brief glance of the sort important people reserve for those with whom they clearly have nothing in common. He did it so well I would have been insulted had I not been trying my damnedest to look like someone with whom Doctor Feigenbaum clearly had nothing in common.

I did a slow ten-count, and then followed him into the lobby and along the corridor that led to the new wing. As I passed Mary's reception counter I heard her tell someone on the telephone that Doctor Feigenbaum had arrived and was on his way back.

Doctor Rothenberg moved his office to the new wing when it was completed, so I figured that was where Doctor Feigenbaum was heading. Upon learning my guess as to his destination was correct, I continued on to Sally's room, which now contained only Sally and Russ.

Russ was adjusting Sally's pillow for her. She saw me and said, "Hello, Johnny. Susan told us you went for a walk."

"She was correct. I went out to see if I could catch a chipmunk as a playmate for Mister Whiskers, but they were all too quick for me. How are you?"

"I'm fine, thank you. Russ was explaining the difference between blimps and dirigibles to me. He's quite knowledgeable on the subject."

I smiled. "He should be. Russ flew two-thirds the way across the country in a blimp not long ago."

Looking at Russ, Sally said, "Oh, you did? That must have been really fun."

Russ shrugged. "Not too much. Those blessed things only go fifty or sixty miles per hour. Traveling two thousand miles in one took darn near forever."

Still excited about blimp travel, Sally said, "Yes, but cruising along at a leisurely pace you got to see so much of the countryside."

"Actually, what I got to see were the tops of a lot of clouds, and after seeing one cloud, you've pretty much seen them all."

"Oh, you!"

I said, "If I may be permitted to change the subject a little, I just witnessed the arrival of Doctor Feigenbaum."

Sally sounded even more excited about that than she did about blimps. "He's here?"

"Yes, he is in Doctor Rothenberg's office. I suspect they are conferring about your case."

Sally asked, "Does he look smart?"

"Very smart." Turning to Russ, I said, "Russ, I'm going melt into the background for a while, so I'll let you handle things here."

Russ shot me a questioning look. I said, "No problems. I just want some time to do a little checking on Doctor Feigenbaum and his driver."

"Okay, sir."

I hurried back along the new wing corridor to the lobby. There, I approached Mary's reception counter. "Hello, Mary."

"Hello, Mister Spicer. Isn't this a lovely day?"

I hadn't really noticed what sort of day it was, but I remembered lots of sunshine and warm temperatures from my earlier outing, so I said, "Yes. Very pleasant."

"May I help you with something?"

"Well, yes, a small thing. Actually, two small things."

Her eyes lit up. Mary liked helping people.

Do you know the man who arrived about ten minutes ago?"

"Doctor Feigenbaum? Yes, I know him."

"You've seen him before?"

"Oh, yes. He's been here many times. I think Doctor Feigenbaum is a good friend of Doctor Rothenberg's."

"Good. I just wanted to be sure of who he is. Now, the second thing. Do you know Miss MacLure, the new patient who arrived yesterday?"

Mary thought about that for a few seconds. "No, not really. I mean I've heard her name, but I haven't met her or anything."

"That's fine. If any calls come in for Miss MacLure, I need you to fib a little and tell the caller you have no patient by that name, and if you can do it without sounding too interested, ask the caller for their name in case Miss MacLure should be admitted. Also, if such a call comes in, please let me or Sergeant Pierce know right away. Okay?"

"Sure, Mister Spicer. Do you want me to tell the evening operator to do the same thing?"

"Yes, please. I don't want to make a bigger deal out of this than it is, but we're trying to keep Miss MacLure's whereabouts quiet until she's better. Okay?"

"Sure. I'll do exactly what you said."

"Thanks, Mary. You're tops in my book."

That set Mary to giggling. "Oh, Mister Spicer, I bet you say that to all the girls."

Smiling, I said, "Only the pretty ones."

Having thus cemented a lifelong friendship with Mary, I went outside and looked for the big black Caddy limo. It was parked on the far side of the lot overlooking the beach below. The Caddy, however, was backed into the parking spot so the driver could watch for his employer's return. Said driver was leaning against the driver-side fender studying the seagulls circling overhead. He was probably hoping none of them bombed the immaculate limo.

The fellow didn't miss much. He lost interest in the seagulls and was watching me a little warily as I approached. Borrowing a line from Mary, I said, "Nice morning."

He gave me a single head nod and continued studying me. I gave him a little more to work with. Offering my hand, I said, "My name is Johnny Spicer."

As we shook hands, he said, "Gary Henson."

"Mister Henson, I'm with the US Army Military Intelligence Division. Here's my identification."

He looked at my MID ID without comment and said, "How can I help you, Major Spicer?"

"First, I would appreciate it if you would keep this

conversation between us. We don't need to create a fuss if there is nothing to fuss about."

Obviously curious, Henson said, "Okay."

"I'm here in connection with Doctor Feigenbaum's patient. She is a government witness in an espionage case. My question for you is have you seen anyone unusual hanging around your employer or following you to the clinic, maybe this woman?"

Henson studied Marjorie Yount's mug shot and shook his head. "No, I haven't. I can say that with some assurance because, besides being the doctor's driver, I am also his bodyguard, so I pay particular attention to our surroundings."

"Good. I have no reason to suspect the doctor is being followed, but I wanted to put you wise to the situation. Forewarned is forearmed."

"Thanks, Spicer. If I see anything unusual, are you usually here at the clinic?"

"For the time being I am. Do you mind if I ask you a question purely out of curiosity?"

He chuckled. "You want to know why a retired doctor needs a bodyguard, right?"

"You guessed it."

"Well, to be honest, he probably doesn't need a bodyguard these days, but there have been times in the past when he did. As you've probably guessed, the doctor is Jewish. He is very involved in improving the plight of German Jews and helping Jewish refugees escape from Germany. That makes him unpopular with the Nazis."

"I can see how it would."

"On two different occasions they tried to do him in. I was a detective sergeant with the LA Police Department then and happened to be nearby when the second attempt on his life was made. I nailed the Nazi, but I took a round in the hip.

Even though I get around pretty well, the department had to furlough me on a disability. Doctor Feigenbaum offered me a lifetime job at a salary I could not afford to turn down, so here I am."

"Great. Good to see one of the hometown boys make good. Before the Army got me, I was a private cop in Hollywood. Say, I bet you know a friend of mine at the Sixth, Detective Sergeant Mackie?"

Henson got a big grin on his face. "C. K.? Sure, and his boss, Bobby Winfield. Great guys. I was last assigned to the Fourth, Hollenbeck, but I still got out to Hollywood once in a while."

The former detective sergeant and I were playing the "who do you know that I know" game to check each other out. He played the game well and we agreed to get together for a drink sometime.

I felt pretty good when I headed back into the clinic. Whether he knew it or not, I had an ally in the parking lot if more trouble than Russ and I could handle turned up. An armed ally, at that. I can spot a shoulder holster a mile off.

There seemed to be a convention going on in Sally's room when I got back. I stayed out in the hallway and took inventory. The crowd included Doctor Rothenberg, Doctor Feigenbaum, Susan, Russ, an orderly, and of course, Sally.

The doctors seemed to be discussing surgical strategies and Sally wore a wide-eyed expression. That was a shame. The girl needed reassurance, not a litany of all the things that could go wrong.

When the conference ended, the doctors left the room. Feigenbaum noticed me in the hallway. That this was the second time he'd seen me registered with him. I wondered if he would be curious enough to ask Rothenberg about me.

The next to leave Sally's room was Susan. She was carrying a clipboard and stopped to update me.

"Well, surgery is scheduled for tomorrow morning. Doctor Feigenbaum wanted to do it this afternoon, but one of his surgical nurses is ill, so they need a replacement for her, and the replacement can't get here until tomorrow morning. Doctor Feigenbaum isn't happy about not having both of his usual nurses, but he feels we need to move ahead without any further delay. His primary nurse, however, will arrive tonight to make sure we prep Sally according to Doctor Feigenbaum's liking."

"Okay, thanks. Sally looked terrified in there. The doctors must have scared the daylights out of her."

Susan nodded her agreement. "Yes. That was Doctor Feigenbaum's doing. He insisted on talking through the entire surgery in front of Sally. Doctor Rothenberg kept trying to steer him out of the room to continue the conversation elsewhere, but Feigenbaum wouldn't take the hint. He may be a brilliant surgeon, but his bedside manner leaves a lot to be desired."

"I'd say so." Looking into Sally's room, I saw Russ talking like a Dutch uncle about something, but Sally wasn't having any of it. "It looks as if Russ isn't having much luck improving her mood. Should we give it a try?"

Susan held up her clipboard. "I have some details for tomorrow to attend to before the rest of the day gets away from me. Why don't you see what you can do?"

I sighed. "I'll have to look at my job description sometime and see if it includes patient morale boosting."

Susan smiled. "It should. You're better at it than most doctors I know."

Scowling at her, I muttered, "Horse feathers," and walked into Sally's room.

Russ saw me first and gave me a frustrated look. I said, "Russ, go take a turn around the parking lot and get some fresh air. Oh, and introduce yourself to the guy who drives Feigenbaum's limo. He's a former LA cop by the name of Gary Henson. Nice guy."

All Russ said before leaving the room was, "Yes, sir."

I turned to Sally. Her eyes were puffy and red. "What's going on? Did Doctor Feigenbaum upset you with all his doctor talk?"

"Now I know for sure I'm not going to make it. This is awful! I don't know what to do."

"Well, it seems to me, the first thing you have to do is point your thinking in the right direction."

Sally looked up at me with a pitiful expression. "I don't understand what you mean."

"Try looking at it this way: Feigenbaum is the best in the business and he certainly isn't a guy who wastes time on lost causes. If he didn't think you could make it, he'd be on his way back to LA by now. And remember, he's doing this pro bono. He doesn't make a dime whether you live or die."

"He doesn't?"

"Nope. In fact, my impression is he's bound and determined to get you well and he isn't going to take 'no' for answer. It's like you are a personal challenge to his skill and knowledge."

"You think so?"

Fibbing a little, I said, "I do. He as much as said so a while ago. Now, what kind of cat are you gonna get when you're home again, a Siamese, a Persian, or a good old American alley cat?"

"Oh, definitely an alley cat. He'll remind me of you."

Twenty-Five

Casa Sobre El Mar, Santa Barbara

After lunch I sent Russ back to the Biltmore for a little more sack time. That meant I was pretty much confined to Sally's room and the immediate area around it for several hours. With Sally sleeping and Susan off doing nurse stuff, it wasn't long before boredom set in.

Boredom is one of the biggest hazards of stakeouts and guard duty. It dulls the senses and sends your mind wandering off to other places it has no business being. To stay sharp, I concentrated on thinking of ways Dragon Lady could sneak into the clinic and kill Sally.

Actually, I thought of several ways it could be done. Casa Sobre El Mar was no fortress by any means. Our first line of defense was secrecy. I was counting on it taking Dragon Lady a while to figure out where I'd taken Sally. Of course, that assumed Marjorie Yount was still hunting Sally after three failures—four if you count Dragon Lady's attempt to kidnap North American engineer Michael Wilkins from his home near Mines Field.

It was possible her bosses reassigned her. On the surface that might sound like a good thing, but it was anything but good. If Marjorie Yount was reassigned, the Japs would put someone else on the case. That was bad because whoever they assigned would be an unknown. Better an enemy you know than one you don't.

Sally moaned and cried out. I quickly went to her bedside. She appeared to be asleep, but she was moving around a lot in the bed, so I guessed she was having a nightmare. Torn between letting her toss and turn and waking her up, I noticed the "nurse button" hanging over the headboard of her bed.

Casa Sobre El Mar had all the latest gadgets and gizmos, and this one was a humdinger. When a patient pushed the little red button at the end of a cord by their bed, several things happened. First, a light began flashing on a console at the nurses' station. Each room had its own light on the console, so the nurses could quickly see who was calling for them. The flashing light was accompanied by an annoying buzzer that would quickly bring someone to the station if there was no one there.

At the same time a light outside the patient's room goes on so a nurse in the hallway could immediately see who needed help. I pushed the damned button.

Susan arrived in less than a minute. I said, "Sorry to bother you, but Sally seems to be having rather violent nightmares. I didn't know if waking her was the thing to do."

Susan put her hand on Sally's shoulder and shook it gently. "Under the circumstances waking her is best. We don't want her jerking around this way."

It took a surprising amount of shaking to wake Sally, which I presumed was probably due to the medications she was receiving. Finally, she groaned, and her eyes flickered open.

Susan said softly, "Hi Sally. You were having some nightmares. I thought you might like to wake up for a little while."

Sally's eyes darted around the room anxiously. "Oh, God, it's awful!"

Susan said, "It was just a dream, Sally. You're awake now and it's all over."

Sally stared at her. "No! No, it isn't over! They're still trying to kill me. I know they are!"

I was standing on the opposite side of the bed from Susan and she looked up at me. I reached down and took Sally's left hand. "We don't know that for sure, Sally. And even if they are, that's why I'm here. Anyone who wants to get to you has to get past me and Russ first, and that isn't an easy thing to do."

She looked at me for a long moment, and then she surprised me by asking, "Johnny, do you have . . . do you have your gun?"

I opened my sport coat so she could see my shoulder holster. "I do, even though I'm pretty sure I won't need it."

Seeing the Smith & Wesson under my coat apparently reassured her. Sally relaxed and squeezed my hand. "Thank you, Johnny. Please stay close by."

"I've been here just about the whole time, and when I wasn't here, Russ was. We've got you covered, kiddo. All you have to worry about is getting well. We'll take care of the rest."

Sally's eyes were drooping. She started to say something but drifted off to dreamland before she got the words out. At least I hoped she drifted off to dreamland and not back to nightmare land.

Susan signaled me to follow her out into the hallway. "I was hoping letting her get some sleep would reduce the anxiety and fear, but they're very strong."

"I'm not surprised. Hell, I have nightmares about Dragon Lady, and I'm not even the one she wants to kill."

Placing her hand on my shoulder, Susan said, "I know, darling."

I was wondering just how Angel knew I had nightmares about Dragon Lady when a movement up at the lobby end of the hallway caught my eye. I turned to see an orderly leading a nurse I didn't recognize in our direction. Susan said, "Oh, that's Frances Hughes, Doctor Feigenbaum's head surgical nurse. Fran is one of the best in our business."

Nurse Hughes was an older woman, perhaps in her late forties or early fifties. Her hair was short and gray. Her eyes were bright and blue. Her smile was warm and friendly. "Susan! It's so good to see you again."

The nurses embraced each other, and Susan said, "Welcome to Casa Sobre El Mar, Fran. This is your first time here, isn't it?"

"It surely is. What a lovely place! If there are any openings on your staff, give me an application!"

They both laughed, and then Susan said, "Fran, I want you to meet Johnny Spicer. Johnny, meet Nurse Frances Hughes."

As I smiled and said, "A pleasure to meet you, Frances," Susan held up her left hand and wiggled her ring finger. At the same time, she pointed in my direction with her right index finger.

Fran's eyes brightened. "Oh? Well, how about that? Johnny, you must be a pretty special fellow. I happen to know Susan wouldn't accept anyone but the best."

"Thank you, Frances. I don't know if I'm special or just darned lucky."

"Maybe both. Forgive my curiosity, Johnny but what is it you do that requires a shootin' iron?"

I was careless about remembering to button my sport coat after showing Sally the Smith & Wesson, and my jacket hung open a little when I leaned forward to shake hands. Apparently, Nurse Frances didn't miss much.

Susan came to my rescue. "Johnny is a major in the Army's Military Intelligence Division. They decided they couldn't fight this war without him. Our patient is a witness in his care."

Frances Hughes seemed impressed. "My goodness. I'd best mind my Ps and Qs!"

Susan winked at me. "I don't think you have anything to worry about. Johnny has a soft spot in his heart for nurses. He hardly ever shoots them."

Frances laughed heartily. "Well, I'm certainly glad to hear that!"

Changing the subject, Susan asked, "Would you like to meet your patient?"

"Please." She gestured toward Sally's door. "In here, I presume.?"

I waited in the hallway while Susan and Frances went into Sally's room. I also buttoned my jacket.

I heard Susan say, "Sally, I want you to meet Nurse Frances Hughes. She works with Doctor Feigenbaum."

Frances said, "Hello, Sally. How are you feeling?"

I wondered why nurses and doctors always ask that question. They shouldn't have to ask, they're supposed to know how their patients are feeling. Nonetheless, Sally groggily answered her. "Hello, Nurse Hughes. I'm okay, thank you."

"Well, Sally, we're going to make you feel much better than okay. Your surgery is scheduled for tomorrow morning and I'm here to help you get ready, and that includes answering any questions you might have."

"Thank you, Nurse . . . Nurse Hughes. Do you really think you can make me better?"

I saw Frances take a quick glance at Susan before she said, "I do, but I will not lie to you. The surgical procedure Doctor Feigenbaum will perform for you is not by any means simple or easy and there is some risk involved, but he is the best cardiovascular surgeon in the business. I've seen him perform many a miracle."

Sally simply said, "I see."

Susan chimed in. "I know you're worried, Sally, but you have a knowledgeable and experienced medical team on your side."

Sally asked, "Is Johnny here?"

Frances glanced at Susan again and said, "Major Spicer is right out in the hall. Nurse Susan and I are going to take care of a few pre-operation chores for you now. I expect he'll come in to see you when we leave."

I did. Sally held out her left hand and I took it. "What do you think of Nurse Frances? I like her."

"She's okay. Will you be here tomorrow morning?"

"You bet I will. Russ will be here, too."

Sally nodded, and her eyelids drooped. A few moments later I felt her grip on my hand weaken and I lowered her arm to the bed.

Around 1600 hours Susan and Fran returned to Sally's bedside. Nurse Roger and an orderly pushing a cart loaded to the gunnels with linens and medical paraphernalia followed closely behind them. The first thing they did was change Sally's bedding. That required rolling her to one side and then the other. Despite their care in moving her I heard Sally moan in pain.

Next, Sally's blood pressure, temperature, and heartrate were recorded yet again. Nurse Roger drew more blood samples and the orderly hurried them off to the lab. After that, Nurse Roger left the room and closed the door.

I asked, "How's she doing?"

Nurse Roger said, "They're inserting a urinary catheter because she won't be able to use a bedpan for a while."

"As I remember catheters aren't much fun."

He shook his head. "No, they aren't. They're also somewhat risky because they can cause infections. It will be removed as soon as possible after her surgery."

"What other fun and games does Sally have in store for her?"

"Well, once the catheter is in, we'll remove the dressing from her wound to clean and disinfect the area thoroughly. After that we'll apply a temporary dressing that can be removed easily for the surgery."

"There's a lot to this, isn't there?"

"Yes, there is. You were lucky. You were out like a light while we did all this for your surgeries."

"Roger, if I'd been lucky, I would have ducked sooner and avoided the bullet in the first place."

He grinned. "Well, there is that."

Sally's door opened, and Susan said, "Okay, Roger, we're ready to remove the dressing."

Roger said, "Looks like they can't get along without me in there. See you later, Mister Spicer."

The door to Sally's room was closed for quite a long time. Meanwhile, Russ showed up. "Good afternoon, sir."

"Hi, Russ. They're starting to get Sally ready for her surgery tomorrow morning."

He nodded. "That can't be much fun."

"No, I don't think it is. We also have a new nurse. Her name is Frances Hughes, and she's Doctor Feigenbaum's head surgical nurse. Susan knows her and says she's a nice gal. So far, I agree with Susan."

Russ nodded, and a young fellow came hurrying along the hallway in our direction from the lobby. It took me a minute to recognize him. He was Mary's nightshift replacement at the reception desk. His expression warned me I was about to hear something I really didn't want to hear.

"Mister Spicer, Mary just gave me your instructions about what to do if someone calls asking about Miss Sally MacLure."

"Yes?"

"Well, I'm afraid the horse is already out of the barn."

Frowning, I asked, "What the hell is that supposed to mean?"

"Somebody called asking about her last night."

Russ looked alarmed and I said, "Swell. What did you tell them?"

"I followed our usual instructions for surgical patients. I told her Miss MacLure was a patient but was only allowed visits from family members for the time being."

"Her? The caller was a woman?"

"Yes. She said her name was Mary Adams."

I sighed. "All right. Thanks for letting us know."

"You're welcome, sir."

As he jogged off back to the lobby, Russ swore. "Damn! Dragon Lady knows Sally's here."

"That's my fault. I didn't think to give them instructions about Sally until today. As the fellow said, the horse was already out of the barn by then."

"How do you want to handle this, sir?"

"We need to step up our security, that's for sure. I think one of us probably needs to be outside the clinic at all times. That might give us some advance warning if trouble shows up. We can switch off between Sally's room and outside. Of course, we don't know who we're watching for, but if you see Dragon Lady, herself, don't hesitate. Shoot to kill."

Russ was wearing his thoughtful look. "But why would she show up instead of sending someone else? She must know we've identified her."

"Sure, she knows. Dragon Lady is even taunting us by using an alias on the telephone we're sure to know. That makes me wonder if she's been ordered on a suicide mission. The Japs do crazy stuff like that. As I said, do not hesitate. Shoot that woman on sight.

"You take the first shift outside. I need to tell Susan what's going on. Come back here in two hours and I'll spell you. And not a word of this to Sally. She already has plenty to worry about."

"Yes, sir."

Russ headed out and I mentally kicked myself several times for not talking to Mary at the reception desk about Sally the moment we got to the clinic. I dropped the ball and now all we did to get Sally undercover was shot to hell.

Worse, there was no way Russ and I alone could provide the kind of security we needed now that there was a clear threat. The clinic grounds were too large and secluded. We needed more manpower and to get it, I had to let Colonel Beecher in on the gag. If he knew General Davis was after my hide, I was done. I might as well cut out the middleman and call Davis directly.

Suddenly the door to Sally's room opened and everyone came trooping out. Susan took one look at me and whispered, "Johnny, what's wrong?"

I wasted no time in coming to the point. "I'm sorry, Angel, but I messed up. Dragon Lady knows Sally is here."

Her expression said more than her words. "Oh, no. What can we do?"

The truth was I had only one option, to call General Davis and confess my sins. Any other course of action was too risky. "Russ and I can't keep this entire complex secure by ourselves. I have to call General Davis and ask for some help."

"After your talk with him last night?"

"I don't have any choice. He'll bail me out of this jam, and then permanently assign me to a desk in a basement somewhere."

"He won't do that. You're too valuable to him."

I shook my head. "Not when I disobey orders and mess up on top of it."

At that point Frances Hughes surprised us by joining the conversation. "It might be none of my business, but from what I just overheard, I'm guessing there is a problem. Can I help?"

Susan looked at me and I said, "No, I don't think . . . ." Suddenly seeing Nurse Hughes gave me an idea. "You know, maybe you can help. Do you know where Doctor Feigenbaum is tonight?"

She gave me a questioning look. "Certainly. He's spending a few days at his summer home, which is just a few blocks from here."

"Do you think Gary Henson is there, too?"

Her expression changed to puzzled. "Gary Henson? Oh, you mean Doctor's driver. Yes, I imagine he is. What are you getting at?"

"Fran, we have a minor crisis brewing here. I have reason to believe a Japanese agent has discovered where Sally MacLure is and I won't have the manpower to protect her properly for a few days. Talking to Henson yesterday, I learned he is a former Los Angeles police officer. That's just the sort of fellow I need to help me out. Do you think Doctor Feigenbaum would loan me his driver for a day or two?"

She thought for a moment, and then said, "If the situation is as serious as you say and Mister Henson is willing, I don't see why Doctor Feigenbaum wouldn't go along with it, especially if I call and make the request on your behalf." She smiled. "I'm pretty good at talking Doctor into things. When do you need Mister Henson here?"

"Right now, wouldn't be too soon."

"Then I will call Doctor posthaste. I'll be back in a few minutes."

As she walked off toward the nurses' station, Susan held up both hands with her fingers crossed. I said, "This is not by any means a perfect solution, but it buys me a little time. Henson impresses me as a guy who can handle himself pretty well, despite a minor disability."

"Good. I need to go take care of a couple of things, but I won't be long. Just so you know, we've sedated Sally a little more heavily, so she will get a solid night's sleep. She's going to need it."

Turning the room light off, I hardly gave Sally a glance as I walked quickly past her bed to the windows and pulled the curtain a little to the side for a look. The sun was already down and the only natural light was a faint glow on the western horizon and some pale moonlight. I took my time and looked as deeply into the shadows as I could. I saw nothing to raise my level of concern any higher than it was already.

Next, I stopped by Sally's bed. She appeared to be in a deep sleep, so I quietly returned to the hall. I hadn't been there more than a few minutes when Fran Hughes showed up with a smile.

She gave me an exaggerated salute and said, "Mission accomplished, Major. Mister Henson will be here shortly. Is there anything else I can do to help?"

"Thank you, Fran. You have no idea how much I appreciate your help. Oh, and if you are going back to the nurses' station, would you please ask the orderly to see me when he has a minute?"

Frances smiled. "Will do, and you are very welcome."

Pulling my notebook from my jacket pocket, I wrote Russ a quick note to the effect that Gary Henson would be showing up to give us a hand, and if he got there before Russ and I switched places, to please send Gary in to see me. When the orderly arrived, I asked him to take the note out to Sergeant Pierce who was outside on the grounds somewhere. Then I set what was left of my mind to work figuring out the best way to make use of our additional manpower.

That endeavor was briefly interrupted when Susan returned. Having already spoken with Frances, Susan knew help was on the way. She gave me a quick kiss on the cheek.

"I knew you'd think of something, darling. Sometimes I think I have more faith in you than you have in yourself."

"That could be because I know me better than you do."

No more than ten minutes later I saw Gary Henson walking down the hall from the lobby. The slight limp that got him furloughed from the LAPD on disability was hardly noticeable. He said, "Hi, Spicer. I met Sergeant Pierce outside. He filled me in a little on what's going on."

"Hi, Gary. Thanks for coming to bail us out."

"Sure. How can I help?"

I pointed toward Sally's room. "The witness we're protecting is in there. Jap agents have made five attempts on her life in the past ten days or so and we've been very lucky, although the outcome of one of those attempts is up to your boss at this point. What we need is help filling in the gaps so we can cover Miss MacLure's room and still keep an eye on things outside."

"Okay. And the person we're watching for is that woman you told me about earlier?"

"She's one possibility, although it could be someone else, so we're watching for anyone who looks out of place."

"All right. What's the procedure if I see such a person lurking in the shrubbery?"

"Challenge them but do it from cover. If it's Dragon Lady— the woman in the photograph I showed you—she's just as likely as not to take a shot at you. If it's her, shoot to kill. She won't give you a second chance."

He looked surprised. "She's that good?"

"You bet she is. This woman is well trained, and her past behavior proves she has no compunctions about killing anyone who gets in the way of her mission."

"Sounds like a real sweetheart."

"Not exactly the kind of girl you take home to meet mom and

pop."

"All right, what's next?"

"Have you had dinner yet?"

"Not yet. I was just thinking in that direction when Doctor Feigenbaum told me to get over here and do whatever you needed doing."

"I gotta remember to thank him for loaning you to us. In the meantime, please hike down that way about fifty feet and tell whoever is at the nurses' station that Major Spicer would appreciate it if they could order a couple of dinner trays sent to the empty room next to Miss MacLure."

With a grin, he said, "I take it this mission doesn't require shooting anyone?"

"Only the chef if you don't like your dinner."

We ate at the small table next to the open connecting door that gave me a view into Sally's room. As I devoured my last bite of some very tasty Swedish meatballs with noodles, I glanced at my wristwatch. It was time to relieve Russ.

"Gary, I hate to make you eat and run, but it's time for me to replace Russ outside. Would you please go out and tell him to come on in, and then keep an eye on things for a few minutes until I can get out there?"

"On my way."

The rest of Monday night continued along the same lines. There were no unwelcome guests, and Russ and I even managed to sneak in a few hours of sack drill. To tell the truth, though, I was a little disappointed the night went so well. The Japs were going to show up; that was inevitable, and I was anxious to get the confrontation over with. I'm not a patient guy.

Twenty-Six

0545 Hours – Monday – 9 MAR 42

Casa Sobre El Mar, Santa Barbara

Monday morning dawned with a frosty chill in the air. I knew that because I had the outside duty as the eastern sky began to lighten and I was wishing I'd worn something a little warmer than my sport coat. So, it was in the hope of generating a little warmth as much as my sense of duty that I began another brisk circuit around the clinic grounds.

My route took me in a counter-clockwise direction around the access road circling the buildings. The new wing—the one Sally was in—runs roughly north and south on the west side of the complex. After rounding the northwest corner of the loop road, I stopped and looked down the length of the new wing. I studied the area for several moments to make sure the shadowy movement I thought I saw was just my imagination playing a trick on me.

The moon was down and with the sun rising on the other side of the building, my side was dark as night, so it seemed unlikely I actually saw anything, and I was just about to move on when I sensed the movement again. This time there was no doubt. Someone or something was slowly moving toward me along the wall of the new wing. I hurried toward the side of building at my end and flattened myself against it.

The movement I'd seen was about one third the distance between me and the far end of the building. Sally's room was at the midpoint of that distance. I set off in that direction, listening and looking for all I was worth. Whoever or whatever I glimpsed was quiet as a ghost.

Making steady progress, it only took me a couple of minutes to cover half of the distance to the windows of Sally's room. I paused for a moment there and that's when I heard a faint scraping sound, something like the noise a single hung window makes when it's opened, at least that's the description my imagination came up with. It was ample motivation for me to abandon stealth for the sake of urgency.

Stepping a few feet out from the building, I drew my Smith & Wesson and broke into a trot. The ground between the building and the access road was planted with some kind of ground-covering vine that threatened to trip me up with every step. I zigzagged through it like a halfback going for six points.

I glanced up to gauge my progress just in time to see a dark trouser leg disappear through an open window about thirty feet away. I changed course slightly toward my goal, and an arm replaced the leg in the window. I had a moment of déjà vu when I made out a pistol in the hand attached to the arm, a pistol aimed at me. I'd seen something very similar in Sally's room at Letterman Hospital, except the arm was pointing through a doorway then and I was in a position to do something about it.

This time all I could do was try to step out of the line of fire. I jogged left just as the pistol's muzzle spit flame at me and ended up sprawled face down on the ground. I didn't know if dodging to the side or tripping over one of the damned plants saved me from a bullet with my name on it, but I had no time to think about it. Within seconds of the gunshot a woman screamed from inside the building.

I had not returned fire for fear of hitting Sally, but from the position of a small tree near the road I realized the gunman wasn't in Sally's room, he was in the vacant room next door. Then who the hell screamed?

A second later the answer to that question dawned on me and it made my blood turn ice cold. Sally wasn't in the vacant room, but Susan was. She'd gone in there to catch a cat nap.

I got back on my feet and moved to the window for a look but the curtain was pulled. Figuring this was a good moment for prudence, I used the short nose of my Smith & Wesson to push the curtain aside just far enough to see what was going on.

The room lights were off, but a small nightlight above the bed showed me the gist of what was going on. None of it was good. Susan was in front of the gunman and being held there by his left arm which was around her neck. The pistol, a nine-millimeter German Luger from the quick look I'd gotten when he shot at me, was pressed against the right side of Susan's head. The worst of it was I had no clear shot without the hitting Susan.

My mind raced trying to picture the parts of the situation I couldn't see. Where was Russ? Odds were he was either in Sally's room or in the hallway right outside it. There was no doubt he'd heard the gunshot and Susan's scream. The unknown was what he planned to do about it. I'd made it very clear to him Sally was his highest priority.

What about Gary Henson? The last time I looked at my wristwatch it was about quarter to six. Oh-six-hundred was the time Russ and I were to trade positions, so it was possible Henson was outside looking for me. In the still early morning air, it was hard to imagine him not hearing the shot and scream. That probably meant he was looking for the source of the sounds. I recalled telling him he should shoot to kill and hoped to hell he recognized me at the window before he got trigger happy.

I got the idea from the gunman's movements he was confused. At first, I thought he'd gone for the vacant room intentionally, but now I wasn't so sure. His attention was divided between the hallway door and the connecting door. Both doors were closed, and he looked like he might be deciding which one to use. That he didn't look in my direction led me to conclude he thought his shot through the window finished me off.

The way things stood, my only hope of a clear shot was if he went for the connecting door, otherwise he was between me and Susan, and at that close range, a thirty-eight round was likely to go right through the gunman and hit Susan too. The connecting door was hinged on the right and opened into the room, so he couldn't use his left hand to open the door without letting go of Susan. He would have to open the door with his gun hand, presenting me with his profile for a split second before the door opened far enough to shield him from my direction. The table at which Henson and I ate our dinners helped some because its position prevented the door from opening all the way into the room. I wouldn't have a completely clear shot or a long time to take it, but it was better than . . . .

The hallway door interrupted my thoughts. The door and large pieces of its wooden frame exploded into the room with a thunderous crack and light from the hall flooded the room. In what seemed like one motion, the gunman shoved Susan aside and spun toward the hall in a crouch. Susan landed on the floor and scurried under the bed.

Whoever kicked the hall door in jumped to one side, so the Jap had no target. As the gunman looked for something to shoot at, a second explosion of lumber sent the connecting door flying into the room. It tipped the table over and landed on the gunman, knocking him to the floor. The gunman got his gun hand out from under the door and swung it around in an arc, still looking for a target. I was lining up the Smith & Wesson's sights with my silhouette view of the Jap's head when Russ's Colt semiautomatic popped twice from the connecting doorway.

The best thing about a large pistol like a point-four-five-caliber Colt is that very little will stop its slug from reaching your target, including a solidly-built wooden door. The gunman, still prone on the floor, let the Luger slip from his fingers and his head hit the hardwood floor with a solid thump I heard clear over at the window.

Next Gary Henson appeared in the hall doorway and yelled, "Nurse Jackson?"

A timid voice answered from under the bed. "I'm here."

Russ said, "It's okay, Miss Jackson, you can come out now."

As Susan slid herself out from under the bed, it dawned on me I was still standing at the window with my Smith & Wesson unfired. The whole scene played out in front of me as if I was watching an Edward G. Robinson film. I'd contributed absolutely nothing to the elimination of the Jap spy.

Pushing the curtain aside slowly so nobody would be surprised and shoot at me, I said, "Nice work, guys."

Gary, Russ, and Susan all looked in my direction. Gary said, "What the hell are you doing out there, Spicer? Come on in and join the party."

Since my knees were still a little wobbly as a result of being shot at from point blank range, I decided to walk around to the new wing's rear door rather than climbing through the window. Inside, a surprisingly large crowd for that hour of the morning was forming in the hallway outside the empty room. I also saw Nurse Hughes rush into Sally's room.

Pushing my way through the folks in the hallway, I climbed over the remains of the hall door and entered the formerly empty room. Susan was sitting on the bed but when she saw me, she jumped up and ran into my arms. I held her and neither of us said a word.

Russ, however, had something to say. He picked up the Jap's Luger, and handing it to Gary, he said, "Well, let's see who we've got here."

Finding my voice, I said, "If he's not a Jap agent, I don't want to know about it."

Watching Russ slide the door from the dead man's body, Gary

said, "Well, whether or not you want to know about it, HE is not a Jap spy." Chuckling, he added, "I'm pretty sure SHE is, though. Our visitor is none other than Dragon Lady, herself."

Astounded, I looked over Susan's shoulder. There was no question about it, especially when Russ pulled the knit watch cap off Marjorie Yount's head.

Even Susan turned to gawk. "You mean that's the woman who caused Sally all the pain and suffering?"

I said, "That's her." To Russ and Gary, I said, "Thanks, guys. I'm afraid you got stuck with all the dirty work this time."

Russ stood. "I wouldn't say that, sir. If you hadn't made her take a shot at you earlier, we wouldn't have known she was here."

I grumbled, "At least we know I'm good for target practice."

Feeling the need to be elsewhere, I led Susan around the body and into Sally's room. Frances Hughes turned from Sally's bed and removed her stethoscope. "Our patient is fine." With a smile she added, "Sally slept through the whole thing."

Turning to Susan, Fran said, "How about you, Susan? Are you all right?"

"Yes, I think so. I'm afraid my knees are a little weak and I managed to scratch my arm somewhere along the line, but otherwise, I'm fine." Looking at me, Susan asked, "How about you, darling. Russ said something about that awful woman shooting at you."

I smiled a thin smile. "The Japs are better off without Dragon Lady. She was a lousy shot."

Susan said, "Thank God!"

Frances came over and took Susan's arm. "Come on, let's get you cleaned up and dress that cut on your arm. Excuse us, Johnny."

Susan looked up at me and we kissed. Frances laughed. "Here we are in the middle of a war zone and you two are smooching!"

Back in the room next door, I watched an orderly place a bedsheet over Dragon Lady while Russ and Gary moved the broken doors out of the way and into a stack by the window. Russ noticed me. "What now, sir?"

I was tempted to say, "Let's all go home," but it wasn't time for that yet. "Gary, would you mind doing outside duty for a while? I need to call Washington and I'd like Russ to stay close to Sally and Dragon Lady, here."

"I don't mind at all. Do you think anyone else will show up from the opposition?"

"I really don't think so, but they've fooled me before. It would really stink to lose our witness after all this."

Gary nodded. "Yeah, I see your point. I'm on my way."

To Russ, I said, "I'm going to call General Davis, although I'd almost rather go another round with Dragon Lady."

"I can understand that, sir. Do you plan to tell him where Sally is?"

"I don't have much choice. The only saving grace is we . . . or you and Gary nailed Dragon Lady. That might get me off the hook."

"I hope so, sir. Good luck."

Stopping at the nurses' lounge where Frances was applying a dressing to Susan's arm, I said, "How is it, Angel?"

"Not bad, just messy. I'm fine."

"You don't know how glad I am to hear that." Then, turning to Frances, I asked, "Will you be going ahead with the surgery this morning?"

She was vehement about her answer to my question. "Absolutely. Doctor Feigenbaum will be here as soon as Elsie Olson reaches his house this morning. She'll be his other surgical nurse. Doctor does not want to delay this any further."

I nodded. To Susan I said, "I have to make a call to Washington from a public telephone. I'll be back as soon as I can. Meanwhile, Gary Henson is patrolling outside and Russ is with Sally."

"All right, darling. Please hurry back."

It was going on ten hundred hours at the other end of the country and General Davis was in his office. His first words were, "Come to your senses, have you, Spicer?"

"Not really, sir. I just need to arrange for someone to stop by and pick up one dead Dragon Lady."

"Well done! I'd rather have her alive, but I was pretty sure that wasn't going to happen. I'll send a couple of agents up to Santa Barbara from LA to remove the body."

I started to reply but stopped short. "How . . . ."

"How did I know Miss MacLure was at that private clinic where your gal friend works? Hell, I figured that out practically before you got her there."

"But how?"

"It was easy, Spicer. I know you. I sat down with your dossier as soon as we knew Miss MacLure wasn't at Letterman any longer. That clinic was the most likely place for you to go, so I sent a couple of agents disguised as gardeners or some such thing to see if I was right. I was."

I remembered watching the two gardeners planting daisies around the parking lot yesterday morning. It also occurred to me I should look into that dossier Davis was talking about. I simply said, "Yes, sir."

"Don't sound so discouraged, Spicer. I put you through the ringer last time we talked to keep our little masquerade going. I figured there was a fair possibility Marjorie Yount might come to the same conclusion I did. It wouldn't do for either of us to give the game away by being complacent. You and Pierce did well."

"Terrific, sir. Now tell me how to get out of this chicken outfit."

"Only way to do that is with a Section Eight."

I pictured the smart aleck grin I knew was on the general's face. "Keep this crap up and I'll qualify. Anything else, sir?"

"Yes. I've sent you First Sergeant Tiner and a couple of his men from the Presidio, so you and Sergeant Pierce can get some rest. They'll be there this afternoon."

"I take it you want us to continue the same assignment?"

"Yes. Stick with your witnesses for a few more weeks and then you can cut 'em loose. I'll tell you when it's clear. Oh, and send me an AAR on what happened today as soon as you can."

"Yes, sir."

On the short ride back to the clinic I cursed General Dwight Davis no more than a thousand times. When I got there, Gary Henson met me at the front steps. "You'd better get in there, Spicer. Feigenbaum and his nurse arrived a few minutes ago and preparation for your gal's surgery has shifted to high gear."

"Thanks, Gary. We have some help on the way down from San Francisco. They should be here this afternoon. Can you stick with us until then?"

"Oh sure, just when things get interesting you hand me my walking papers."

Opening one of the lobby doors, I said, "Hell, stay as long as you want. You might even have another opportunity to get your brains blown out."

I didn't hear his reply. Sally's room was a beehive of activity when I got there. Susan met me in the hall.

"How did it go, darling?"

"Turns out General Davis figured out Sally was here and all that hogwash about a court martial was just camouflage to keep up the act."

"That's rotten."

"That's sort of what I thought. How are we doing here?"

Susan smiled. "Almost ready. I'm glad you got back. Your cute blonde has been asking for you."

"Is okay for me to go in?"

"Yes, darling."

Susan rushed off with her clipboard and Russ appeared at my side. "Everything okay, sir?"

"Yeah. General Davis says, 'good work' on nailing Dragon Lady, so we're off the hook. Also, he's sending that Sergeant Tiner and a couple of his men down from the Presidio to cut us some slack. Davis said they'll be here this afternoon."

"That will help."

"Yeah. Oh, do we have any After Action Report forms in the Dodge?"

"Yes, sir. There's a stack of various forms in the trunk compartment. I saw them just the other day."

"Good. Go get some rest. I can handle things here for now and Henson is outside."

"Thanks, sir. If you don't mind, though, I'd like to stick around and see how the surgery goes."

"Sure. Whatever suits you. I'm going in to see Sally before they haul her off."

Nurse Frances saw me come into the room. "Major Spicer, I want you to meet Nurse Elsie Olson. She and I will be assisting Doctor Feigenbaum this morning."

Nurse Olson was younger than Nurse Frances. She was also tall and slender with brown hair and all business. I got no smile when she said, "Hello, Major Spicer. I am very pleased to meet you."

Frances said, "Now go say hello to our patient before we take her to the operating room. She's very anxious to see you."

Nodding, I walked over to Sally's bed. She was awake, but only barely. "Johnny?"

"Yup, it's me, kiddo. How are you doing?"

"Sleepy. Are they going to do it pretty soon?"

"Yes. I just stopped by to wish you luck, but you aren't going to need any luck. You've got the best doctor and nurses in the business taking care of you."

I wasn't sure what I said registered with her. Sally just stared up at me.

"Johnny?"

"Right here, kiddo."

"Johnny, if I . . . if I don't make it, I want you to know I appreciate all you've done . . . done for me."

I started to tell her she was going to make just fine, but she wasn't through. "And . . . I . . . love you."

Leaning over, I kissed Sally on the forehead. "You, too, kiddo. You're aces in my book."

Sally whispered something that might have been 'thanks,' and having said what she felt she needed to say, she drifted off again.

I gave Nurse Frances a nod and she understood. "Good. They'll be taking her in into the operating room in a few minutes. I'm glad you got back before they took her. It was important for her to see you. You're her rock."

"Do you have any idea how long the surgery will take?"

Frances looked up at me as if she was trying to understand my thoughts. "It's very difficult to say, Johnny. My estimate would be at about two hours. Doctor doesn't like to keep patients under much longer than that."

"I see."

Just then a pair of orderlies came in and began rolling Sally's bed toward the door. Frances said, "Looks like we're on our way."

"Good luck, Fran, and thanks."

I took my usual place at the tail-end of the parade and off we went. Behind the hallway doors labeled "Surgical Theater," was a prep area where doctors and nurses dressed and scrubbed. Beyond that was the entrance to the actual operating room. All of this could be seen through large windows in the hallway doors. There was only one way in and out, and I planned to be outside that hallway door until Doctor Feigenbaum finished.

Conveniently, the operating room was across the hall from the nurses' station, where Doctor Rothenberg and Susan were deep in conversation. When Rothenberg saw me, he and Susan came over.

"Hello, Mister Spicer. I understand we had some excitement early this morning."

"We did, and Uncle Sam owes you a couple of new doors."

Rothenberg chuckled. "I'll put them on his bill. I'm just grateful our only casualty was the enemy. As Susan tells it you and your men were very courageous."

I smiled at Susan. "She was the brave one. Personally, I was scared as hell."

Susan hooked her arm through mine and Rothenberg said, "Johnny, if I may be so familiar, I'm fairly certain if you experienced fear it was on behalf of Susan."

Trying to make light of things, I said, "Oh, I was plenty scared enough for both of us."

The doctor smiled at that, but said, "I don't want to sound like an expert in the science of psychology, because I'm certainly not, but I subscribe to the theory that some people deal with frightening situations instinctively. When faced with a crisis these people shift mental gears and function automatically with very little actual thought as to what they are physically doing. I call it the 'hero quality' because it is a trait shared by all heroes. I think you are one of those people."

"If you say so, Doctor."

Susan sensed I was uncomfortable with all the hero talk, so she changed the subject. "Oh, I almost forgot. Russ came by and left some sort of form he said you needed. I put it over there behind the counter."

"Good. It's an After Action Report form so my boss will know the details of what happened here this morning. If you don't mind me taking up some space, I'd like to begin filling it out while everything is still fresh in my mind."

Rothenberg said, "Certainly, Johnny. Have at it. Susan, I will be in my office. Please let me know when they finish up in there."

Susan smiled and said, "Yes, Doctor."

Sitting at an empty spot on the desk surface that ran along the inside of the nurses' station counter. I glanced at my wristwatch. It was 0835. Taking my pencil from my inside jacket pocket, I began filling out the AAR form.

Twenty-Seven

0930 Hours – Monday – 9 MAR 42

Casa Sobre El Mar, Santa Barbara

I finished the AAR form around 0930 and got up to stretch my legs. Looking down the hall I saw some activity involving a couple of Army enlisted men, so I investigated. Russ explained the fellows were MID and arrived with a panel truck and a body bag for transporting Marjorie Yount's remains to Los Angeles. What would happen to her there, I didn't know or care.

Back at the Nurse's station, I paced some until I realized I was annoying one of Susan's nurses. She was trying to concentrate on some paperwork and my nervous meanderings distracted her. I apologized and stepped outside for a smoke. The new wing's back door was just a few paces beyond the operating room.

While I was outside, Gary Henson came by. He stopped, and we chatted for a minute or two. Henson was impressed with MID's efficiency in hauling Dragon Lady away so quickly. He said even the Los Angeles County coroner's office wasn't that quick.

He also asked if there was any news from the operating room. I told him there wasn't. He continued his rounds and I returned to the nurses' station to twiddle my thumbs.

Susan came by about 1015 and we stood in the hallway to talk softly so we wouldn't disturb the work going on at the nurses' station. She consulted a clever little upside-down watch pinned to her apron, so it read right side up when she looked down at it.

"They should be closing soon. I sometimes think I should have pursued a career in surgical nursing. This waiting around without being able to help drives me crazy."

I got the idea there was something else on her mind. I knew she would get to it in time. "I can certainly understand that. As

260

you've noticed, I have very little patience to begin with, and situations like this are torture."

She got to it. "Johnny, assuming everything goes well in there, Sally will have several months of recuperation ahead. She'll spend some of that time here, but what happens after that?"

"I'm not sure. I think Russ told me Sally is originally from the Portland area and her folks are still there, but I don't think they know anything about what's going on here."

"I meant what will you have to do about protecting her?"

"Oh. General Davis told me to stay with our witnesses for a few more weeks. After that, the event they have some knowledge about will be over and done, so there won't be anything to protect them from."

"I'm glad to hear that. Sally needs some normalcy in her life."

"And I suspect you think I need some normalcy that doesn't include any cute blondes."

Susan smiled. "Am I that obvious?"

"No. I was just practicing my mind reading."

She studied my face for a moment, and then shrugged. "Well, you can't very well blame me for protecting my interests, can you?"

"No, I would feel the same way if our situations were reversed, but I'm also fairly certain you know your interests are not in need of protection. You're stuck with me come hell or high water."

Susan opened her mouth to say something, but some movement she saw through the windows in the operating room doors stopped her. "Oh, oh. It looks like they're done in there."

"Good. What happens now?"

"Well, in a regular hospital, Sally would be taken to a surgical recovery ward, but here she will be taken back to her room, where she'll be observed twenty-four hours a day until it is safe to leave her alone for short periods of time. While she is being wheeled to her room, Doctor Feigenbaum will tell us how things went. Excuse me a second. I need to tell Doctor Rothenberg they're done."

Watching the activity beyond the window gave me no clues as to the outcome of the surgery. Then Russ showed up. "Susan told me they're through in there."

"It seems that way. We don't know anything yet. Susan said Doctor Feigenbaum would tell us how it went after Sally is back in her room, and there will be a nurse with her 'round the clock until they think she's stable or some such thing."

"I see, sir."

"I'd like you to take the Sally watch while I find out the score. I'll let you know as soon as I know."

"Yes, sir."

No sooner had I given Russ his marching orders than the operating room doors swung open and the orderlies rolled Sally's bed through them with Nurse Olson backseat driving. As they passed us in the hall, I got a glimpse of Sally. Going strictly on appearances, I would have pronounced her dead then and there. Her face was deathly pale, and I saw no signs that she was even breathing. I hoped Feigenbaum's report would be more favorable. Russ joined the parade to Sally's room.

Susan and Doctor Rothenberg arrived on the scene only a moment before Doctor Feigenbaum walked out of the operating room with Nurse Frances. He didn't shillyshally about Sally's condition.

"Well, we've done what we can. The matter is in Yahweh's hands now. The best news I can give you is there were no unexpected complications."

I glanced at Frances Hughes. She gave me a small nod. I took that to be a good sign.

Rothenberg said, "Ferdi, you look exhausted. I have some fresh coffee in my office."

The doctors walked off toward the lobby and Frances said, "Don't let Doctor's lack of enthusiasm discourage you, Major Spicer. He really is tired. Two hours of precision work in an operating room is exhausting."

Susan nodded. "But no surprises?"

Frances said, "None. X-ray pictures are wonderful things."

Susan slipped a folded sheet of paper out of her apron pocket. "This is the monitoring schedule we talked about. As you requested, I put you down for the first four hours, and then my staff will take over for the late afternoon and night shifts."

Frances studied the schedule for a few seconds. "Looks fine to me."

"I'm going to post it on the bulletin board here at the station. Are there any special instructions you want added?"

"No. We'll just take care of anything that needs doing as we change shifts."

Turning to me, Susan asked, "Do you have any questions, Darling?"

Nodding, I said, "One. How soon will she be conscious and aware of her surroundings?"

Frances gave my question a moment's thought. "It's hard to anticipate that at this point. Doctor wants her immobile, so we'll keep her sedated for a while, maybe eight hours. What happens after that will depend on what we can tell about her condition. I'll keep you and Susan informed as we go. Speaking of which, I'd better get down to Sally's room." With a smile, she added, "Nurse Olson doesn't like to be kept waiting."

As Frances walked briskly down the hall, Susan said, "Johnny, why don't you go home for some sleep. Nothing will be happening here for a while."

"I would rather stay here and make sure nothing will be happening."

Susan gave me a questioning look. "Do you think there will more trouble like we had this morning?"

I shrugged. "I hope not, but we have to figure Dragon Lady was expected to report the success of her mission to someone. Since that won't be happening, the enemy will know she failed. I don't know what they'll do about that. So, until our reinforcements show up this afternoon, Russ and I have to stay on our toes. That goes for Gary Henson, too. In fact, I should go out and let him know where things stand."

Susan frowned. "I was hoping we'd seen the end of all that."

"I hope so, too, but as Doctor Feigenbaum said, it's all in Yahweh's hands now."

"I take it Yahweh means God?"

"In Hebrew, yes."

Susan stood on her tiptoes and gave me a peck on the cheek. "Be careful, darling."

"I will. If you see Russ, please tell him what Doctor Feigenbaum had to say if Nurse Frances hasn't already told him. I'll be in to relieve him shortly."

Old Sol was in his full glory now, warming the sea breezes and making sparkles dance across the surf rolling in toward the beach. It was the kind of day that makes you glad you're alive. Since only a few hours earlier I'd come within a gnat's eyebrow of not being alive, I was particularly grateful for being around to see it.

I was following the same counter-clockwise route around the facility I followed earlier when I spotted Dragon Lady. This time around I spotted Gary Henson.

Noticing me, he turned and gestured skyward. "Swell day, huh?"

"Yes, indeed. I came out to tell you the patient survived the surgery. Doctor Feigenbaum says it's up to God now, or words to that effect."

Smiling, Henson said, "She damned well better survive after all we went through to keep her alive for that operation."

We left the empty room's window open and it caught my eye. Something about it gave me an uneasy feeling but I didn't know why. I said, "Yeah. You okay to hang around for a few more hours?"

"Sure. Feigenbaum drove himself here this morning in the Talbot, so he's not counting on me to drive him home."

"Great." I looked at my wristwatch—1100 hours. "Our reinforcements should be here not long after lunch. I'll send Russ out to spell you for lunch in a while."

"I'm gonna miss the food here. If all hospitals served grub as good, there would be a lot more patients."

"Not if all hospitals charged what Doctor Rothenberg gets for a room here."

Gary caught me glancing toward the open window. "Something bothering you, Spicer?"

I shook my head. "Guess I'm just remembering how lucky I was this morning."

He nodded as if he understood exactly what I meant. "I'd better move along. Don't forget to send Russ out so I can get lunch."

Absently, I said, "Will do."

Gary headed off at a brisk pace and I stood there staring at the open window. A question kept asking itself in my head. How did Dragon Lady end up in the wrong room? Surely, she would have found out which room Sally was in. It just wasn't the sort of mistake a pro would make.

I took a few steps toward the window and more questions jumped up. Okay, supposing she deliberately chose to come in through that window instead of Sally's, why? Did Dragon Lady think she was less likely to be spotted coming that way? Maybe, but how did she know the room was empty? When I looked in I had to push the curtain aside to see anything, and even then I couldn't see much in the dark. The way I remembered things, she wasn't there long enough to open the window and spend any time looking through it to see what or who was inside the room. That being the case, Susan's scream would have surprised the hell out of her.

Also, she would be certain we were guarding Sally, but she couldn't know where the inside guard was because we moved around. Dragon Lady had to be counting on being so quiet the inside guard didn't know she was there until she took him down. That was the only practical advantage I could come up with for breaking into the empty room instead of going directly to Sally's room. It was either that, or Dragon Lady simply fouled up and broke into the wrong room. Maybe.

Susan was at the nurses' station when I came in. She looked up. "Everything okay outside?"

"Sure is. How 'bout in here?"

"Fine. We're just getting things back to normal . . . cleaning up the O.R. and trying to get our maintenance people to replace a couple of doors."

I gave her an apologetic smile. "Sorry about the damage."

She shook her head. "Like Doctor said, I'd rather have damaged doors than damaged people."

A question occurred to me. "Angel, when Dragon Lady broke in this morning, you were napping in the empty room bed, right?"

"Yes, but I wasn't napping. I was, pardon the expression, dead to the world."

"Can you remember specifically what woke you up?"

Susan thought about my question for a moment. "I think it must have been a gunshot. She shot at you through the window, right?"

"Yes."

"The first thing I remember seeing was a dark shadow close to the bed. It was turning away from me. That's when I screamed."

"Which way was she turning?"

"From the window to the inside of the room."

"Yes, but do you recall whether she was turning to the left or the right? You were on her right as she faced the window. Did she turn toward you or to the left?"

"Oh, gee. I think to the right. Yes. She was turned past me toward the hall door when I screamed."

"So, she turned back left to face you when you screamed?"

"Yes, I'm pretty sure that's right."

"What happened then?"

I could tell Susan wasn't having any fun remembering the experience, so I said, "I know you'd sooner forget the whole incident, but this could be important."

"Oh, I understand. I'm just trying to remember the sequence of events. When she turned back toward the bed, she saw me right away because I was trying to get up and out of there, and she said, 'Shut up or I'll shoot you,' or words to that effect. She had a throaty voice."

"From what you said just now, though, she was facing the bed right after she climbed through the window. I wonder why she didn't see you then."

Susan shook her head. "That's a good question and I don't know the answer."

"Okay, what happened then?"

"She grabbed my wrist and pulled me to my feet and held the gun to my head. It was so close I could smell that metallic oil odor guns have. I resisted, but she was very strong, as strong as a man. In fact, at that point, I still thought she was a man."

"You have a good memory, Angel. I've just got one more question. This is kind of vague, but did you get the impression she knew where she was, or did she seem confused?"

Susan didn't need to think about that. She shook her head. "I don't think she was confused. She dragged me toward the connecting door right away and was about to open that door when there was a noise in the hallway. She turned toward the hall door and a second later it crashed in at us."

Apparently, I'd misread the situation when I thought Dragon Lady looked undecided about what to do after grabbing Susan. I said, "All right, thanks, Angel. I've just been trying to figure out if she broke into the empty room instead of Sally's on purpose or if it was a mistake. I'm getting the idea it was intentional, but I can't figure out why. Maybe it doesn't make any difference. I'm just curious about what she was thinking."

"I hope I helped. Any idea when your reinforcements, or whatever you call them, will get here?"

"I don't know for sure, but from what General Davis said, I imagine early afternoon, maybe around two."

Susan touched my cheek with her right hand. "Do you think we could go home for a while then? You look like you could use some rest. I know I could."

Nodding, I said, "I imagine so. I'll need to brief the new team and show them around, but after that we can probably sneak out for a while."

Susan smiled a coyish smile. "I bet Mister Whiskers has been missing you. I know I sure have."

"In that case, we will certainly head for home. I don't want to disappoint Mister Whiskers."

She gave me a whack on the arm. "Oh, go soak your head! Some romantic fellow you are."

When I got to Sally's door, I spotted Russ standing near the chair Nurse Frances was using. He saw me, and I gave him a "come here" gesture. Out in the hall, I asked, "How's it going?"

"Quiet, almost too quiet, sir. I keep looking at Sally to make sure she's still breathing."

I looked through the doorway at Sally. "I hear you, Russ. Listen, I'll spell you for a while. Go get some lunch, and then you can relieve Henson outside."

"Yes, sir. A change will do me good. I need to move around some, but I didn't want to disturb Sally. See you in a while, sir."

Russ headed off in the direction from which I'd come, and I walked into Sally's room. Nurse Frances smiled. "Hello, Major Spicer."

"Hello, Nurse Frances. How's the patient?"

"I hope she's healing like crazy, but that's on the inside. We can't tell much from the outside yet."

We chatted quietly for a while about nothing much in particular until I heard Susan's footsteps in the hall. She brought a glass bottle in that looked like the one already hanging from a metal stand next to Sally's bed.

"I brought you a replacement saline bottle. The one that's up should be close to empty."

Frances said, "Thank you, Susan. I'll hang it in a minute. It's time to check vitals, anyway."

"I ordered a lunch tray for you. Chicken à la King on rice today. Anything else I can bring you?"

"No, thank you. Why don't you go home and get some rest? Surely this place can get along without you for a while."

She looked in my direction. "I plan to do that just as soon as Major Spicer can tear himself away from his duties for a while." With a mock glare, Susan added, "He wants to make sure Mister Whiskers doesn't get lonely." Then she stuck her tongue out at me.

Frances laughed. "Oh, oh. Major Spicer, I suggest you reconsider your priorities. A nurse scorned is not to be trifled with."

"So I've learned, Fran. I plan to escort Nurse Jackson home as soon as my replacements get here."

Susan folded her arms in a defiant pose. "That would be a very good idea, Major."

I tossed a salute at Susan. "Yes, ma'am."

On that note, Susan turned to leave the room. At the door, she stopped and said, "Oh, I forgot. I remembered something else from this morning."

I followed her out into the hall. "What did you remember, Angel?"

"I doubt if it means anything, but before I was fully awake and screamed, it felt like that woman was right next to the bed and I thought I heard something sliding on the floor, like a cardboard box or something. Maybe it was just her shoe."

I didn't remember Dragon Lady carrying anything, especially a cardboard box, when I first spotted her outside, but it was pretty dark. I could have missed something. I said, "If she put something on the floor, where would it be? I didn't see anything when Russ and Gary moved the broken doors out of the way."

"Maybe she slid whatever it was under the bed. That could explain why she didn't notice me until I screamed, and when I hid under the bed, I felt something against my left ankle. I didn't remember that before because there was so much going on, but now I remember it clearly. I thought perhaps the sheets were untucked and slid to the floor. That happens sometimes."

"Were you on your stomach or your back when you were under the bed?"

"I was on my tummy."

"So, what you felt would have been back in the corner between the window wall and the wall the bed was against, right?"

Susan nodded. "Well, let's go take a look and see if it's still there."

We walked into the empty room through the hallway door, and kneeling next to the bed, I looked under it. There was something there, all right. It looked like a blue canvas duffel bag, the kind with a zippered opening on top and a leather carrying handle on each side of the opening.

Looking at the expression on my face, Susan said, "What is it?"

"A duffel bag."

I took another look to judge the bag's position relative to the bed. The hospital bed looked to be high enough off the floor that it could be moved out from the wall without disturbing the bag. Not disturbing that bag suddenly seemed very important.

"Susan, how difficult is it to move this bed?"

She looked at me curiously. "There is a lock on each wheel, but pushed up against the wall like this, they probably only locked the outer two wheels."

"Can you tell if they're locked by looking at them?"

"Yes. The locks are designed to be operated by foot. They have a red foot pedal and a green one on each wheel. If the red side is down, the wheel is locked, but if you just want to get the bag, I could slide under the bed and reach it."

I shook my head vigorously. "No, Angel, we won't be moving that bag until we have a better idea what's in it."

Susan frowned. "Why not? What could be in . . . Oh! A bomb?"

"That's what we need to find out. Now, the wheels on this side of the bed are locked, right?"

"Yes."

Still on my knees, I leaned over and looked at the other two wheels. The red ends of both were up. That meant we could move the bed by simply unlocking the two outer wheels. "Susan, would you please find Russ and send him in here on the double? He was going to get some lunch."

"On my way."

In not much more time than it took me to get back to my feet, Russ ran into the room. "What did you find, sir?"

"A canvas duffel bag. Susan thinks Dragon Lady slid it under the bed this morning. Take a look, but don't move anything."

It was Russ's turn to get down on his knees. He bent over to look under the bed. "Yes, sir, I see it."

As he got back to his feet, Susan came in. I said, "Susan, what's on the other side of this wall?"

"A linen room."

"All right. The first thing we need to do is get Sally and Fran out of the next room. Would you please get that done?"

Susan's expression was grim. It was her crisis face. I haven't seen it often, but I know it means she's in her "all business" mode.

Again, she said, "On my way."

As she hurried off, Russ asked, "What's the plan, sir?"

I glanced at my wristwatch. The time was 1215 hours. The duffel bag had been there for about six hours. Knowing that might be important if we determined there was a clock-activated bomb in the bag.

"Well, the first step is to clear the area. If there's a bomb in that bag, it's probably booby trapped somehow. We don't want anyone in the area except the dumbbells who are going to try getting that bag the hell out of here."

"Us, sir?"

"Well, yeah, unless General Davis shows up to help."

Russ just nodded.

Twenty-Eight

1245 Hours – Monday – 9 MAR 42

Casa Sobre El Mar, Santa Barbara

Halfway under the bed in the empty room next to Sally's room, I studied a canvas duffel bag that looked anything but innocent. At least now I had a pretty good idea why Dragon Lady climbed through what I'd been thinking of as the "wrong window." She intended to leave some insurance behind where it wasn't likely to be discovered in case her first plan failed.

Of course, I didn't know for sure there was a bomb in the canvas bag. It might just be full of Dragon Lady's dirty laundry.

Standing behind me, Russ said, "They're wheeling Sally out of her room, sir."

I slid out from under the bed. "Good. I guess we should also evacuate the room across the hall. There are at least a dozen other rooms to consider. Russ, you know anything about bombs, like how much damage this thing could do?"

"I know a little, sir, but until we actually see the bomb, we won't know what it can do."

Getting back to my feet, I said, "I just knew you were going to say that. I guess the first thing to do is move the bed out of here, so we can get to the damned thing."

"Yes, sir, but we have to be very careful not to jar the bag."

I gave his concern a moment's thought. "Yes, but from what Susan said, it sounds as if Dragon Lady just slid the bag under the bed with a good push. That means a motion booby trap isn't likely. It wouldn't hurt to be careful, though."

Susan came back into the room. "Sally and Fran are in a room up at the lobby end of the hall. What now?"

"Is there anyone in the room directly across the hall?"

270

"Yes, a young sailor who was injured at Pearl Harbor. Should we move him, too?"

I nodded. "Yes, that's next. After he's out, make sure the hallway doors to the other rooms are closed."

Susan left to evacuate the fellow across the hall and Doctors Rothenberg and Feigenbaum arrived at the party. Rothenberg seemed upset. Feigenbaum was calm.

Rothenberg said, "Nurse Jackson told me you found a suspicious bag in here. Is that true?"

I said, "It is. We're about to move the bed out of the way so we can get to the bag and find out what's in it."

"Do you think it is some sort of explosive device?"

"That is a possibility, but we won't know for sure until we open the bag."

While I was talking with Rothenberg, Feigenbaum lowered himself to his knees for a look under the bed. "I see the bag. How can I be of help?"

"We could sure use a couple of flashlights and a pair of diagonal cut pliers."

Feigenbaum turned to Rothenberg. "Ham, please see to your staff. Make certain they are clear of the area. Also, please find us a flashlight or two and a pair of dikes."

Doctor Rothenberg hurried off up the hall and Feigenbaum said, "I didn't mean to take over your job there, but I know Ham is quite nervous about all this. I thought if I appeared calm and gave him something to do, it might take his mind off that bag under the bed."

"Thanks, Doctor. Our next step is to move the bed out of the way. You might want to step out into the hall."

He took my advice and I turned to Russ. "The bed wheel locks on the far side are off. I checked that earlier. To release the ones on this side, we step down on the green end of the lever next to the wheel."

I released the outside wheel lock at the head end of the bed, and then a thought occurred to me. The wheels on the beds at the clinic worked like casters to make turning in tight spaces easier. I got back down on the floor to see which way the wheels on the other side of the bed were pointing. The one in the corner was aimed straight at the bag.

"Hang on a minute, I need to turn the corner wheel away from the bag."

Back on my feet, I said, "All right, we want to move the bed at least three feet straight out from the wall. Ready?"

Russ said, "Ready."

"On three. One . . . two . . . three."

The bed moved easily. When it was three feet or so from the wall, I said, "Okay, hold it a minute."

I pushed my wheel lock on and laid across the bed so I could see the bag. We hadn't touched it.

I said, "All right, the bag is okay. Now let's push the bed out through what's left of the hall doorway."

We got the bed rolling again and took it out into the hallway, where we locked the wheels and left it. When we got back into the room, Feigenbaum was standing next to the duffel bag. Two flashlights and a pair of diagonal cutters were on the floor near the bag.

He said, "I hate to be the bearer of bad tidings, but I definitely hear ticking from inside that bag."

I said, "Then I guess we need to take a look inside."

Russ said, "That's where we need to be careful. Even if there aren't any motion sensitive booby traps, there are sure to be some kind of traps to prevent disarming the bomb."

"Point taken. Russ, if you and Doctor Feigenbaum will step outside for a minute, I will open the bag."

Russ looked as if he was going to protest being sent out of the room, but he didn't. I watched the two of them go out into the hall, and then turned my attention back to the bag. Lifting the metal zipper tab, I gently pulled it. The zipper opened half an inch. Taking a deep breath, I held the bag in place with one hand, grabbed the zipper tab firmly in the other, and applied a steady, even pull. The zipper slowly followed the curve of the opening until it reached the end of the zipper track.

I picked up one of the flashlights, turned it on, and used the fingers of my left hand to spread the bag open while I pointed the light beam inside. What I saw first were four sticks of dynamite with two lengths of black friction tape holding them in a square, two-by-two configuration. The blasting cap, a three-inch thin metal tube, protruded from the end of one dynamite stick. The blasting cap's two wire leads disappeared into the jumble of wires in the bottom of the bag.

The ticking was coming from a white Westclox Big Ben wind-up alarm clock with more wires attached. Its alarm indicator pointed halfway between the numerals one and two. The clock hands indicated the more or less correct time, 1300 hours.

Another item I could clearly see in the bag was a red and black cardboard box that looked to be about four inches tall by two inches by one-and-a-half inches. A pair of clamp-type wire connectors were fitted to the top of the box, and the label said, "RCA Radio B Battery—67.5 Volts". It was the sort of battery used in portable radio receivers and was probably the power source for detonating the blasting cap, which in turn, detonated the dynamite.

The wire jumble in the bottom of the box was colorful to say the least. The cloth insulations on the wires were red, green, orange, and black, and there seemed to be miles of them.

I yelled, "Okay, come on back. The bag is open."

Still on my knees, I described the contents of the duffel bag. Russ said, "Sounds like a homemade time bomb. "Let's see how it is wired."

He knelt next to me. "Would you please hold the bag open while I take a look, sir?"

I cautiously spread the opening using both hands. From the corner of my eye I saw Feigenbaum watching from the hall doorway.

Russ pointed a flashlight into the bag and looked. After a few moments he moved the clock slightly, so he could see underneath it.

"Sir, whatever you do, don't lift the bag. It seems to have a kind of motion booby trap after all. There's a small hole in the bottom of the bag with a pushbutton switch sticking through it. I suspect it's a momentary contact switch that is depressed when the bag is on a flat surface and released when the bag is picked up. I can't see what the switch does, but it's there for a reason."

"If it's a booby trap, how the hell did she carry the bag in here?"

"If I had to guess, I'd say the switch operates a normally closed relay. When the switch is pressed, power to the relay holds it open until the switch is released. Then the relay closes and completes a detonation circuit. That set up would also prevent the trap from being deactivated by disconnecting the power, and it probably means there's more than one battery in there. Apparently pressing the switch initially activated the circuit somehow. Actually, it's pretty slick."

"You can commend the Japs on their creativity later. Any other good news?"

"Well, there is no doubt it's a time bomb. It's set to go off at thirteen-thirty and, with four sticks of TNT, it will destroy this room and the rooms on both sides, plus the room across the hall. I'm pretty sure the bomb wiring, itself, is also booby trapped.

There is much more wire in there than there needs to be to make the clock set off the dynamite. The only explanation for that is another booby trap or two."

"So, like in the movies, if we snip the wrong wire we get a one-way ticket to the next world?"

"That's about the size of it, sir. I would strongly recommend not snipping any of the wires."

"What would happen if we just kept moving the time back on the clock until it runs down?"

"I'm afraid we can't do that, sir. They cut the adjusting stems off inside the clock, so we can't get to them without removing the case, and I'm sure whoever built this thing anticipated we might try that and booby trapped the clock case."

"All right, how about sliding something flat, like a cookie sheet, under the bomb to keep that switch gizmo depressed, and then carrying the thing out of here on the cookie sheet?"

"That's about the only solution I can think of, sir, but whatever we slide under it would have to be absolutely flat with no lip around the edges. I don't know how sensitive that switch is."

I glanced at my watch again. "We're running out of time. We've only got about fifteen minutes depending on the clock's accuracy. I'll see if I can find a cookie sheet or something similar."

Just about everyone at the clinic was gathered in the lobby. Susan was standing with a small group that included Nurse Roger and Feigenbaum's second nurse, Elsie Olson.

To Susan, I said, "It's a bomb, all right, but I think we can safely move it out of the building with the aid of something flat, like a cookie sheet with no lip around the edge, but we need it fast."

Nurse Roger heard my request. "Would a two-by-three-foot sheet of tin we use to firm up bed mattresses work?"

"How thick is it?"

"Eighth of an inch, maybe less."

"Yeah, that might work. Where is it?"

He began to move toward the hallway. "There's one in the linen room next to the room you're in. I'll get it."

I stopped him. "Thanks, but I'd rather you stayed out here. I can get it. Where is it in the linen room?"

Frowning, he said, "Should be on one of the shelves to your left at the back of the room."

"Thanks, Roger."

Russ was out in the hallway with Doctor Feigenbaum. He gave me a questioning look.

"There's a sheet of tin in the linen room that might do the trick."

Feigenbaum followed me into the linen room. I said, "It's supposed to be at the back on the left."

Someone apparently moved the tin sheet since Roger last saw it. Doctor Feigenbaum found it just inside the door on the right. I took the tin sheet into the room where Russ was waiting for me. I held the sheet up and checked its flexibility. It was not the ideal tool for the job. If held by the edges with weight in the middle, it would bow, probably enough to release the tension on the pushbutton under the bag.

I said, "We'll have to support the tin from underneath as we carry it. Otherwise, it has enough flex to release that switch."

Russ said, "I see that." Glancing at his watch, he added, "Looks like we'll have to make it work. We have less than ten minutes left."

I moved to the window and pulled the curtain aside. "We can save some steps if it will fit through the window."

"Looks like it will. I'll run around to take it from you on the other side."

"All right. I'll wait until you're out there before I try to pick the damned thing up."

Less than a minute later I saw a movement at the window, and I was trying to figure out how Russ got out there so fast when I realized it was Gary Henson. In the excitement I'd forgotten he was waiting for someone to relieve him for lunch.

"Sorry, Gary. I've been a little distracted. We've got a damned bomb in here."

Henson leaned in the window to see the bag on the floor better. "Those Japs don't give up easy, do they?"

"No. Russ will be out there in a second, so I can hand the bag to him through the window. Then he'll carry it away from the building and try to leave it somewhere without detonating it. I suggest you put some distance between yourself and this window."

"Hell, we don't need to wait for Russ. Hand the damned thing to me."

"It's not that easy, Gary. The bomb is booby trapped. We figured out how to move . . . ."

Russ arrived at the window. I heard him repeat my suggestion about moving to Gary. Henson took off at a trot.

"Okay, sir, let's get that damn thing out of there."

"All right. By the way, watch your footing in that ground cover out there."

He looked down. "I will, sir."

I looked at the duffel bag and decided to do the whole process on my knees. I could reach the window on my knees and that eliminated the need to perform a balancing act with the bomb while I stood up.

I avoided looking at my watch and went to work sliding the tin sheet under the bag. It slid just fine until the edge of the tin hit the button. The spring in the switch was too strong to let the eighth-inch thickness of the tin slip under it. I grabbed a flashlight and looked into the bag to see if there was any way to lift the button from the inside. There wasn't that I could see.

The only option left was to push down on the canvas bag to see if I could tilt the switch enough to get shove the tin under the edge of the button. I yelled, "Stand back, Russ, I have to tip the bag to get the tin under it."

Russ wisely stepped to the side and I began to depress the canvas on one end while pushing the tin against the pushbutton from the opposite direction. Nothing happened. I pushed down harder. The tin sheet moved.

With the tin sheet now under the pushbutton and sweat was pouring off me like Niagara Falls, I released my pressure on the end of the bag and slid it until I had an edge of the tin sheet visible on each side of the bag. I yelled, "Okay Russ, here I come."

With my right hand on top of the bag and the fingers of my left hand under the edge of the tin sheet, I tipped the bag and tin sheet far enough to get my entire left hand completely under the tin. From there, I lifted the whole works, pushing my hands toward each other to maintain pressure, and shuffled along on my knees to the window.

Russ reached through the window and got a hand under the tin sheet. I supported the rest of the bag until Russ got the sheet and bag sandwiched between his hands the way I'd carried it. He said, "I've got it, sir."

He slid the bag out of my hands and through the window. By the time I got to my feet, Russ was clear of the planting area and crossing the road. He was almost in position to set the bag down on the far side of the road. That was the last instant I saw Staff Sergeant Russell Pierce alive.

Twenty-Nine

Casa Sobre El Mar, Santa Barbara

I will never know if we were too slow and the clock triggered the bomb or Russ inadvertently relaxed his pressure on the tin plate holding the booby trap button in. I can't see that it makes the slightest difference which it was.

The concussion slugged me hard in the chest, I was hit with a hail of broken window glass, and several seconds passed before a dazzling afterimage of the brilliant white flash began to fade. By that time Susan had her arms wrapped around me and she was saying something like, "Johnny, Johnny, are you all right? I was so afraid . . . ."

"I'm all right, Angel, but Russ isn't."

Susan instantly shifted into her nurse mode. "Oh, no. Russ is hurt? Can we help him? Where is he?"

With my free arm I gestured out the window toward a blackened section of the concrete roadway. "He's out there, but there isn't a piece of him left that's big enough to help."

"Oh, Johnny, I'm sorry."

At that point lots of folks who were concerned about my welfare began showing up. Gary Henson, for one, appeared in the window. "Geez! That was a hell of a bang! You okay, Spicer?"

"Yeah, I'm fine."

"The way your luck is running, you should to head for Santa Anita. That's twice you've cheated death today!"

My mind wasn't quite back to its usual level of mediocrity yet, but I think I glared at him. Henson mumbled something that sounded like, "Sorry," and left.

The empty room suddenly was full of people, among them

277

Doctor Rothenberg, Nurse Frances, Doctor Feigenbaum, and Nurse Roger. My first inclination was ordering Russ to get all those people out of here.

Instead, I said, "Angel, I need to call Washington from a payphone. Make apologies for my sudden disappearance, will you?"

"Of course, darling."

I drove the Army's Dodge to the Seaside gas station at Hill Road and Highway One. I was becoming a frequent customer of their public telephone. It sounded like General Davis was on his way out of the office. "Yeah, Spicer, what do you have for me?"

Even though I didn't feel very military, I did my best to sound that way. "Sir, I'm calling to report an incident. We discovered a timed explosive device at the clinic. Marjorie Yount planted it before we got her earlier."

Davis said, "I see. What . . . ."

I kept talking, "We were attempting to remove the device from the premises, but we were either too late or we triggered one of the booby traps. Sergeant Pierce was killed in the explosion."

It wasn't until then that I realized what I must sound like to the general. I didn't care. He did.

"Okay, Spicer, relax a minute. Are you okay?"

"Yes, sir."

"All right. I'll send another cleanup crew from LA. Have Sergeant Tiner and his men arrived yet?"

"Not yet, sir."

"Then they should be there any time now. When Tiner gets there, I want you to turn the protection assignment at that clinic over to him and resume command of the overall mission. Got that?"

"Yes, sir."

"Good. Also, write me an After Action Report as an addendum to the first one and bring both to that transport center the Army Air Force has at the Los Angeles airport. I'll meet you there tomorrow at . . . twelve-hundred-hours your time. Can you be there by then?"

"Yes, sir."

"All right. Listen, Johnny, I understand how you feel. I've lost men in combat, too. You will never forget what happened to Sergeant Pierce, but keep it together for a while and things will begin to fall into place.

"Oh, and put a medal recommendation for Pierce into that AAR. Meanwhile, I'll have someone find his next of kin, so Graves can make the notification."

"Sir, I'd like to make that notification."

"I figured you might, Spicer. First, let's find out where his family is and see if it's practical for you to do that. Then, ..."

"Sir, I don't care if it's practical or not, I owe Russ Pierce at least that much."

"All right, we'll discuss that tomorrow. See you then."

General Davis was right. By the time I got back to the clinic, I was feeling a little more settled and my thinking was clearer. So much so that I immediately noticed some things had changed in the Casa Sobre El Mar parking lot during the short time I was gone.

For one, Doctor Feigenbaum's Cadillac limo and the blue Talbot coupé the doctor drove to the clinic that morning were gone. In their place was an olive drab Plymouth four-door sedan with a white star on each rear door. Sergeant Tiner had arrived just in time to miss all the excitement.

One of Tiner's men, a corporal I didn't recognize, challenged me at the clinic's entrance. I showed him my MID ID and explained he was not to challenge anybody, but merely report any unusual visitors to Tiner. I also told him an MID clean-up crew from LA would be arriving in a while, and to send them to see Sergeant Tiner. The corporal was used to taking his orders from Tiner and I got the idea he didn't like anyone else telling him what to do. TS.

I found Tiner talking to Susan at the nurses' station. I heard her say, "Oh, here's Major Spicer now."

Tiner turned and saluted. Not bothering to return his military courtesy, I said, "At ease, Sergeant. Let's go outside for a smoke and some talk."

I gave Susan a nod and briskly walked a few paces down the hallway to the new wing's back door. I didn't wait for Tiner. The rear door had one of those self-closing gizmos and the door was almost closed by the time the sergeant caught up with me.

I offered him a Lucky Strike, which he accepted. We lit our cigarettes with the brushed chrome Zippo lighter Susan gave me. I kept it in my hand for a while because if felt good.

"Tiner, when you arrived I was out making a secure telephone call to General Davis. He has some new orders for both of us. I'll give you a rundown on why you're here and what's been going on in a minute, but first the orders. Davis will be sending the actual orders out later, but for now, take my word for it."

"Yes, sir."

"From this point on you and your team report to me and are responsible for protecting an MID witness—the same woman you delivered to Letterman Hospital last Saturday. Her name is Sally MacLure, and she had major surgery a few hours ago, so Miss MacLure will not be too sociable for a few days.

"A Jap agent made two attempts on her life today. Fortunately, we headed them off, but a damned good soldier— Sergeant Russ Pierce—died in the process.

"Understand this: Pierce did not die protecting a cute blonde with a nice smile, he died protecting a secret that goes all the way to the top. Should it be necessary, I expect you and your men to do the same. Are we good so far?"

"Yes, sir."

"All right, here's what's been going on."

I spent several minutes giving Tiner the short version of Dragon Lady's demise and our attempt to remove the bomb she planted. After that, I told him I wanted one man with Sally and one outside at all times. I also told him if he needed more manpower, to call General Davis or Colonel Beecher.

My next stop was the nurses' station because that's where Susan was. I explained about Tiner taking over security at the clinic, and that I was to meet Davis in LA at noon on Wednesday.

Susan was watching me closely. When I finished nattering, she said, "Are you okay, Johnny, I mean really okay?"

I sighed. "Yeah, Angel, I'm okay. Losing Russ that way kind of threw me. He deserved better."

"Yes, darling, he did. Oh, that man who drives for Doctor Feigenbaum stopped by while you were out. He said since reinforcements had arrived he was leaving. He also told me to tell you he was sorry for the comment he made to you about luck."

"I'll get in touch with him later, so we can straighten things out. Henson is a nice guy and he did us a big favor. I owe him."

Susan smiled. "I'm so glad you weren't hurt. When that bomb exploded . . . ."

"I know, Angel. It was scary, but I think we're through with all that now."

"I hope so. Fran asked me if she should move Sally back to her room. I said I would ask you but fixing the damage in the room next door will be noisy and it might be better to leave her where she is."

"If you can spare the room, I see no reason not to leave her where she is. Also, would you please introduce Tiner to Frances and anyone who ought to know him?"

"Yes, I'll do that."

"How's Doctor Rothenberg holding up after I damn near destroyed his clinic?"

Susan smiled again. "He's all right now. I talked to him. Doctor was just upset. He likes things to run smoothly and it got a little chaotic here for a while."

That made me smile. "Chaotic? That's the understatement of the year. When can we get out of here and go home for a while?"

Susan looked at her upside-down watch. "In about thirty minutes. I imagine you'll also want to straighten out the automobile situation. If you want, we can drop your car off at Elton Bishoff's, and then I'll bring you back to get the Army car."

I hadn't thought that far ahead yet. "That would be helpful, Angel. Thanks."

With some time to kill, I walked outside to the area where I'd last seen Russ. My intention was to retrieve any loose things he had on him at the time of the . . . when he died. I found only two items worth picking up: one of his dog tags and his slightly singed billfold.

I put the wallet in my jacket pocket. Some of the money in it was Uncle Sam's and I thought his family might appreciate the rest of its contents—mostly some photos and a couple of cards. It didn't seem like much of a legacy for a man who lost his life in the service of his country. I gave myself a kick in the rear with a reminder that we were at war and the same thing was happening to men all over the globe.

Catching up with Tiner, I gave him the dog tag I found and showed him where the explosion had taken place. What remains there were would be centered around that point. I also told him to tell the clean-up crew they would need to go by the Biltmore to pick up Russ's personal gear.

It was 1700 hours by the time Susan and I got all the cars where they belonged and arrived at her apartment. Once there, we decided we were hungry, so I walked over to the Chinese take-out place in the next block of State Street and took out some of those little white boxes full of stuff like Chow Mein and fried rice. We shared a few morsels of chicken with Mister Whiskers as compensation for leaving him on his own so much. He seemed to think that was an excellent tradeoff.

After dinner, Susan went off to take a shower and I sat at the kitchen table to fill out a second After Action Report. On the table before me was a new blank form and the one I'd filled out that morning, along with the aforementioned Mister Whiskers, who sat quietly watching me.

I really believe cats sympathize with their humans in times of pain and sorrow. Since I'd become one of his adopted humans, Mister Whiskers seemed to think he could help by staying close and occasionally purring at me. He was right.

Susan, in her bathrobe, joined us and rewarded Mister Whiskers with some pets while I finished up the AAR addendum. After I gave it one last read through and signed it, Susan asked, "All done with the paperwork?"

"Yes. Now I can hand it over to General Davis tomorrow."

"It's none of my business, but is the general coming all the way to LA just to see you?"

I looked up feigning surprise and said, "Wouldn't you?"

Susan smiled a warm smile. "Yes, darling, I would, but I suspect my feelings for you might be somewhat different than the general's."

"True. To answer your question, it sounded like he was making the trip just to be sure one Major Johnny Spicer wasn't due for a Section Eight."

Susan frowned. "Section Eight?"

"Yeah, that's a discharge for someone who is mentally unfit for service, also referred to as a psycho."

Nodding, she asked, "And are you?"

"If I was sure it wouldn't land me in a nut-house somewhere, I'd do whatever it takes to convince him I am, but I'm afraid I'm not quite that far gone yet."

Susan put her hand over mine. "My professional medical opinion is you would benefit greatly from some recuperative leave. Isn't that what they call it?"

"It is. I suspect, however, I won't have any leave coming for a few more weeks. There is some unfinished business I have to take care of. Then, by God, I'll take some time off even if it means going A-W-O-L."

Susan gave me another frown. "A-W-O-L? What's that?"

"It's an acronym for Absent Without Leave."

Susan nodded. "Oh. I suppose the Army frowns on such behavior?"

I chuckled. "It does, indeed."

With the help of Mister Whiskers and Susan, I was feeling a bit more human when we went to bed. What followed is best described as a celebration of being alive that left us both exhausted. In that state you would think I'd sleep like a baby. I might have if it weren't the nightmares that came marching into my head each time I managed to fall asleep.

I'm afraid Susan didn't get much sleep either. She roused me out of bad dreams several times. To be honest, I wasn't too unhappy about getting out of bed and into the shower. I put my soldier suit on, and after some coffee, Susan and I headed out to Casa Sobre El Mar in separate cars. The clinic was only my first stop of the day. Mister Whiskers went back to bed.

Thirty

Casa Sobre El Mar, Santa Barbara

I guess, when I got right down to it, I objected to giving up direct control of security at the clinic, and from my conversation with General Davis the day before, I got the idea I would be spending my time elsewhere from now on. That disappointment probably accounts for me stopping at the clinic before my drive to LA, even though the stop wasn't really necessary.

Sergeant Tiner briefed me on his first night at the clinic. All went well. I told him I was headed for a meeting with General Davis, but beyond that I didn't know where I'd be going. I promised to let him know.

Next, I looked in on Sally and got a good sort of surprise for a change. She was awake. Nurse Frances was with her and smiled when I walked into Sally's new room. She also gave me a thumbs-up gesture, and the corporal Tiner assigned to the room stepped out into the hallway.

Sally was groggy, but she recognized me and immediately held out her hand. I took it and said, "Good morning to you, Miss MacLure."

Her voice was hoarse, and her words were a little slurred, but the spirit was still in them. "Hi, Johnny. I was hoping . . . hoping you would come . . . to see me."

"I'm not going to ask you how you feel yet but judging by Nurse Frances' smile when I came in, I'm betting you are well started on the road to recovery."

Sally stared at me for a minute, as if thinking about what I said. Finally, she said, "I think so. I don't know. I hope so."

I smiled. "Trust me on this one, Sally. You're doing fine, and you've got lots of folks rooting for you, so keep it up."

Her eyes were drooping, but she managed to say, "Thanks."

She drifted off and I laid her hand back on the bed. When I turned toward Nurse Frances, she gestured to the hallway.

Tiner's corporal traded places with us and Frances said, "I'm glad you came in. Seeing you gave her a boost."

Nodding, I said, "How's she really doing?"

"Well, at this stage we can only go by outward signs, but her mind seems sharp, at least as sharp as can be expected in her state of sedation, and her vital signs are all in the normal post-surgery range. Even more encouraging is that she woke up all by herself. She'll be in and out for a few days, though, as we reduce the sedation."

"Thanks for the report. It sounds hopeful."

"It is, Johnny. For what it's worth, I have a feeling she's going to be just fine."

"Listen, Fran, I should have said something to you yesterday, but I didn't think of it. I'd rather nobody told her about Sergeant Pierce's death. Sally was close to him."

Nurse Frances smiled. "I already decided we wouldn't tell her any of what happened yesterday for a while. She needs good news right now, not tragedy. If she asks, I will simply tell her Sergeant Pierce has been reassigned to another duty."

"Thank you." I glanced at my watch. "I guess I need to get going. I've been ordered to LA today and I'm not sure when I'll be back. Hopefully, I'll at least be back here for the night."

"I hope so, too. I trust you are doing all right. I imagine Susan is seeing to that."

I returned Fran's smile. "She is."

Frances stood on tiptoes and kissed me on the cheek. "You take good care of yourself, Major Johnny Spicer."

At the nurses' station Susan and I drank a cup of coffee, and then she walked me out to the Army's Dodge. "Drive safely, Johnny. Come back as soon as you can. I'm going to miss having you around."

"I'll miss being here. Despite everything else that happened, it was good to spend some time together."

We kissed, and I climbed into the Dodge. Susan was standing on the clinic's front porch waving to me as I drove off. I waved back and looked at my wristwatch. It was 0900.

It was a good day for driving down the coast and the miles seemed to roll by much more quickly than usual. Before I knew it, I was parking outside the military hangar at Mines Field and it wasn't quite 1130 yet.

As I got out of the Dodge, I noticed at least one change since I was there last. Sentries now kept watch on the building and aircraft parked around it. The Army was apparently finally realizing it was fighting a war.

After retrieving my dispatch case from the Dodge's trunk, I walked into the building. An MP standing inside the door asked for my ID. I showed it to him and he gave me a spit and polish salute in return. From there I walked to the operations counter, where a first louie was holding forth. He asked if he could help me.

I showed my MID ID again. "Are there any messages for me?"

He checked an in-basket on his side of the counter. "No, Major Spicer, no messages."

"I'm expecting to meet Major General Chester Davis here in a while. He's flying in from Washington. Any word on his plane?"

He consulted a clipboard and said, "Yes, sir. The last we heard he was on time and expected here around twelve-hundred hours." He glanced at his watch and added, "He should be in the pattern any time now."

"Thanks, Lieutenant. I'm going to grab a cup of coffee and wait for him outside. It's too nice a day to be inside."

As I turned away from the counter, the lieutenant said, "Sir, if you'll wait just a moment I'll get you a cup from the pot we keep back here. It's fresher. Do you take anything in your coffee?"

Reminded that rank has its privileges, I said, "Just black, thanks."

With a cardboard cup of fresh hot coffee in hand, I walked out of the hangar and sat myself down at a picnic table in the sun on the east side of the building. The coffee was good, and I was glad I had it because the sun's warmth immediately made me sleepy.

I wasn't there more than fifteen minutes when I heard a big twin taxiing nearby. I turned and saw a familiar white and silver Army Air Force DC-3 coming my way. A few minutes later I saluted General Davis and we shook hands. I offered to get him a cup of coffee, but he declined.

We sat opposite each other at the picnic table and Davis said, "How are you, Johnny? Feeling a little better about things?"

"Yes, sir. You were right. I'll never forget what happened yesterday, but I'm already beginning to see it in a different light."

"Good. Now, I'd like to begin by reading your AARs."

I removed them from my dispatch case. "Here you are, sir."

He accepted the reports, each of which consisted of four

pages. "Relax while I read these, so I can discuss them intelligently."

I lit a cigarette and finished my coffee while he read. That was when I realized I was no longer angry with Davis. Twenty-four hours earlier I was ready to kick his butt, but now I felt differently. It seemed Chester Davis was a guy you just couldn't stay mad at.

When Davis finished, he stacked the reports neatly on the table without saying anything. Then he stared at the traffic going by on Century Boulevard a hundred yards to the south.

Finally, he looked me in the eye and said, "Those reports make dramatic reading. They help me understand your situation a little better. I had a rough idea from what you told me on the telephone, but this . . . ." He picked up the reports again. "This includes all the details you left out over the telephone and makes it all seem real to me."

"I'm glad, sir, because it seemed very real to me at the time it was all happening."

"I'll bet it did. And this fellow . . . ." He thumbed through the first AAR, found what he was looking for, and said, "Henson. He was a big help. We owe him a letter of commendation."

"Yes, sir. He's a former Los Angeles cop furloughed on disability. Now he's a driver-bodyguard for the cardiovascular surgeon who operated on Miss MacLure. The minute I met him I knew he'd be a good man to have around, and when I asked for his help, he didn't hesitate a minute."

"Good grief, Spicer, do doctors need bodyguards in this damned town?"

"Well, not most of them. Doctor Feigenbaum is involved in anti-Nazi movements and they took a couple of whacks at him. After that he put Henson on his payroll."

"I see. All right, you've included his address here so when I get back to Washington, I'll get a letter off to him. And while we're on the subject, how is Miss MacLure? Did she make it through her surgery yesterday?"

"Yes, sir. I stopped by the clinic this morning to see how Tiner was making out and found Miss MacLure awake. She was still pretty loopy from the anesthetic, but her nurse said she's doing well."

He held up the AARs again. "Good. I'd hate to think we went through all of this just to have her die during the operation that was supposed to save her life."

"Yes, sir."

"Now, about recognition for Sergeant Pierce. I'm going to put

287

him in for a Distinguished Service Cross. That's the Army's second highest medal for valor, and he certainly earned it." The general thought for a moment, and then added, "I see now that it could have just as easily been you receiving that medal posthumously. That's a very sobering thought."

I nodded without comment. I couldn't help thinking how an MID enlisted man receiving a DSC would certainly benefit the outfit when budget time came around. Davis was nobody's fool, he played the Washington games with the best of them. That was okay with me. All I cared about was seeing Russ's family receive their country's acknowledgement of his courage.

Thinking about Russ's family reminded me of something else. "Sir, were you able to track down Sergeant Pierce's family?"

"Yes. His mother and a younger sister live in a little berg called Corvallis. Ever hear of it?"

"No, sir, but I can find it."

"The fellow in our records department who dug up the address once lived up in Oregon. He says Corvallis is about 90 miles south of Portland.

"As for finding it, I want you to wait a few days and take care of some other business first. Then you can take a day off and have Slu Irvin fly you up there. You should be able to do that early next week. Will that make you happy?"

I nodded. "Yes, sir. Thank you."

"Now, about replacing Pierce as your ADC, I think you can handle the rest of this assignment on your own. If you need help, we'll get you someone, but I don't want any unnecessary staff issues slowing you down right now."

"Yes, sir." I wanted to ask what the rest of my assignment was, but I figured Davis would get to that in his own sweet time. He did.

He put on a thoughtful expression and said, "Sometimes there is a tendency in this business to get so focused on a specific enemy agent that we lose track of the overall assignment. In this instance you've spent three weeks chasing this Marjorie Yount and her pals around, and you successfully put all of them we know about out of business.

"Now that part is good, but we don't want to overlook the possibility that other Japanese agents could also be assigned to sniffing out the mission we're protecting. If what this Yount woman dug up sufficiently interested her bosses, it's likely they've put more people on it.

"For example, we are providing heavy protection for a couple of North American Aviation employees, so the Japanese are sure we have a special interest in those people—they must know something important. That by itself is enough to make Jap agents suspicious. In other words, they've stumbled on something that looks big and they want to find out what it is. Understood?"

I nodded my understanding and agreement. "Yes, sir. And the fact that they've lost four agents trying to find out what's going on is more of an encouragement than a deterrent. In my experience, the Japs don't give a damn about the people they lose. Taking out their agents just makes them more determined."

"That is exactly right. So what I want you to do is go back up to the Presidio and spend a few days going through all of our recent activity reports on known Japanese agents. See if you can connect any of the information you find in those reports to your assignment. If you can, it might give us an idea of who to look for and where to look for them."

"That's kind of a long shot, sir. Besides, we have analysts who are much better at that sort of thing than I am."

"Yes, we do, but you know what you're looking for. Because of the tight security on this assignment, they do not."

"Yes, sir. What do I do when I finish reading the reports?"

"Listen, Johnny, I know you don't like sitting around an office reading reports, but I think this is worth the effort. When you're done, let me know what, if anything, you found. Then you can go see Pierce's family. After that I want you at McClellan Army Airfield in Sacramento. That's where the action is going to be shortly when a whole bunch of B-25s show up more or less unannounced. I want you to hang around the field and do what you do best, keep your eyes open. You are to stick with those planes until they are aboard the Hornet and on their way to Tokyo. Understood?"

"Yes, sir."

"Do you have any questions or thoughts?"

I nodded and dug into my dispatch case. "Yes, sir. I have Sergeant Pierce's wallet. I found it at the explosion site and I picked it up because there's cash in it that belongs to Uncle Sam."

Davis took the wallet and looked through it. "All right, add up the cash so we can account for it as expenses, but leave it in the wallet. Give the wallet to the family when you go up there. It isn't much, but they might be able to use it."

"What about a service for him, sir?"

The general sighed. "Graves will put whatever remains were picked up in Santa Barbara into a sealed coffin. I know there wasn't much left of Sergeant Pierce, but his family doesn't need to know how bad it really is. The coffin will be shipped wherever the family wants it for burial. Anything else?"

"No, sir."

Davis stood up and offered his hand. I stood and shook it. "Johnny, you've got some leave coming when this is all over. After that we'll talk about a new assignment. Take good care of yourself."

"Thank you, sir."

I gave General Davis my best salute. He returned it and marched off toward his DC-3. The ship's crew had the props spinning by the time he got to the boarding ladder at the hatch. He turned and gave me a wave. No more than a minute later, the ship was taxiing away.

All of a sudden, I felt sad and a little lonely. I can't explain it, but I didn't like it. I picked up my dispatch case, flipped the empty cardboard coffee cup into a nearby trash can, and headed for the Army's Dodge.

I turned south on Sepulveda Boulevard and drove a couple of blocks to Rod's, a pretty decent hamburger joint I discovered a few months back when I was working in the area. I picked up a burger and a soda for the trip back to Santa Barbara.

It was 1330 when I pulled out of Rod's parking lot and turned north on Sepulveda, which is also California Route One. Following that road for a couple of hours would bring me nearly to the clinic's front door.

I parked in front of that door a few minutes after 1600. In the lobby, Mary told me she thought I would find Nurse Jackson somewhere in the new wing. I thanked her and took off in that direction.

Passing Sally's room, I saw Sergeant Tiner and one of Susan's nurses inside. He looked up when I stopped in the doorway. I gestured for him to join me in the hallway.

"Yes, sir?"

"Sergeant, I have my marching orders for the next few weeks. I'll be away for a while. If you should need me, call the Presidio number. They should be able to get a message to me. If you need a quicker response, General Davis is your back-up."

Tiner smiled. "That's some back-up, sir."

"As I said the other day, this thing we're involved in goes all the way to the top. Do you have Priority Able clearance?"

"Yes, sir."

"Okay, the only other thing I can tell you is you won't be stuck with this detail much beyond mid-April, and at some point around the end of this month they'll likely transfer Miss MacLure out of here. They may even send her home to Inglewood with a nurse. If and when that happens, you and your men tag right along. Understood?"

"Yes, sir."

"All right, Sergeant, I'll check in from time to time. Good luck."

"Thank you, sir."

As I passed Sally's old room a minute later, I noticed new, unpainted doorframes in both doorways to the room next door. It seemed, however, work had stopped for the day.

Susan was speaking into the telephone when I got to the nurses' station. She ended the call quickly and was in my arms kissing me a few seconds later. I remembered a time when she was much more reserved about demonstrations of affection in public. I viewed the new policy as an improvement.

An hour later Mister Whiskers gave us a royal welcome and I gave Susan a censored account of my meeting with General Chester Davis. My report included an edited version of the schedule Davis laid out for me.

Shaking her fist in the air for emphasis, Susan said, "Someday I will meet that man, and when I do, I'm gonna give him a poke right in the nose for keeping you too far away from me."

I laughed. "Oh, he'd charm you out of that idea before you got around to slugging him. The General can be very beguiling."

In her sternest tone of voice, she said, "No chance of that, is there, Whiskers? We've spent far too many nights alone."

Mister Whiskers looked up at Susan, looked up at me, and purred loud enough for the downstairs neighbors to hear him. He enjoyed being the center of attention.

Deciding we were more tired than hungry, we heated up leftovers from the little white boxes in the fridge instead of going out. It seems Chinese take-out is just as good the second day as the first.

After dinner we retired to the couch, where we listened to the radio. I tuned in KNX, "broadcasting from Columbia Square on Sunset Boulevard in Hollywood." Hearing KNX made me feel a little homesick. Columbia Square is not more than a dozen blocks from my old office at Hollywood Boulevard and Highland Avenue. At 1930 we heard George Burns and Gracie Allen, after which we yawned our way through Gene Autry's Melody Ranch, where he climbed back in the saddle yet again.

291

By 2100 I could barely keep my eyes open. Since Susan was suffering from the same affliction, we turned off the radio set and went to bed. Neither of us had the energy for love-making, so we invested the time in some much-needed slumber.

Thirty-One

1400 Hours – Saturday – 14 MAR 42

Presidio Building 100, San Francisco

After nearly three days of staring at Enemy Agent Activity Reports, my original stack of 304 was down to one. I began the ordeal by asking the archivist in MID's intelligence library for all the EAARs meeting several specific criteria, including date, location, and nationality. Some of the reports were no more than a paragraph or two, while those written by the outfit's more loquacious field agents were several pages in length.

I tossed EAAR number 304 on top of my "finished" stack and picked up number 305. Of course, the last report was the only one in the entire stack containing anything even remotely related to my assignment. The report was filed from someplace called Fairfax, Kansas. That location triggered a memory of Sally telling us the B-25D variant was built in a plant North American hastily constructed in Kansas City, Kansas to speed up production.

Curious if Fairfax was anywhere near Kansas City, I got up, stretched, and opened a big world atlas kept on the archive room's counter. Turns out Fairfax is actually a district of Kansas City tucked into a large bend of the Missouri River north of town. It is also home to the Fairfax Municipal Airport, which happens to be the location of the NAA plant Sally told us about. It's handy to have an airport around when you're building airplanes.

Returning to my table and EAAR number 305, I found the report concerned a Japanese agent by the name of Abe Yuta, which would be said last name first something like AH-bay YU-tuh. Mister Abe, according to the MID agent who filed the report, was observed on the Fairfax Municipal Airport grounds wearing white coveralls with the word "Maintenance" stenciled on the back.

When our agent questioned the airport maintenance supervisor, the man claimed he'd never heard of Abe Yuta and certainly had no Japanese employees on his crew. Whether or not the supervisor would know a Japanese person if one came up and bit him on the butt is unknown. Something or someone must have tipped Mister Abe off, however, because the report concluded by saying there have been no further sightings of him.

You might think finding someone who looks Japanese, assuming that to be the case with Abe Yuta, would be easier in these times than locating a western-looking agent like Marjorie Yount, but that's not always the case. Because of his appearance, Abe Yuta would have sense enough to stay out of sight whenever possible, whereas Yount could move around in public without attracting attention.

So, was the Abe sighting meaningful in terms of my assignment? Probably not. Even though I didn't know where Doolittle's B25s were, I was pretty sure they weren't at a municipal airport in Kansas. It was more likely they were someplace the squadron could practice landing their ships in the short length of an aircraft carrier deck without anyone paying much attention.

While I don't believe in coincidences, this had all the earmarks of a rare instance that might actually be one. Still, following up on the Abe lead couldn't hurt, so I added EAAR number 305 to the stack and took all of the reports back to the counter. There, I exchanged the reports for the Jap spy mug book.

Back at my table, I opened the mug book and found Abe Yuta on the second page. The photo was so out of focus and grainy it made the snapshot of Marjorie Yount I was carrying around look like a studio glamour portrait. About all you could tell for sure from Mister Abe's photo was that he had two eyes, a nose, and a mouth in more or less the usual places.

The information accompanying the photo wasn't much help either. We knew him to be a Jap spy because he was seen meeting with another known Japanese agent. Sightings of Abe were few and mostly in the west or Midwest. That was it.

The woman behind the counter remembered me from when Sally and I found Marjorie Yount's photo in the same mug book, and I'm sure she was not looking forward to another "rush" request for a copy photo. I gave her a break and told her I didn't need the copy of Abe's mugshot until Monday morning at 0800 hours. She did not seem appropriately grateful.

Glad to be out of Building 100 and into the fresh air, I took a leisurely stroll down to Crissy Field. Stu Irvin's AT-7 was there, so I figured he wouldn't be too far away. I found him in the main hangar drinking coffee that resembled old motor oil from a filthy ceramic mug that looked like it hadn't been washed since the Great War.

He saw me coming "Oh, oh, run for it boys, here comes trouble."

"Hell, Irvin, you should be grateful to me."

"Oh? And for what act of kindness and/or generosity on your part should I be grateful?"

"I've made you famous. Why, just the other day General Chester Davis mentioned you by name. Now, just how many Army Air Force prop jockeys do you think the general knows by name?"

Taking a swallow of the sludge in his mug, Stu said, "One too many. Where to this time, spook?"

"Corvallis, Oregon tomorrow morning."

If anyone could nod boringly, Irvin could. "Oh, we're back on the Oregon kick, huh? I don't know, Spicer, I'd have to miss church to take you up there tomorrow morning."

"Irvin, if you walked into a church, lightning would surely strike and turn the place to ashes."

He looked genuinely hurt. "Hey, that's not a nice thing to say. I'll have you know I went to Sunday school religiously as a kid."

"The Sunday school teacher must have been a tomato."

He grinned. "She was."

"Well, if it's any consolation, we're going up to Corvallis for a notification."

Stu's expression got serious in a hurry. "Oh? Who bought the farm? Anyone I know?"

"Yeah, my ADC, Russ Pierce."

"Oh hell, Spicer, I'm sorry to hear that. I liked him. How did he go?"

"We were trying to defuse a Jap time bomb in a clinic full of wounded soldiers and we failed. Russ succeeded in saving a bunch of lives, though, by getting the bomb out of the building before it blew. General Davis put him up for the DSC, but I'm pretty certain Russ would swap the medal for another chance at that bomb."

"I get that. What time do we leave in the morning?"

I shrugged. "I don't know. How long a flight is it?"

"That's near Portland, isn't it?"

"Yeah, I'm told it's about ninety miles south."

"I usually figure Portland at three hours, so take half an hour off that."

I did some mental arithmetic. "Okay, how about we leave at oh-eight-hundred? That should get me to the family house around eleven-hundred-hours."

Stu nodded. "Oh-eight-hundred it is. How long will we be up there?"

"I imagine a couple of hours."

"Got it. See you at oh-eight-hundred, and Spicer, I'm sorry about Pierce. He was a good guy."

"Yeah, he was. See you tomorrow morning."

Returning to Building 100, I used a secure telephone to call Washington and make my promised report to General Davis. He wasn't any more impressed with the fruits of my Enemy Agent Activity Report labors than I was. I told him I planned to see Pierce's family on Sunday. He said fine, and that was the end of the conversation.

I took it easy the rest of Saturday, ending the day with a call to Susan from the payphone out in front of the Presidio's Visiting Officers Quarters. She said all was well at the clinic. Sally was still making progress and Mister Whiskers sent his love. I hit the sack early and spent some time thinking how I would break the news to Russ's family. I decided there was no way to plan something like that. You just had to do it and hope for the best.

Sunday morning, I put on a uniform and transferred Russ's wallet from my dispatch case to my blouse pocket. Then I went downstairs and dropped a dime into the kitty next to the coffee pot in the VOQ lobby. The dime bought me a cardboard cup of fresh coffee. I drank most of it before putting the cup into one of the car cup holders Stu gave me, and driving down to Crissy Field.

1100 Hours – Sunday – 15 MAR 42

Corvallis Army Airfield, Corvallis, Oregon

Two hours and some change after we lifted off of Crissy's runway, we turned into the airfield pattern at Corvallis. Stu said, "You've got the luck of the Irish, Spicer. A week ago, we would have had to land in Portland and drive back to Corvallis. They just approved the new runway here for military use. The only other functional parts of the base are the tower and the ops shack. They're still working on the rest of the place."

With little appreciation in my voice, I said, "Fortune doth smile upon me."

Stu looked over at me in the copilot's seat. "Hey, I can let you out right here in the pattern if you'd prefer."

"No, go ahead and land. You need the practice."

He muttered, "Spooks."

Once on the ground, Stu parked the AT-7 beside the operations shack and we climbed out. It felt good to stretch and move around without airplane controls in the way. It seems the AT-7 cockpit shrinks in direct proportion to the length of the flight.

I told Stu he didn't have to go with me to make the notification and he seemed happy to stay with his beloved airplane. I went into the ops shack, where a staff sergeant behind the counter asked if he could help me. I told him I needed transportation into Corvallis.

"I'd be happy to loan you a staff car, sir, but we only have one so far and it's in use. I can call a taxi for you, if you'd like."

"Yes, please do that."

I told the woman driving the cab I wanted to go to 509 Northwest Polk Avenue. She said, "Oh, the Pierce place. You a friend of the Pierce's, are you?"

Apparently, everybody really does know everybody in small town America. I said, "A friend of their son's."

"Which one? They have two, Russell and Ricky."

"Russ."

"He's in the Army like you. That where you know him from?"

"Yes."

The woman was blessedly quiet for several minutes. It took her that long to figure things out. When she did, she asked, "Say, you wouldn't be bringing the Pierce's bad news, would you?"

"My mission is classified, ma'am, I've said all I can say."

That shut her up until we pulled up to a large white farmhouse in a rural neighborhood without curbs or streetlamps.

"That will be thirty-five cents, Major."

I dropped two quarters into her outstretch hand and said, "Would you please wait a couple of minutes while I make sure somebody is home?"

"Well, we usually charge for waiting."

"Think of it as a contribution to the war effort."

The woman glared at me and I walked up a path to the front door of the Pierce's house. There was no doorbell, so I knocked. When a young woman with the same sort of clean-cut features as Russ and a white apron over her blue dress opened the door, I said, "Good morning. My name is Johnny Spicer. Would you be

June Pierce?"

A hint of concern crossed her face. "Yes, I'm June."

I glanced back over my shoulder to wave the cab driver off, but she was already making a U-turn to head back the way we'd come. To June Pierce, I said, "Miss Pierce, I've come to see you and your mother regarding Russ. May I come in?"

She opened the door wide to let me in. "Yes, of course, Major Spicer. I should have recognized your name from Russ's letters. I'm afraid mother isn't home, though."

Removing my cap, I stepped into a cozy living room with crocheted doilies on the arms of the chairs and sofa. Maroon and white chintz window curtains were pulled wide to let the sun in. "Will your mother be back soon?"

"I'm afraid not. She took the train up to Seattle to visit my aunt. Is there something I can help you with?"

"Miss Pierce, I'm sorry, but I'm here with some bad news."

June Pierce nodded slowly. "I was afraid of that. Something has happened to Russell."

"Yes. He was killed in the line of duty last week."

With tears already rolling down her face, she sank into an overstuffed chair. After a moment spent composing herself, June asked the first question that occurs to most service family members when they learn about the death of a son or brother. "Can you tell me how he died?"

"Yes. I can. He and I were removing a Japanese explosive device from a clinic full of wounded military personnel and the device exploded while he was carrying it away from the building."

Looking up at me in shock, she sobbed, "Oh, no. That's horrible!"

"I know it's not much consolation, Miss Pierce, but Russ died a hero. The wounded soldiers and sailors, nurses, and doctors at that clinic are alive today because of his bravery. He's been nominated for a Distinguished Service Cross, one of the country's highest honors for soldiers."

June pulled a hanky from a pocket of her apron and wiped some tears away. "Thank you for that, Major Spicer. It really is some consolation to know he died saving others. That is so like Russell."

"Yes, it is. In the relatively short time we worked together I came to appreciate his loyalty and dedication. Russ was more than a good soldier, he was a good man."

A new wave of sobs hit June Pierce. Between them, she said, "Yes . . . yes, he . . . he was. You should . . . should know Russell thought highly . . . of you. He . . . said so . . . often in his letters."

"Thank you, Miss Pierce. I'm pleased to know that. Can I get you anything? A glass of water or something?"

She shook her head. "No, thank you, Major Spicer. I'll be all right. This is just . . . such a shock."

"I understand. I keep thinking of things I want to tell Russ, and then realize I can't."

She nodded. "Major Spicer, I have a favor to ask."

"Name it."

"Would you please stay for a few more minutes while I call mother? She may have some questions I can't answer."

"Certainly. I will tell her about Russ if you want me to."

June shook her head. "No, I think it would be better if it came from me. I'll call her now, if that's okay."

"That's fine."

"The telephone is in the kitchen."

I followed her down a hallway into what struck me as a typical farmhouse kitchen, even though I couldn't recall ever actually being in a farmhouse. The telephone was a combination of old and modern, an upright candlestick instrument with a dial attached to its base.

While she placed her call with a long-distance operator, I looked out the kitchen window. The Pierce's backyard fit with everything else about the house. Besides a sturdy clothesline and a neatly painted toolshed, there were several flowerbeds containing a variety of healthy-looking plants. The only ones I recognized were roses.

June broke the news to her mother, they consoled each other for a few moments, and then the call was over. The women of the Pierce family were made of stout stuff.

June said to me, "Mother asked me to thank you for coming all this way to see us. She wishes she could meet you."

"Perhaps we can meet another time. I'd like to come back for a visit when the war is over."

She smiled what I suspected was the best smile she could muster under the circumstances. "Yes, Major Spicer, please do that."

"Plan on it. Shall we sit at the kitchen table for a few minutes while I cover some details?"

"Yes. Forgive me. I'm not being very hospitable. Would you like some coffee?"

"No thanks, and I think you're doing quite well under the circumstances."

At the table I explained she would soon receive a letter from the Army Quartermaster Graves Registration Service regarding the disposition of Russ's remains. His body would be transported in a military coffin wherever the family specified and would be accompanied by an honor guard.

I also told June she would be hearing from the Department of Veterans Affairs regarding benefits to surviving family members of soldiers. I knew Russ carried GI life insurance, the premium for which was deducted from his pay. The Army would also be contacting her about back pay Russ had coming and similar matters. I gave her a typed information sheet with addresses and telephone numbers for various Army and government agencies she might need to contact.

Finally, I gave June one of my MID business cards. "Miss Pierce, if you need help with any of this, here's my card. The number on the card is our west coast headquarters at the Presidio in San Francisco. As Russ probably told you, we travel quite a bit, but if you leave a message for me at that number, I will receive it and call you as soon as I can."

"Thank you so much, Major Spicer. I really appreciate you going to all this trouble for us. I'm sure mother is grateful to you as well."

For some reason that made me feel kind of bad. It wasn't right that I should be praised just for treating Russ's family with the respect they deserved. I said, "Miss Pierce, I have a favor to ask."

June looked a little surprised. "What can I do for you, Major Spicer."

"From now on, would you please call me Johnny? I'm not a career military man and I still have trouble getting used to all the Army's protocol. I would have told Russ the same thing, but he had to go by the rules. You don't."

She gave me a sweet smile. "Okay, Johnny. I'd be honored to do that if you will call me June."

"Deal."

Next, I reached into my blouse pocket and removed Russ's wallet. I handed it to June, saying, "This is Russ's. The rest of his personal effects—clothes and things—are being packed up and shipped to you, but that could take some time and I wanted to be sure you got this promptly."

Taking the wallet, she opened it and looked at the photos Russ carried with him. She held one up. It was a fairly recent picture of June. "That's yours truly on a family picnic last summer. Thank you, Johnny. It feels kind of good to know I was with Russ in his last moments."

A stray tear found its way down her cheek. "You definitely were. Russ loved his family more than anything."

June wiped the tear away and smiled the same sweet smile. "I know, and we loved him. Russ was the best brother a sister could ask for."

"I would have guessed that. Well, June, unless you have any questions I haven't answered, I should be going. Would you mind calling a taxi to take me back to the airfield?"

With vehemence, she said, "Yes, I would mind. I will drive you back. That's the least I can do for all the kindness you've shown mother and me."

We rode to the airport in a spotless two-year-old black Ford convertible. When we got into it, June said, "This is Russ's car. He lets me use . . . I mean . . . ."

"I understand, June. It's a beauty, too." I didn't mention that seeing the Ford convertible reminded me of the big smile on Russ's face when I saw him driving Sally's similar Mercury convertible. He was definitely a convertible sort of fellow.

At Corvallis Army Airfield, I got out of Russ's Ford and walked around to the driver's window. "Thank you for the lift, June. The woman who drove the taxi to your house was as nosy as they come. She wanted to know what business I had at the Pierce place. I think I insulted her when I told her my business was classified and I couldn't tell her."

June smiled again. "Good for you, Johnny." After a short pause, she added, "Thanks again for all you've done, and please don't forget your promise to come and see mom and me after the war."

"I won't, June. Now, you take good care of yourself and remember to call me if you need anything, and I mean anything."

"I will, Johnny. Have a safe flight home."

With that we shook hands and June drove away. I didn't envy her the next few days. They were going to be tough for her and her mother. I hoped I'd helped to make that time just a little easier.

Stu was waiting for me in the ops shack. He saw me arrive with a pretty girl in a convertible and I could just tell he was going to say something about it. I gave him a look that clearly said I would not appreciate any smart comments.

We touched down at Crissy at 1612. I thanked Stu for the ride and headed for the VOQ, grateful to be back home, or at least back to what I would call home for the next sixteen hours or so before I started my drive to McClellan Army Airfield in Sacramento.

Before going to bed Sunday night, I called Susan. Ever since I left Corvallis I'd been thinking about Susan being in a similar situation to June Pierce's. I needed to talk with her. I didn't have anything in particular to say, it was just good to hear her voice.

Thirty-Two

1100 Hours – Monday – 16 MAR 42

McClellan Army Airfield, Sacramento

Nearly three hours after leaving the Presidio, I showed my MID ID to an MP at McClellan Airfield's Palm Street gate. From there I drove straight to the Air Service Command building, where I was pleased to see their increased security measures still in effect. Inside, I asked for First Sergeant Joe Richards. He was surprised to see me.

"Hello, Major Spicer! It's good to see you again, sir."

"Hello, Sergeant Richards."

"What brings you back to our little corner of Paradise, sir?"

"I guess I just can't get enough of your hospitality. Tell me, have they replaced Captain Ellis yet?"

He shook his head. "Not yet, sir. I've heard they're working on it, but you know how that goes."

"I do, Sergeant. So, you're still running ASC here, right?"

"Temporarily, yes sir."

"Good. Let's you and I take a short walk and get some fresh air."

"Yes, sir. I'll just grab my jacket. Some of that fresh air is a little chilly today."

We crossed the street behind the ASC building and strolled along the flight line. Sergeant Richards was right, the air had a nip to it, enough so that I could see my breath when I spoke.

"Sergeant, I expect you'll be happy to know all of the Japanese agents we know of who were directly involved with Captain Ellis' death have joined their honorable ancestors."

"That's good news, sir. My wife is getting pretty annoyed at sharing our bed with a Colt forty-five."

"I wouldn't put that Colt back on the top shelf of your closet quite yet."

"No?"

"Do you remember Captain Vernon Carlson?"

"Yes, sir. You were asking about him the last time you were here."

"Correct. It seems Carlson turned and was working for the Japs."

Richards looked flabbergasted. "Wow! I sure never expected that. Do you think he'll be back, sir?"

"I can assure you he, personally, won't be back, but you have to remember whatever he knew about the mission involving those field conversion kits North American is building for you, is also known by the Japs, and after all the effort they've put into finding out what's going on, I'm pretty sure we haven't heard the last of them yet."

Richards did not look happy. "I see, sir."

"You are aware, are you not, that a whole flock of Mitchells will be descending upon you soon?"

"I have no direct knowledge of that, sir. Twenty-four refueling kits were ordered and we've also received a shipment of thirty-two low-speed B-25 propeller assemblies. Putting two and two together, I can conclude we would be installing those kits and propellers on something, but I have no specific orders as of yet."

"Well, here's something else to include in your equation. Those B-25s on which you conclude you will be hanging all that stuff are the reason I'm here. My specific orders are to stick with those ships until they leave the country, that is, assuming they will be leaving the country."

"Yes, sir. I assume there is concern about sabotage while they're here?"

"That's a possibility, but not the only concern. Sergeant, do you have any idea where those Mitchells might be going when they leave here?"

He shook his head vehemently. "No, sir, I do not."

"Good. Neither do the Japs, and my job is to make sure they continue not knowing the answer to that question until such time as it no longer matters."

"Understood, sir."

"So, you've received no specific orders regarding the aircraft?"

"Not officially. Captain Carlson told Captain Ellis we would be making field modifications to some ships using parts supplied by the Army Depot. Typically, we are also expected to go over ships that come through here and put them in the best possible shape. That's one of the base's primary roles."

"Have the in-flight refueling system field modification kits arrived yet?"

"They have not, sir. I've been calling the depot about every other day, urging them to contact the supplier and make sure they're on the ball."

I smiled. "Good idea. I'm sure the mission commander will appreciate your persistence in this matter."

"Yes, sir. So, you will be here for a while?"

"It looks that way."

1000 Hours – Friday – 27 MAR 42

McClellan Army Airfield, Sacramento

While sitting on my hands for days on end waiting for something to happen, nothing did. Well, almost nothing. On Friday, 20 March, a deuce-and-a-half showed up outside Sergeant Richard's building with a load of 24 in-flight refueling system field installation kits from North American Aviation via the Sacramento Signal Depot.

Then, early on the morning of Tuesday, 24 March. Sergeant Richards sought me out. He had a piece of pale yellow teletype paper in his hand. He said nothing but handed me the teletype. The message was short and to the point:

MCCLELLAN AIR SERVICE COMMAND
24 MAR 42 1607 Z
8 AAF HQ

EXPECT ARRIVAL OF 22 B-25B AIRCRAFT BETWEEN 26 MAR AND 27 MAR 42 FOR SERVICE AND MODIFICATION AS DIRECTED. FLT UNDER COMMAND OF LT COL JAMES DOOLITTLE.

I nodded and handed the slip back to Sergeant Richards. He returned my nod and hurried off to alert his people.

Thursday, 26 March came and went with nary a B-25 on the horizon. Around mid-morning on 27 March, however, they showed up in droves. Before long, impatient pilots had the McClellan flight line looking like rush hour in the Cahuenga Pass.

I was standing next to Sergeant Richards on the flight line while he sorted out what was surely the largest aircraft traffic jam in Army Air Force history. Part way into the landing operations, a short Lieutenant Colonel in a well-worn leather flight jacket and an overseas cap marched up, took a chewed-up stogie out of his mouth, and demanded, "Who the hell is in charge of this God-awful foul up?"

Richards snapped to attention. "I am, sir."

"Sergeant, if you damage any of my airplanes in this mess, I will personally see to it you spend the rest of this war in the stockade. Got that?"

"Yes, sir."

About that time Doolittle noticed me standing off to the side. "Who the hell are you?"

"Spicer, MID."

He studied me for a moment. "Oh yeah, I heard about you. You're the guy who's been stacking up dead Jap spies out here like cordwood. That right?"

"I'm one of the guys."

"Well, keep up the good work for another couple of weeks or so and it won't matter what the hell they find out about us."

"Will do, sir."

He walked away patting his pockets. He didn't find what he was looking for and turned back to me. "Hey, Major, you got a light?"

I handed him my Zippo. He lit his cigar butt and dropped my lighter into a side pocket of his leather flight jacket. As he turned to leave, I said, "Colonel, that Zippo was a birthday gift from my fiancé. If I show up without it, she's gonna come lookin' for you and the Japs will be the least of your worries."

He stopped short and looked me square in the eye. He just stood there doing his best to intimidate me and I just stared right back at him. Finally, he grinned. "Spicer, you're okay."

Doolittle tossed me the lighter and turned back to Sergeant Richards. "Briefing with your maintenance crew chiefs at eleven-hundred hours in your office, assuming you have an office."

"Yes, sir." Pointing at the ASC building, he added, "In that building, sir. I'm Sergeant Richards, acting ASC commander."

Nodding and ignoring the hell out of the "No Smoking" signs plastered all over the place, Doolittle disappeared into the hangar where his B-25 was parked. The guy walked with a swagger that inspired confidence because it said he'd been there and back. From what I knew about Doolittle, he'd earned the right to swagger.

Not knowing how many people would be in on the briefing, Richards decided to hold it the ASC's conference room instead of his office. I spoke with the MPs around the ASC building and the one in the lobby about who would be allowed in.

I included myself on the guest list. Since I was supposed to keep an eye on the proceedings it would help if I knew what the proceedings included. At 1100 hours sharp, Doolittle and a First Lieutenant walked into the conference room. Richards and his three staff sergeants came to attention. I stood at the farthest corner of the room from the door.

Of course, Doolittle noticed me the minute he walked in the door, but he said nothing about my presence. "At ease. Take your seats, men."

Doolittle studied the ASC men in the room for a moment, and then said, "As you may have noticed, we brought you a few B-25Bs this morning. They will be used in a highly specialized and very secret mission. The ships have already received some modification. Your jobs are to finish the modifications and make sure each ship is in top combat condition.

"While you're doing those jobs, you will say absolutely nothing about what you're doing to anyone—not to your wives, not to your mamas, not to your bookies, nobody! You need to impress that point on your men daily. The MID major at the back of the room has orders to shoot anyone who opens his big yap. So, keep your traps shut. Is that correct, Major Spicer?"

"It is, Colonel Doolittle."

"Good. Now that we have the basics covered, I'm going to turn this briefing over to First Lieutenant Bower. He's our engineering officer on this mission and he'll bring you up to date on the aircraft and what we expect from you men. Also, if you have any specific questions regarding work on a specific ship, he's the guy you ask. Go ahead, Bower."

Lieutenant Bower stood and filled up a large part of the room. He was a burly guy with something like a perpetual smirk on his face. His voice was deep enough to sing bass with the Ink Spots. "First, we actually only brought you twenty-two of our twenty-four aircraft. The last two weren't up to the trip. You will find a few others that need more attention than we have time to give them. The lowest acceptable number of combat-worthy ships for this mission is sixteen. That's your target number, and you must meet it, no excuses.

"The aircraft are all B models, and most were fairly new but not combat-worthy when we got them. Since then, we've beat the hell out of them while training for this mission. That couldn't be helped. Now it's your job to make 'em right again.

"Some modifications were made to the ships at the base where we did our training. The most significant of these mods include removal of the lower gun turrets, installation of de-icers and anti-icers, addition of steel blast plates around the upper turrets, removal of the liaison radios, and the installation of dummy fifty-cal gun barrels in the tail cones as a deterrent to attacks from the rear. We've hung 160-gallon neoprene auxiliary fuel tanks in the bomb bays and mounts for additional fuel cells were added in other locations around the aircraft. With the addition of the in-flight refueling kits you will install, we will end up with eleven-hundred gallons of fuel, useable, in each aircraft.

"The only other modification you need to be aware of concerns bombsights. These ships were originally equipped with Norden Mark Fifteen units. They're the ones with stabilized bombing approach autopilot systems. For our application, those sights are worthless. They were removed along with all of their mechanical autopilot linkages. Instead we're using a bombsight that costs 20-cents a pop to build and were put together by one of our pilots, Captain Greening, in his spare time. For our purposes his 'Mark Twain' bombsight is considerably more reliable than the Norden.

"Now, the time available for the work you will do is limited. We need to be out of here on 31 March. That gives you four days including today to get everything done. On top of that we need to fly a few more training missions. We'll fly those missions in the ships you've finished as you finish them. Obviously, you'll have to work round the clock to meet that schedule, so let's get humping!"

Doolittle stood again. "All right, men, there's a lot riding on this mission and we're counting on you to help us get it done. As Lieutenant Bower said, let's get humping. Dismissed."

The conference room emptied in a matter of seconds. Lieutenant Colonel Doolittle, however, stayed behind to ask me a question. "Major, level with me. What security problems are we really facing here?"

"Colonel, any answer to that question will be an educated guess at best, and my guess is the Japs will send at least one agent in here before you leave. I don't expect a sabotage attempt, though. It's too late for that."

"Yeah? If the aircraft aren't their target, why would the Japs be here?"

"Information. That's what they've been after all along. If they'd gotten it earlier, they might be after the aircraft, but at this point they desperately need to know what you're up to."

Doolittle nodded. "All right, how will they go about trying to get the information they want?"

"Mostly by watching what's going on and listening to what's said. The technical term is 'intelligence gathering.' For example, they already know in-flight refueling systems will be installed here. That tells them you're going on a long-range mission. What they need to know are the targets of that mission and when you will attack those targets. Now, the Air Service Command people don't know that stuff, but I assume your crews do, or they at least know enough to narrow the possibilities down, so they can't assume it's safe to discuss the mission in the open here."

"They know that, but I'll remind them. Anything else?"

"Yes. They need to keep their eyes open. Your guys all know what is normal on a flight line. If they see anything that seems out of whack, they need to let me know about it, pronto."

"Got it. How many people do you have here?"

"Just me."

Doolittle's bushy eyebrows shot up in surprise. Sounding incredulous, he asked, "You're it?"

"Yes. The Japs know most of our agents and they would quickly spot a large number of MID people hanging around the base. That, in itself, would be a dead giveaway as to the mission's importance. Me being the only MID presence here has the opposite effect—it makes the activity here seem less important. Of course, a bunch of base MPs will be patrolling the line, but that would be a normal occurrence with this many aircraft around."

Doolittle shook his head in something like amazement. "I hope to hell you're right."

"Like I said, Colonel, it's an educated guess."

"Well, your batting average has been pretty damned good, so I guess we'll do it your way."

On that note, Lieutenant Colonel Doolittle turned around and left me alone in the conference room. I hoped to hell I was right, too.

1300 Hours – Saturday – 28 MAR 42

McClellan Army Airfield, Sacramento

With all the activity in the hangars and on the flight line, even my Aunt Tilly would have figured out something big was happening. There was no hiding that fact.

After inhaling a sandwich at the Feathered Prop Café, I returned to the line and continued trolling for enemy agents. So far, I'd seen a sum total of zero, which either meant I was missing something or I was overestimating the Japs' desire to know what Doolittle and his gang were up to.

Strolling into one of the repair hangars, I spotted a small group of the Colonel's people gathered near one of the B-25s undergoing a propeller swap. I was casually walking in their direction to see what they were discussing when a movement over their heads caught my eye.

The hangar had a peaked roof supported by vertical I-beams of incremental lengths rising from several latitudinal girders spanning the width of the building. The girder nearest where I thought I'd seen movement was equipped with a special catwalk for access to the lifting mechanism of a gantry crane which could be positioned to lift heavy aircraft parts and move them from one side of the hangar to the other.

I slowly followed the length of the catwalk with my eyes until I saw the movement again. There was someone up there, all right. A fellow in olive drab fatigues was lying on the catwalk almost directly over the B-25 where Doolittle's fliers were having their confab.

Had a Jap spy finally showed up? It seemed that way. All I had to do is figure out how to nail him. His location, twenty feet above my head, meant that would take some doing. From his position he could watch both of the two overhead access ladders, diagonally opposite each other at the ends of the hangar. If I climbed one, he would spot me and head for the other ladder.

Okay, if I couldn't get to him, maybe I could get him to come to me. Base MPs were providing security up and down the flight line, including one posted just outside the hangar I was in. I stepped through the big overhead door and gestured for the husky corporal with a black MP armband to come over.

When the MP was standing next to me to one side of the open hangar door, I said, "Corporal, don't try to see him from here, but there is someone I suspect might be a spy up in the rafters of this hangar."

I could tell he was fighting the urge to look. "What do you want me to do, sir? Should I get help?"

"No, I think we can handle this. The fellow is on the catwalk next to the overhead crane. In a minute I want you to climb the access ladder at this end of the hangar as if you're coming to get him. When he sees you coming, he'll head for the other ladder at the back of the hangar, which is his only escape route. I'll be out of sight back there waiting for him."

"Yes, sir. Is he armed?"

"I don't know. Hell, I'm not even positive he's an enemy agent, but he's sure acting like one."

"Well, if he is armed and shoots at me, should I return fire?"

"No. Stray rounds will bounce around this metal hangar like ping-pong balls. Someone is bound to get hurt. Just stay low and keep flushing him in my direction."

He gave me a dubious look but nodded. I said, "Wait here for three or four minutes while I get into position, and then climb the ladder."

The MP nodded again. I turned around and casually strolled through the hangar. At the back, near the second access ladder, I slipped behind a tall stack of shipping crates that concealed me from the Jap spy, assuming that's what he was.

A minute later the MP walked into the hangar and over to the access ladder on the opposite side and opposite end of the building. He leaned his Tommy gun against the wall and opened the flap on his sidearm holster. I was glad he had sense enough not to try climbing a vertical ladder with the Thompson hanging on his shoulder.

As he started up the ladder, I chanced a look at the fellow on the catwalk. He was still there, and since his back was to me, I couldn't yet tell if he saw the MP coming after him yet. A moment later, he shifted his position toward the MP climbing the ladder. Then he turned to look at the back ladder. The guy now knew he was officially in trouble.

I'm certain he couldn't see me, but he must have figured we'd set a trap for him. Instead of heading for the back ladder, he turned left and ran down the catwalk toward the crane hoist mechanism, which at that moment was on my side of the building. A lifting hook suspended from a stout chain was supporting a Wright-Cyclone engine about to be hoisted into position in the wing of a B-25.

In a flash he was over the railing and shinnying down the chain. A moment after he grabbed the chain, the crane operator, concentrating on the load he needed to raise and oblivious to what was happening in the rafters, put the hoist in motion to lift the engine. To his surprise, the Jap suddenly found himself going up instead of down. To counter the movement of the hoist, he increased his rate of descent.

I came out of my hiding place at a dead run. Unless he jumped, the Jap was going to end up on the wing of the B-25. He spotted me and, hanging onto the chain with one hand, he reached into the right-front pocket of his fatigue pants, intending to pull a pistol—a Japanese eight-millimeter Nambu by the look of it when he got it out. The pistol, however, got hung up in his pocket, and before he got it all the way out the thing discharged. I heard the muffled pop and saw his right leg jerk.

It looked very much like my Jap spy had just managed to shoot himself, but if he did, it wasn't slowing him down much. With the pistol finally out of his pocket, he let off a round in my direction and went back to shinnying down the chain.

The round he fired at me ricocheted off the concrete floor, near my feet and again off of a metallic object off to my left. His second shot did just about the same thing. The sound of gunshots and ricocheting slugs got the attention of the mechanics working under the Jap, and they scattered, including the guy controlling the hoist. The ship they were working on was nosed into the wall on my side of the hangar and the engine being installed had been headed for the port wing, but was now dangling just above its intended destination.

Coming from the starboard side of the B-25, I ducked for cover under the wing on that side of the ship. Ahead of me, beyond the belly of the aircraft and next to the port wing was a roll-around platform on which two of the mechanics who'd scattered had been standing so they could guide the engine into position. I made for it and reached the platform's ladder just as I heard a solid thump over my head, indicating the Jap was now on top of the wing.

My plan was to climb the ladder, so I could get a shot at him from above the wing. With the Jap on top of the wing now, that didn't seem like such a smart idea because it made me a clear shot for him, too.

I could hear him moving around up there on top of the wing because the hangar had gone completely silent. It was like everybody was tuned into Gangbusters to find out what was going to happen next.

Being a mid-winged aircraft, the top of a B-25's wing is only eight or nine feet above the ground. A jump to the ground from that height was entirely possible, but if I was right about the Jap shooting himself in the leg, he was more likely to try descending by way of the roll-around platform. With my Colt in hand, I waited to see which route he was going to take.

I could hear him moving over my head, but what I heard didn't make any sense. It sounded as if he was moving to the opposite wing. If that's where he was headed, he had to climb over the fuselage to get there. It sounded like he was doing exactly that.

Turning toward the port wing, I was about to duck under the bomb bay door again when I heard a scraping sound behind me. It was the sound of a boot on the metal crew boarding ladder. In that instant I realized there was another route down from the wing and my Jap pal had taken it.

He climbed into the ship through the escape hatch in the cockpit canopy and dropped down through the crew boarding hatch in front of the bomb bay. I had just enough time to spin in his direction and throw myself to the concrete floor before the Jap dropped to the ground in a crouch and we were face to face with no more than five feet between us. We fired within a split second of each other. At that range, neither of us was likely to miss. We didn't.

His small eight-millimeter slug went through my uniform blouse and poked a hole in the fleshy part of my left shoulder. My big point-four-five caliber slug poked a hole in his chest. I went to the base infirmary to have the slug removed from my shoulder and get a tetanus booster. The Jap went to the morgue.

After getting patched up, I went to Joe Richards' office and used his telephone to call Washington. General Davis listened to my report with interest and showed about as much sympathy for my gunshot wound as it deserved.

"Send me the bill for having the hole in your uniform patched. I don't want you running around with an MID shield on a moth-eaten uniform."

"Of course not, sir."

"You say you don't recognize the agent? Are you sure he was a Jap?"

"He carried no ID, but he has Japanese facial features, and when I spotted him, he was eavesdropping on a conversation among a group of the mission's fliers. Also, he shot me with a Nambu 94, a Jap pistol. If he wasn't a Jap agent, he'll do until one comes along."

"And they took him to the Mather Army Airfield hospital morgue?"

"That's what I was told, sir."

"All right. I'll have Colonel Beecher send someone over there and figure out who this guy was. You fit to continue your assignment?"

"Sure, I'm all patched up. I might have a sore shoulder for a while, but nothing disabling."

"Good. How are things going there otherwise?"

"The prevailing opinion here is everything is on schedule."

"Okay, when you've seen them off from their final departure point, clean up the loose ends and let me know. After that you've got two weeks."

"Thank you, sir."

Toward the end of my telephone conversation with General Davis, Lieutenant Colonel Doolittle barged into Richards' office and paced around impatiently until I hung up the telephone. "I heard you got yourself shot, Major, but you look okay to me."

"I am. As they say in the movies, 'It was only a flesh wound.'"

"They tell me the guy who shot you was a Jap spy. That right?"

"It seems that way. MID is sending someone from San Francisco to try and ID the guy, but I have no doubt about him being a Japanese agent."

Doolittle smiled a rare smile. "Then good work, Spicer. Keep it up."

After that he was gone, and I used the phone again to check for messages at the Presidio. There were none, so I called Santa Barbara to check with Sergeant Tiner, or at least that's the story I'll tell anyone who asks why I called Santa Barbara from one of Uncle Sam's telephones.

I spoke with Tiner for a grand total of about fifteen seconds, and then had him get Susan on the line. "Hi, Johnny. How are you?"

I'd already decided not to tell her about getting shot. It was no big deal. "I'm fine. How are you doing?"

Susan hesitated, and then said, "Something happened that you aren't telling me. Are you okay?"

"I'm fine, Angel. I'll give you a complete report when I see you in a few days."

She sounded more cheerful. "A few days?"

"Yup. Possibly Thursday night if everything goes according to plan."

"That's swell, Johnny!"

I agreed with her and we ended the conversation. After that I went back to trolling for Jap spies.

Thirty-Three

0700 Hours – Thursday – 2 APR 42

Naval Air Station Alameda

Standing in a light foggy mist out near the end of a pier at Alameda Naval Air Station, I could see the Hornet and the escort vessels comprising Task Group 14.2 anchored about half a mile out in San Francisco Bay. Despite the fog, I could also clearly see Doolittle's B-25s crowded together on the aft half of the Hornet's flight deck.

The bombers began arriving at NAS Alameda from Sacramento on Wednesday, and by dusk Thursday, all sixteen Mitchells were aboard the Hornet. At that point the carrier left the dock to spend the night anchored in the bay with two cruisers, four destroyers, and a tanker.

Now there was smoke rising from the stacks of all eight ships. Around 0700 hours Task Group 14.2 began their journey. I watched them pass under the San Francisco-Oakland Bay Bridge and make a turn to the west, putting the ships on a course that would take them out under the Golden Gate. Next stop, Tokyo.

The Hornet's departure felt like the culmination of a six-week assignment that resulted in the death or injury of at least ten folks, including yours truly. It felt that way, but the assignment wouldn't be completed until the last bomb from the last B-25 landed on Tokyo.

It was expected to take the Hornet two weeks and change to reach its destination—a point at sea from which Doolittle's crews could reach Tokyo, and from there, safe landing spots in China. During that time a security slip-up could leave the task force open to attack by Japanese ships or aircraft.

So for the next two weeks all of the people the Doolittle

mission left behind were still potentially at risk from Jap agents. That group included everyone at the Sacramento Army Signal Depot and McClellan's Air Service Command; engineer Michael Wilkins, stashed at the Presidio; and of course, Sally at Casa Sobre El Mar.

Sergeant Joe Richards and the McClellan ACS people were surrounded by base MPs, so there wasn't much more I could do for them. I heard the Signal Depot's security got a swift kick in the pants from Colonel Beecher and security there was improved. Wilkins was covered by MID in San Francisco, and Sally had Sergeant Tiner and his team watching out for her at the clinic.

Of course, if the Japs learned the Mitchells went to Alameda from McClellan Army Airfield, it opened a whole new can of worms. A good agent would know base Naval personnel could make intelligent guesses about where their aircraft carrier might be going, even if they hadn't been let in on the specific details, but that was the Navy's problem . . . sort of.

In the meantime, the only thing I had to go on was a fuzzy photo of a Jap spy in Kansas City, who very likely had absolutely no connection to my assignment. MID might make an identification of the guy I'd shot in a McClellan hangar, but I couldn't see how knowing who he was would do me much good.

About all that was left for me to do was to keep my fingers crossed and my eyes open. Oh, and I needed to report the Hornet's departure to General Davis. I decided to get that chore out of the way next.

The sun was warming things up early for a change, so I slipped out of my uniform overcoat and drove the Army's Dodge to a Chevron station not far from the Navy's digs at Alameda. There, I placed a long-distance call to Washington.

Davis sounded as if he would have been surprised if the Hornet had not departed on schedule. I, on the other hand, was surprised and very happy to have survived a lousy mission to this point with nothing more than a minor shoulder wound.

"All right, Spicer, anything else going on I need to know about?"

"I don't think so, sir. I'm tying up a few loose ends, but nothing new."

"Then it looks like were over the hump on this one, but it might be a good idea for you to keep a low profile for a while."

I knew what he was thinking. "You figure the Japs have targeted me for a hit?"

"We haven't heard anything definite, but I would not be

surprised. You've been a real pain in the butt to them lately. I know you can handle yourself, but I wouldn't like to see any innocent bystanders hurt."

"Yes, sir. Point taken."

Having said all that needed to be said, we ended the conversation and I stood there in the telephone booth for a moment debating my next move. My plan was to head back to Santa Barbara and I was going to give Susan a call to let her know I would be there this afternoon, but remembering General Davis' final words, I decided to begin lowering my profile by not broadcasting my plans over the clinic's telephone system. Susan would be happy to see me whether she knew I was coming or not.

I filled up the Dodge's gas tank and pointed myself south through the east bay communities of San Leandro, Hayward, Fremont, and Milpitas, ending up on US Highway 101 in San Jose at the bottom of the bay. I rolled into Santa Barbara around 1530.

As I neared Casa Sobre El Mar I paid closer attention to my surroundings. I was reasonably certain nobody followed me from Alameda, but I wanted to be certain the Japs didn't have the clinic staked out. I saw nothing to indicate their presence, so I parked and walked into the lobby.

Mary greeted me enthusiastically. "Hello, Mister Spicer! You've been away a long time."

"Yes, and I'm glad to be back. Do you happen to know where Susan is?"

"I think she's at the new wing nurses' station. Do you want me to check?"

"No thanks, Mary. I'll track her down."

The door to Sally's room was closed and I nodded to one of Tiner's corporals standing in the hallway as I passed by. Further down the hall no signs of destruction remained next door to Sally's old room. At the nurses' station I found Susan posting something that looked like a schedule on the bulletin board.

She turned, saw me, and hurried into my arms. "Johnny! Gosh, I'm glad to see you!"

"The feeling is entirely mutual, Angel."

We shared a quick kiss and Susan asked, "Can you stay for a while?"

"Yes and no." Leaning close to her ear, I whispered, "Can you meet me at the Biltmore after you get off work? I'll explain things there."

She looked a little puzzled and whispered back, "Should I come prepared to stay?"

I nodded and changed the subject. "How's our patient?"

Susan smiled. "She's terrific. We're all really happy about how quickly she's recovering. Doctor Feigenbaum stopped by yesterday and was very pleased with her progress."

I grinned back at her. "Chalk that up to getting proper care."

"Chalk it up to spunk. That girl never gives up. Oh, and she asks about you and Russ frequently, especially you."

Nodding, I said, "I guess I ought to stop by and see her."

"Yes, you really ought to, and you don't need to worry about me being jealous. Sally and I have talked a lot. You're her hero and she loves you for that, but she also understands about us. Actually, I've enjoyed getting to know her."

"I'm glad to hear that. I'll stop by and see her, and then I've got to get going."

I got a kiss on the cheek and in a conspiratorial tone, Susan said, "I'll see you soon."

The door to Sally's room was open when I got there this time. Tiner's man was still in the hall. I nodded to him as I walked in. One of Susan's nurses was sitting in a chair chatting with Sally, and then I realized Sally was also sitting in a chair.

She even stood when I came in and took a few shaky steps with a cane to meet me. I said, "Well, look at you! Next thing you'll be out dancing all night."

Despite the cast that was still on her right arm, we hugged for several moments. Sally said, "You've been away a long time. I got better."

"I'll say you did."

The nurse stood. "Would you like me to leave, Major Spicer?"

I shook my head. "No, thanks. I've only got a few minutes."

The nurse nodded, and Sally said, "Only a few minutes? Gee, don't you love me anymore?"

Smiling, I said, "Sure I do, kiddo, but you seem to be getting along just fine without me hanging around."

Sally gave me a coy look. "Yes, but I might do even better if you were around a little more often." Returning to her chair, she said, "How's Russ?"

The nurse gave me a look that seemed to say this wasn't the time to tell her Russ was dead. Bowing to her judgement, I said, "Behaving himself."

Sally's expression changed to suspicious. "Are you sure about that?"

"Positive. We've been busy, and I'm happy to report all this security stuff will be over in another two or three weeks. Then I'll

318

be able to tell you what this has all been about."

"Good, but do I really want to know?"

I nodded. "I think you'll be pleased you were part of it."

"I hope whatever it is was worth all this."

"All I can say is to a lot of people you'll be a hero. Now, I need to get a move on."

Smiling, Sally said, "Okay, be that way. Say hello to Russ for me if you see him."

Something about the way she said that told me Sally knew damned well I wouldn't be seeing Russ. I just nodded and said, "Okay, kiddo. Behave yourself and I'll see you again soon."

I looked back over my shoulder from the door and Sally's expression had turned sad. I felt a little sad, too.

I drove into the Biltmore's circular drive remembering good times Susan and I shared there before the world went to war. The hotel manager, Edwin Dekker, remembered me from those times and gave me a warm welcome. He even put us in Suite 2101 the same rooms with a terrific view Susan and I had during our last visit.

After the bellman, an older fellow I didn't recognize, hauled my bag up to our suite, I parked the Dodge and sat outside on a bench near the lobby entrance. I lit a Lucky and wondered if Jimmy, the young bellboy I was used to seeing at the Biltmore, might have enlisted. Otherwise, I just stared out across the Biltmore's meticulously landscaped grounds at the Pacific Ocean. I must have been daydreaming because I didn't notice Susan's snazzy Pontiac convertible coming until it passed right in front of my nose.

The doorman opened Susan's car door for her, and as she got out, I gave her a wolf whistle just as I did the first time we met at the Biltmore after I returned to the Army. She turned, but this time I got a smile and a wink instead of a glare.

Susan had swapped her nursing togs for a dark green dress that brought to mind one of the reasons I fell in love with her in the first place. She caught me looking and stepped back to pirouette like a fashion model and give me the whole effect. "You approve?"

I gave her my best lecherous grin. "Let me put it this way, if we don't get up to our suite soon, the folks in the lobby are going to see quite a show."

"Well, what are we standing around here for?"

The activities that followed in Suite 2101 concluded with Susan in my arms and both of us thinking the world was not such a bad place after all. I was also remembering what General Davis said about how he'd hate to see any innocent bystanders hurt if the Japs were out to get me. To me, Susan was a very important bystander, which was why we were at the Biltmore instead of Susan's apartment. It was also the reason I wouldn't be spending much time with her until I was certain the coast was clear.

Susan, of course, noticed the dressing on my shoulder. While she removed the dressing to take a look, I explained how it got there, making it sound a lot less exciting than it really was. Either Susan was getting used to such explanations, or she was getting better at hiding her reactions to the dangers of my job. She didn't quite take the whole thing in stride, but she didn't make a big deal about, either.

After Susan inspected the wound and pronounced it healing nicely, she redressed it from supplies in a little nurse travel kit she always included in her suitcase. Then, not really feeling like traipsing down to the Biltmore's restaurant, we ordered from room service and spent the rest of the evening being lazy.

Biltmore Hotel, Santa Barbara

Friday – 3 APR 42 – Saturday – 18 APR 42

We ate breakfast in the Biltmore's coffee shop, after which we went our separate ways, Susan to the clinic, and me down US Highway 101 in the direction of Los Angeles. Our goodbyes were particularly poignant that morning.

I'm not very adept at killing time. Oh, I had a few minor chores to help pass the next couple of weeks, but they didn't amount to much. Mostly, I was making a target of myself to lure any would-be assassins out of the bushes.

Every few days I made the rounds of Sally's empty house in Inglewood and the North American Aviation plant at Mines Field. I followed a random schedule, hoping to spot anyone who might be watching either place. I also made a couple of trips up to Santa Barbara for the purpose of checking the clinic and Susan's apartment. It wasn't much fun being that close to Susan and not seeing her, but I did make it a point to talk with her by telephone every night.

During one of those telephone conversations Susan reported that Doctor Feigenbaum gave Sally her walking papers, saying she could manage just fine at home with visits from a nurse to change her dressings and handle other medical chores. That meant I had to get Sergeant Tiner and his men ready to transport Sally home and set up a security routine there.

Sally went home on Friday, April 10, and Tiner was overjoyed when I met him in Inglewood that afternoon and told him he would likely be resuming his normal duties in about a week. It seems the sergeant wasn't any better at killing time than I was.

I passed the same good news on to the MID security people guarding Michael Wilkins at the Presidio. Things were winding down and it appeared the Japs had given up on the whole deal. It was not yet time to accept that as a sure thing, but matters were definitely looking up.

On a whim I called Gary Henson, Doctor Feigenbaum's driver who helped us out at the clinic and arranged to meet him for lunch in Hollywood. We agreed to meet at Eli's Deli up Highland a block or so from my old office at Hollywood Boulevard and Highland. It felt good to visit the old neighborhood again.

I was looking forward to seeing Danny Cohen, Eli's son, but it was Eli behind the counter when I walked into the deli. We greeted each other like the old acquaintances we were, and when I asked after Danny, Eli told me he enlisted in the Navy to do his part for democracy. Eli said Danny was getting along fine as a Navy cook. I've always heard the Navy has the best food in the services, and I was pretty certain it just got even better.

When Henson arrived, I introduced him to Eli and suggested what I always thought was the best item on the menu, the Fancy-Schmancy Hollywood Reuben. It was a corned beef Reuben, the only true Reuben, taken up a couple of notches with marbled rye bread and a smear of yellow mustard. For our sides, Gary and I both chose the German potato salad, which I noticed was now simply called "warm potato salad" on the menu board.

We sat at one Eli's tables to await our sandwiches and Gary said, "Spicer, I owe you an apology. My comment at that clinic about you being lucky was a lousy thing to say after you'd just lost your partner. I've felt bad about saying it ever since."

"Forget it, Gary. We were all a bit edgy that day, but while we're on the subject, I don't think I properly thanked you for helping us out up there, so thanks. Without you we might have lost Miss MacLure before your boss ever got to operate."

"Hell, it gave me a chance to do a little something for my country. I tried enlisting, but the military doesn't want me anymore than the LAPD. Oh, and speaking of that, I got a nice letter of commendation from a General Davis in Washington DC.

I gather he's your boss?"

"Yes, he is. Tell you what, Gary, keep your eye on the headlines during the next week or so and you'll find out what was going on and how important your help really was."

In addition to making the rounds of various places where I might spot Jap agents, I checked in regularly with Washington, more for something to do than because I had anything to talk about. I made one of those calls on Friday, 17 April around 1330 hours west coast time. When I got through to General Davis, he sounded a little more wound-up than usual.

"Johnny, the first thing you do tomorrow morning, you find yourself a copy of the LA morning paper and read the headlines, and then you call me. Got that?"

Knowing damned well he wasn't going to give me anything more than that, I said, "Yes, sir."

That night I stayed at my usual lodgings near Mines Field, Patmar's Motel. After dinner in the coffee shop, I called Susan.

"Angel, when you get up tomorrow morning. Turn on the radio to KNX and a whole lot of stuff will suddenly be clear."

"All right, darling. I'll do exactly that."

After calling Susan, I went to bed with my fingers crossed. I was pretty sure there were 80 Army Air Force flyboys somewhere out over the Pacific Ocean who needed all the luck they could get.

Thirty-Four

Patmar's Motel, Inglewood

Wearing civvies as a small personal celebration for what I anticipated I would find on the front page of the *Los Angeles Times*, I walked over to Patmar's coffee shop and stopped in front of the newspaper rack outside the door. The banner headline below the masthead was printed in bold three-inch letters. It said, "TOKYO BOMBED!"

I fished around in my pocket for a pair of nickels and bought the last two copies in the rack. Inside the coffee shop the *Times* headline was in evidence at nearly every table. It was the news everyone had been hoping for. It was payback for Pearl Harbor.

After ordering coffee, I read the article below the headline. I was not at all surprised to find the story full of holes and deliberate inaccuracies ranging from the type of aircraft used to the location from which the raid was launched. The article even implied the bombers were launched from a secret island airfield somewhere in the Pacific. Also, little was said about the amount of damage done by the raid, except to report that three Jap cities were bombed. In addition to Tokyo, Doolittle's bombs also landed on Kobe and Yokohama. Despite its inaccuracies the story was damned good news for Americans.

I finished my coffee, paid my bill, and stepped into a public telephone booth outside. General Davis was expecting my call.

"Congratulations on a successful mission, Major Spicer."

"Thank you, sir. It has definitely been interesting."

"I'll say. Do you have anything new for me?"

"Yes, sir. I thought it might be a nice gesture to recognize Miss MacLure somehow for her service. She really was a big help in our investigation and helping us sure as hell cost her a lot. Is there anything we can do for her?"

"I was wondering if you'd get around to thinking of that. To answer your question, yes, there is something we can do for her. In fact, I've already put the wheels in motion. Miss MacLure will be receiving the Secretary of War's Medal for Outstanding Public Service. It's a medal for civilians who've gone beyond the call of duty in the service of their country. She should be getting notification before too much longer."

"Thank you, sir. I think she'll appreciate the gesture."

"You're right, she does deserve the recognition. Do you have anything else for me?"

"No, sir. I haven't seen anything the slightest bit suspicious anywhere during my travels for the past couple of weeks."

"Good. Your leave begins tomorrow. Report back to the Presidio on Four May. Have fun."

My next call was to Colonel Beecher at the Presidio. His opening comment was, "Would I be correct in assuming this morning's headlines have something to do with the hush-hush assignment you and General Davis have been conducting?"

"Yes, sir, that would be a correct assumption."

"Well, congratulations on whatever part you played in giving the Japs a good swift kick in the pants."

"Thank you, sir. All we really did was help the flyboys keep things under wraps so the mission would be a surprise."

"From what I'm hearing, it was definitely a surprise . . . a damned big surprise."

"Yes, that's my impression, too. Sir, I have a favor to ask."

"I guess you've earned a favor or two. How can I help?"

"Would you please turn that North American Aviation engineer we have under wraps up there loose and see that he gets transportation back to Los Angeles?"

"Sure. I'll get it done today. Anything else?"

"Yes, two items. First, I'll be sending Sergeant Tiner back to you today. Second, you should be seeing some new orders come through for me. General Davis ordered me to take a two-week leave."

With surprise in his voice, Beecher said, "He ORDERED you to take two weeks' leave?"

"Yes, sir. This has been a pretty rough assignment, losing Sergeant Pierce and all, so the general thinks my work would benefit from a few days off."

"Yeah, I heard about Pierce. That was a damned shame.

Pierce was a good man."

"Yes, sir, a very good man. I miss him."

"All right, Spicer. Have a good leave. I'll see you in two weeks."

My third call was to Air Services Command headquarters at McClellan Army Airfield. When I got Joe Richards on the line, I said, "I take it you've seen or heard the big news this morning?"

"Yes, sir! Colonel Doolittle really gave 'em hell, and we helped. Everybody around here is feeling pretty good about that."

"As they should, Sergeant. I just called to say it's probably safe to put that forty-five back up on the closet shelf for now."

"Thanks, sir. I'll do that when I get home tonight. I'm also thinking about cutting back a little on our security here at the office. We're tying up a lot of manpower."

"That's up to you, Sergeant, but I wouldn't cut it clear back to what it was before. You guys will no doubt be handling more classified missions in the future. It's better to stay prepared than start from scratch every time extra security is needed."

"Understood, sir. That's essentially what I had in mind."

"All right, Sergeant. Congratulations on a job well done. Have a beer on me."

"Will do, sir. Thank you."

My last call was to Susan's apartment. She answered on the first ring.

"Hello?"

"Hi, Angel."

"Hi, darling. I did as you suggested and turned on the news this morning. All I can say is wow!"

"Yeah. I'm sure glad the raid came off as planned. Most people will never know the total cost of that mission, especially the cost on this side of the Pacific."

"So, you played a part in all of this?"

"Yes, Russ and I were assigned to look for holes in the Army Air Force security that might result in the Japs knowing what was coming their way before it got there. That's how we got on to Dragon Lady, and it's a darn good thing we did. She knew way too much already when we found out what she was up to."

"Johnny, I'm so proud of you . . . and Russ, too. What happens now? Do you have new orders already?"

"I sure do."

That disappointed her. "Oh. I was hoping maybe we could . . . ."

"Yeah, General Davis has ordered me to take two weeks'

leave."

"Oh! I could kiss that man!"

"I wish you'd make up your mind. A few days ago, you wanted to poke him in the nose."

"I'm a woman; it's my prerogative to change my mind."

"Well, I noticed the woman part. I don't know about . . . ."

"Just take my word for it, darling. When will you be here?"

"Probably tonight. I have one more job to do down here. I need to see Sally and tell Jim Tiner and his crew their job is done. I also suspect Sally will have some questions for me."

"Yes, darling, I'm pretty sure she will."

"Say, is there any chance you can get a few days off for an ocean voyage?"

"I've got some time coming, but how long will this ocean voyage take? I might not have that much time."

"Well, I haven't checked the sailing schedule lately, but I imagine it will take about two and a half hours each way."

Susan caught on immediately. "Oh! Catalina! I'd love it! How about I ask Doctor for a week? Now isn't a real good time for me to be gone for much longer."

"Well, until we can have forever, a week will have to do. Can you find out today? Maybe we can even leave tomorrow."

"Yes. I'm on duty in a little while and I'm sure Doctor Rothenberg will be in today. I'll get a schedule worked out first thing, so I can get his approval. Gosh! I'm all excited now!"

"All right, Angel, I'll stop off at the Catalina terminal in Wilmington and pick up a steamer schedule. See you in a while."

My telephone calls completed, I loaded up the Army's Dodge and settled my bill at Patmar's. After that, I pointed the Dodge toward 235 West Hillcrest Boulevard in Inglewood, Sally MacLure's home.

The drive only took a few minutes, and when I got there, I saw Tiner outside the front door. As I walked toward the porch, I held up one of my copies of the *Times*.

"Have you seen this, Sergeant Tiner?"

He stared at the headline for a moment, and then said, "No, sir. I hadn't seen it until now. That sounds like good news."

"It's very good news, Sergeant. Aside from giving the Japs a little taste of their own medicine, it means you and your team can pack up and go home."

He looked pleased. "Is that what all this has been about, sir?"

"It is. We needed to keep all the preparations under wraps, so Colonel Doolittle and his crews could surprise the Japs. We did, and he did."

"That's great, sir. I'll round up my team and we'll get headed north. Thank you, sir."

Inside, I found Sally sitting in the living room reading a book. She looked up and said, "Johnny!"

"Hiya, kiddo. I brought you something else to read this morning."

I handed her the *Times*. Sally took it from me with her left hand, probably so I would notice her cast was gone. She read the headline and said, "Holy smoke! Is this what all the fuss has been about?"

I sat across from her in an overstuffed chair and said, "Yes, ma'am, that's what all the fuss was about, and you are now officially a free woman again."

"Really?"

"Yup. I just told Sergeant Tiner to pack up his team and get lost. He's doing that as we speak."

As if on cue, Tiner stepped into the living room and said, "Forgive the interruption. I just wanted to say goodbye, ma'am. It's been a pleasure knowing you."

Sally smiled. "It's been a pleasure knowing you, too, Sergeant. Thank you for keeping me nice and safe. Have a good trip home."

Tiner said, "My pleasure, ma'am." He tossed me a salute and said, "See you soon, Major."

Then we were alone again, and Sally held up the *Times*. "Does this mean you can give me some honest answers to a couple of questions?"

I knew what was coming and I wasn't looking forward to it. "Probably. You certainly deserve some straight answers."

"Okay, Major Spicer, here's my first question: Something has happened to Russ Pierce, hasn't it?"

I nodded. "Yes, Sally, he's dead."

Sadness clouded her pretty face. "Did he die because of me?"

"He died for everyone who was at the clinic that day. Dragon Lady showed up early on the morning of your surgery. She came in through the window of the empty room next to yours. I was outside then, and Susan was napping in the empty room. She woke up to see Dragon Lady shooting at me through the window."

"Oh, God!"

"Fortunately, Russ and Doctor Feigenbaum's driver figured out what was going on and broke into the room. They killed Dragon Lady on the spot.

"What we didn't know then was she slid a time bomb under

the bed in the empty room as insurance in case we got her before she got you. Susan remembered something about that later, so Russ and I went to investigate and found the bomb. We weren't sure how to disarm the thing, but we could see it was set to go off in a few minutes, so we figured the best thing was to get the bomb out of the clinic. Russ went outside and stood at the open window while I picked the thing up and handed it to him.

"He was taking the bomb away from the building when it detonated. Russ was killed instantly."

Tears welled in Sally's eye. Softly, she said, "How awful."

I sighed. "Yeah, I miss him."

"Russ told me his family lived up in Corvallis. Do they know?"

"Yes, I flew up there and talked to his sister, June. I told her Russ died a hero. I think that might have helped just a little. We didn't tell you because the doctors thought the news would upset you and interfere with your recovery."

Sally wiped at her tears with a tissue from a box on an end table next to her chair. "I see. I guess that was the right thing to do. Thank you for telling me now. I don't imagine you enjoyed reliving the experience."

"I'm feeling a little better about it now, and when I'm honest with myself, I think part of my initial reaction was because it just as easily could have been me instead of Russ."

In a solemn tone of voice, Sally said, "I know. What did Susan think about that?"

"I think you can guess how she felt about it."

Sally nodded. "Yes, I suppose I can. May I ask another question?"

"Sure. Ask away."

"Who shot me?"

That question surprised me. I shrugged as if I didn't see why the answer to that question was important. "A Jap espionage agent."

She looked at me for a moment, and then said, "Remember, you said 'straight answers.'"

"Why is his name so important?"

"Because I have an odd feeling I know who it was. I don't know why I feel that way, but it's a very strong feeling."

I sighed again. "Okay, who do you think it was?"

Looking me square in the eye, Sally said, "It was Vern Carlson, wasn't it?"

Wondering how she came to that conclusion, I nodded. "Yes it was. It turned out he was working for Dragon Lady and to her you were a loose end."

Sally sat there staring at the floor for quite a while. Finally, she said more to herself than to me, "How could he do that?"

"I'm not going to tell you he didn't have a choice, but he may have felt he either had to kill you or they would kill him. I know that hurts, but he isn't worth your tears."

She nodded. "What happened to him?"

"Russ and I caught up with him shortly after he shot you. I returned the favor."

Sally frowned. "You shot him?"

"Yes. He was shooting at me and I shot back."

She shook her head. "I ought to join a convent and become a nun or something. Every man I fall in love with is either rotten or already taken."

Smiling, I said, "Seems to me joining a convent is a bit drastic. Give it a little time. You'll find the right guy, and when you do, it's a sure thing he'll thank his lucky stars."

Sally tried to give me a small smile in return. "Johnny . . . I . . . I . . . ."

I walked over and knelt next to her chair. "I know, kiddo. Believe me, if Susan wasn't in my life, I'd be lined up at your front door and I wouldn't take no for an answer."

She leaned over and put her arms around me. "Johnny, would you please hold me . . . just for a minute?"

I held her until she said, "I'm sorry. I know I shouldn't be doing this. I just . . . ."

"It's okay, kiddo. Susan would approve. If fact, she knows I'm here."

Sally wiped away more tears with another tissue. "Susan is wonderful. It's easy to see why you love her so much."

"Just so you know, Susan thinks you're pretty wonderful, too. She's told me so more than once."

She looked surprised. "She has?"

"She has. There's someone else who thinks you're pretty special."

Puzzled, Sally asked, "Who?"

"A fellow by the name of Henry Stimson, the United States Secretary of War. His office will be sending you a letter before long to say you have been selected to receive the Secretary of War's Medal for Outstanding Public Service. My boss requested you receive the medal in recognition of the help you've given us at great personal cost."

She stared at me for a moment apparently digesting what I

told her. Finally, Sally said, "I suppose I should be grateful for the recognition, but I really don't feel much gratitude. I didn't serve my country; my country USED me and damned near got me killed. If it wasn't for you and people like Susan and the doctors at the clinic, I'd be dead. Please tell your boss where he can pin that medal. I don't want the damned thing."

Sally was right about her country using her and nothing I could say would change that, so I simply said, "All right, I'll tell him. Now, I have to be going. Is there anything else I can do for you before I go?"

"No, thank you. I'm getting along well. Doctor Feigenbaum says I can go back to work in a couple of weeks."

"That's good news. If you have any problem getting your job back, don't hesitate to call me."

Sally smiled. "Thank you, Johnny. I can't think of anyone I'd rather have in my corner."

I gave her a kiss on the cheek, got one in return, and then I was out the door. It was time to get on the road. I had one more stop to make before I could head for Santa Barbara, and it was in the opposite direction. I headed south out of Inglewood for Wilmington and the Catalina Steamer Terminal.

As I drove through the shirttail communities of Hawthorne and Torrance, I got Sally's tirade out of my mind by thinking about visiting Catalina with Susan. We'd both been there before, but not together. For my part, Catalina and the little town of Avalon were the perfect getaway. I always enjoyed the steamship trip over, and once there, I felt like I was a million miles away from life's troubles.

Wilmington and the Catalina Steamship Terminal were at the north end of Los Angeles Harbor, and I could tell I was getting close because of the changing scenery. As tract houses turned into warehouses, fuel storage tanks, and docks, I turned my attention to my route. I knew my way around the port of Los Angeles because I'd spent quite a bit of tine out there during a recent assignment. Still, the port is a maze and one wrong turn can leave you completely lost.

At the first street past the harbor power plant, I turned south, and that's when I noticed something in my rearview mirror I didn't see before. What I saw there was a beat-up faded red Chevrolet pickup truck. Now, there's nothing unusual about seeing such a vehicle at the harbor. The place is lousy with trucks of every description running hither and yon.

No, what concerned me about this particular truck was I'd

seen it somewhere else recently. It, or one identical to it, was parked on West Hillcrest Boulevard in Inglewood, a block from Sally's house. I wasn't positive it was the same truck, but it sure looked like it. I gave myself a mental kick in the butt for letting my mind wander off to Catalina instead of paying attention to what was going on around me.

Water Street was coming up on my left. The Catalina Steamship Terminal was the only building on that street, so I made the turn to see if the pickup truck followed. It did. I breezed right by the terminal, and when the truck did the same, that clinched the deal. Beyond the terminal building the street turned to gravel, and then to dirt before dead-ending against the back side of a tank farm.

I kept right on going until I was off the gravel and on the dirt. There, with my right foot still on the gas, I stabbed the brake pedal with my left foot and cranked the Dodge's steering wheel hard to the left. The little coupe did exactly what I expected it to do. It swapped directions end for end amidst a great cloud of dust.

The Dodge fishtailed a time or two, and when straightened itself out, the pickup truck and I were face to face, with the distance between closing rapidly. I pulled my Smith & Wesson from its holster and transferred it to my left hand.

The wide-eyed truck driver and I both braked to a stop, ending up about fifty feet apart with the truck slightly offset to my left. That's when I got a clear look at the pickup's driver. His features were as Japanese as they could be. The antics of Jap agents were getting downright annoying.

We sat there like Jack Dempsey and Max Schmeling sizing each other up before the bell, and then he tipped his hand. He leaned to his right as if to get something from the floor on the passenger-side of his cab. What he came up with was one hell of a big shotgun. I saw it clearly through his windshield while he turned it end for end in the cramped space of the truck's interior.

Making sure the Dodge was in first gear, I waited for what was certain to happen next. There it was. The driver-side door swung open. In order to use that big gun, he had to get out of the car. He figured he'd be safe behind the truck's open door. He was wrong.

When he swung one foot to the ground I popped the clutch and floored the gas pedal. I heard the clatter of dirt and rocks hitting the Dodge's underside as I aimed its left front fender at his open door and nailed it shut just as his second foot hit the ground. The Jap let out a piercing scream as I went by, so I figured I'd done some damage. I couldn't see how much damage until I got the

Dodge turned around.

The Jap agent was in a heap on the ground below the mangled driver-side door of his truck. The shotgun was still in his hands. I would have to do something about that.

I pulled around the right side of his vehicle and made another U-turn, so I was facing him again. I pulled up about ten feet away and looked down at him through my open driver-side window. From that distance, the guy looked like he was in a lot of pain—his eyes were tightly closed, his jaw was clenched, and his mouth was twisted into a grimace.

He sensed me there and opened his eyes a little to squint up at me as he swung the barrel of the shotgun in my direction. I rewarded his persistence by cursing the guy and shooting him squarely between the eyes.

After that, I just sat there for a while waiting for my pulse to drop back down into a more normal range and keeping an eye on my surroundings for anyone who saw or heard the skirmish. Apparently, no one did, or if they did, they didn't care.

While sitting there, I also did some arithmetic. This guy was the seventh Jap we either killed or put out of commission since I'd started the Doolittle assignment. I wondered how that tally stood up against the bombing fatalities in Tokyo.

Finally, I stepped down and walked around to look at the front of my Dodge. The little business coupé was wounded, but not beyond repair. I gave it a sympathetic pat on its crunched fender, and then drove back to the Catalina Steamship Terminal.

There is a row of public telephone booths just inside the terminal entrance. I stepped into one and placed a Priority Able call to Washington DC. A radio playing music in the background made me think Davis might be at home.

"What's up, Spicer?"

"I just tangled with another Jap agent. He followed me from Sally MacLure's home, so it seems they have more interest in me than in her now."

"What happened?"

"Damned fool tried to shoot me with a shotgun that was bigger than he was, so while he was trying to get the thing pointed in the right direction, I ran over him with the Army's Dodge. Even after that he still thought he ought to kill me, so I shot him."

"All right, where are you?"

"I'm a block or so east of the Catalina Steamship Terminal located at one hundred West Water Street in the town of Wilmington."

"Is your car drivable?"

"Yeah. It will need a little bodywork, but that can wait."

"How about you? You need medical attention or anything?"

"No, all I need is a few less Japs who want to kill me."

"Hell, Spicer, you don't need my help with that. I've lost count, but you've taken out at least five or six on this assignment alone."

"Correction, sir; we've taken out seven on this assignment."

"Maybe you ought to get lost for a while, Major."

"Yes, sir. I plan to do exactly that. Oh, and sir?"

"Yeah, Spicer?"

"I mentioned the Secretary of War's medal to Miss MacLure and she said I should tell you to pin the medal on your butt, . . . sir."

Nothing but long-distance static came down the line for several seconds, and then General Chester Davis said, "You, know, Spicer, I don't blame her one bit. In fact, if it were me, I wouldn't have been nearly so polite."

1600 Hours – Sunday – 19 APR 42

Saint Catherine Hotel, Santa Catalina Island

I sat in front of a window in our fourth-floor room at the Saint Catherine Hotel and watched the sleek *Miss Catalina* speedboat roar past the Avalon Casino while Susan changed the dressing on my shoulder. Angel noticed *Miss Catalina*, too.

"Gosh, that looks like fun! Can we take a ride on it?"

"Sounds like a good idea to me."

After arriving on the first boat over from Wilmington Sunday morning, Susan and I strolled through the exotic little town of Avalon and got slightly sunburned on the Saint Catherine Hotel's beach. As a result, I was already beginning to feel rejuvenated. Santa Catalina was still working its magic despite indications the island was gearing up for war.

Checking into the hotel I learned that as of late August the *SS Catalina* steamer and her sister ship, the *SS Cabrillo*, will no longer be available for carrying passengers to and from the island. Both ships were being pressed into service by the Navy to haul sailors back and forth across San Francisco Bay.

Further evidence of Catalina's transition to a war footing greeted us in the harbor when we arrived. An angry looking navy-gray destroyer bristling with guns was anchored in the bay just fifty yards from the Avalon Pleasure Pier. The plan was for the military to take over Catalina for coastal defense operations and specialized training.

Susan finished with my shoulder and said, "There you go, darling. Now please try not to get shot for a while."

I wrapped an arm around her waist and pulled her close. She leaned over for a kiss and I said, "Why not, Angel? I've got a great nurse to take care of me."

"Because this nurse can think of activities that are a lot more fun than patching you up, that's why not."

"Really? What kind of activities might those be?"

"The kind that involve lots of hugging and kissing and . . . ."

I pulled her onto my lap and kissed her for a long time. When we came up for air, I said, "You mean like that?"

In a slightly breathless tone of voice, Susan said, "Yes, darling, exactly like that."

THE END

MEET H. P. OLIVER

H. P. Oliver began his career with a degree in journalism from San Jose State University and spent the next twenty-some years writing award-winning entertainment and educational media. Now he applies his creativity and imagination to writing historical mysteries.

About mystery writing, Oliver says, "To be truly engrossing, a mystery needs a little meat on its bones—something more than just figuring out who did the evil deed. Taking a story back in time or even basing it on actual historical events is a great way to endow a good yarn with even more color and depth. Historical periods and locations give the writer an opportunity to take most readers where they've never been before."

H. P. Oliver lives in northern California and spends much of his time working on projects throughout the western states. In addition to his love of history, Oliver's interests range from vintage film to restoring classic cars.

For information about H. P. Oliver's books, including synopses, previews, video trailers, and purchase links, visit his fan site at www.HPOliver.com, where you will also find illustrated history articles and other fascinating features. Plan to stay a while.

BOOKS BY H. P. OLIVER

H. P. Oliver's books are available at Amazon.com

www.ingramcontent.com/pod-product-compliance
Lightning Source LLC
Chambersburg PA
CBHW061927170626
46813CB00006B/2330